D1388226

Carolina Skeletons

Carolina Skeletons

David Stout

OVERLOOK DUCKWORTH
New York • London

This edition published in the United States and the United Kingdom in 2014 by
Overlook Duckworth, Peter Mayer Publishers Inc.

NEW YORK:
141 Wooster Street
New York, NY 10012
www.overlookpress.com
For bulk and special sales, please contact sales@overlookny.com,
or write us at the above address.

LONDON:
30 Calvin Street
London E1 6NW
www.ducknet.co.uk
info@duckworth-publishers.co.uk
For bulk and special sales, please contact sales@duckworth-publishers.co.uk,
or write us at the above address.

Although based on a crime that actually occurred in South Carolina in 1944, this book
is a work of fiction. The characters who live and die in these pages were born out of the
author's imagination and are not meant to resemble any real persons.

Cataloging-in-Publication Data is avaliable from the Library of Congress
A catalogue record for this book is available from the British Library

Printed in the United States of America

ISBN: 978-1-4683-0854-9 US
ISBN: 978-0-7156-4912-1 UK

2   4   6   8   10   9   7   5   3   1

For Ruth D. Furie, my close friend of many years, whose intelligence and strength sustained me in this as in so much else.

BOOK ONE

CHAPTER 1

Alcolu, South Carolina

Late March, 1944

First light, and the shack village where the colored live comes to life. A rooster crows, a dog yelps, a baby cries. Shout of a woman, shout of a man, a hand hitting flesh, a scream. In the barn over near Mr. Tyler's sawmill, the horses grunt, annoyed at the feel of bridles, reins, saddles. A whip cracks across a horse's flank, bringing a whinny that rises to a shriek of pain.

The sun goes from orange to yellow. More sounds from the shacks, really a low rumble as the sounds blend into one. And smells—smells of people too close together, of this morning's cooked possum and last night's vomited peach wine. And, from over by the mill, smells of horses and their straw, smells of wood, cut and soon to be cut. Smells, all mixed, rising with the mist coming from the dirt and grass between the shacks.

A whistle sounds, beckoning men to the long, gray dirty mill hunkered down next to a pond. White foremen on horses use the heads of the animals to nudge the slower colored through the gate. White mill workers, dressed cleaner than the colored and carrying black lunch pails, shuffle through the gate, too. The white men talk to each other in tired drawls.

The saws go on, one by one. No matter how many times you hear it, the sound of the saws is terrifying. When a big log is fed into a saw, the scream is horrible, like an animal being tortured.

The white men run the saws and cranes and other machines, and the colored force the logs into the saws, not seeming to mind the noise and heat and flying dust. In that way, the whites and colored are a team.

Some of the colored are down at the pond. You can hear the splashes as the logs bump and roll in the water, prodded by colored men with long poles. A wonder to watch, how the colored balance on the logs, laughing and talking to each other in grunts and shouts unfathomable to white people. They seldom fall, so fine is their sense of balance, and when they do fall they laugh and kid each other, teeth flashing in dark faces, as only the colored can kid each other. But when something bad happens—an ankle broken, toes smashed between logs—they jump to help each other.

Some of the older workers have boys off in the war, just like the white workers. That's one of the reasons there's some real friendship between the whites and colored, when they're at the mill. Of course, at night, when they shut off the saws, the whites go home to Manning, or some other place nearby. They ride four or five to a car, mostly, to save gasoline.

The colored don't have as far to go. They just walk back to the shacks Mr. Tyler built for them. He just charges them enough to break even on the rent. Not only that, he fixed up some showers for the colored workers—actually a row of spigots in a little shed right next to the mill, so those colored who want to can smell better. Makes it easier for the white workers, too. The colored seem happy enough, getting up with the sun, working at the mill, buying tobacco at the company store, getting drunk on peach wine, and getting up with the sun the next morning to do it again. Over and over.

We're talking about the men, of course. The women work even harder, probably, finding energy from God knows where, taking care of the young and finding time to raise vegetables next to the shacks. It's the women, mostly, who go to Green Hill Negro Church, singing and praying loud enough for their whole families, making up for the men, who would rather drink and chew tobacco.

This is a good time of year to be working at the mill. For that matter, it's a pretty time all over South Carolina. Winter is just about gone, and even when the sun is yellow and bright, at its highest point in the sky, there is no hint of that smothering heat that makes the mill workers sweat so much the dust sticks to their skin all day.

Way up north, there's still snow on the ground, some places. But here, it's already spring. Flowers are out.

CHAPTER 2

Cindy Lou Ellerby was surprised and very happy when her paper came back with a gold star, and the teacher told her, loud enough for the class to hear, that she had enjoyed reading it, especially the part about how the world "feels like it has a runny nose" in the winter. The class had laughed at that. Cindy Lou thought those words were the reason she got the star, because writing wasn't that easy for her. If she could do whatever she wanted in school, she would spend all day with the crayons and paintbox.

It was a Friday in late March, and getting the paper back with the star on it gave Cindy Lou a second reason to be happy. The first was just that it was Friday, and Friday afternoon after school was her favorite time in the world.

Sometimes she went into Manning with her parents. Her father had told her once that three thousand people lived in Manning, or right around it, but she could not picture that many people. She sure couldn't picture all the people who lived in Columbia, which was a lot bigger even than Manning. She thought she would like to go there, maybe with her parents, or with her big sister, Marcia, who was nine years older than Cindy Lou, or her brother, Roy, who was two years older still.

Sometimes Cindy Lou prayed for a baby brother or sister so she wouldn't be the littlest. She had asked her mother and father whether God would send her a baby brother or sister. Sometimes her mother and father thought it was funny, when Cindy Lou asked that. Other times they hushed her. She didn't understand all the way why God couldn't do that, if she prayed as hard as she could. After all, God saw the sky and everything under it and could make the pines seem like they were on fire when the sun went down. If He could do that ...

But Sue Ellen Clark was almost like her little sister. Sue Ellen was three years younger but was still her best friend. Cindy Lou liked the way Sue Ellen followed her almost anywhere she wanted to go and took her word for almost anything and never told on her when they did something they weren't supposed to. Sometimes Cindy Lou teased Sue Ellen, telling her things that weren't true just to scare her or make her mad. But Cindy Lou almost always stopped before Sue Ellen got really mad. And Cindy Lou looked out for Sue Ellen on the playground.

"Come on, Sue Ellen," Cindy Lou said, after school that Friday afternoon, getting on her bicycle and holding it straight while Sue Ellen slid onto the back fender. Cindy Lou hooked their lunch pails over the handlebars, stood up while pedaling until they got going, then sat down. It felt good riding the bike, with a breeze in her face and Sue Ellen's arms around her waist. The breeze tasted good; it smelled like grass and mud and ... spring.

"Let's go and pick flowers," Cindy Lou said.

"I have to ask my mom."

"Me too."

They rode to Cindy Lou's house first, and she asked her mother if she could go with Sue Ellen to pick flowers down past the shacks and the mill. Her mother said yes, but that they should both be careful not to get their clothes dirty and not to cut themselves on bushes or on cinders near the tracks. Cindy Lou knew her mother would say yes, as long as she promised to be home for supper, because they had gone down past the shacks and mill before.

Cindy Lou left her lunch pail at her house and went to the bathroom, and then she ran to her bicycle, and Sue Ellen got on the fender again (even though Cindy Lou's mother and father had told her it was not a good idea to let her ride on the fender, because it could get bent), and Cindy Lou pedaled hard. She was eager to get to the flowers and was glad that Sue Ellen was in her house, for only a minute to talk to her mother and go to the bathroom.

The breeze blew gently into Cindy Lou's face and up her dress as she turned the bicycle onto the dirt road that led past the mill and the shacks. She could smell cut wood and pine sap. Cindy Lou could see colored men balancing on logs, and she heard the rumble from the mill.

She was proud of her father; he must be very brave to work in such a place and not be afraid.

The shacks were a faded gray (Cindy Lou made the same color at school by dipping her brush in black when it was very wet, then running it again and again over the paper till the paper was almost soaked through), and Cindy Lou could smell colored people's food cooking. She knew the smells were from garden things and animals that white people usually didn't eat (except maybe to keep from hurting the feelings of colored people who were especially courteous and helpful), but they were good smells all the same.

Cindy Lou could hear shouts of children playing, barking and growling from dogs, and here and there a cry from a colored child whose behind had just been spanked.

It made Cindy Lou nervous to ride through the colored shacks, but it was the shortest way to get to the mill. Her parents had told her not to stop to talk to any of the colored, nor to make them angry by teasing them, but just to go straight through minding her own business. If anyone tried to stop her, she was to shout for help as loud as she could, and one of the mill foremen would hear her. He would be able to tell it was a white girl calling for help, and he would ride up quickly on his horse.

Actually, she was more afraid of the foremen than she was of the colored. The foremen wore clothes dark from sweat, and they looked mean on top of their horses as they rode from shack to shack. Cindy Lou didn't understand what the foremen did, except that they talked mean to the colored families. Her parents had explained that it was up to the foremen to collect money from the colored and take it to the mill or to the store right next to the mill. The money was what the colored had to pay to live in the shacks and what they owed the store; it was no wonder the foremen looked grumpy, her parents had said, because they not only had to make the colored pay what they owed, but they had to make sure the colored men went to work on time and didn't lie about being sick.

Now they were past the shacks; the cooking smells were gone, and the breeze in Cindy Lou's face smelled only like spring and wood again.

She had to stand up on the pedals to make the bicycle go up the hill for a short distance. Now she was on level ground again.

"Good for you, Cindy Lou," Sue Ellen said.

"Good for me. Good for me," Cindy Lou panted, and laughed with her friend. It was what they always said to each other when they were riding the bicycle and Cindy Lou had to pedal uphill.

Cindy Lou turned the handlebars to make the bike go down the road to Green Hill Negro Church. The church was on their left, a low wooden white building with a small graveyard next to it. The girls had heard the hymn-singing and shouting from the church on Sunday mornings. The first time she heard it, Cindy Lou laughed and told her parents how funny she thought the sounds were. But her parents had told her that that was the way good colored people talked to God, and that God heard them, because the colored people who went to church were sincere in their hearts and meant well.

Past the church they went, Cindy Lou stopping her pedaling, resting her legs and getting ready to work the brakes when the bicycle got to the bottom of a little hill where the old tracks ran off to the left, cutting through patches of woods and fields of clover.

Blossom was enjoying herself in the clover. Linus Bragg held her tether loosely, letting the patient old cow nibble at her own pace. She was in no hurry, and neither was he. His mama had told him to give the cow a good walk and feed and never mind hurrying back, 'cause it wouldn't make supper come any faster. What I care when supper come? Linus had asked, knowing that was a game. Mama, knowing too, had said, 'cause you like catfish and onions and buttered tater skins, and there be a nickel for you to get a strawberry ice cream cone with for dessert at the company store. That's why. That good enough, Linus had said.

Linus had liked catfish and onions and buttered tater skins for as long as he could remember (his brother and sister teased him about it). At fourteen, he still liked them. Who needed a reason? The only times he got mad at the teasing was when his brother and sister made fun of his size. He had hardly grown since he was twelve, and other boys his age in the mill shacks were at least a head taller. Never mind none, mama and daddy said. Some people grew early, and some grew later.

There were things about his body that Linus thought he would never understand. No one had told him that he would begin to have fun touching himself a certain way; this frightened and puzzled him, even though it was more fun than anything else, enough fun to make him blink.

He knew it was what animals did on farms, and he knew that people did the same thing. His mama and daddy ...

Impatiently, Linus yanked on Blossom's rope. The cow tugged back; the line went taut across his coveralls, flicking him where the magic feelings came from. He put his hand inside his coveralls and felt himself growing. The grass and dirt were cool under his feet.

Spring rode on the gentle breeze that licked his face. The birds felt it too; they sang in the trees when the breeze went by them.

Linus was startled when he heard the voices and laughter. He pulled his hand out of his coveralls. More voices, girls' voices, and the rattle of a bicycle. Now he saw them, off to his left, a white girl a few years younger than he pedaling a smaller girl. The older girl's hair was blonde and trailed behind her in the breeze. The older girl's dress blew up for a moment, showing Linus milk-white thighs and a glimpse, almost faster than he could see, of white underpants.

What he saw made Linus gasp. But it frightened him, too, and made his face burn, because of what his mama had told him once. You don't even look at white girls, she had said. You sit far away if you see them playing, because you don't want any habits that get you in big trouble later, when you closer to being a man.

What you mean? Linus had asked.

Tell you plain, his mama had said. You even look at a white girl like you might like her, some white boy, white man, gonna come after you eventually. You see them little white girls playing, jumping around, you walk the other way, far away. 'Course it should be up to their mamas to keep them acting proper, but that don't matter none, far as you're concerned.

You even look at a white girl like you might like her, some white boy or white man gonna cut your thing. And once you're older and look at a white woman, God help you. You really gonna get cut then. Cut so bad, ain't nobody gonna be able to sew you up.

Linus was embarrassed and frightened when his mama told him that, and it didn't help much when she saw how bad he felt and laughed and cuffed him behind the head, playfully, to make him feel better. He had never forgotten what she said.

Now, he had just looked at a white girl's underpants. He wondered if anyone had seen him.

Linus felt the magic start up in him.

Cindy Lou saw the boy holding the cow, saw by his face that he was a few years older than she, although not much bigger. She was not afraid, for her parents had told her how to talk to colored people. They are creatures of God, too; just speak up, firmly but kindly, so there's no misunderstanding, like you know your place. They'll almost surely know theirs, assuming they're the good colored, her parents had said. And there's nothing wrong with being extra kind, extra friendly to them once in a while, so long as there's no misunderstanding.

Cindy Lou was tired from the pedaling and braking, and so she stopped near the colored boy.

"That's a pretty cow you have," Cindy Lou said. "What's her name?"

"Blossom," the boy said, just loud enough for Cindy Lou to hear.

"I'll bet she gives a lot of milk for your family," Cindy Lou said.

"Yessum," the boy mumbled. Cindy Lou thought he looked very shy. His eyes were large and maroon.

Cindy Lou's legs were spread as she straddled the bicycle bar. The breeze came by again, lifting her dress slightly, and she smoothed it down with her hand.

"We're going to pick flowers now," she said. "Take good care of Blossom, and she'll give good milk for years. Watch she doesn't eat any strong weeds."

"This be clover here," the boy said.

"Bye, now," Cindy Lou said, pedaling off again.

The older girl had made Linus feel the magic more strongly than he had ever felt it before. He saw again, in his mind, how the breeze had lifted her dress. But Linus was afraid; he had looked at what his mama had told him he should never look at. Slowly, trying not to let his face show anything, Linus looked around him. There was a breeze on his face and birds singing and Blossom grunted. He was alone.

Linus wanted to see the flash of white again. Maybe, when they stopped to pick flowers, the breeze would come by and lift up the dress. . . .

Linus tied Blossom loosely to an old fence post. Just tying her up made him afraid, because his mama had told him that if he ever left Blossom alone, and she found out about it, she would whip him real bad. But Linus wanted to see. He could hear the blood rushing in his ears, the sound right alongside the sweet calls of birds, as he set off in the direction the girls had taken.

Though he tried to shove the picture out of his head, he could not help but see himself putting his hand there, in there, where he had seen the flash of white underpants. The picture made him dizzy, and afraid.

If he could not put his hand there, he might at least see . . .

He had walked only a few minutes when saw the bicycle on its stand just to the side of the tracks in a flat, clear area. Linus knew where he was, knew the flat, clear area soon sloped down to a little field, hardly bigger than the yard around his family's shack. In that little field, bordered by a patch of woods and by a ditch, the grass was especially rich and green, the flowers as colorful as a watercolor box.

Linus's ears were filled with the sound of his own heart beating. No, no . . . something else? The slow clop, clop, clop of a horse, the sucking sound of a horse pulling its hooves from mud. The clop, clop, clop went away, and Linus wasn't sure if he had really heard it or imagined it.

Linus heard the girls laughing. He stopped, listened and looked around (he was still alone), then walked toward the sounds.

The first moment Cindy Lou realized they were not alone was when she saw the fear in Sue Ellen's eyes. Sue Ellen was kneeling on the grass, just a few feet away, and clutching a bunch of flowers so tightly that the stems were turning to green paste in her hand.

Cindy Lou turned to look in the direction that Sue Ellen's terror-bright eyes were staring. And there he was, standing still. It was like a dream. For a long time he stood, and Cindy Lou stared at him, unable to take her eyes away, even though the look in his eyes was one she had not seen before. It was a look that terrified her.

The birds sang and darted in and out of the sun and shadows of the trees, oblivious.

And then he started toward them, the look on his face hardening, his eyes wide. The breeze lifted Cindy Lou's dress a little, and she smoothed it down with a trembling hand.

Sue Ellen screamed. She did not stop to breathe in and out, she just screamed. Loud enough to drown out the bird sounds, loud enough to make him put his hands to his ears to stop the noise.

He was upon them now, grabbing Sue Ellen's bird-thin wrist, shaking her.

"You be quiet. You be quiet …" Cindy Lou heard him pant.

Sue Ellen stopped screaming; her face told Cindy Lou that her younger friend wasn't sure if what was happening was real. Cindy Lou didn't know whether to be happy or sorry for her friend.

He spun her away, and Sue Ellen fell to the ground. Then he started toward Cindy Lou.

Cindy Lou had never been so afraid, had never imagined there could be such fear. Once, in the second grade, she had been really bad in school, and the teacher had stood up and walked toward her and said she might paddle her in front of the class. Cindy Lou had been afraid then, more than ever before, so afraid she thought she might wet her pants. The teacher, seeing how afraid she was, stopped and told her not to do it again, not to misbehave in class, and Cindy Lou had prayed her thanks to God, right there in the classroom, she was so thankful.

This was so much worse. He had hurt Sue Ellen, now he was coming toward her. He was reaching; he wanted to put his hand where she would never let anyone put a hand. Cindy Lou jumped away.

"Run, Sue Ellen," she said, barely able to get the words out. "Run and cry for help. Run fast."

Sue Ellen was on her feet again, screaming again. Don't make him mad, Cindy Lou wanted to tell her, but she could not find her voice.

Cindy Lou prayed that it was a dream after all. She saw him stoop down. He's looking for a rock, she thought.

"I won't tell if you don't hit me," she heard herself say.

But he did not seem to hear, and the look in his eyes was worse than anything she had ever seen, even in a dream. She saw the track spike in his hand. The spike was covered with rust.

Sue Ellen screamed even louder than before when he raised the spike over his head. He brought it down on Sue Ellen's head, and Cindy Lou saw more blood than she had ever seen before. Sue Ellen's hair was getting wet with it. The sound of Sue Ellen's screaming changed, to a lower, moaning sound. Cindy Lou had never heard anything so terrible, and she knew it was because Sue Ellen was hurt real bad. Cindy Lou saw the spike come down again; she could not believe he could still be mean enough to hit Sue Ellen after hearing the terrible noise she made.

Cindy Lou was mad as well as afraid, mad because of how he had hurt Sue Ellen. Cindy Lou grabbed for his wrist; she would bite him as hard as she could, hard enough to make him cry. She would!

Cindy Lou tried to grab his wrist, but her fingers could not hold on. Then his wrist was right in front of her face, because he was trying to put his hand over her mouth.

Then the big part of his hand was over her mouth. But her mouth was still open, and part of his hand came inside. Cindy Lou bit as hard as she could; she was surprised at how loud he hollered, how much it seemed to hurt him. She bit as hard as she could, so hard that her mouth hurt, so hard that she still had a hold on him, with her teeth, as he shook her head one way, then the other way, shook her so hard that it made her dizzy looking at the sky.

Then the spike covered part of the sky. There it was, now covering the whole sky. There was pain all over the side of Cindy Lou's head, like a hard slap that hurt way underneath the skin and a knife cut all at once.

She had cut herself bad on a knife in the kitchen one time, but this pain was even worse. It made her weak and dizzy. She was surprised that the second blow did not hurt as much as the first, though it made her even more weak and dizzy. She was whirling around now, the blue sky and green treetops spinning faster and faster.

The spinning stopped. Cindy Lou believed in God.

* * *

Sometimes on the playground, Linus got to laughing so hard and having so much fun that he giggled, his giggle almost as high as a girl's.

Linus had heard the girls with the bicycle talking and giggling. Then their voices had gone real high, only it did not sound like on the playground. Now, as he came near the clearing, Linus heard nothing. He did not understand, because he thought the girls were nearby. He stopped, trying not to make any noise, but he stepped on a branch. Linus listened as hard as he could, but he heard only his own heart and breathing. Then he thought he heard a horse's hooves, like before, but he was not sure.

He tiptoed, listening as hard as he could for the girls, but there was no girl sounds. Then he was standing at the edge of the clearing, looking at the girls lying on the ground. They were playing a game, looking up at the sky to see who could be still the longest.

Then Linus saw their heads, saw the red. It was not a game.

One time, when he was little, Linus had peeked through a crack in the shed wall and watched his daddy kill a pig. Linus had never forgotten the squeal and the gush of blood. It made him dizzy, made his knees weak to remember.

Linus had cried then, cried because of the squeal, cried because the pig was dead.

This was worse. He wondered if he was dreaming. No. His knees were so weak, his ears so full of the sound of his own heart, that it could not be a dream.

Linus stood still. He heard his heart and his breathing, then he thought he heard the horse sound again. Then nothing.

He remembered tying Blossom to the fence post, remembered the magic feeling, remembered walking toward the sounds, remembered looking—

The girls lay still. The older one's eyes were open, but they were shiny-dead. Hair flat against the head, held there by blood, the breeze stirring little hairs near her neck.

Linus could not believe how much blood there was. It was worse than the day of the pig.

Linus was afraid. Should he go tell?

He was sorry he had looked at the girls. He had not meant to look, the breeze had done it. Picked up her dress and let him see . . .

He touched his face, felt it covered with sweat, felt his shirt sticking to his back. He would go tell.

Just then something hit Linus in the back, hard enough to hurt real bad, and suddenly he was looking right at the ground, so close he could see the dirt real close, smell it. Something big stuck in his back, then something was across his neck and his head was being pulled up, up, off the ground and he could hardly breathe. He was more afraid than he had ever been.

Linus waited a long, long time, until the cattails and lily pads stopped bobbing up and down, until the water was still. His legs were still weak. He felt his heart pounding.

Slowly, Linus walked back through the woods, back to where he had left Blossom. It hurt too much to even think about his mama and daddy.

The breeze came by. Linus heard the birds. He could not believe they were still singing.

The cow looked up as he came to her. She looked mad because he had kept her waiting.

"You, cow. What you look at?" Linus swatted her nose with the tether, hard enough so she grunted with surprise and hurt, hard enough so that the end of the leash came around behind him and stung him on the arm.

Linus wanted to cry. He had left the cow tied up, then he had hit her.

"Sorry, Blossom. Sorry . . ."

The cow grunted, forgiving him, and Linus wanted to cry.

Linus led Blossom back down the tracks. He had to walk slowly, because his legs were trembling, and he had to try as hard as he could just to put one foot in front of the other, one in front of the other.

He wanted to cry, but he couldn't. He felt sick.

One foot in front of the other, one in front of the other . . .

Linus remembered the feeling he had had once when he played a mean trick on Mr. Crooks, a scary old man who live a few shacks away.

Linus's papa had told him to pay no attention to Mr. Crooks, that he only seemed mean because he was old and hurt a lot but still had to work at the mill.

One day, Linus had snuck up behind Mr. Crooks's shack and pulled the plug in the barrel where Mr. Crooks kept his catfish. At first, sneaking away and then running, Linus had been proud and excited, happy and laughing to think how mad Mr. Crooks would be when he looked in the barrel and found the water gone and the fish dead. Then Linus had thought of the fish, imagined them flopping all over each other like snakes in the empty barrel, afraid to die. He had felt sorry for them, and for Mr. Crooks.

So Linus had snuck back to Mr. Crooks's shack, afraid of being caught yet hoping very hard that he would not be too late. The barrel was half empty, the fish beginning to swim faster and faster in circles, bumping into each other.

But it was not too late. Linus plugged the barrel up again and took buckets of water from Mr. Crooks's pump, pumping as hard as he could without being noisy, and filled the barrel again. Then he ran away, as fast as he could, ran until he knew he was safe. When he stopped to catch his breath, he felt light and happy, knowing the fish had enough water.

He must not tell. He must keep the secret about the girls until he died and went to heaven . . .

One foot in front of the other. His knees shook. He felt sick.

He was almost at the Green Hill church. He could smell the cut wood and hear the screams of saws from the mill. Almost quitting time . . .

When he got to his family's shack, he would tie Blossom up and stay outside until it was almost dark . . .

"You hold that cow right, hear? Ain't some dog you pullin' around . . ." It was Mr. Crooks, standing in the doorway of his shack. The mill foremen sometimes let him quit early, so he was the only man around.

22

"I lead her okay." Linus's mouth was dry.

"Your folks gonna hear, you give me any sass …"

Linus went by Mr. Crooks's shack. From the corner of his eye, he thought he saw Mr. Crooks take a step toward him, then stop.

Linus was so afraid, he tried to make himself think of something else. He thought of the color poster he had seen in the company store, the one with the plane that had a red tiger's mouth behind the propeller. He loved the picture of the tiger plane, shining silver except for the tiger mouth and the orange flashes from the guns in the wings. He had gone by the big trash barrel behind the store, picking up almost-empty cans of paint and scraps of pine. Before long, he had enough scraps of wood to paint on.

He could never get the tiger plane to look just the way he wanted, but he still loved to try. He painted blue for the sky, a whole lot of orange for the flashing guns, and yellow for the bad planes that the tiger planes shot at.

Linus knew the tiger planes were in the war, way across the ocean. He used to hope it would last until he was big enough to fly a tiger plane.

Once, two white men from the mill had come by and stood over him when he was trying to paint a war picture (he liked the colors, but he could never make it come out as good as he saw it in his head). Linus had felt funny when the white men laughed. Boy, you thinkin' of flyin' one of them planes? Yes sir. For whose side, boy?

Linus had felt his face burn when the men laughed. They meant he could never fly a tiger plane, that it was funny to even think about it. It took Linus a long time to get the thought out of his head and tell himself that he could fly a tiger plane, maybe. If the war was long enough.

Linus tied Blossom to her stake in the backyard, next to the garden. Then he walked to the back door of the shack and listened. He could hear his mama humming, could smell food. He thought he would be sick.

"I be home, Mama. I be out here for a while."

He heard his mama grunt that it was all right. Then he went to the shed and got out his wood scraps and paint. But he did not feel like painting a tiger plane.

Linus stared at the red tiger mouth behind the propeller, at the red spot on the bad planes. Back there, where the girls were, the red had been just as bright.

He knelt and stared at the picture for a long time. It did not look as real as he had remembered it. Blossom chewed on grass; she was happy. He smelled food cooking in the shack, but he was not hungry. It would be dark soon.

Linus wanted to cry, but he was afraid. His mama would ask him why.

"I ain't gonna fly no tiger plane," he whispered.

CHAPTER 3

Hiram Stoker winced when the phone rang. For a fleeting moment, he was tempted to ignore it. But he had never ignored the phone, and he never would as long as he was sheriff of Clarendon County.

His years as a law man—too many years, he sometimes thought—had not only honed his gifts for hard work and common sense. They had given him an intuition as well. That was why, as soon as the phone rang this particular evening, he knew his whole night was shot.

He was already late getting out of his cramped office in front of the jail. That afternoon, he had had to straighten out a messy colored thing: two big bucks, drunk on peach wine, carving each other with razors. Lucky for them (though not so lucky for the sheriff, since they were now sleeping it off in their cells out back, until he could get them shipped off to a highway work gang to straighten them out), they had been so drunk that neither had been able to do a real good cutting job. Still, there had been the smell (a lot of human blood in one place smelled, white and colored both), and the unpleasantness of hearing them whimper while being sewed up.

Anyhow the sheriff had just got the bucks bedded down, warning them that they had goddamn well better keep quiet till his deputy came by for the night trick, when they could have some supper if they had the stomach for it, when the phone rang.

Goddamn. He was looking forward to getting home, getting some dinner, maybe some cards and part of a jug ...

Trouble. The sheriff knew it by the hairs on his arms.

"Sheriff's office."

"Hiram, this is Wilbur Clark. Me and the wife are worried. Sue Ellen went to pick flowers down past niggertown and she ain't back."

"Who she with, Wilbur? Maybe she just stopped somewhere. Wish I had a dollar for every time my sons—"

"Uh, huh. She went with Cindy Lou Ellerby. She ain't come back either. Her folks are here now, at our place. We all worried."

"Hmmm. Down by the mill they went, you say …"

"Yep."

"Tell you what. I be by your place in a little while. If the tykes ain't back by the time I get there, we can figure a little bit what we're gonna do. And if they is, I'll scare 'em so bad they'll never worry you like this again."

Stoker hung up and dialed home to tell his wife he would probably be late. A moan came from a cell.

"Shut up back there!" he shouted, annoyance having chased compassion from his heart. "Your own goddamn fault. Sorry-ass niggers." He gave his wife a terse message, turned out the lights, locked his door, and got into his car.

To get to the Clark house, the sheriff had to drive by the mill. He liked Mr. Tyler well enough (not a bad sort at all, especially for being so rich), but he had to admit Mr. Tyler made his job tougher, at least indirectly. The mill had been busier since the war, and Mr. Tyler had taken on some unfamiliar help. Had to, with so many men away. Still, that made Stoker's job harder. Any sheriff knew that the fewer strangers around (whites and colored both), the quieter things were. With more strangers at the mill, there had been a few more fistfights, a few more wrecks, a few more ruckuses in the colored shacks.

Twilight came as he was passing the mill. Just a few lights on, the saws quiet, the smell of cut wood in the now-chill air. He drove slowly, half-expecting to see two little girls walking in a big hurry, knowing they were late and fearing for their fannies.

He slowed to a crawl, opened his window all the way. Frogs and crickets thrumming away, telling the new spring they were alive. A pretty sound, but Stoker frowned. If they were out there and lost, the girls would be scared.

The sheriff heard a horse cry in pain from the shed near the mill gate. He stopped his car and got out.

Even in the gathering darkness, Hiram Stoker easily made out the stooped, shuffling form of T. J. Campbell. A sneaky, no-good way about him, the sheriff thought, knowing his dislike was not particularly rational but not caring, either.

"Evenin', T.J.," Hiram Stoker said.

"That you, Sheriff?"

"None other. You here kinda late, aincha?"

"Lotta work to do. Never seems to get done . . ."

"Hmmm." There was a laugh, Hiram Stoker thought. In the sheriff's opinion, T. J. Campbell was not a candidate to work himself to death. The sheriff thought he had one qualification to work at the mill at all, let alone be a foreman, and that was his kinship to the owner. Short on brains, long on mouth, mean to the workers, white and colored both. And horses.

"You happen to see two little girls in these parts?" the sheriff said, forcing his mind to the task at hand.

"Nope . . ."

Silence hung in the dark.

"Well, they were down by the mill a while back, down where there's some flowers. Off the track there . . ."

"I said no. . . ."

Smirky shit, Stoker thought. Mouth always set in a sneer . . .

"Well, they're missing. Or lost. Young girls. Their daddies work at the mill. Ellerby and Clark. Always together. Went pickin' flowers this afternoon after school and ain't been seen since."

"I'll keep my eyes open."

"You do that."

"That it?"

The sneering quality in T.J.'s voice angered Stoker no end. It didn't matter that the sheriff knew T.J. was masking a basic cowardice; it still angered him.

"Something else, T.J. There's a law on the county books against treating animals bad. Lest you think this is a bluff, and it surely isn't, you best be gentler to them horses. I like horses. Like some better than people, truth to tell. Got that?"

"Sure, Sheriff." A sneer in the dark.

"And you know what else, T.J.? When I was growing up around here, a guy who behaved like you was known as a shitass."

Driving on, the sheriff became thoroughly angry. There was something in T.J. that he couldn't put his finger on, something that made him pissed off and uncomfortable at the same time. Seemed like a person ought to feel sorry for T.J., almost. All those damn pimple scars on his neck, front and back . . . Parents up and died on him young . . . Still, T.J. was damn lucky—more lucky than most people around Clarendon—that his uncle owned the mill. Hell, Tyler wasn't the warmest guy, and he made T.J. keep some long hours, but so what? T.J. had a job, a foreman's job, and he'd be well off someday because his uncle owned the mill.

Oh, the hell with it.

Up ahead were the lights of the Clark house. As soon as Stoker saw them, he knew the girls hadn't come home. There were too many lights on, for one thing. Extra people in the house, come there just to worry with each other, moving from room to room with their fretting, leaving lights on. More than that: The house itself, spilling its light through windows onto glistening night grass, seemed to be lying low with pain.

The sheriff knocked twice and entered through the kitchen door without waiting for it to be opened.

"Howdy," he said, trying to make his greeting friendly and low-key but not too jovial.

He could read the pain and fear in the faces. There were the girls' parents, Wilbur and Catherine Clark, and Jason and Wilma Ellerby. The four of them were sitting at the kitchen table, drinking coffee. In the other room, worn-out furniture and sagging floors groaned slightly as several men and women and a few children—relatives, friends, siblings, the sheriff knew at once—got up to look into the kitchen.

Jesus, look at the faces, the sheriff thought. Looking at me like I can make things better for them. "Howdy, folks."

"Sheriff, I was out looking for 'em," Wilbur Clark said. "Figured after a while my place was here, with Catherine."

"Same with me, Sheriff," Jason Ellerby said.

"You did right, both of you," the sheriff said. "Did all you could, I know." He had seen worry get the better of people before. He felt sorry for Clark and Ellerby for thinking they had to explain. They were simple, physical men, sawmill workers. He wondered how they would deal with—

"Coffee, Sheriff?"

Someone handed him a cup. "Thanks, but it's probably too good for me. I'm used to the paint thinner my deputy brews."

Laughter. The sheriff welcomed it. He had seen people so torn apart that they couldn't talk straight.

"So," Stoker began, his face serious now. "I sure don't want to make light of your worrying, not at all. But the chances are the girls are someplace safe. I seen so many cases like this, the years I been doin' this job, that I can say that honest-like. You folks already checked with all their friends? Every one?"

Several voices replied at once, but Stoker let them talk. Their message was simple enough—they had checked everyone they could think of—and he knew it made the parents feel better to tell what they had done.

"And you checked down past the colored church? Somebody?"

"We did," Wilbur Clark said. "Catherine hollered real loud. Scared us not to get an answer. Happened before that they'd go down that way, explorin' like. Sure, sometimes they'd lose track what time it was, we'd have to go holler for 'em. Ain't that far away that they went; they'd always hear and holler back . . ."

"And right smart, they would," Catherine Clark broke in. "They'd be scared, whenever we had to go and fetch 'em."

"Bet they would," the sheriff said. "My Bob, he was always runnin' off, more'n my other son. Get into scrapes, come home late, his clothes all tore and stuck with burrs. Used to worry as much about him then as I do now that he's off in the war—"

The sheriff stopped abruptly; he didn't want his listeners to think he was minimizing their concern. And he sure as hell didn't want to get himself thinking about his son Bob.

"Now, here's what's what," Stoker began again. "Them tykes could still walk in here two minutes from now. Wouldn't surprise me a bit. But assuming they don't: I'm gonna call my deputy. Then I'll get in touch with the highway patrol, have them watch—"

"Somebody might have taken them away in a car?" Catherine Clark said, voice pitch rising with each word.

"Hold on, now," Stoker said. "Didn't say that at all. Ain't likely. Can't remember the last time we had a kidnapping in these parts. Ain't enough money to make it worthwhile. What we need is some more manpower. Get the state to send us some bodies. Then I'll head over to Darryl Lee's place and get him to bring out his hounds. I'll need a piece of clothing from each girl."

A starry Carolina night, a blue-black sky dotted with silver. Incessant thrumming from legions of frogs in the swamp, and now and then a splash from God-only-knows-what.

"Got any notions?" Deputy Dexter Cody asked the sheriff. They were sitting in the sheriff's car, taking a break from searching, trying to dry their pant cuffs and sipping coffee from a Thermos.

"A few," the sheriff said. "None pretty."

Theirs was one of three cars parked in a clearing a hundred yards from the rear of the lumber mill, which squatted black and silent now. Another car belonged to the highway patrol, which had sent four men. The third, its rear seat ripped out to make a wagon-like interior for farm chores, belonged to Darryl Lee. The car had brought four good tracking hounds, whose wondrous voices could be heard a few hundred yards away. Directly behind them was the mill; off to their left was the colored church and beyond that, far enough away so that there were hardly any sounds, the colored shacks. If the sheriff turned on his headlights (which he just might do, and honk his horn to signal that the search was over for the night), they would shine down the tracks leading away from the mill. It was down there, the parents had said, that the girls had said they were going.

The sheriff felt comfortable with his deputy. Dexter Cody was tall and bony, but strong. He was in his early thirties and lived with his widowed mother, whose health was very poor. Dexter was celibate, near as the sheriff could tell. Taking care of his mother didn't leave him a lot of time to do much courting. And he wasn't a whole lot to look at, truth to tell.

Dexter worked hard, and he was loyal. He didn't want to be sheriff himself (Jesus, who would want that?), which meant Hiram Stoker could trust him. Dexter was so plain, so without guile, it seemed to the sheriff. Dexter could be scary, too, especially to the coloreds. If they had one who was, say, making a fuss in his cell, Dexter would tell him— once, that's all—that if he didn't shut up, he'd have a cracked head and an empty belly. Worked every time.

If Dexter had any fault, it was that he was too hard on the colored sometimes. The sheriff had cautioned him on that a few times, but ... well, that's how Dex was. And mostly he was a damn good deputy. Not much imagination, just plain horse sense. Which in the present situation was more valuable anyhow.

"Dex, what do you think?"

"If they's alive, they ain't out there, not along them tracks or in the woods. Makes no sense."

"No, it don't."

Damn. The coffee had helped to string out his nerves, and the chill of the early spring night was coming into the car. Two sets of parents were tearing their hearts out with worry this very moment.

Time to decide. The sheriff could let the search go on through the night, knowing one of the searchers could drown in a creek in the pitch dark. He could call it off for the night, though that would give the message to the parents that their little girls just might not be coming home. And if he acted now—right now, not a half-hour later—he could get authorization for a National Guard company to be on the scene by first light, or shortly thereafter. If he did that, and it turned out that the girls were safe and snug somewhere all along, some people would hold it against him.

Goddamn.

"This job don't get no easier, Dex. And I don't get no younger."

The sheriff turned on his headlights, blinked them repeatedly, and leaned on his horn. The search was over for the night. He would call the highway patrol watch commander, who would call the nearest National Guard officer.

The light in the kitchen of the sheriff's house was still on—an answered prayer. It meant his wife, Effie, was not only still up but probably making something for him.

"How you spoil a man," he said, smelling the warmed-over stew and muffins as he hung his gun belt over a chair.

"I married the sheriff."

He hugged the plain, round-faced woman with clear blue eyes and hoped she knew how much he loved her.

Then the sheriff sat down to eat and found that he was ravenous. He ate, she poured him some milk, and they talked a while.

Before long, he was bone-tired and ready for bed. He thought for a moment of his son Bob (must be dawn in England, he's probably having breakfast right now), then he thought again of the girls. Two things bothered him. One was the way the dogs had seemed to pick up the scent along the tracks, then nothing; the other was his wife's casual remark that if the girls had been planning some all-night mischief, they would have changed out of their school clothes.

CHAPTER 4

Middle of a Carolina morning in spring, the sun sucking mist up from the trees. If one could have hovered up there in the mist, one would have seen the National Guard troops poking slowly through the woods, would have seen a dozen or so men in highway patrol uniforms mixed in with the troops, now and then telling a soldier to poke this way or that, kick under this or that bush. And in a group by themselves, their voices unmistakably different, a score or more colored mill workers hacked and poked their way through the grass, pines, and brush. Minute by minute, the sun got brighter and the mist thinner, so that if one were hovering, magically, above the entire scene, he would have seen the railroad tracks shining like silver. And if one's eyes had happened to pause for a moment on a water-filled ditch, he would have seen something (ah! part of a bicycle pedal) protruding from the water.

Hovering magically above, and staring for several minutes at the ditch, one would have seen reflections of cloud wisps on the water surface, would have seen, now and then, brief images of pine tops, then the gentlest of ripples, then back to almost perfect stillness, with just the cloud wisps and the sun on the water. Or was there more? If one had had that magic vantage point and stared at the ditch, by and by he would have seen a trace of yellow beneath the surface, just barely visible when the surface was still and the light shone a certain way. Yellow from a schoolgirl's dress.

Private Luke Reddy paused, leaning on his pole as he took deep breaths and pulled his canteen from its holster. He was thirsty and his feet were tired and there were scratches on the backs of his hands. Still, it was not a bad feeling; it was sort of like the feeling after a day of hunting. He would be damn glad when the chow truck came out with the midday meal (assuming they were still searching by then, which looked like a sure thing).

Reddy was sure that if he ever got into combat (and God, he wanted that so, to be there and know what it was like and be able to know it all the rest of his life!), he would find the little things—the sweat running down his ass, the scratches on his hands, the bug bites—as bad or worse than being shot at. He wouldn't be able to choose when to hit the ground, either. Enemy bullets start flying your way, you get down. Dive into the mud if you gotta. Hell, dive into cow flops; better that than get killed.

He had been searching as conscientiously as he knew how. Part of it was pride: He knew he wasn't a bad woodsman, and if he was a good rabbit and quail hunter, knowing more times than not when to approach a particular bush quietly, when to stop dead in his tracks, then start up again, all the while getting the shotgun half into position so he was ready to fire as soon as the rabbit or bird was flushed—why, if he was that good, he would sure as hell do a good job this morning. No one would ever say he had walked right over where the girls lay and he had not seen them.

Damn. Wonder what the hell happened to them. Some of the niggers behind him were laughing it up like they were on a fucking picnic.

A thought filled Reddy with a killing rage. The thought of two little girls, probably tied up, clothes ripped off, being held prisoner in some nigger shack was more than he could stand. Fingers the color of rotten bananas roaming all over them, dick like a big lump of coal. . . .

The way to deal with something like that—the only way!—was a rope around a black neck, tighter, tighter, tighter. . . . Or cutting. Niggers loved to cut, loved what a razor could do. How about what a bayonet could do, especially in the right place, where a nigger's soul lived. . . .

He stuffed his canteen back into its canvas container on his belt and tried to stuff the murderous thoughts into a corner of his brain. Wasn't anything worse than being near crazy, you were so pissed off, and not being able to take it out on somebody. That was one of the things that pissed him off the worst about the Guard, getting pissed off at some sergeant and having to swallow it.

"You, you boys there! Easy lookin' along the tracks. Back into the woods where you can do some good."

Reddy smiled as the state trooper shouted at the gaggle of niggers to quit moping along the tracks (it was true, anybody could look along the tracks, not have to get scratches or burrs). Just plain no-fucking-good, lazy-ass bunch of niggers.

Well, he was sure as hell entitled to a little easier terrain. He had been stomping through the rough stuff all morning. Time for him to get out in the open a bit, get his pant legs dry. And what the hell, there *was* a clear patch of grass and flowers up ahead, right by the tracks, where somebody had to look.

He walked up to the tracks and stood on a rail, stretching his legs to make himself as tall as he could to see as far as he could down the straightaway. It was a game he had done since he was a child.

He left the tracks and walked across the little flower-adorned clearing, swinging his pole gently at the yellow and blue petals. Reddy stopped at the ditch. Wide, maybe a few feet of water, considering all the rain ...

Here and there a lily pad, over there part of a rotted stump ... and something there was no accounting for. The black of the bike pedal sticking up caught his eye. He stood at the edge of the ditch and extended the pole. He tapped the end of the pedal; it turned easily.

Reddy could hear the birds, now joyous and gentle, now raucous and scornful, in the trees above. He prodded beneath the surface of the water, just around the pedal. The hard "ting" feeling of the bicycle fender was unmistakable; so was the feeling when the end of the pole jammed between spokes. It was hard work with the pole, at once pushing down and trying to pull the bicycle toward him. His hands and wrists ached. Finally, he could feel the bicycle come free, the pole still wedged in the spokes, the bicycle coming to him more easily now, sinking slowly now that it had been pulled loose from whatever it had snagged on. The momentum from the sinking plus what he could generate with the pole brought the bicycle toward the edge.

He had it now, one wheel resting in the muck near his feet, the rest lying in shallow water. He bent down to look, and it was then that he noticed the flap of yellow fabric on the surface. Knees trembling, hands and wrists aching, Reddy poked at the yellow cloth.

Not so many months later, Private Luke Reddy would get his wish. He would indeed go into combat, on a couple of tropical Pacific islands with names he had never heard of. He would sweat and get diarrhea and malaria, see men's intestines lying next to them, see flies crawling on purple corpses. He would hear men scream in pain, their agony heard over the exploding shells, and he would smell burnt flesh. He would remember those things and not want to talk about them. But what he would remember more than any of that—what he would dream about years later—was the face of Cindy Lou Ellerby bobbing up out of the water.

"Found 'em," Dexter Cody told Sheriff Hiram Stoker, who swallowed the last of his coffee and nodded. The deputy hadn't said the word "dead," but there was no need.

The sheriff sighed, took a deep breath and swallowed hard, mentally steeling himself for what he was about to see. At least there would be no decomposition, not with their just being dead a day or so and out in the cool night. The coroner, he had a trick to keep from puking around rotting corpses. Just swallowed his tobacco plug; it did the trick every time.

The sheriff didn't chew tobacco. Besides, he wasn't worried about his stomach; he was worried that what he was about to see would do something to his spirit, take something out of him that could never be put back. He had seen enough bodies to be almost used to death, except when the dead were children. White or black, dead children still bothered him. Come upon a bad fire or a wreck (worst of all, maybe, had been the time that tyke on the Folsoms' farm had got run over by the tractor) and, well, it took something from you. . . .

"Okay, Dex. Now we do our job, I guess."

A couple dozen Guardsmen and state troopers had formed a circle on the grass clearing. As he approached, the sheriff could see flashes of color—the girls' dresses—between the shifting legs of the onlookers. Stoker was dimly aware of birds singing in the trees, of the word "sheriff" being whispered as he drew near, of the men parting to let him through. Just inside the circle stood a Guard sergeant with the name "Hansen" on his chest and, next to him, a private.

"Reddy here spotted 'em in the ditch, Sheriff," the sergeant said.

"They was underneath that bicycle there," the private said, somewhat breathlessly. "I shouted for help soon's I saw the one's face in the water. Couple my buddies came, and we dragged 'em out."

"Good work," Stoker said quietly.

"Guess you don't need the men anymore," the Guard sergeant said.

"No," the sheriff said. "Mind, tell 'em there ain't no sense blabbing all over, what they saw. Wouldn't be human if they didn't talk, but let's not get things all stirred up with rumors and such. Got that, Reddy?"

"Yes, sir."

"Good. Now, if I asked you official-like, for reasons of evidence, if you did anything to the bodies except pull 'em out of the ditch, I assume you'd say no. Correct?"

"Sure, Sheriff." The private looked puzzled.

"Okay. That's just what I figured. That's all."

The sheriff walked to the bodies, tiptoeing as if he didn't want to wake the little girls, took off his hat and knelt down at their feet. They were side by side, face up, their clothes wet, strewn with stringy green-water weeds. Mouths open; eyes open, too. That glassy look, staring but not seeing, that chilled his soul whenever he saw it. He saw the head wounds at once; actually, he couldn't have avoided seeing them. They were grotesquely, horribly large and deep, through the bone and into the brain. The sheriff looked at them for a long time, then he was conscious of being looked at himself. His eyes came up, and he saw that a number of Guardsmen were still standing there, staring in fascination.

"Goddamn it!" the sheriff heard himself bellow. "What the fuck you lookin' at, you men? Get the fuck outta here. If they's any evidence in these parts, your fuckin' boots gonna tramp it outta sight. . . ." Stoker stopped, his throat sore, his anger spent, his anguish bottomless. He heard the Guard sergeant hustling his men away from the scene.

"Dexter," the sheriff shouted, but not as loudly, "get your ass on over here with some state law-men types, hear?"

Now, before his deputy and a bunch of state people arrived, the sheriff had a few moments of privacy with Cindy Lou Ellerby and Sue Ellen Clark. He stood up and stared down into their eyes.

Hiram Stoker honestly did not know if he was religious or not. What he did know is that he sometimes wondered just what it was, this spirit, or breath, or whatever, that was in the body when a person was alive and that vanished—forever—when a person was dead. And he knew that, at that moment, he ached terribly inside.

"Now listen, you two honeys," he whispered. "If God knows any better, you two are someplace better already. I know that . . ."

Liquid seeped slowly from the girls' terrible wounds, and their eyes had the stare of the dead. For a moment, Stoker thought of bending over and closing them.

He stood up, blinked and swallowed hard, business now.

"Coroner's been notified," Dexter Cody said. "On his way. With a camera."

"Good," the sheriff said. "Now, Dex, take some notes for me, okay? And you men"—the sheriff spoke to several state highway patrolmen nearby—"you look on and remember, case we need you in court."

The sheriff knelt down, close to the bodies. "Deep wounds . . . Ax or hammer, maybe . . . Or else a rock . . . We'll look around a bit, maybe find some stones with red on 'em . . . Their panties are in place . . . Rest of the clothes too . . ."

The sheriff stood up.

"Somebody strong?" Dexter Cody said.

"Could be. Maybe not. Don't have to be too strong with a hammer or a hatchet. Come to think of it, them wounds aren't even enough for a hatchet. Deep, but partly mashed in, like. See what I mean?"

"Hmmm . . ."

It was getting on toward noon, and the sheriff knew he had best go to the Clarks' place and break the news before they heard it from someone else.

"This ain't been the best day of my life," the sheriff sighed.

CHAPTER 5

The mill was quiet. The pond was still, logs lying calm in the water. There was no spinning and splashing from the colored with their incredibly nimble feet and their poles.

"How'd they take it, when you broke the news?" Cody asked quietly as the sheriff stopped the car at the edge of the shacktown.

"Pretty hard." The sheriff had put an edge on his voice, intentionally, because he did not want to remember how it had been, and if he had to talk about it with his deputy, it would just stir up the memory.

Not that he would be able to forget it completely, ever. It wasn't so much the way Jason Ellerby had sobbed and bellowed—he had seen grown men cry before, and where was the shame in that?—but the woman's scream that had stayed with the sheriff. Jason's wife had shrieked so loud that the sound rang off the pots and pans in the kitchen. The sheriff had felt like he'd been punched in the stomach. Then she had screamed again. . . .

"We gonna get help from the state?" Cody asked.

"I hope not. Pretty sure I convinced 'em we don't need it. Hell, they'd only interfere and get in our way. Besides, if I know these colored at all, the answer's right here. Somebody here knows."

The sheriff prided himself on knowing the colored in his jurisdiction. It made his job easier—hell, made it possible. And it wasn't all that tough. You just had to treat the colored as human beings.

He had learned as a boy (and he had taught his own sons) that if you wanted to know where the fish were biting, follow the colored. Sometimes they would try to be clever, kind of shuffling along, lazy-like, toward their special fishing places. You had to laugh at that; nobody could hide a long cane pole.

But the sheriff had learned from his father, and had taught his sons, that if you didn't step all over the colored, moving right in on their fishing spots, sticking your line into the stream right next to their lines, they would not only welcome you but would offer help. They knew so many tricks, the colored: how to bait a hook just right, how to flick the wrist to set the hook. There were so many things that had made the colored such good fishermen.

Hiram Stoker and his deputy stood by the car for a moment. The sheriff took a deep breath to get used to the smell. With no sawing going on today, the aroma of wood cut from the day before and sap still burning on the blades was faint, and easily overpowered by the smell from the shack colony. The latter smell was pronounced, what with so many more people in the shacks. A smell that blended bodies that were too seldom washed and lived very close together. Odors from a hundred stewpots bubbling with possum and collards.

A man shouted, drunkenly, a woman screamed back, a dog barked, a baby cried, a hand struck flesh. Momentary silence, then the same cycle: shout, scream, bark, cry, slap ...

"Let's see what we see," the sheriff said.

They started down one of the main paths between the rows of shacks. The sheriff could hear (no, more like he could feel) voices in the shacks subsiding to whispers or silence. Stoker felt that he started out with an edge when dealing with the colored (they were instinctively afraid of authority), and he had found he got better results by sweet talk than by threats. He wasn't above using the latter, however.

"Afternoon," he said to a young woman. Her skin was purple-black and her breasts already pendulous.

"'Lo ..." the woman said, nervously cuddling a half-naked infant only slightly less dark than she was. The woman was standing a few feet from her door. Two other children, the same shade as the infant but a couple of years older, stood in the doorway, curious but unsmiling.

"Handsome youngsters," the sheriff said, taking off his hat. "Real nice ..."

Stoker could feel her fear and suspicion.

"Pretty terrible thing happened down yonder," the sheriff said, waving his hat in the general direction of the murder scene. "Reckon you heard."

"I hear, yes, sir, but I don't know nothin'. . . ."

"Well, I sure hope you keep your eyes and ears open for me, 'case you do run across anything suspicious. Anything, anybody at all. Hear?"

"Yes, sir . . ."

"Good. Your man be at home?"

"No, sir . . ."

"Hmmm." The sheriff put his hat on, and he and Dexter Cody started down the path. Suddenly, from around the front corner of the cabin came a yellow dog, its teats swinging and its mouth snarling and slobbering.

"Turnips!" the woman shouted—more like screamed, since she was afraid the sheriff would kick, or shoot, the animal.

"Whoa, there," Stoker said, taking his hat off again and swatting the animal, just hard enough to stun her, across the snout. "Who you be trying to scare, old girl?"

The sheriff let the dog chomp on his hat band for a moment, let the animal tug and growl (a friendly growl, now) and plant its paws. Then he gently took the hat away and rubbed the dog along the throat.

"Right good dog here," Stoker said to the woman. The baby in her arms and the children who had been in the doorway looked at him wide-eyed. "Yep, a right good dog. You feel safe with her, I bet."

"Yessir . . ."

"Good. Good. Mind what I said . . ."

Stoker and Cody walked away slowly. The sheriff was pleased; he knew his encounter with the dog had gone more than halfway toward dissolving that colored girl's fear of him. The sheriff sensed that Cody was nervous (Dexter just didn't cotton to dogs).

The sheriff had fired a deputy once, years ago, for kicking a dog for no good reason. The deputy had at first thought the sheriff was kidding, then had been flabbergasted to realize that he was not.

"Tell you what," the sheriff had told him. "You just accomplished a lot of things, all bad. Filled that nigger with resentment, so next time he gets drunk he's apt to hurt someone. Fixed it so I can't ever get any truth out of that nigger, or any of his friends, if I need it. And you hurt a dog for no good reason. . . ."

The sheriff and his deputy walked at an even pace now, nodding and waving to whomever they saw. Mostly, they got nods in return. The sheriff usually went out of his way to be gentle with the colored children. There was nothing soft about that, only practical. They would grow up someday, sooner than anyone cared to think, and he would just as soon they grew up tame and gentle. It would make his job a hell of a lot easier, down the road. Assuming he was around that long.

"Hi, you," the sheriff said as an old man came into view. He had a cane pole in one hand and a string of long, fat catfish, glistening and squirming like snakes, in the other.

"Evenin' . . ." the old man said. He stopped, uneasy.

"Reckon you heard about the trouble down yonder."

"Yes, sir. I hear."

Clearly, the man was nervous. The sheriff could tell by the way his stomach moved in and out and the shuffling of his feet.

"Well, you hear any gossip, know anything, I'd sure expect you'd tell me. Sure would appreciate it . . ." The sheriff put a hard edge onto his voice to test the reaction. The man seemed slightly more nervous each moment.

"Sheriff, I surely would. Yes, sir . . ."

"Well, I figured you would, truth to tell. How come you're all agitated, like?"

"Sheriff, I truly is sorry, but can I trouble you to let me by so I can get these here fish in my barrel? Otherwise, they gonna die. . . ."

Instantly, the sheriff felt foolish and apologetic.

"Hell, yes, old man," Stoker said. "I shoulda known. If I had a catch like that, I'd sure want to keep 'em fresh till I feasted. . . ."

"Yes, sir . . ." The old man's teeth flashed white and nervous. "I glad you understand. . . ."

"You don't mind I walk with you?" The sheriff let his voice become more gentle. Without another word, he and Dexter turned and began walking, slowly, with the old man.

"No, sir. Glad to have you, Mr. Sheriff. . . ."

"Good. Good."

They walked only a few more yards until the man turned onto a short path that led to the rear of his shack. There, he took the stringer of fish and slid them, one by one, into a barrel.

"Now, how the hell you slide them fish off like that without gettin' stung by them whiskers?" Stoker asked good-naturedly.

"Practice make perfect. Sure do. I been fishin' long time."

"I see that. Worked at the mill a long time, too, I bet."

"Yes, sir. Mr. Tyler, he be good to me. Lets me off early many days, 'cause I be lame."

"Well, Mr. Tyler appreciates a hard worker, no doubt about that. I bet you been around these parts so long you know pretty much everything. . . ."

"Almost. Yes, sir . . ."

"What you call yourself?"

"Crooks. Elijah Crooks."

"Well, Elijah, you hear anything, anything at all, you let us know, hear?"

"Yes, sir . . ."

"Enjoy them fish, now. . . ."

* * *

There had to be better ways to spend Saturdays. The sheriff and his deputy were tired and edgy as they got into their car to head back to Manning. It was already past six.

"Depressing, ain't it?" Cody said.

"Sure as hell. You can already see, some of 'em are gonna grow up willing to work, those with the clean cabins and their daddy home. Some of the others . . . Well, too damn many gonna grow up trouble. . . ."

Despite the chilly dusk, the sheriff unwound his window. He wanted to rid his clothes of the smells of colored people's sweat and their shacks and their greasy fried food.

The sheriff and his deputy had spent an exhausting afternoon, talking to dozens of colored men and women and their children, trying to make small talk in their crowded shacks (actually, the sheriff had had to do the talking; Dexter was no good in that department), ignoring the squealing of babies, spending half the time just breaking down the barriers before they could even ask questions. . . .

Godalmighty, there had to be an easier way to make a living, Stoker thought. His feet hurt from walking, his throat hurt from talking, and he dearly wanted to be home. But first, he had to go back to the office and tell the other law men that he and Dexter had found nothing. It was a safe prediction (Stoker could feel it in his bones) that they would say they'd found nothing either.

Well, one good thing: If nobody had any progress to report, they could all go home early.

Which is almost what happened. The highway patrol had recorded only a routine number of incidents (which was to say very few, considering most people didn't have easy access to gasoline), and none that seemed promising. Which allowed the sheriff to say, with great relief, "Good night, you all. See you here Monday morning." The sheriff wasn't sure what, if anything, he and Dexter would do Sunday; he didn't plan to think about it till Sunday morning, in fact.

The sheriff said good night to Dexter, opened his car door, and tossed his gun belt onto the seat. He was just about to get into the car when he sensed the man's approach.

"Mr. Sheriff?"

"Who's that? Come in outta that dark. . . ."

"It be Elijah Crooks, Sheriff. From over by the mill . . ."

"Huh? Oh, yeah. You had all them catfish."

"I jes' remembered somethin'. Hitched a ride over here to tell you . . ."

Liar, the sheriff thought. Just got his nerve up. Never mind.

"I seen somethin' yesterday, Sheriff. Long about late afternoon, it was. . . ."

"Yeah, well, go on. Don't let it get to be daylight before you tell me."

"Young boy leadin' a cow. Name's Linus Bragg. Liked to pull that cow's nose off . . ."

"So? That ain't no crime I know of." Careful, the sheriff thought. Tired or not, be patient. Else you'll scare him off.

"No, sir. It sure ain't. Thing is, and I knows this is so, 'cause I seen him there before, he oftentimes walks that cow down the tracks there. Down where them little girls were . . ."

"Well, now. That sure is interesting. Tell me more, old fisherman."

"He ain't but fourteen or so, but he be mean. One of the meanest ones I see. I think he the one let the water outta my fish barrel one time, though I can't prove it. . . ."

"How did he act? When you saw him yesterday, I mean?"

"Sheriff, he be like in a daze. His eyes, they be all bustin' right outta his skull. . . ."

"Hmmm . . ."

"And his clothes . . . Mind, I can't be sure, but I swear they sure looked wet, some spots. Like he been splashed, or wash hisself off . . ."

The sheriff felt a rush of feeling, felt a chill on his skin, and not from the night air.

"Well, now. I sure appreciate your trouble, Elijah. I really do. If I come out your way tomorrow, you can point me to this Linus's shack, hear?"

"Yes, sir . . ."

Now the sheriff pushed his face up to the colored man's ever so slightly and injected an unmistakable, though quiet, touch of steel into his voice. "And I know I can count on you to keep quiet tonight."

"Yes, sir, yes, sir. You can."

"Knew I could. Don't let the sun go down on you, hear."

CHAPTER 6

Linus Bragg sat with his back against the tree, not caring that a sharp piece of bark was jabbing him. His raised knees cradled the cane pole. He was at his favorite spot, a little pond formed by a curl in the stream. The water was deep and still. The fish were lucky, to be able to hide in the deep, dark water, where nobody could see. . . .

He tried to remember how his world had been, but he couldn't. And he couldn't forget how much he had hurt, how much he had been afraid.

He had let his younger brother, Will, and his sister, Jewel, who was older, eat most of his food the night before. Linus had not been hungry. He had been afraid he would throw up.

His mother had asked what was the matter with him, and he had said nothing, but he could tell from her face that she didn't believe him. She knew he had a secret. Linus's father didn't know. His eyes were squinty, not as shiny as his mother's eyes. Linus felt bad to think that his father wasn't as smart as his mother.

Linus wished he had not left the cow tied up, wished he had not gone to see the girls, wished . . .

The cork float began to move, slowly. Then down and away the float went, the fish diving like a knife. Linus grabbed the pole and pulled back. The line swung to one side, and Linus stood up. The fish was heavy, heavy. Now Linus could see it. Its underbelly flashed silver. With one motion, Linus pulled the fish up and out of the water. It was a giant catfish, bigger than Linus had ever caught before, twice as long as his father's boots.

Linus swung the pole to the side; the fish swung by, its huge back dark brown, thrashing like a snake. Back the same way the fish came, Linus dropping the pole so the fish landed on the grass, instantly tangling itself in the line. The fish thrashed and flipped with unbelievable force, its sides flecked with blades of grass and sand-like dirt.

There was less thrashing now, and the great fish's gills worked furiously, futilely, behind the frightening, stinger-like whiskers. Its eye was wide (Linus could see only one), looking at him, angry, angry. Linus knelt down by the edge of the pond and cupped some water in his hands. He dropped it on the fish's head; the gills opened wider. More thrashing. Again, Linus brought water in his hands; again, the fish gulped for it, then thrashed.

He had never seen such a fish. He was sure that not even Mr. Crooks had ever caught such a fish. Its thrashing and gulping, and the wide angry eyes, were all the more pitiful for the fish's size. Linus could not bear to watch.

Linus took out his jackknife and grasped the line about a foot from the fish's mouth. He had to saw on the line, his knife was so dull. He dragged the fish to the water's edge. Bringing his hand as close as he could to the fierce, gulping mouth, Linus sawed the line again. The hook was set deep in the mouth, but the fish had not swallowed it. No blood was coming from the gills.

Finally, Linus cut through the line. Only a little was left on the hook. Still no blood from the gills. Linus was glad. He knelt again, cupping water in his hands and dropping it on the fish's head. More thrashing, as if the fish knew—*knew*—it was close to the edge. Linus stood up, shoved the fish the rest of the way with the bottom of his foot (there was a cool slime-feeling for a second before he put his foot on the grass), and watched the fish slide into the water. A flick-splash of the tail and the fish was gone like lightning.

"I ain't hurt you, do I?" Linus whispered to the water.

He returned to the tree and sat down, the sharp piece of bark sticking the same spot on his back, his knees shaking. The noise in his ears went away slowly. Time went by, the light fading slowly. It was almost as though there were no time.

The face of Linus's mother shone bronze in the light from the kerosene lamp. The teeth were white and beautiful (though he had never allowed himself to feel it before, Linus knew he loved her smile), and the eyes were friendly. His father's face was darker, forehead wrinkled like a prune, eyes not as shiny. His father worked hard in the mill.

His father was tired. He hadn't been able to rest, even though it was a Saturday, because he had been one of the lookers for the lost girls. Turned out one of Guardsmen had found them, his father said.

Terrible thing. Terrible thing. Oh, Lord. Terrible thing. The words came out in whispers, flickering softly off tongues the way the kerosene lanterns made the flame shadows dance on the plank walls.

The whispers flickered again, were alive in the air like the flames. They gonna come through here. They be lookin' for him here, whoever do it, lookin' through the shacks. Lord, yes ...

The thought of men coming through the shacks was scary. Linus imagined the shack on fire, with his mama on fire and Will and Jewel inside, screaming. . . .

"Linus, you not like Mama's food no more."

"I be all right, Mama. I feel bad. Didn't catch no fish today . . ."

"Even Mr. Crooks, he not catch one every day. You eat."

He could only eat a little. Mr. Tyler had given his father (and all the workers who had looked for the girls) some bacon to say thank you. His mother had cooked it with beans, carrots, and potatoes. Linus felt bad that he couldn't eat more. Let Will and Jewel have his share.

That night, he lay on his back on his mattress, eyes trying to take all the darkness inside him. He listened as hard as he could to the breathing of his brother and sister on the floor next to him. Will snored; Jewel breathed like a puppy.

A tear ran down Linus's cheek; it was hot. He tried to take in all the darkness of the room, all its smells, the sound of Jewel and Will.

He did not remember falling asleep. He knew it had taken a long time, because his eyes itched. Now it was morning, Sunday morning, and he heard his mother moving around in the other room, heard her hurrying Will and Jewel to get ready for church. Their father never went.

Linus got up and went to the outhouse and peed, holding his breath against the smell and shivering from the chill.

"You, Linus. You hurry yourself up. . . ."

Linus felt like he was in a dream as he pulled on his overalls and shirt. He heard his mother's voice, and Jewel's and Will's, outside. Linus wished he could go to sleep forever.

Other voices. White men's voices!

"Linus, you come out here, boy," his mother called.

His legs would barely hold him up. One foot in front of the other, one in front of the other ...

Linus could hear the hymn-singing starting up at Green Hill Church, hear the hymns between the heartbeats that thundered in his ears. Outside now, the chilly gray Sunday morning starting to spin around him, his legs shaking. One in front of the other ...

The sheriff! Linus could tell him, he could make the man— But there was another man, a thin, bony-looking man with a mean face. Maybe he ...!

Linus saw the sheriff stoop and look at Will and Jewel. "Reckon you two gonna be singin' loud and proud this Sunday. Reckon you is."

Linus saw the sheriff whisper into his mother's ear, saw his mother turn and look at him. Her eyes were afraid.

The sheriff looked big and strong. His clothes were pressed and clean.

"Run to church, Jewel and Will," Linus's mother said. "I be right along." Linus saw his brother and sister run up the path and away from him. He wondered if he would ever see them again.

"We got some big trouble to talk about," the sheriff said. His voice was low, but it rolled like thunder.

Linus's knees were shaking.

"Big trouble. Ain't that right, boy? Down where you walk the cow."

Now the sheriff was talking to his mother and father. "You folks know me, know I always tell the truth, know I leave you be 'less I got a necessity to do otherwise."

"Yes, sir," Linus's father said.

"Well, today be one of them times, when I got a necessity. My deputy and me, we take Linus here with us. Got some questions to ask him. Truth to tell, we think he knows about them little girls. Think he was there when it happened ..."

There was a moan and a sob from his mother, and she fell against his father, but he could barely hold her up, his own knees shaking. His father's knees shaking!

The thin, bony deputy stepped toward Linus. Linus stepped back, afraid. The deputy had a mean, pock-marked face.

"Come on, boy," the sheriff said quietly. The sheriff was not angry. "Ain't gonna do you no harm …"

The sheriff would keep him safe.

"Linus!" his mother screamed, then sobbed on the chest of Linus's father.

The sheriff put his big hand on Linus's shoulder and they began walking up the path (one foot in front of the other …), with the deputy with the mean face walking a few feet behind. If only Linus could be alone with the sheriff.

The hymns coming from the church were loud. Will and Jewel were in there singing.

The deputy brushed against him, hard. "Reckon your first taste of white meat gonna be your last, boy."

"Dex." The sheriff hushed him quietly.

The sheriff held open a back door of a big black car. Linus had only been in a car a few times in his life, and this one was the biggest of all.

"In, boy," the deputy said.

Linus got into the backseat, felt his body slump into the cushion, his legs still shaking. The door slammed shut. The sheriff and the mean deputy got in front, the sheriff in the driver's seat. The doors slammed shut, the engine started, and the car was taking Linus away from his mother and father, past the mill where his father worked, away from Will and Jewel and the catfish pond.

Way past the mill now, and past the railroad siding that led into the mill, the big car took Linus. Onto the main road, the paved road that led into Manning, where Linus had hardly ever been.

He hoped he would see the shack again someday.

CHAPTER 7

The door that connected the cell block with the sheriff's office opened and the deputy with the mean face appeared. Linus felt himself start to shake.

"Hungry, nigger?" the deputy said.

Linus shook. He was afraid that he would make the deputy mad.

"I be talking to you, nigger. I asked if you's hungry." The deputy grabbed the bars; his fingers were long, scarred, strong.

"No, sir," Linus whispered.

"Can't hear you, nigger."

"No, sir."

"Well, maybe you better think about food, nigger. How you gonna swing a sledgehammer unless you eat? Ever think about that?"

"No, sir."

"Best you do. You gonna be swinging a sledgehammer till you's an old man, till your mommy and daddy are buried in the ground and your sister's retired from the whorehouse. Long time, nigger. How you gonna break rocks without eatin'?"

"Don't know, sir."

"Don't know ... You givin' me shit, boy? Nigger shit?"

"No, sir."

"Better not. My gun belt can cut a mean stripe across your ass. Got that, boy?"

"Yes, sir."

"Good. Lemme tell you, boy, we got quite a say as to which chain gang you get sent to. Some of 'em treat you right human. Meat and potatoes if you break them rocks good, even lemonade on hot days. Else we can send you to one where they feed you pigs' ears and only give you water when you drop. Got that?"

"Yes, sir."

"Hungry, nigger?"

"Not yet, sir."

"Anything you got to tell me? 'Bout them two girls?"

Linus shook; he had never been so afraid in his life. He heard the deputy put a key in the cell door. The door opened. The thin deputy had a mean smile and was loosening his gun belt.

"Dex?"

Linus recognized the voice of the sheriff coming from the office. The deputy frowned and retightened his gun belt.

"You just got a break, nigger," the thin, mean deputy said.

Cody went into the office and shut the door to the cell block.

"Reckon he's ripe," Cody said to Stoker.

Linus sat on the bunk, pressing his back against the wall as hard as he could. He was afraid to move, afraid that he would make the thin, mean deputy mad.

Linus felt sure the door would open again, and there would be the deputy with a knife, come back to cut him where his mother had warned him they would cut him if he even looked at a white girl that way.

Linus shivered. He could almost see the deputy with a knife in his hand, feel the deputy trying to pry his legs apart so he could get at him there with the knife.

The door between the cells and office opened.

"Hungry yet, boy?" It was the sheriff.

"Dunno, sir." Linus felt joy come into him where the fear had been. The sheriff was big and his face was kind.

"I got a problem, boy." The sheriff opened the cell door, but Linus was not afraid. It was so good to have the sheriff there instead of the deputy.

"It's about them two girls." The sheriff sat down on the bunk next to Linus. "You mind helping an old sheriff with a problem?"

"No, sir."

"Good, good. I figured not. I ain't so old I don't remember how it is, it being spring and all and just learning what it feels like to be growin' up. Follow me so far?"

"Yes, sir."

"Good. Figured you did. Figured you for quite a smart young boy, truth to tell. You go to the colored school over there near Alcolu, boy?"

"Yes, sir."

"Teach you to read and write some, do they?"

"A little, sir." The sheriff was friendly.

"Good. Now, Linus, my problem is, I gotta know what happened with them little girls. Gotta know the truth. Understand?"

"Yes, sir." Linus was afraid the sheriff wouldn't keep a secret.

"Good. Now, the way I figure, you didn't mean for anything bad to happen. I mean when this all started. That right?"

"Yes, sir."

"Probably didn't mean anything bad at all. I mean, when you got a little peek at them girls . . ."

Linus didn't know what to do. He wanted to tell the sheriff everything, but he was afraid. If only he had not left the cow . . .

". . . things started to happen, and before you knew it, without meaning it to turn out that way, they was dead. Right?"

"Yes, sir." Linus wished he could tell.

"Ain't that right, Linus?"

The sheriff's voice was low and soft. Linus was trying as hard as he could not to be afraid.

"Yes, sir."

"Good. Now, if you tell me what happened, the whole thing, I won't be mad. I'll understand. I just have to know. Can you help me? Then maybe I can help you. I can fill in some of the words, 'case there's anything you don't feel right about sayin' . . ."

"Yes, sir." Linus let out a deep breath. The sheriff would not make him tell.

"Good," the sheriff said.

Then the sheriff started asking questions, his voice low and soft, using some simple words, letting Linus fill in his own words sometimes, smiling in a kind way when Linus's words tumbled over themselves.

The sheriff nodded now and then, showing that he understood why Linus had had to throw the spike into the water, and then the girls too.

What Linus didn't understand though, was why the sheriff kept bringing him back to the part where he was cleaning up, dragging the girls to the ditch, dragging the bicycle, then throwing the spike away …

"I'm mighty grateful, Linus," the sheriff said when Linus was all done and out of breath. "Now, if we look back there, back where we found the girls, we'll find the spike, the one you saw had all the red and the hair on it. That what you're telling us?"

"Yes, sir."

"Good. Now maybe you can do one last thing for me, seeing as how you told me you can read and write. Will you sign a paper, a paper just saying in so many written words what you just told me? That would help me a lot, truth to tell."

"Yes, sir."

"Well, ain't that great. Tell you something, boy. I'm right proud of you. Now, would you like something to eat?"

"Yes, sir."

"Figured. Sometimes clearing things up gives a body more of an appetite. I'll send my deputy in with a tray—"

Linus shivered.

"No, tell you what," the sheriff said softly. "I'll bring the tray myself, you done helped me out so much with my problem."

In a little while, the sheriff came back with a metal tray of biscuits and chicken and gravy and milk and fruit. He put the tray on the bunk, knelt down next to Linus, and showed him a sheet of paper.

"Linus, this is what I was telling you about, what you promised me you'd sign. It just says here what you told me, almost the same words. You sign for me, boy?"

Linus looked into the sheriff's face. The sheriff was smiling, and Linus thought he winked at him.

"Yes, sir."

"Good. That's what I wanted to hear, boy." The sheriff took a pen from his khaki shirt pocket and handed it to him. Linus tried to keep his hand from trembling; he wanted to show the sheriff how good he could write. Linus made the clearest strokes he could as he signed his name.

"Right proud of you, boy. You eat hearty, now."

Linus was very, very tired, and some of the sheriff's words had been too big, but he was happy. It was almost like before ...

Alone, Linus picked up a big piece of chicken with the spoon and ran it through the gravy before scooping up part of a biscuit. He had never tasted such good food, and he had never been so hungry.

CHAPTER 8

For Judah Brickstone, the luncheon at the Calhoun House, two miles outside of Manning, was both an opportunity and an obligation. His feelings were appropriately ambivalent.

Weeks ago, he had circled the date in red on his law calendar. It was at least as important—as inviolate, really—as the more official dates on his calendar: those for filing motions to be heard in the upcoming Special Term of Circuit Court, dates when friendly judges would be sitting, dates when unfriendly judges would be sitting.

Actually, he had originally not thought of going to the luncheon at all. Oh, the food at the Calhoun House was good enough (Judah was partial to their filet of bass and peach shortcake), but the prospect of listening to a soldier address a ladies' War Bonds auxiliary booster organization made him wince with anticipation of boredom.

Judah Brickstone was twenty-eight, a new lawyer, and he was exempt from military service because his heart had been weakened by rheumatic fever in his childhood. With only moderate guilt, he occasionally reflected on the head start he could have, what with so many men his age off to the war.

Yet whenever he saw a man in uniform, he was sad somewhere deep in his soul. In his boyhood, he had imagined himself born a century earlier, had seen himself atop a chestnut horse, resplendent in his Confederate gray. . . .

So he was not eager, not at all, to hear a soldier (a *hero* soldier, at that) speak over the cackle of women and the clink of silverware.

The luncheon had become an event he *must not miss* when Circuit Judge Horace Tallman had called him into his chambers some weeks before. . . .

"Good to see you, Your Honor."

"Likewise, Judah. Sit down."

The judge was redolent of cigar smoke and bourbon and had a coarse, backslapping manner that made him appear out of place in his book-lined chambers.

"Judah, you know Edna Ritchie died last week."

"Yes, sir. A grand old lady indeed. A full life ..." He hoped his eyes did not sparkle from the excitement he felt. It was common knowledge that the widow Ritchie had left an estate whose stocks and real-estate holdings were worth quite a lot.

"Hmmm. Full life. Well, maybe. Anyhow, somebody's gotta see that her estate gets administered properly, that everything's in order when it comes before the court. Think you could handle it?"

"Why, I'd be glad to. Yes, sir." Judah was sure that his eyes must be sparkling like a child's, was hoping that he didn't sound too breathless with joy. The judge had just played Santa Claus, had just offered him the chance to make several thousand dollars, based on a percentage of the estate, for a few hours of routine work and one or two trips to the courthouse to be sure the appropriate tax stamps were affixed to the appropriate papers in the appropriate pigeonholes.

"Good. All right, then. The court will assign you."

"And I guess I'll be opening a few books to bone up on my tax law. Yes, sir," Judah said, thinking that he had coated his words with just the right mix of self-deprecating levity and conscientiousness.

"And you can do the court a favor, if you would," the judge went on.

"Of course, Your Honor."

"My wife is one of the ladies in charge of setting up a War Bonds luncheon ..."

Which was why Judah Brickstone had circled the date on his calendar, had persuaded a couple of friends to buy tickets, and had bought a pocketful of tickets himself and given them away to courthouse clerks.

Judah parked his car under the shade of a palmetto tree; though it was only mid-spring, the days were getting hot, and by noon on the day of the luncheon the temperature was in the low eighties.

He walked briskly from his car to the main door of the Calhoun House, quite consciously appearing and sounding more enthusiastic than he felt. "Hi, you . . . Ladies, how you all doing this lovely day? . . . . Afternoon to you, ma'am . . ."

Keeping his mouth fixed in a smile (though if anyone had looked closely, he would have seen no smile in his eyes), he paused for a moment just inside the restaurant. The carpet was a rich maroon, and on the oak wall near the main door stood a life-size portrait of the restaurant's namesake in a splendid oratorical pose. Flanking Calhoun's portrait were two slightly smaller paintings of Confederate cavalry officers from Clarendon County who had served nobly in the War for Southern Independence.

The receiving line was just outside the door to the main dining room. There was Judge Tallman, his plump, smiling wife, a few other women next to their uncomfortable-looking spouses, and the hero soldier. The hero soldier, Judah knew, was from Manning, the son of a farmer. He was a private first class and had been wounded at a place called Anzio less than three months before.

Working hard on his smile, Judah got into the receiving line. "Why, Mrs. Tallman, how nice to see you indeed. You're looking lovely."

"And so nice to see you, Mr. Brickstone. The judge has spoken so highly of you."

"I'm honored indeed, ma'am." He winced slightly from Mrs. Tallman's denture breath, but he had known it was coming and prepared himself.

"Your Honor, a good day to you, sir."

"Likewise, Judah." The jurist's palm was moist, his suit smelled of perspiration and tobacco smoke, and his person had an aura of bourbon vapors. The judge held Judah's hand a moment longer than was normal and bent over to whisper in his ear.

"A word with you after lunch, eh?" the judge said.

"Surely, Your Honor," Judah said. He was immediately curious, vaguely apprehensive, and longed to take out his handkerchief to wipe the droplets of his honor's spittle from his ear and neck.

"Well, soldier! Welcome home to you, and proud to have you back!" Judah Brickstone said.

"I'm mighty happy to be back, sir."

Judah disliked the soldier immediately. His face was thin, his eyes dull, his mouth loutish, his breath stale. Moons of underarm sweat showed on his khaki. He wore a bronze star and a purple heart.

After a moment, Judah felt himself being pushed along. At the end of the line, seated in a wooden wheelchair and attended by a middle-aged nurse and a colored orderly, sat a very old man. His toothless mouth had long before collapsed onto his gums, and great turkey wattles of skin hung from his neck. His hair was white as snow, and his eyes a bright, fierce blue.

"Won't you say hello to Mr. Cantrell," a woman's voice cooed in Judah Brickstone's ear just before he could sidestep the old creature. "He fought with Stonewall Jackson."

"Well, sir. You look like you still have a lot of fight left in you," Judah said. By now, it was a strain to smile.

"I was a drummer boy, start of the war," the old man croaked. "War's end, I had a rifle. Shot at some Yankees. Think I hit some, too. . . ."

"I bet you did, yes, sir."

"Yankees freed the niggers. . . ."

"Well, sir. I sure do hope you enjoy the luncheon."

Sweet Jesus in heaven, Judah thought. Do deliver me.

Judah Brickstone experimented with several sitting positions before he found the most comfortable—or, rather, the least uncomfortable. Finally, he discovered that if he planted his elbow firmly between his dinner plate and butter dish, and rested his chin in his hand, he could endure the boredom and look (or so he imagined) attentive and very serious.

A succession of ladies trooped to the dais to giggle and cackle, speak flatteringly of the hero soldier (whose expression remained dull-eyed and loutish), and talk of flags and patriotism.

Judah was seated beneath a fan. At first he welcomed the refreshing, cool stir of the air. Later, after the restaurant had warmed from the food and people, the air that swirled about his head was sleep-inducing. The thrumming and whirring of the blades was almost hypnotic. . . .

The words sounded farther and farther away, as though they were from a dream. Fight for your home and mine . . . Our way of life . . . Our pride in doing our part . . .

His arm teetered slightly, and Judah was startled. He recovered in time to prevent his head from falling into a gravy boat. He concentrated: Which of the words had he *really* heard, and which had he dreamed? But if he *had* dreamed some of the words, then he must have been asleep. Oh, dear Lord ...

Slowly, he turned his head toward the end of the main table, where Judge Tallman was seated. The judge was looking directly at him, his face stern. Judah Brickstone was horrified.

He sat up, ramrod straight, and listened with his most practiced rapture to the conclusion of the soldier's monotonic address. Actually, he could think of nothing but the awful unfairness of what had just happened to him. He had dozed off for a minute or two, at most, and had perhaps destroyed what it had taken him months to cultivate: the good graces of Judge Tallman. The judge was a man of great influence, from Columbia to Charleston, among lawyers and legislators. His power to make life rewarding or intolerable for a lawyer, especially a young lawyer, was quite simply incalculable. Dear God, please let his honor not have seen my eyelids droop, and I will think pure thoughts all the rest of my days. ...

As the last of the diners were leaving, Judah inched toward the end of the main table, where the judge and his wife were chatting idly with several luncheon organizers. The judge appeared to be relieved when he spotted him.

"Ah, Judah. Darling, please excuse me. Judah and I have something to discuss."

The judge led the way to a small private room off the main dining room. Judah followed, trying not to betray his terror.

The judge sat in a large stuffed chair and beckoned him to sit in its twin. The judge took off his glasses and laid them on the small table that separated their chairs. A middle-aged colored waiter in a spotless white coat approached.

"Jerome, bring us two double-bourbons from the private stock," the judge said.

"A very nice affair ..." Judah began, his fear not abating in the least.

"Hmmm. Well, Judah, let me thank you twice. Once for coming, and secondly for confirming my own feelings."

"Sir?"

"Yes. I was feeling guilty about feeling so bored. Until I looked over and saw you nodding off in your chair."

Flushed, Judah Brickstone began to stammer an apology, but it was all but inaudible in the laughter that rumbled like thunder from the judge.

"Well, I guess I'd better plead *nolo contendere,*" Judah said, immensely relieved.

"Awful chatter. Just awful. My duty as a husband to come of course, but just awful. And that soldier. Godalmighty, he's an infantryman, not a speaker. Awful stuff . . ."

"Well, Your Honor. Perhaps the old Confederate *could* have been more entertaining."

The judge laughed good-naturedly, and raised his bourbon in a toast. All was good with Judah Brickstone's world again.

"To your health, Your Honor," Judah said, letting himself savor the bourbon's warmth from his lips down to his stomach.

"Business," the judge said, switching instantly to a serious, almost confidential manner. "The court approves of your handling of the Ritchie estate and will think of you in the future on similar matters."

"I'm most flattered and grateful."

"No need. Speaking now as an old attorney rather than as a circuit judge, I wonder if you'd be interested in serving on a state bar association committee for planning our convention next year in Charleston? A little work, not much, and a great opportunity to make contacts."

"I would, indeed," Judah Brickstone said, meaning it.

"Done, then. I'll arrange it. You know, the years have gone by awfully fast. It doesn't seem that long ago to me, it really doesn't, when I was a young lawyer."

"Yes, sir." Judah knew something was coming.

"So I like to help out, I really do, help out a young fellow with a bright future. Like yourself."

"Sir, I'm most grateful for your kindnesses. I can't put it any better than that."

"I know you are. You know, the court needs a favor now and then, too. Oh, I'm quite aware of my official powers to tell people to do this and that, but I still think in terms of favors on some things."

"Yes, sir."

"That messy business over at Alcolu, down past the mill. The two little girls that got killed?"

"A terrible thing, yes, sir ..."

"Worse than terrible. Anyhow, the sorry-ass young nigger boy who did it needs to be defended. Can't get justice done without him having a lawyer. The court would be most grateful if you would undertake this assignment."

Judah Brickstone was stunned. He had practically no interest in criminal law, and his total experience consisted in having defended a neighbor's son in a minor assault case.

"I know, I understand," the judge continued, soothingly. "A murder case, and a messy one. You're a little uneasy. Well, relax. Nothing to it. The boy confessed, and he's got enough reading and writing to understand, and the state has a birth certificate showing he's old enough to know what he did. Simple as can be. Guilty as can be. But there's gotta be a lawyer to stand next to him. Simple as that."

"Of course, Your Honor."

"I said nothing to it. And of course, there's not much money in it either."

"I assumed not, Your Honor. What about his folks? Decent stock and all?"

"From the mill shanties. Nigger's daddy works in the mill. Right good folks. Never any trouble, sheriff says."

"Hmmm." Judah groped for words, but it took him but a moment to realize there was only one way to say what he had to say. "Begging the court's pardon, Your Honor. But what do I do now?"

The judge smiled as though he understood. "First thing, I guess you go see your client."

Hot and humid, more like August than May, and Judah's white shirt stuck to his back. He had splashed shaving lotion on his cheeks and neck, even dabbed some on his armpits to mask the smell of sweat. He carried a roll of mints, and one after another he had been putting them in the back of his mouth. He had no desire to visit Linus Bragg in his oven-hot jail cell, and he hoped desperately that the vapors from the shaving lotion and the mints would deflect the odor of colored sweat.

The gray work shirt on the deputy was perspiration-stained despite the fan on the desk. The deputy's face glowed with moisture. He looked up, unsmiling.

"I'm attorney Brickstone, here to see the colored boy."

"Ain't you lucky," Dexter Cody said, rising.

"Don't feel lucky at all," Judah Brickstone said, trying to sound jovial.

"Sheriff told me you was coming by. Said it was all right for you to talk to him alone. Guess I can take your word you ain't got no hacksaw blade in that briefcase."

"No indeed."

"Too bad. Nigger could run it 'cross his throat and save us all some trouble."

The deputy pulled his lanky body lazily out of the chair, unselfconsciously pulled at his pants to unstick them from his legs, and pulled a ring of keys from the desk drawer. "You can hang your coat over there," he said.

Linus had learned long ago that you did not fight the heat. You moved through it evenly, neither too fast nor too slow, but you did not fight it. It made no sense, but it was true: You tried as hard as you could *not to try at all*, in the heat. You just did not fight it, no matter what.

His daddy had told him many times that the white men in the mill, most of them, had never learned that trick. They fought the heat, futilely, by cursing it, cursing their own sweat that ran into their eyes and made sawdust stick to their clothes and their clothes stick to their skin.

The colored did not defeat the heat; they just did not fight it, and thereby they won a truce that let them move through it.

Every day was the same. He was tired and bored and mad. His mama and daddy must have got really mad at him, because they hadn't come to visit. He couldn't bear to think that something might have happened to them. The sheriff would have told him. . . .

By practicing, and pretending, every day, Linus had learned to make himself float on his back, like his bunk wasn't really there under him. His head floated, too, with his eyes closed, and instead of the wool blanket under his head, there was the back of the tree at the catfish pond.

Linus could remember fishing at the pond, could remember the great big fish he had caught (Linus hoped that fish was happy way down in the deep, dark water, and he wondered if he would ever be able to keep any fish he caught, as soon as they let him go home), but he was finding it harder to remember what was real and what wasn't.

He wished he had not looked, wished he had not tied the cow up to walk after the girls. . . .

The keys clanged, and Linus was afraid when he saw the thin deputy with the mean face by the cell door.

"Getch your ass up, boy. Lawyer's here to see you."

The deputy went away, and a white man came in. He was wearing a white shirt and a tan tie, loosened around the neck, and pants that looked to be part of a suit. He carried a tan briefcase. Linus had seen only two or three white men dressed so fancy in his whole life: Mr. Tyler, who was so rich he owned the mill and the land around it, and some of Mr. Tyler's relatives.

The white man pushed open the door and came in slowly. His face was wrinkled, like he was smelling something bad.

Linus thought he smelled perfume on the white man. The white man put perfume on to smell better in the heat! He had to be rich, maybe as rich as Mr. Tyler, to do that!

"How you today, boy," the white man said. "I'm Mr. Brickstone, here to defend you."

The white man moved closer to Linus, seemed to be ready to sit on the bunk next to him, then wrinkled his face some more and stayed standing.

Linus waited. He did not know if he was supposed to say anything.

"This here's a serious thing, boy. This here's a capital case. You know that?"

Linus knew that the capital of South Carolina was Columbia.

"About as serious as it can get, boy. You understand that?"

"Yes, sir." Linus guessed it was all right to give answers to the white man. He must be a friend of the sheriff to be able to visit him.

"Now, boy, I want you to tell me the truth. . . ."

Judah felt uncomfortable; he was tired of standing, but he did not want to sit down too close to the boy in the oven-like cell.

"Yes, sir." Linus would talk with his best manners, no matter what.

"Boy," Judah said, wrinklng his face some more, "you signed this here document, and it says . . . You know what it says? That you came upon the two girls . . ."

"Yes, sir." Linus did not know what a "document" was.

"And then you . . ."

"Yes, sir." Linus thought the white man didn't like him.

"Anybody make you sign this?"

"No, sir."

"The sheriff asked you to sign, and you signed. Willing, like?"

"Yes, sir."

"And you told them about the spike. . . ."

"Yes, sir." Linus was afraid of the man's voice. He didn't sound very nice for someone who was a friend of the sheriff.

Judah Brickstone loathed the colored boy, loathed the way he looked, the way he smelled, the way he so matter-of-factly admitted killing two little girls. Judah paused; he must try to step back emotionally. The boy was his client, and that was how the law worked, the price he had to pay.

"Boy?"

"Yes, sir?"

"Ain't nothing to do but throw yourself on the mercy of the court. Your age and all. You understand that?"

Linus did not really understand, but he was afraid to say so.

"Boy?"

"Yes, sir." Linus was sure the man did not like him very much. Still, Linus wanted to say something. He swallowed, trying to be brave, hoping the man would understand.

"Boy?"

"Didn't want nothin' to happen …" Linus whispered.

"What's that, boy? I can hardly hear you."

Linus felt a hot tear on his cheek. ". . . to the shack," he whispered.

Judah wished he were somewhere else. "Boy," he said, summoning all his patience and charity. "Are you telling me you were forced to do something?"

"No," Linus whispered, turning away.

* * *

The office was only slightly less hot than the cell, but Judah Brickstone was still immensely relieved when the deputy came in to escort him out.

"He tell you all about it?" Dexter Cody said in a monotone that was, somehow, challenging.

"Much as I need to know," Judah said, draping his suit coat over his arm. He did not like the deputy's manner, not at all. After all, he, Judah Brickstone, had not chosen to have anything to do with this sorrowful case.

"Pathetic little shit, ain't he? Even for a nigger boy," Cody said.

"I've seen worse," Judah said. But in fact, he hadn't, not ever. He was immediately self-conscious, regretting his words, for he knew he was anything but a hardened, savvy criminal lawyer. He thought he saw the deputy smirk. "No money in this for me," Judah said. "The court—"

"I know," the deputy interrupted, sliding open a desk drawer as he spoke. "I don't envy you a bit, Counselor."

"Well, I just want that understood—" Judah Brickstone stopped, puzzled. The deputy had taken a large brown envelope from the desk drawer; now he stood and handed it to him.

"Sheriff and me, we got feelings like anybody else," the deputy said. His eyes were bitter and dark, his angry mouth ringed by perspiration.

"Be honest about it, I used to feel sorry for him in there. Young and all. Ain't nobody come and see him, not even his folks, they's all so scared."

Judah Brickstone knew, somehow, that he was not to open the envelope until the deputy told him to.

"The sheriff, he's easy on the niggers," Cody said. "Go on over by the mill, try and find any of 'em say anything bad about Sheriff Stoker. Bet you can't. Treats 'em fair, gentle even, long as there's no trouble. . . ."

"I'm sure he—"

"Now, the sheriff's gotta carry a shotgun around, afraid he might have to use it on a friend, just to stop a lynching. Ain't every sheriff would go that far. This one would, and it tears him up. White and colored around here, got along fine for a long time. Till this."

The deputy gestured toward the envelope, and Judah Brickstone knew it was time for him to open it.

"Chain gang's way too good for that nigger," Cody said.

Judah saw the photographs of the dead girls. At once, he felt weak in his stomach and knees. The girls lying side by side, after being pulled from the ditch; close-ups of each girl, taken from several angles and showing the sickening wounds; the older girl's eyes wide open, a horrible death glaze on each orb.

He studied them, horrified by what he saw, yet almost unable to look away. His mouth was dry as chalk, his heart heavy with pity.

"Oh, my . . ." The words came out of Judah Brickstone's mouth almost involuntarily.

The autopsy pictures, the girls lying naked and innocent, next to a long work sink, heads propped up on blocks. The smaller girl had been still very much a child; the older one had started to develop breasts, had just begun to grow pubic hair. Judah Brickstone felt ashamed for looking.

The deputy took the pictures back. "Chain gang's too good for him," the deputy said quietly.

Judah Brickstone turned and went out the door. He closed his eyes and took deep, slow breaths to keep from getting sick.

CHAPTER 9

The sheriff had driven only a few yards down the path toward the pond behind the mill when he knew he had made a mistake. The ground was softer than it looked—a sucking ooze of mud barely concealed by the little bit of grass that hadn't been trampled by horses and mill workers. Stoker stopped, slammed the shift into reverse, and worked the clutch. Backwards the car sped, lurching from one side of the path to the other. Through the rear window, he could see a group of colored workers scampering out of the way. Finally, he made it to a hard, clear area at the head of the path. He stopped, shifted into first, and parked off to the side.

Annoyed, he got out, slammed the door, and took a deep breath. He knew they were watching him, fear and curiosity in their hearts, and he wanted to break that fear down, fast.

"All right, goddamn it! Which one of you boys tried to trap the sheriff like that, plantin' that mud where you knew I was gonna drive?"

White teeth flashed in joyous, relieved smiles. Laughter from deep in their chests rolled like barrels.

"Weren't me, Sheriff. Weren't me . . ."

"Tell you what, you damn lucky, that's what," Stoker said. "Only way I coulda got out was by you boys hitchin' some chains to my axle and pulling with a team of horses, truth to tell."

"Weren't me, Sheriff. It was Tyrone. He soak the ground to make that mud. . . ."

"Shit, I ain't plant no mud," said a large, powerfully built young colored man with soft, vulnerable eyes. "Don't you go gettin' me in no trouble. . . ."

The man called Tyrone was now the butt of waves of good-natured laughter with a touch of cruelty. He smiled, even managed to laugh, but his shyness almost stripped him naked. He was the one Stoker would single out.

"Rest of you boys, you get along with your business," the sheriff said. "Tyrone, he gonna help me with my car. Gonna clean off the mud underneath. Ain't that right, Tyrone?"

The big colored man slumped with dismay, his face gone gloomy from the anticipated humiliation. More than that: The sheriff knew Tyler's mill workers didn't earn enough to buy extra clothes.

"Yes, sir, Sheriff. I help. . . ."

"That's mighty fine. Rest of you boys, you be moving along. Git about your chores. Wouldn't do to have Mr. Tyler see you loafin' . . ."

Smiles gone, the colored shuffled off, casting sympathetic glances at Tyrone.

The sheriff and Tyrone walked to the car. Stoker knew they were alone. The only sounds were from birds, the distant shouts of workers, and the muffled roar of the mill.

"Sit yourself on the running board a spell, Tyrone."

Tyrone did as he was told.

"You go to the Green Hill Church, Tyrone?"

"Sometimes, I do. When I ain't too tired . . ."

"Believe in God?"

"Yes, sir. I do, for sure. . . ."

"You swear to God right now that you and me are having a secret talk, and that you'll never tell another soul in the world what we say? You do that?"

"Oh, yes, sir. I swear. . . ."

"And you swear to God that you're gonna tell me the truth when I ask you some things? You do that?"

"I swear, I swear. . . ."

"Good. Now, you hear any talk about them little girls, the ones that got killed down the way there?"

"We all heard that mean little boy, he do it. . . ."

"Sure, sure. But you know, it's my job to kind of tidy up loose ends. Now, do you remember where you were that day?"

"Oh, yes, sir. I do, Sheriff. Honest. I was down on the pond back there. Mr. T.J., he can vouch. Honest . . ."

There. The sheriff looked into the big brown eyes and saw fear—the natural fear of authority—but no guile, no lies. Stoker felt satisfied he was getting the truth. And that's what he needed, to be absolutely sure none of the mill workers were involved, white or colored. Or even . . .

"Mr. T.J., he had his eye on us the whole time. We be there at the pond, working hard. That the truth . . ."

"You remember T.J. watchin' over you boys. That right? Think there's any need for me to talk to Mr. T.J.?"

"No, Sheriff. No need, no need . . ."

Eyes wide, without guile, only fear. Telling the truth.

"T.J., he with us whole time," Tyrone went on. "I remember, he give his horse a good sock when the horse misbehave. That right."

The sheriff remembered T. J. Campbell's sneer in the dark.

"Tyrone," the sheriff whispered with a wink, "you think T.J. does about as good with horses as he does with the girls?"

The colored man's laughter exploded like a thunderclap. He tried not to laugh, then laughed harder. Stoker got a kick out of it.

The sheriff felt good. A man, a law man, had to decide for himself where the loose ends were. A good one always tried to tie them up. He could sleep easy.

"Tyrone, do me a favor and knock that big clump of mud off the back there. You best get a little mud on your hands and knees so them other boys won't suspect we had a little talk. And thanks for your trouble." The sheriff stuffed a dollar bill into Tyrone's shirt pocket.

CHAPTER 10

A few days later, Hiram Stoker stopped at Leon Winkler's station, halfway between Manning and Alcolu on the road past the swamp, to gas up.

"How you be, Leon. Won't take but a buck's worth, if that."

"'Day to you, Sheriff."

The sheriff got out of his car, stretched, and tried to be casual. Normally, Winkler was an easygoing sort, not a deep thinker and not the least bit moody. This day, he had avoided the sheriff's eyes and had not even faked a smile.

"Get a chance, appreciate you be checkin' the oil," the sheriff said, knowing the oil was full.

Looking around, the sheriff saw four young men working on a jalopy in a corner of Winkler's lot. The jalopy's parts were laid out on a tarp next to the car, along with assorted wrenches and greasy rags, but the men were, for the moment, ignoring their work and staring at Hiram Stoker.

Something didn't fit. The men looked familiar to Stoker, particularly the one who was staring most intently, but he had not seen them at Winkler's station before. Nor, the sheriff was sure, had he ever arrested any of them.

"They from close by?" the sheriff asked Winkler, nodding toward the men.

"Sumter," Leon Winkler said, his face behind the raised hood of the sheriff's car. "Oil be right up there."

"What they be doing around here?"

"They say they're looking for engine parts. These days, I let just about anybody work on their cars here, they pay me a little and return my tools proper-like. Ask me, they's stirring up shit more'n lookin' for car parts."

"What kinda shit?"

"'Bout them girls. How they was raped, before and after they died. They be talkin' about how a jury's too good for that nigger, how he deserves the same chance he gave them girls. Same treatment before he dies, maybe."

"That what you think, Leon?" Stoker had put steel into his voice.

"Normally, no. But if he did—"

"Listen here, Leon. The truth is ugly enough, so don't let's be making things worse. Truth to tell, neither of them girls was raped, before or after, near as the autopsies could show. That's the God's truth."

Winkler looked surprised, relieved, sullen all at once. He said nothing.

The sheriff spoke more quietly, like a friend. "Lot of people come by here, Leon. I be counting on you to not give them any false rumors, hear? Don't let's stir up any shit."

Hiram Stoker was about to ask Leon Winkler if he had talked to many people about the murders, if he had passed on any information that he knew now to be untrue. Just when he was about to ask the question, the shadow of guilt on Winkler's face told him the answer.

"I better be having a talk with these master mechanics," Stoker said. "Check the tires, willya, Leon?"

The four stood facing Sheriff Hiram Stoker, not threatening, stopping just short of being disrespectful, but with slightly challenging scowls. Damn, where the hell did he know them from?

"How you all be today?" the sheriff said, hands on hips.

"Fine, Sheriff," the one who had been staring the hardest said.

"Good, good. Understand you know a whole lot about the murder of them girls."

Sullen silence.

"Funny, 'cause I'm the sheriff hereabouts, and there's a whole lot I don't know. How come you folks know so much?"

"Luke here found the bodies," one of the four said, pointing to the one with the hard stare.

Of course. They looked familiar because they were Guardsmen, had taken part in the search; Hiram Stoker hadn't recognized them without their fatigues.

"Never forget it," Luke Reddy said. He tried to sound confident, but the sheriff smelled fear. He thought he knew why.

"You know them girls had all their clothes on," the sheriff said.

"He coulda put 'em back on. Afterwards," Luke Reddy said. This time, his voice was unmistakably shaky.

Sheriff Hiram Stoker drew a deep breath. He knew what had happened, plain as jam on toast. Luke the Guardsman liked being the center of attention, liked being asked about finding the bodies, which is why he had found it easy to add details that weren't true. Once he'd done that, he was stuck with his own story.

What Hiram Stoker dearly wanted to do—what he had done before with other hard cases, and always with good results—was talk to Luke the Guardsman in private. Slap his face and take him down two notches, truth to tell. But now, he must not embarrass Luke the Guardsman too much in front of his buddies. More to the point, he would just shoot off his mouth all the more about the murders.

So Hiram Stoker swallowed hard and got ready to flatter.

"Well, now," the sheriff said quietly, stretching his words to sound as casual as he could. "Lotsa things coulda happened. I tell you this, the autopsies don't show no sign them girls was violated. God's truth."

The sheriff saw Luke the Guardsman's face pale, saw his friends look at him with doubt. A delicate moment. The sheriff must not shame him. Must not.

"Don't get me wrong, now," Hiram Stoker said. "I ain't saying you're wrong to be goddamn mad about what them poor girls went through"—there, blur the truth and go on—"but all I can work with is what the docs tell me."

Silence. Everyone was uncomfortable.

"I owe you folks in the Guard, 'specially Luke here, for finding them poor things. Best maybe now we don't say too much about it, else we stir things up. You folks help me on that score, I be much obliged."

Face burning, the sheriff nonetheless smiled. Then he paid Leon Winkler for the gas and drove off.

"Goddamn, Hiram," the sheriff said to himself in the privacy of his car. "You wiser or just older? Was a time you woulda kicked that kid's ass. Today, you did everything but rub peach jelly on his balls. . . ."

The sheriff was still annoyed when he got back to his office. Dexter Cody was sitting at the sheriff's desk, doing paperwork and drinking coffee.

"How's our boy?" Hiram Stoker asked.

"Appetite's fine. Funny what confession'll do. He sure as hell ain't no Catholic either."

Stoker smiled. "How can you tell?"

"Today's Friday, and he ain't asked for fish."

Stoker sat at his desk after Cody respectfully yielded the chair. The sheriff picked up an envelope lying on the desk.

"Prosecutor's office sent that over while you was out," Cody said.

The sheriff read a one-paragraph, handwritten note from an assistant prosecutor he knew well:

Just to assure you that the confession of Linus Bragg looks to be in order, especially as he has some reading and writing and there is a birth certificate on file to show he turned fourteen in December, putting him comfortably above the State of South Carolina's age of reason, which is seven. A conviction will be assured. God willing, it will be in another county, assuming his lawyer routinely asks for a venue change.

Best,
J. Donaldson

"Can't come quick enough," the sheriff said.

"What's that?"

"Change of venue. Boy's sure to get it, once his lawyer asks. Can't get a jury in Clarendon that don't know the girls' families and hate that boy in the cell. Meantime, word's goin' around that he had sex with them girls. . . ."

"Before and after," Cody said.

"So. You heard the talk too. Means trouble."

Sheriff Hiram Stoker had the same feelings as any other decent man.

He had the same wish for revenge (almost an animal need, it burned so hard sometimes) any other man might have, and never mind that "turn the other cheek" shit from the Bible, which his wife read more than he did anyhow.

Sometimes he thought the hardest thing about being the sheriff was trampling down, within himself, that urge for revenge. Part of him inside, and not so deep, would gladly have turned Linus Bragg over to a couple of strong men. Fetch a rope from the hardware store and head for the nearest tree. Wouldn't even need a thick limb, Linus being so small. But he was the sheriff, goddammit. First thing, he was running the law in Clarendon County; anybody think otherwise, he wasn't doing his job tough enough. Law says you do something by the letter, you do it. Works out better in the long run, he knew that much. And maybe some of it was stubbornness: If a mob came and took Linus away, it would mean that Hiram Stoker wasn't really the sheriff, that he just had the title.

The sheriff went to the door between the office and cell block and opened it quietly. He saw Linus Bragg lying on his bunk, eyes closed. The prisoner looked laughable, pathetic, in his jail clothes. Stoker had told Cody to give him the smallest set he could find; they were still several sizes too big.

"Sleeps a lot," the sheriff said.

"Sad and bored. He be needing his energy the next fifty or sixty years," Cody said.

The sheriff shut the door as quietly as he could. Not for the first time, or the last, he wondered how such terrible things could happen. Some people thought he should know, because he was the sheriff. If anything, the more he saw, the less he knew.

Oh, some things were easy to figure. A mean man beats his wife, she stabs him one day; sad, but easy to figure. Young guy gets drunk on peach wine and goes to a whorehouse, he's apt to have a busted car, sore head, and clap all at once.

But Linus, shit. He wasn't but a kid who liked to fish. Family not only know their place, they live damn good lives. Hell, they were on their way to church when they arrested him. All but the mister, but that was normal enough. The saddest, worst things were beyond figuring.

CHAPTER 11

The sheriff had slept well and had awakened in fine spirits. His first look out the window, at the gray light and the dew-soaked grass, had added to his good feelings. A new day, and a day off from work. God, he needed one.

Effie had spoiled him again with a big breakfast. God, he loved her. He could still taste the bacon and sausage and grits and the strong coffee.

Best of all, he was going fishing with his son Junior.

Junior Stoker's feelings, as he sat next to his father on the ride over to Lake Marion, were hard to sort out. Junior liked to fish (sort of), though his brother, Bob, had always been better at it and liked it more, and Junior was pretty sure his father would rather be going out with Bob than with him.

"You been writin' to your brother in a while?" his father asked.

"Just last week," Junior said.

"Good, good ..."

Junior was happy enough for his father's company, glad enough to be going fishing, and all in all it was a pretty morning.

"Should be bitin' today," the sheriff said. "Ain't too cold, ain't too hot, and we got a good, early start."

"Hmmm."

The sheriff parked on hard sand by the lake shore, and he and Junior unloaded the gear.

Hiram Stoker paid fifty cents for a bucket of minnows and a rowboat, and in no time he and Junior were in the water. The sheriff rowed strongly, evenly, the oars making delicious noise.

Then he had a thought—really, a wonderful, spontaneous collection of feelings—and was about to tell Junior. But he stopped himself; he wasn't sure he could put it right, or at least so it wouldn't sound stupid to his son. What Hiram Stoker felt was that there must be nothing more beautiful in the world than a cool lake on an early morning, mist rising from in toward shore, and the birds in the woods a few hundred yards across the water just waking up. He prayed, for a moment, to whatever power had made the lake and woods and birds. For a moment (and only that, for he would let nothing spoil the morning) he asked that power to bring his son Bob home safe.

"This is about right," Stoker said, bringing the oars into the boat almost noiselessly. He let the boat's momentum carry it as far as it would go. Then he silently dropped the anchor—two cement-filled soup cans attached to a half-inch rope—over the side. "'Bout what I figured. Twenty-five feet or so."

The sheriff rigged a number-six hook onto his leader, bit a split-shot sinker onto the line just above the leader, and took a medium-sized minnow from the bucket. In no time, he had baited his hook, closed his tackle box, and played out his line. Then he noticed that Junior was still fumbling with his leader.

"Need help, say so," the sheriff said quietly.

"I'm okay," Junior said. It was several minutes before he had satisfactorily tied the hook to the leader and the leader to the line. He took two split-shot sinkers from his tackle box and tried to bite them onto his line, as he had seen his father do. He bit one of the sinkers shut, hurting a tooth in the bargain, without even getting it on the line. As inconspicuously as he could, he put the ruined sinker into a pocket and took another from his tackle box.

"Don't forget to close that box—Oh, I didn't know you were still getting ready," his father said.

Junior's face burned with shame and anger. Not for a single goddamn second could his father stop being the boss, the sheriff. Junior knew, he knew, that his father had been no better at rigging a line when he was seventeen. It took practice. Like anything else.

Finally, minnow on hook more or less securely and two split shots to carry the line down, Junior was fishing.

"Nice morning," Hiram Stoker said.

"Yep," Junior said.

Hiram Stoker was relieved that Junior had finally got his line into the water. He had felt for the boy, he really had, when Junior was fumbling around. Hiram Stoker remembered his own father (impatient he was, all his life), and tried to curb his own impatience. Watching his son's discomfort, Hiram Stoker had felt both amusement and compassion.

Well, sometimes there was nothing to say. Just nothing. Shit, Junior thinks I been the sheriff all my life. Like I don't recall what it's like, being young. He ain't that easy himself sometimes, truth to tell. No seventeen-year-old is.

Junior had been fishing only a few minutes when he had a nibble.

"Got somethin'," he said.

"Let him walk with it."

Seconds ticked off, the nibble persisted, and Junior fought the urge to jerk the rod. The line began to slant; the fish was going away, hook full in its mouth, ready to be set. Junior flicked the rod up slightly and immediately felt the heavy, furious resistance.

"Way to go. He's hooked. Rod end up. Up, up, up. Right ..."

Junior found himself praying that the fish would not get away. His father kept up a steady, calm volley of instructions ("Up, up, right ... Taut, taut, wind, right ... Attaboy"), and Junior found himself glad for his presence, his words. If his father told him what to do with this fish, and if he just did it, the fish would be in the boat....

"He's comin' up ... I see him now, a biggie ... all black and silver. Fine fish, Junior. Up, up with that rod end, and I'll get the net under him."

Up, out of the water, the bass in the net, black and green and silver-white.

"Attaboy, Junior. He'll go a few pounds. Wait till your ma ..."

The fish fell onto the bottom of the boat now, its body writhing with great force. There was a metallic clatter and crash as Junior's tackle box fell over on its side. Rattles and rolling noises as the fish in its death struggle scattered artificial plugs, bobbers, sinkers, a can of light oil, hooks, everything.

"Goddammit, Junior. That's why a fisherman always has his tackle box closed when he's fixing to land a fish— Aw, shit. No harm. Damn fine fish. Damn fine."

His father put the bass on the stringer and let it into the water with a few feet of slack. The fish flopped quietly. It was several minutes before Junior got his tackle box straightened out, but he didn't care. He felt the delight of a child. Damn good fish, damn good fish, he said to himself, over and over; he glanced at the bass repeatedly as he patiently sorted his gear. When he snapped his tackle box shut, his father looked at him and smiled.

"Good, huh?" the sheriff said. He didn't know whether to mention the tackle box again, didn't know whether there was anything to make up for, and if so, whether he would be doing more harm than good to try. Finally, he decided.

"Didn't mean to jump on you back there, about that tackle box being open. Hell, I been fishin' a lot longer than you. . . ."

"It's okay," Junior said. "Won't happen to me again."

"Hmmm."

The morning got older, minute by minute, and the sheriff and his son said little. The sheriff did not feel like saying much. It was good to just sit in the boat, smelling the water.

"My turn," the sheriff said after a while. Within moments, he had boated a respectable bass, about two-thirds the size of his son's. A few minutes later, the sheriff pulled in another bass, almost identical to his first.

"Damn, Junior. I got more pounds of fish than you, but you still got the biggest. . . ."

Junior had another nibble, but he made his move a little too soon, and the fish slipped away.

"Get him next time," the sheriff said. "Call it a morning now? Got some fine fish for Mom to cook."

Quickly and expertly, Hiram Stoker pulled up the anchor, slipped the oars into their locks, and began rowing toward shore.

"You know, son," the sheriff began, pretending that it was the effort of rowing rather than self-consciousness that contorted his face, "when

I was your age, I remember, uh, you know … wondering about various things …"

Junior's face was burning. He felt waves of embarrassment, yet— how could it be—he wanted to burst out laughing at the same time.

"… juices get to flowing a certain way … only natural that a man, 'specially a young man …"

On and on the sheriff's anguished voice went groping for the words but not finding them, while Junior tried to bat them all out of the air, mentally, to pretend they had never been uttered.

"… questions you have about anything … don't always have as much time … with your problems, of course feel free …"

Junior knew that his father was far too good an oarsman to be twisting his face, his red face, with the physical effort. Maybe the boat could capsize; that would stop the lecture in a hurry. Was it wrong for Junior to pray for that? It seemed an odd thing to pray for, since he so seldom prayed for anything. They were close to shore now. Perhaps if the boat overturned, they would be in no danger at all. Maybe the water was not even over their heads; they could save the rods and tackle and the fish—

Suddenly, Junior was aware of the silence. His father had stopped talking, stopped rowing. Though his father's back was to the shore, in the rowing position, the sheriff had turned his head all the way around to see something.

There were four men—no, five—waiting on the shore. They looked at their feet, scuffed their toes in the sand, put their hands on their hips. They were waiting, impatiently. Their postures were, somehow, challenging.

Junior had heard no sound. He did not know how his father could have heard a sound, since there were no voices coming from shore, and the men were still several hundred feet away. Junior had seen it happen before, had seen his father size up a situation with a sense that seemed to have nothing to do with sight and hearing.

Abruptly, the sheriff turned around again and resumed the normal rowing position, back straight toward shore, his eyes staring at Junior in the stern. The sheriff's face was unsmiling, all business.

"What you suppose—?" Junior began.

"Suppose, shit. Don't have to suppose. Been the sheriff long as I have, don't have to suppose. Men don't come out to meet the sheriff's fishing boat unless there's trouble. You can bet our catch of fish it's got to do with that sorry ass little colored boy."

The men looked appreciatively at the bass on the stringer.

"Had some luck there, Sheriff," one of them said.

"Some. Boy here, he caught that big one."

"What you use?"

"Minnows. What brings you fellas out here?"

Out in the lake a bit, a fish leaped and splashed. Waves lapped gently onto the shore.

"Must be gettin' too old for this job," the sheriff said. "I ask a question, don't get no answer."

The sheriff knew the men; they worked at the mill and, no doubt, knew the fathers of the dead girls. None of the men were troublemakers, none would lead a lynch mob. But all might join one.

"We hear that nigger got hisself a lawyer," one of the men said at last.

"So?" Hiram Stoker said. "You know any way to run a trial, official-like, without him having a lawyer? Maybe you know somethin' I don't."

"We hear they gonna move the trial someplace else," another man said. "Like maybe all the way over to Columbia."

"Could be," Stoker acknowledged. "I got no control over that. Lawyer's right to ask for a venue change, if he wants one. Too much emotion here, maybe." More silence, and the sheriff knew he had made a mistake, talking about emotion. That was just what they felt, all right. Them and a lot of others.

"What'll he get? What kinda sentence?"

"Life. Chain gang, maybe. He ain't but fourteen. We'll all be long dead and he'll still be making big rocks into little pebbles. . . ."

"Too good for him, what he did."

"Now, hold on there," the sheriff said, trying to mix reason with authority in his voice, knowing it was probably too late already. "I don't know what you fellas been hearin'. . . ."

"We hear he diddled with them. Before and after they was dead."

"No, goddamn it," the sheriff said. "ain't no truth to it. You men can do me a big favor and stop swallowing every horseshit rumor you hear."

The men stared back, uneasy but unconvinced. Too late to stop rumors. Way too late. Time for straight talk. Fear, if it had to be that.

"I'm sorry I don't have time to chat with you men, but me and my boy, we gotta get home and clean our fish. Ain't much to talk about anyhow. Any you men got ideas about doing my job for me, wearing a sheet instead of a badge, you best forget about it. Some of you got wives, kids to worry about. Best you be home taking care of them. That clear?"

The men didn't move.

"C'mon, Junior. Got three good bass to clean."

CHAPTER 12

Linus was bored—bored with the four walls, with his blanket, with the tin plate and dull spoon he ate with; bored with the food, bored with the smell of the jail, bored with the smell of his own clothes and his own body.

He did not understand anything. His mama and daddy and Will and Jewel had not come to see him. It was getting harder and harder to tell what was real and what wasn't. Sometimes, in his head, he saw the shack burning up.

The sheriff told Linus there would be a trial pretty soon. Linus didn't know what that meant and was afraid to ask. But he hoped that was where the sheriff would tell him he knew that Linus had not meant anything, had not meant to look, and so he could go home.

Linus thought he heard the door between the cell block and office open. His eyes popped open wide, and he sat up. He was wide awake now, afraid. It was still light out, still light and hot in the cell. The deputy must still be outside.

The fear went away, leaving him hot and bored and angry again.

It had been so much easier with just the heat. You could make yourself not feel it, almost. Make yourself get sleepy, and dream. Now, he had to work that much harder to not feel things. He had to lie on his back and swallow hard, again and again, whenever he felt a sob coming. Had to work hard to let himself float on his bunk, float away where there was no feeling ...

* * *

Sheriff Hiram Stoker studied Linus's face for several seconds before quietly closing the door between the cell block and office.

"Think he's got all his marbles?" Stoker asked Dexter Cody.

"Relatively speakin'," the deputy answered. "Ain't seen him jerkin' off, though I ain't looked. He hasn't bashed his head against the bars yet."

"Hmmm. I seen his face twitchin' away, like he was having a bad dream."

"His whole life's gonna be a bad dream from here on. Serves him right. He probably be dreaming about nigger heaven."

"Wish he'd go there and get outta my life, truth to tell."

"Change of scenery might do him good."

The sheriff had decided that morning, after the face-off with the men at Lake Marion, to move Linus Bragg. He had not lost a prisoner to a lynch mob yet, nor had he ever had to shoot one of his neighbors.

Hiram Stoker had cleaned the fish with Junior (the kid wasn't half bad with a knife), eaten an early dinner, and told Effie he'd be driving to Columbia that very night.

"These guys come out to the shore to greet me, means there's gotta be a lot more thinkin' just like them. 'Specially with those young bigmouths from the National Guard," he'd told his wife.

There were a lot of things a sheriff simply could not anticipate: farm accidents, kids drowning, one colored slashing another across the puss with a razor. So the trick to the job was knowing what you *could* anticipate.

The sheriff might be premature, driving Linus to Columbia. Could be there wouldn't be enough mob fever to bring a lynch mob together for a week, two, three. So if he was acting earlier than he had to, he would never know it. But he would sure as hell find out if he waited too long.

"You, Dex. Call the highway patrol. Ask for that sergeant. Baldwin, whatever his name is, or whoever's filling in. Make 'em feel important. Tell 'em we request they be on the lookout for two, three cars traveling close together. Any guys with sheets, take their names and send 'em home."

"Tell 'em what it's for?"

"Yeah," the sheriff said, shaking his head ruefully. "Tell 'em we got a dangerous, desperate prisoner that we gotta transport, and we don't want any distractions."

CHAPTER 13

It had been weeks since Judah Brickstone had felt so good. Part of it was simply the weather; he had lost count of the days and nights when the heat and humidity had hung on him like a slimy skin. The night before, he had awakened to the sound of a mighty thunderclap. For an hour, he had lain awake, smiling, watching the lightning, listening to the thunder roll like barrels from heaven to hell and back. God almighty! You must have sent that storm yourself.

It had broken the heat. So now, as he walked into the Calhoun House (envying, as always, the immortal portrait soldiers in Confederate gray), he felt dapper and comfortable in his freshly pressed suit. He had chosen the suit because this luncheon was potentially very beneficial as well as enjoyable. He was to be the guest of Clement Burger and Cyril Hornsmith, attorneys from Columbia. No, more than that: two of the most influential and wealthy lawyers in the state, men whose company he would not be in were it not for the entre provided by Judge Horace Tallman.

Even as he smiled at the hostess, Judah cautioned himself. Overconfidence, smugness could be fatal professionally. Still, as a not-so-bad lawyer (if he did say so himself), he had very good reason to be optimistic.

He had met Burger and Hornsmith only once, at a bar association meeting in Columbia. He had thought that they enjoyed his company. More important, they had seemed impressed by some of his ideas for streamlining future association conventions.

"Mr. Brickstone? Mr. Hornsmith asked me to tell you to come directly to the old oak room." The hostess was smiling but acted as if she was conveying an order.

"Gentlemen, a pleasure indeed!" Judah said after entering the room.

"Ah, Judah ..."

"Pleasure's mine, Judah ..."

There were three men, which surprised Judah. Burger, tall and angular, seemed to take half a minute to get out of his chair and offer his hand, though he moved with more grace than the potato-shaped Hornsmith.

"We'd like you to meet a friend," Burger said.

"I'm Richard Kraft, Mr. Brickstone. Executive assistant to Governor Olin Johnston."

"Ah! Soon to be United States Senator Johnston, perhaps," Judah said cheerfully, glad that he kept up with politics.

Kraft was a much younger man, perhaps even younger than Judah. His smile was thin, his hand stiff.

"I'm working eighteen hours a day to help that happen," Kraft said. He had pale blue eyes, like ice behind rimless glasses. Measuring him, Judah knew.

A colored waiter appeared with four brandies, bowed, and closed the door silently behind him.

"Richard is here with our blessing," Burger said. Hornsmith nodded.

"Eighteen hours a day," Kraft said. "Because I believe in my heart that Olin Johnston should be Senator. He can help F.D.R. do more for the state of South Carolina than that relic we have now."

"Ed Smith was fine for his time," Burger said. "But it's time he was retired."

Judah Brickstone tried to keep his face free of dismay. He hadn't the time, interest, or energy to be anybody's campaign worker. God, not now! His estate work would suffer irreparably. He sniffed his brandy deeply, felt the bite on his tongue.

"We can win this primary," Kraft said. "Uphill, but we can do it. Olin is strong in the cities. With the right issues and speeches, he can cut into Smith's strength in the center of Carolina. Right here, and Sumter, Calhoun ..."

Bewildered, Judah took a long sip. The old oak room—a sanctuary of warm man-to-man talk the last time, with the judge—was getting to be a most uncomfortable place indeed.

"It's unfair," Kraft went on, "unfair to Olin that he should have a problem because of the colored. But Smith could paint him into a corner, if anyone could ..."

"Rumor is, he's got a Confederate uniform and a white sheet for each day of the week," Hornsmith said, his first and last attempt at humor.

"Which would get him a lot of votes, if it could be proved," Kraft said mirthlessly. Not a man at ease with levity, Brickstone reflected. He remained baffled.

"Unfair," Kraft went on. "Unfair, because Olin is still a traditional Southerner, New Deal or not. I know; I've had to write letters to the families of servicemen, letters for his signature, to the effect that even though the war makes it temporarily necessary for the colored to exist more closely than desirable in the military, things aren't going to change back home."

"Hmmm." Judah felt like he was dreaming.

"Sometimes the most unlikely event can become a damaging political issue. . . ."

"We're talking about the young nigger you represent," Burger said.

"I'm the counsel appointed by the court," Judah said. "I would never—"

"Judah, we understand completely that no lawyer ever is entirely free to pick his clients," Hornsmith said soothingly.

"What we don't want . . ." For the first time, Kraft seemed embarrassed, hesitant.

"Gentlemen," Burger said. "Let me try to help. We can all take an oath, over brandy, that what's said in this room stays here."

"Yes," Hornsmith said quietly. "In fact, this conversation is not even taking place."

"I would like to know if you are going to seek a change of venue for that boy," Kraft said.

"I—why, I'm still undecided," Judah said, truthfully.

"Because if a venue change were granted," Kraft said, "the case might be tried in Columbia."

"I realize that," Judah said.

"Where it would get a lot more attention," Kraft said. "And place Olin Johnston in a terrible position. I'm not even sure the Governor's thought this through the way I have. The same compassion that impels him to run for the Senate would, I think, cause him to agonize over this boy's fate. Colored, but only fourteen. I promise you, the Governor will have some soul-searching nights for this case, no matter where it's tried. He reads his Bible."

"Do you see, Judah?" Burger prodded gently.

"I'm not sure I do," Judah said. An understatement.

"I do not want the Governor to be put in a position where he has to say 'Yes, I hereby spare this boy' in Columbia, where the papers will blow it up bigger than the war. If that happens, Ed Smith wins the primary without saying a word."

"Also," Burger said, "if that happened, the Governor's chances in Clarendon, Sumter, and Calhoun would go down the drain. People around here would be furious. Denied their justice first by a change of venue, second by the Governor's clemency."

"But would the Governor grant it?" Judah asked.

"I honestly don't know," Kraft said. "I don't. I swear, I haven't talked to him about it. All I would like is for the Governor to be able to make his decision without a glare of publicity. I have some influence with him ..."

"Would it go against your ethics not to seek a change of venue?" Hornsmith asked. There, the point of all this. Finally.

"Don't answer yet, Judah," Burger interrupted. "If I may, Cyril. You may know, Judah, that I've served several terms on the state bar's ethics committee. I know a little about difficult questions. Hell, I've faced them myself. It's my deeply felt, personal conviction that you would be doing nothing wrong ethically, that you'd be on perfectly solid ground, to not seek a change of venue. To let the boy be tried here, close to his home."

Close to his home. Odd phrase, that, Judah thought. Linus Bragg's home was the niggertown by the mill. If he was tried in Clarendon, the jurors would be the very men who would gladly put a rope around his neck. Judah Brickstone knew *that* much. No, not a rope. There were men who, if they had a chance, would nail Linus Bragg's hands to a tree, cut away his privates, and light a fire at his feet. And if any of them got a look at what he had seen, the autopsy pictures ...

"Judah?" Burger was waiting for an answer.

"He'll get just as good a trial here, close to home," Kraft said. "It will foster a much more sensible atmosphere, much quieter, for the Governor to consider—"

"Hell, Judah," Hornsmith said. "Let's talk plain. The boy did it, didn't he?"

Judah thought of the pictures. He took a long gulp of brandy. "Uh, yes. He confessed."

"So, then," Kraft said. "I say let justice be done right here."

"So much rides on Olin's election," Burger said. "So much good can come to the state. Economic recovery. Good, honest men in high places, from statehouse clerks all the way up to judgeships—"

An almost palpable embarrassment filled the old oak room.

Judah finished his brandy. He did not know what to say.

"Enough speeches for now," Burger said. "Just consider it, Judah. Now let's get some lunch."

CHAPTER 14

Sheriff Hiram Stoker made a big project out of unbuckling his gun belt and hanging it up, and he hoped his deputy would not notice.

The sheriff felt that his mind was being pulled in several directions, and he was sure it showed in his face. So he turned his back to Cody as he pretended to take extra care in arranging his gun belt.

"What's eatin' you?" Cody asked.

Goddamn. Sometimes Dex had more intuition than he gave him credit for. . . .

"Pour me a cup, will you?" Stoker said.

He sat down, nodded his thanks to his deputy as he accepted the cup.

"Don't know if I got many reasons to feel happy, truth to tell," the sheriff said. "Just ran into the prosecutor. Over at the barbershop. It's his understanding that Judah Brickstone's not asking for a change of venue for Linus."

"Sounds fair and square," Cody said. "He did the crime here. Let him get convicted here."

"Right. And the jury won't take five minutes—"

"Two ought to suffice."

"—to not only convict but to send his ass to the chair. I didn't quite figure on that."

"That bothers you?" Cody sounded surprised.

"Lots of things bother me. It'll be the first time I ever presided over somebody that young being put to death. White or colored. Ain't the prettiest thing, watching that electric go through a man. Or a boy . . ."

"Ain't your doin.'"

"Hell it ain't. I'm the sheriff, ain't I? Actually, I ought to be thankful. Know why? I was worried about a lynch mob before. Now I don't have to fret. The lynch mob's gonna be swore in, all twelve of 'em, legal and honest. Maybe that's it. I feel like I gave in to somethin'. . . ."

"Still ain't your doin.'"

"You know, coming out of the barber's, I ran into a couple of guys, two of the ones met me and Junior down at the lake. Told 'em not to worry, that the boy was gonna be tried right here, by twelve good men and true, and that they could all come and watch him burn if they had the stomach."

"Why you so hostile to that?"

"And they said that was fine. They'd come and watch the burning if they could. Like they was arranging rides already . . ."

The deputy said nothing. Stoker could tell he was puzzled. Good old Dex. There were advantages to thinking in a straight line. . . .

"Politics," the sheriff said. "That venue thing. Way the prosecutor told me, confidential-like, is that Brickstone's got himself connected."

"Who to?"

"Hitched his wagon to some big lawyer types, and they and Olin Johnston's people are talking to each other. Long and short of it, they'd just as soon not have a big trial over in Columbia. Right here is fine, they think. Nice and quiet-like . . ."

"Can't figure you out sometimes. The way things bother you."

"Can't always figure myself out, truth to tell."

The sheriff sipped his coffee slowly, letting his deputy know by the way he put his feet on his desk and swung halfway around in his chair that he didn't want to talk anymore about it just then.

In his youth, the sheriff had worked one summer in a slaughterhouse. One summer only. He had never gotten used to it, the smell of blood and how the animals went wild with fear as soon as they figured it out, how they screamed and bellowed. No one to argue for the animals' point of view . . .

"Oh, almost forgot. There's a letter for you," Cody said, nodding toward the sheriff's desk.

The sheriff saw that the letter was from the state prison. His feet still on his desk, he leaned far back in his chair and read.

Dear Sheriff Stoker,

I am writing as one law man to another, and not to tell you your business. Plain and simple, I am watching the prisoner Linus Bragg extra close, and I urge you to do the same when he is in your hands for the trial.

The guards have seen him acting like he is not really there, if you get my meaning. I have seen this kind of thing before, what with there not being a whole lot to do for a fellow except to reflect on what he did to get himself behind bars, but in your boy's case it could be more serious.

Unofficially, I obtained something from the people in charge of the insane asylum. They say it will calm him down some. He gets a little in his food every day, though in small amounts he can't taste it. Just as well. It might make the world a little fuzzier for him, but then, that's the point.

I think he is more than a little homesick and cuckoo. He is not really a hard case, never mind what he did. Maybe the weight is too much for him. I have seen it before in strong men. Their mind does tricks on them, and before you know it they don't know what's happening and what isn't.

They even believe their own lies sometimes. With the colored, especially, they believe their own fairy tales and get to feeling low. That's when you have to watch them, so they don't make a sheet into a noose and save the state some trouble.

I remind you of this, as if you weren't busy enough, because that colored group with alphabet soup for a name is holding a convention in Columbia a short time from now. I tell you between you and me that I have been asked from high up in state government to be sure nothing happens to this boy outside the law. Read between the lines.

My own opinion is, this Linus Bragg does not entirely understand yet how he got himself in the mess he is in. I advise caution in handling him, and I promise to exercise the same.

Sincerely,
Bertram I. Painter,
Captain of Corrections

P.S. Get here early enough when you pick him up for the trial and we can have some coffee and swap lies about fishing.

CHAPTER 15

On this, the day of Linus Bragg's trial, Judah Brickstone was grateful to God and Sheriff Hiram Stoker, and not necessarily in that order.

The former had seen to it that, although it was early June, it was not oppressively hot. Sitting shoulder-to-shoulder with a dripping colored boy for the better part of a day was not what Judah Brickstone had had in mind when he became a lawyer.

The sheriff had scrounged up a fresh set of coveralls and a clean shirt for Linus to wear in court. How to describe the smell Judah had been nauseated by the day before, when the boy arrived from Columbia in the sheriff's car ...

"All rise ..."

Feet shuffled, chairs squeaked, a door opened at the front of the oak-paneled room.

"All persons having business before the court ..."

Judah Brickstone wished he was somewhere else. Anywhere else.

". . . the Honorable Circuit Judge Byron Bolt presiding. Be seated, please."

Feet scuffled, chairs squeaked, throats cleared. Judah sat with his client at a square wood table. Several yards away, toward the other side of the room, the prosecutor sat at a somewhat larger table on which rested a formidable stack of law books and manila folders and envelopes.

"Proceed." The prosecutor had tipped Judah, in a discreet, friendly way, that Judge Bolt considered this case simple in the extreme and would likely brook no unnecessary delays.

"Good morning, Your Honor. The People of the State of South Carolina are ready to proceed at once, sir."

Judah thought the prosecutor, who was standing now, looked absolutely in control. Self-assured. In friendly territory. With the truth on his side. He wore a well-pressed suit and his hair was held down with copious amounts of brilliantine.

"Very well," the judge said. His honor was a short, thin, stern-looking man with glasses, gray hair, and a cruel, narrow upper lip.

The fans whirred overhead. Moments passed. Judah became aware that there was an air of expectation. The prosecutor was looking at him, his eyebrows raised condescendingly. He, Judah, was supposed to do something!

"Is the defense ready?" Judge Bolt asked, peering over his glasses.

"Ready, Your Honor," Judah Brickstone said, rising awkwardly.

"Are there any motions?" the judge asked.

"We have no motions at this time, Your Honor," Judah said.

"Your Honor," the prosecutor said, "we believe we have an adequate panel of jurors to try this case, and we are prepared, with the cooperation of the defense, to seat a jury before lunch and get started on the evidence."

"Let's proceed, then," the judge said.

Linus felt better than he had in some time.

To be away from the prison, to see faces besides prison faces—these people didn't know how lucky they were! And to be able to come and go whenever they wanted ...

He turned in his seat a little, so that, over Mr. Brickstone's shoulders and through a window, he could see a tree. The leaves moved hardly at all, but they did move. If you watched one leaf long enough, sooner or later you would see it move a little.

He saw himself back at the catfish pond, wondered if anyone else had caught that big fish. He hoped not. Maybe it would still be there when he got back.

"Your Honor, at this time the people would like to call Mrs. Penelope Vine."

Linus was bewildered. He had no idea who she was, the middle-aged, plainly dressed woman who walked to the big chair on a platform and put her hand on a Bible. She mumbled some words Linus could not hear, smiled, and sat down. Linus turned to Mr. Brickstone and thought he saw, in his eyes, that he did not understand either. Linus was afraid.

"Mrs. Vine, you are clerk of the Clarendon County Bureau of Records. Is that correct, ma'am?"

"Yes, sir. For fourteen years." The woman smiled in a friendly way and Linus was no longer afraid.

"Now, Mrs. Vine, not to take up too much of the court's time, or yours, I am going to show you a document, which I will first have marked for identification …"

At first, Linus had thought that the man, who must also be a lawyer, was working with Mr. Brickstone. But after some time passed, and they still sat at different tables and didn't talk to each other, Linus figured they were on opposite sides. The man smelled of hair oil and lotion when he went by.

"Now, Mrs. Vine, I ask you, please, to tell us what this document is."

"Yes. This is a birth certificate for a Linus Bragg, colored, and it shows that he was born December twenty-ninth, 1929, in Alcolu. Over at the mill shantytown."

"So that he was fourteen, turned fourteen, the end of last year. Thank you. That's all, ma'am, assuming Mr. Brickstone has no questions."

"No," Judah Brickstone said. Linus thought he sounded nervous.

"Your Honor, having established that the defendant here has reached the age of reason before the law, I will now call Sheriff Hiram Stoker."

The sheriff had on his work clothes, but Linus thought he looked very much at home. The sheriff nodded and smiled at the judge, some women who seemed to be there to run errands for the judge, and the lawyer who was asking the questions.

"Now, Sheriff, I will show you a piece of paper, which I will first have marked. But before I get to that, will you tell us what you know of the events in this case."

The sheriff was about to speak when the lawyer stopped him with a hand signal.

"Begging your pardon, Sheriff, and may it please the court. Since the events here are rather cut and dried, horrible as they may be, perhaps we could expedite matters if the sheriff, rather than being led step by step by a lot of questions, could just go ahead and tell us what happened."

"That okay with the defense?" the judge asked, peering over his glasses.

"Uh, certainly . . ." Judah said.

Linus thought Mr. Brickstone seemed afraid.

"Well, the night of March twenty-eighth, last, I was just getting ready to lock up and head home when the phone rang . . ."

Linus thought the sheriff's voice was very deep and clear, like he was used to having people listen to him. He sounded easy and kind, too.

". . . and so, finally ruling out that they might have gone to a friend's, it getting dark and all, we started a search. We used dogs . . ."

Linus had asked Mr. Brickstone who the twelve men were sitting in two rows over to the side. They're the jurors, Mr. Brickstone had said. The jurors mostly listened to the sheriff, but now and then some of them looked over at Linus. It made him shiver. More and more, Linus was glad that the sheriff was in the room, because when the men who were called the jurors looked at him, he could feel the hate.

". . . and then my deputy, Dexter Cody, came up to tell me. Didn't even have to say they were dead, actually. I knew they were . . ."

Linus sat up. Maybe the sheriff had found out how the girls had got to be dead!

". . . One of the Guardsmen had found 'em. There they were, lying there. It was clear to me, from the deep head cuts and all, that whoever had hit 'em had hit as hard as he could, meaning to kill . . ."

Linus felt like his head was spinning. He wished he had not left Blossom tied up.

". . . figured whoever done it was from close by, and we figured a good place to start was the colored shacks by the mill. Considering where they was killed, and all. So my deputy and me, we went over there and snooped around, and by and by . . ."

Linus was shivering, he was so eager to hear what the sheriff had found out.

". . . and after talking to a few colored folks, we came across this guy with a big string of catfish. Old fella, he was . . ."

Mr. Crooks! Linus thought.

". . . and later on, just as I was leaving the office, damned—excuse me—if the same old fella, Crooks, didn't come up to me right outside my office. Said he'd seen Linus Bragg, he knew the boy, walking a cow home the same day the girls were killed. Same time, almost . . ."

Linus's face stung, like someone had just slapped him.

". . . said the boy had a funny look on his face, dazed-like, and that his clothes were wet in spots. The old man, he knew Linus, like I said. So the next morning, my deputy and me, we went over to find this Linus Bragg. Found his place, arrested him with no trouble. Brought him in, and at first he wasn't hungry. I let my deputy talk to him for a while. Then I went in, quiet-like, to have a talk . . ."

The sting on Linus's face hurt worse than ever. His eyes felt hot. The sheriff had tricked him.

". . . after a while, he told me the whole story, signed a confession. Then I got him some dinner."

Linus thought his face would burn up. He had felt sure the sheriff understood. No, that was not the worst thing. The worst thing was that Linus had believed the sheriff when the sheriff pretended he liked him.

The man who was asking the sheriff questions came back to his table and picked up an envelope.

"Now, Sheriff, I'm going to show you some photographs and I'll ask you if you recognize what they show."

The sheriff frowned as he looked at the shiny black, gray, and white pictures. "These are the victims, their bodies, where they was pulled out of the ditch and here, lying in the morgue."

The courtroom was silent as death. Judah Brickstone felt naked; the pictures showed what had happened to two little girls, what had been done to them by the nigger boy sitting next to him. His client.

"At this time, Your Honor . . ." the prosecutor began.

Judah was no fool. He recognized the self-conscious smoothness, the extra caution in the voice.

". . . the people would like to submit as evidence this signed confession by Linus Bragg and these photographs. So that we may know exactly what he did, what he admitted."

Judah Brickstone did not want the jurors to see what his client had done.

The judge peered at him over his glasses. "Mr. Brickstone?"

Judah was on his feet, the floor seeming to tilt under him, his knees shaking.

"May it please the Court . . ." Judah said.

"Yes, Counsel?" Judah thought the judge seemed annoyed.

"Regarding the matter of the photographs . . ."

Judah Brickstone could see the hate in the faces of the jurors. Not just hate for Linus Bragg but—no, he was not just imagining it—hate for him as well. It was not fair! Hate on the faces, hate in the eyes. He knew what kind of men they were. Hard working and dirt poor, some of them; all bone and gristle and no love for men who wore suits and ties. Judah knew; he could feel their hate.

"Your Honor," the prosecutor said. "Is Mr. Brickstone trying to make an objection? Does he object to the jury's seeing these pictures? If so, he should say so."

Judah's legs were rubber. He felt faint. "No objection," he said at last, then sat down, out of breath.

The prosecutor handed the judge the pictures, and Linus saw the judge's face wrinkle up, like he was going to get sick. Then the pictures were given to the jurors. One by one they looked at them, and then at him.

A man older than Mr. Brickstone and dressed in a suit (Mr. Brickstone had told Linus he was a doctor) went to the stand and told about the bodies. He said they had been hit hard on the head a lot of times.

The courtroom was so quiet, it was like someone had told everybody to hush. Linus could feel the hate.

"Now, Doctor, could you tell if the girls had been forced to have sex before they died?"

"It appeared not. Of course, we don't know if the defendant tried but wasn't able."

Linus heard a few people laugh, but they were mean laughs. The hate was still there, mixed in with the laughs.

Judah Brickstone stood up. He was in a mood to defend himself at least as much as his client.

"Excuse me, Doctor," Judah said. "You say 'appeared not.' Isn't it true that your tests showed, rather they didn't show, any sign of sexual assault?"

"Your Honor," the prosecutor snapped, "the defense will have its chance to cross-examine. Perhaps Mr. Brickstone is unfamiliar ..."

That was too much for Judah. Bad enough that he was being forced to defend a colored murderer, but even worse, he was being painted as a man who would stick up for the worst kind of sex fiend. Such an impression could ruin his practice. Nor would he tolerate the prosecutor's insults about his lack of courtroom experience.

"Well, all right," the judge said, in the tone of a father breaking up a fight between his two little boys. "But as long as Mr. Brickstone has already asked, the doctor may answer."

"True," the doctor said. "The tests showed no signs of sexual assault. No blood—in the genital regions, I mean—and no ejaculate."

The prosecutor asked the doctor a few more questions, but Judah hardly heard, he was so angry.

"No further questions," the prosecutor said at length.

"No further questions," Judah said woodenly.

"In that case, Your Honor," the prosecutor said, "and assuming Mr. Brickstone has no objections, perhaps the Court would consider a recess for lunch. Except for summation, the people have concluded their case."

The guards took Linus to a small damp cell in the courthouse basement, where he was given a tin plate of beans, a roll, and a cup of water. He ate only a little.

Judah Brickstone, his own lunch lying like a lump of dough in his stomach, sat at the counsel table, making notes for the summation he must deliver in what he hoped, with mounting fervor, would be his last (even though it was his first) criminal case. First the prosecutor came back into the courtroom, nodding perfunctorily at Judah, who nodded in return. Before Judah knew it, the courtroom was filled again. The door to the chambers opened, there was a shuffle of feet, and the judge took his place. He nodded to Judah Brickstone, who rose. Judah felt hot and self-conscious.

What Judah hoped for most of all, as he stood before the jury, was to see less hate on the faces. If the men hated less, they might forget after a while that he had defended the boy. . . .

"I was picked to defend this boy here," Judah said. "You all know that, and you all know what a terrible thing this was. We all know. I ask you to remember that this boy had barely turned fourteen when this happened. True, he's got more schooling than some of the colored, but he's still a boy. Maybe you can find some mercy. . . ."

Before long, Judah Brickstone was finished and back in his seat. He sat slumped in his chair, his face flushed, his legs numb, the smell of his own perspiration blending with that of his hair oil and the vanilla in his handkerchief. His spirit was exhausted.

The prosecutor appeared to be righteous and certain. "My friends and neighbors," he said, "my daddy used to tell me that when you make a man's mistake, you pay a man's price. Now, when you commit an animal's crime, doesn't it make sense that you pay the most? You all been on farms. What do you do with a mean dog, a mad dog? With a diseased animal of any kind? Thing is, an animal doesn't try to be mean.

"This is no boy's mistake. A lot of you have children. I have children. You saw the pictures, you saw what he did. Hell, he admitted it. Told the sheriff, signed the paper, then sat down and ate a great big dinner . . ."

Linus didn't understand. Timidly, he touched Judah's sleeve.

"What is it, boy?"

"I get to tell my side?" Linus was afraid, but he managed to whisper.

Judah Brickstone was flabbergasted. "My God, boy. You can't go up there. What would you say?"

Linus shut his eyes and bit his lip to keep from crying.

Linus was in the backseat of the sheriff's car. The sheriff had given him a piece of ham, donuts, coffee, and an orange for breakfast. Linus had enjoyed the food and thanked the sheriff, trying to get the sulk out of his voice so the sheriff wouldn't leave him alone with the thin, bony deputy.

The men at the prison, where the sheriff was taking him again, had taught him that: not to put too much sulk into his voice, to keep it nice and even.

Linus ached inside. Each tree and field and path that went by the window took him farther away from his mama and daddy, from Will and Jewel, from the catfish pond.

Yesterday seemed long ago. The twelve men were only out of the courtroom ten minutes (Linus was proud he could tell time). When they came back in, the hate was still on their faces.

Linus remembered the judge's face. Before the men came back, his face had seemed so mean, almost as mean as the deputy's, only smarter. But after one of the twelve handed over a piece of paper, the judge's face looked both more kind and sad.

Linus could remember being pulled to his feet, being held tightly, one big man in uniform on each of his arms.

"Linus Bragg," the judge had said. His face was very kind, very sad. "You have been found guilty of murder ..."

Linus could not believe how quiet the courtroom was.

"... and the jury has found that you should be put to death."

Put to death. Put to death. Linus said the words over and over to himself, sometimes making the words with his lips, as the car went by the trees and fields and ponds. When he had heard the words in the courtroom, he could not believe they were talking about him.

Linus remembered Mr. Brickstone's face. He looked all tired, all worn out, like he had been working hard.

"I'm sorry, boy," Mr. Brickstone had whispered. Then he picked up his books and seemed to be in a big hurry to get away. Linus wondered if he would ever see him again.

Linus ached most, even more than he did for the catfish pond and for Blossom, when he thought of his mother and father.

When his mother and father weren't there, Linus guessed it was because the courtroom couldn't hold all the people who wanted to get in, the people who had the same look in their eyes as the twelve men....

Then, when the sheriff put the handcuffs back on him and took him out of the courtroom and back to his cell, Linus was sure his mother and father and brother and sister would be in the sheriff's office. But there was nobody in the sheriff's office except the mean deputy. The sheriff put his hands on Linus's shoulder and steered him back to his cell.

Linus was afraid to ask. He felt like crying. But he had to ask. "Where my ma and pa?"

Linus thought the sheriff's face was sad. "They be long gone, boy. Far away. Up north. For their own good."

For their own good . . . maybe so they wouldn't get burned up in the shack . . .

Linus had started to cry, the tears hot on his cheeks, streaming down his neck, into the top of his shirt, but he was so sad he couldn't stop.

"How you be doin' back there, boy?" The sheriff's eyes were in the mirror.

"I be okay." Linus was still mad at the sheriff for tricking him.

A white boy, the sheriff's son, was sitting next to the sheriff. Linus had first seen him that morning, in the sheriff's office. The sheriff had said his son would be going along for the ride.

Linus was glad when the car stopped at a store with a gasoline pump in front of it. Linus had to pee, but he didn't want to say that in front of the sheriff and his son. He hoped that the sheriff would ask him.

"How you today?" the sheriff said to the man who came out of the store. "Fill up the tank."

The sheriff turned around and looked at Linus. "Feel like stretchin' and such?" he asked.

"Yes, sir."

The sheriff helped him out of the car and led him behind the store. Linus peed hard and tried not to let the sheriff see him.

Hiram Stoker was having more trouble than usual sorting out his feelings. He could not forget—ever—what had happened to the girls, but he had to feel sorry for the boy as he fumbled to urinate.

"Take your time, boy."

The sheriff saw Linus turn away, ever so slightly. Christ, the sheriff thought. Doesn't want me to see.

The sheriff thought of what lay ahead for Linus Bragg, and something inside him was touched. Abruptly, he thought of the girls, wondered if they had seen that coal-black thing that was still firing that remarkable rainbow of piss. His heart went out to them. Then he felt the hate inside himself. He felt his right hand clench into a fist, as though he was grasping a hunting knife. Yes, he could do it; he, Sheriff Hiram Stoker, would be capable of that which he had protected Linus Bragg from.

Well, the point was he *had* protected the boy. Saved him for the law. Guilty, fair and square, and going to pay a man's price. That was it, in the end.

"Let's head back to the car, boy."

Linus settled back into the seat, held out his wrists for the cuffs, and saw the sheriff give the store owner a dollar for gas. Where was the sheriff's son? There, coming out of the store with a doughnut.

"Damn," the sheriff said to the owner. "Think my boy never ate breakfast. Owe you for a doughnut."

Then, as though he had just remembered something, the sheriff got out of the car. "Junior," he hollered, "you watch things for a minute while I go inside. . . ."

A few minutes later the sheriff came out of the store, holding a small paper bag. He opened it to show the store owner, then handed him some money, smiled, and slapped the store owner on the shoulder in a friendly way.

Linus saw the sheriff get into the car, saw that his face was red.

"Junior," he said, "do your old dad a favor now. Check them rear tires for me. Forgot to have the fella do it."

Junior looked surprised, but he obeyed without question.

"Long ride for you, boy," the sheriff said to Linus, not looking at him. "A bit easier with this."

The sheriff took a candy bar and a bottle of root beer, already opened, from the bag and placed them in Linus's hands.

Linus could hardly believe his eyes.

"And something to keep with you. Help you be the man I know you can be when the time comes ..."

The sheriff placed a small Bible on Linus's lap.

"Some good stuff in there, boy. Powerful medicine."

Linus's eyes were hot and his throat all tight. He was still mad at the sheriff for tricking him. Now that the sheriff had given him presents, he didn't know what to feel.

Put to death. Linus turned those words over in his mind again. *Put to death.* He knew what they meant, but he could not picture it happening to him. *Put to death.* At least the sheriff would not let anyone cut him down there. He wondered if anyone could hurt his mother and father way up north. . . .

Sometimes Linus wondered if he should try to talk to the sheriff again. But when he did, he thought of his mother and father and thought they would get hurt. And Blossom ...

No, his mother and father were way up north, on the train. The sheriff had said so.

It was hard to tell when he was dreaming and what was real. . . .

Linus had thought it would be all right when he signed the piece of paper. The sheriff had winked at him, and the food had tasted good afterward. . . .

"Junior," the sheriff shouted. "Them tires okay, we be moving along."

CHAPTER 16

Halfway through the second week of June the sheriff was more tired than he could ever remember being before. Forcing himself not to think about what could happen to Bob was part of it. And arguing with Effie about whether Junior should go with him to Columbia ... well, the sheriff hated to argue with his wife about anything, and the Columbia trip had become a sore point.

Junior wanted to be a law man someday, and he could damn well learn what it was all about, bad and good, and he was going along to Columbia. That was that, as far as Hiram Stoker was concerned.

And then it was the morning of the execution.

The sheriff rose, thought of waking Junior, then decided to let him sleep a little longer. The boy was still recovering from an all-night bender he'd gone on the night before last. Going down the stairs, he smelled coffee and ham and grits in the kitchen. He smiled. God, he loved her.

"Don't you sneak up on me," Effie said, her back to him as she wielded two spatulas over the stove.

"Eyes in the back of your head. You got 'em, truth to tell."

"I just hope you never have to sneak up on anybody to save your life." She poured him a mug of thick, strong black coffee.

"Figured I'd let him sleep a bit longer," he said. "Long trip."

"Be a few minutes before this is done," she said evenly.

"I'll sit out here till then."

The sheriff went through the screen door to the small wooden porch that ran the length of the rear of the house and sat in one of the wicker chairs. He took a long gulp of coffee.

A raspberry and purple sunrise was bursting over central South Carolina. Funny how it seemed to be lighter farther away; he could make out the soybean fields on Bert Roston's spread a quarter-mile away, but the greens in his own garden, which lay practically at his feet, were still sheathed in darkness. But minute by minute, as he watched, it got lighter. The dew sparkled.

"Effie, what time is it in France?" he said, turning his head toward the den.

"Middle of the day," she said from the kitchen. "Almost dinnertime, in fact."

Since the invasion ten days before, he had often wondered what Bob was doing at the exact moment they were doing something at home. He could not even be sure, of course, that he was taking part in the fighting, but his gut told him he was.

"Careful, boy," the sheriff whispered to the morning. "Squeeze them rounds off. You're a damn good shot, truth to tell. . . ."

"Ready," his wife called from the kitchen.

"Comin' right in." He lingered for a moment, savoring the morning. The sky was light enough to show that it would be a blue, clear day. Hot, too.

The sheriff thought of Linus Bragg, wondered if he could see the sun from his cell. Poor nigger never did get to see that many sunrises . . . The sheriff shook his head. God, don't let dying be too hard on the nigger, he thought. Then he thought of the morning they had pulled the girls out of the ditch. Well, he thought, the girls didn't know when they got up that morning that they were going to die. Nigger does. Meant what I said, God. Don't let dying be too hard on him . . .

"Gettin' cold," Effie said from the kitchen.

The sheriff went inside and was surprised to see Junior sitting at the table, head down, concentrating on his breakfast.

"Morning," the sheriff said.

"Morning," his son said.

His face looks a little better, the sheriff thought, both concerned and amused. Took him a few days to get over his first tangle with peach wine. Serves him right, truth to tell.

The sun was still low in the sky, bright through the rear window and onto the mirror, as they headed west out of Manning on Route 521 toward Columbia. Hiram Stoker thought the world was never more beautiful than in early morning. Mist rose from the tobacco and soybean fields. The car windows were open, and the smells of wet, rich dirt and green, growing things filled the air. Thick, country smells, smells of life.

The road to Columbia was narrow, winding in places. Now and then, they passed a hay wagon or a farm tractor.

"How you feel?" the sheriff said at length.

"All right," his son said.

"Better than yesterday morning, I suppose."

Junior's ears burned.

"Matter of fact," the sheriff said, "your eyes yesterday morning— know what they reminded me of?"

"No ..."

"Bass eyes, after a bass been on a stringer all day long."

"Hmmm."

"You and that Cory Wilson fella, that who you with the other night?"

"Yes, sir."

"Thought so. Cory bring the jug, did he?"

"Yes, sir." This was not quite a lie, Junior reasoned. It had been Cory who actually took the jug off the back of Bert Roston's porch, even though Junior had been with him.

"The jug holds trouble as well as fun. You just remember that, hear?"

"Yes, sir."

"You get enough to eat this morning?"

"Fine."

"Reason I ask, you're gonna see things that won't sit so well."

"I'll be okay." But, really, Junior was worried that he wouldn't be.

"Figured. Just sit tight and swallow hard."

They rode in silence for a while, Junior relieved that the lecture was over. At first, when his father had said he could come along, Junior had felt the way he had those early times, when his father took him hunting and fishing. Riding in the car, he still felt that, but there was something more. He did not know what it was exactly, did not even want to think too much about it.

Just as the cool of the morning was turning into the heat of the morning, they saw a car and a horse-drawn wagon by the side of the road. A white man, a colored man, a colored woman, and her two children were in the middle of the road, standing in a rough circle. The white man, grizzled and in overalls, looked to be a farmer. The colored woman and her children had their hands over their ears.

"Little trouble, looks like," the sheriff said, stopping near the wagon.

Now the sheriff and his son could see what the people had formed a circle around. A hound lay in the road, some of its entrails next to it. As the sheriff cut the engine, he and Junior heard the dog moan. It was a sound that cut to the heart, leaving the listener with one wish, only one—that the sound would go away.

"Okay," the sheriff said, his voice controlled but husky. "Let's do what we can."

"Godalmighty, Sheriff," the white man said, seeing Hiram Stoker's badge. "Damn thing jumped off the wagon right in front of me."

"He honk, he honk," the colored man said. "Chillun hold the dog, hold him. He honk, scare the chillun, the dog too, and he jump off. That the truth."

The man was close to tears. A few feet away, his wife and the children, a boy and girl, sobbed.

"Godalmighty, Sheriff. It weren't—"

"Just hold, now," the sheriff said, a slight, commanding edge to his voice. "Just hold, mister. Ain't nobody accusing you. First things first." The sheriff took a deep breath. "Junior," he said quietly, raising his right hand with just his thumb and index finger extended.

Junior understood and got his father's holster and gun from the front seat. He held the holster as his father removed the long-barreled revolver.

"What your dog's name?" the sheriff said to the colored man.

"Blue."

"Well, you get over there and tell your children Blue ain't gonna hurt. . . ."

The sheriff knelt next to the animal, not looking at the entrails, cocked the revolver hammer, and held the muzzle to the head. "Easy, boy," he whispered.

The echo of the shot came back from the nearest ridge as the dog's teeth and parts of his brain came to rest on the roadside.

"He don't hurt no more," the sheriff said quietly.

The sobs of the children filled the air when the echo stopped.

"Godalmighty, Sheriff," the white man said. "Nothing I could do. They shoulda held him. Hell, I got dogs—"

"Nobody blaming you," the sheriff said. "One of those things, that's all." The sheriff put his hand on the man's shoulder; it was a gesture that was meant to express both consolation and, unmistakably, a command. "You best be getting along," the sheriff said.

Without a word, the man got in his car and drove away.

The sheriff faced the colored man. "True what they say, ain't it? About dogs bein' friends?"

"Yes, sir."

"I know you loved that old Blue. I trust you to get him off the road and bury him proper."

"Yes, sir."

"Knew I could. Hell, I had a hound once. Lived fifteen years. Liked to cry when he died ..."

The man was bigger than average, thick-shouldered and bent-backed from field work. His eyes were steady and dry.

The sheriff went over to the children. The boy, nine or ten, cried silently now. His sister, five or six, wailed inconsolably against the chest of her kneeling mother. The sheriff knelt and, not urgently, took the girl's shoulders and turned her toward him.

"Blue be in dog heaven," the sheriff said. "Only thing makes a dog unhappy, once he be in dog heaven, what with all the meat scraps and bones he get, is to hear someone cryin' for him down here. Only thing."

The girl's crying subsided. "Who feed 'em up there?" she asked, timid and suspicious.

The sheriff stood up. "Why, God feed 'em. Who else? He gets scraps and bones anywhere he want. Don't you worry none about that."

The children were quiet now. The man took a flap of burlap from the back of his wagon, tugged and lifted the dog's carcass onto it, and dragged the remains to the side of the road. His wife took a small shovel from the wagon, walked across the road, and took several strides into a field. She turned a clump of rich earth, then handed the shovel to her man.

"Let's be on our way," the sheriff said.

Junior's knees were weak, and his ears pounded with the sound of his blood racing. The morning was laden with suffering and death; it smelled of gunpowder and blood.

Junior looked down at his father's holster, still cradled in his hands, and was amazed to see that his father had placed the revolver back in it. Junior couldn't remember his father having done it.

Back in the car, the sheriff took a red handkerchief and wiped his face and neck.

"Coloreds love their dogs," the sheriff said. "Breaks their hearts when they lose 'em. Can't blame 'em none. Feel that way myself. You gonna be a law man, you best remember what makes coloreds tick. They got feelings too. Some sheriffs forget that, then bye and bye they got trouble with their colored."

The sheriff started the car. The sound of the engine was welcome to Junior, who hoped that the colored boy he was going to watch die would not cry or scream.

"Just set it on the seat," the sheriff said. "My gun and holster."

CHAPTER 17

The hot chocolate made Linus feel funny as the morning got lighter. Fuzzy. Not really sleepy, but fuzzy.

It must be getting close, Linus thought. The other prisoners would be eating breakfast. Doors and keys clanged, and the guard was there.

"Chaplain's here, boy."

The chaplain was a plump, middle-aged colored man with large eyes, sad like a hound's.

"Morning, Preacher," the guard said.

Linus heard the door open and close, as if from far away, and he felt the preacher's hand on his shoulder.

"Boy, I am here to comfort you with prayer, with God's word. Soon, very soon, you shall see Him for yourself. Do you understand that?"

"Yes, sir." Linus's own voice sounded far away.

"You shall see him, I promise, if you repent for your sins. Do you understand?"

"Yes, sir." Linus hoped he would be safe in heaven.

"I have a boy your age. I shall pray for you as I pray for him, son. . . ."

The preacher was wearing a suit, but it was all funny-baggy, not as nice as the Governor's suit.

Linus had not known who the Governor was. The guard had let the Governor into the cell and told Linus to stand up and say hello.

"Hello, boy," the Governor had said in a soft voice. Then the door was slammed shut and Linus was left alone with him.

Linus remembered thinking that the Governor looked very sad.

"Boy, you know you are to be put to death. . . ."

Put to death.

"You are very young, boy. The state has never put to death anyone so young. Did you know that?"

"No, sir."

"Boy, I have the power to—" The Governor looked sad and bit his lip. "Boy, is there anything you want to tell me, anything that would make me want to ..." The Governor bit his lip again.

Linus waited for the Governor to go on.

"Boy, some people did not even want me to come and see you. But I prayed on it, and here I am. Is there anything ...?"

The Governor's words made Linus sad, and before he knew it he felt tears on his cheeks. That made him feel even worse.

"God have mercy on you, boy," the Governor said. Then the keys and cell door clanged, and the Governor was gone.

Linus was glad that the Governor had prayed too, just as the preacher was praying now in his soft, sad voice.

Linus had known the night before that it was getting close, the time when he was going to be put to death. They had brought him a big tray of food—ribs, sweet potatoes, root beer, and ice cream. He had not been very hungry, but he had eaten a little bit of everything.

He had felt sleepy right after eating. He had gone to sleep and dreamed, of the mill where his daddy had worked, his family's shack, Green Hill Church, the catfish pond.

He had opened his eyes a few times. His cell was still dark. He had prayed for his ma and pa and Will and Jewel, for the sheriff and Mr. Brickstone....

His mama had told him that it was better to pray for someone else, because then God would see that he was not selfish, and his prayers would count more. He prayed that he would see his mama and daddy again, after they had lived their lives up north.

Linus had kept the secret, cleaned up where the girls had died, and he had only a little way to go, because the day was here when he was going to be put to death. The morning sounds had told Linus the day was here—sounds of garbage cans slamming onto cement, of water going through faraway pipes, of pails dropping, of men moaning and swearing.

Linus missed the morning sounds from the shacks and the mill, missed the horses and roosters and saws. . . . His father did not work at the mill anymore.

The guard had brought Linus a cup of hot chocolate and told him he had to drink it. It tasted funny.

Linus could hear the preacher, but the voice sounded far away.

"When you sit down for that last moment, and it will be only a moment, imagine that you are leaping across a wide ditch. And when you land, you will be in heaven."

Linus was going to jump over a ditch. . . .

"I shall pray for you now." The chaplain closed his sad hound's eyes and mumbled. Then he opened them and put his hand on Linus's shoulder again. "God bless you, boy."

The door clanged open and the chaplain shuffled out.

Linus was surprised just then to see the sheriff at the cell door, along with a gray-haired man in a suit. The man in the suit frowned and seemed sad. The guard let them in.

"This here's the warden, boy," the sheriff said. Linus thought the voice was far away.

"Linus," the sheriff said, "you know you have only a short time to live, don't you?"

"Yes, sir." It was coming close now. He was going to be put to death.

"Now, Linus, do you have anything to say?"

The sheriff was doing tricks with his voice, making it sound far away. Linus tried to tell him he knew about the trick. Then Linus's own voice sounded far away, and he couldn't remember how to make the words.

The sheriff himself seemed very far away too. From way far away, the sheriff was looking at him. The sheriff seemed sad. Now the sheriff came close again. Linus felt something at his side, felt the sheriff grabbing his arm. He heard the sound of keys.

The sheriff had to bite his lip to keep from snarling at the guard who fumbled with the keys; he wanted out of the cell and away from the boy as fast as he could go.

Ah, shit. Hell, no. The guard wasn't feeling any better than he was. "Obliged," the sheriff said when the door was finally opened.

He wondered if it had been a mistake to bring his son. Maybe Effie had been right. Not a thing for a boy to see, she had said. Could affect him for life.

Hell, not a thing for a man to see, either. They'll find out, the sheriff thought, as he walked into the execution chamber and saw the church-like pews jammed with those who had come to watch the sacrifice.

The sheriff recognized some of the faces from that day in the kitchen when he had broken the news. There were others, too, mill workers and neighbors. And there was Junior, white-faced and staring. The sheriff hoped his son would not throw up.

Everyone stared at the chair. It sat in the center of the room, about ten feet in front of the pews. The wood was dark and shiny and the straps hung like snakes, coiled and waiting. A thick black cord ran from underneath the chair across the floor to a hole in a wall behind which, the sheriff knew, was a generator.

He sat down next to his son and nudged him in the ribs with as much gentleness as he could muster. Junior said nothing.

From around the corner, just out of view, doors clanged and feet scuffed.

Linus's feet felt like blocks of wood, but he was able to move them. The guards held him tight.

One guard had whispered to him to hold on tight to the Bible, to hold on tight. . . . Linus understood that the Bible had been the thing the sheriff had put in his lap that day at the gas station. Linus held tight. He knew the Bible said things about children and lambs being put to death, put to death, put to death. . . .

The guards steered him around the corner, and there it was. Linus had wondered what it would look like, and now he knew. Black and shiny. His father worked at the sawmill. Maybe his father had cut the wood for the chair! Linus tried to tell that to the guards but he couldn't make real words come out. It was like in a dream, what came out of his mouth, and the guards did not seem to hear him.

There was the sheriff. The sheriff's son was next to him, with a white face, as white as in a dream. Linus wanted to say something to the sheriff, but he could not make real words.

So many people. Some of the faces were the same ones he had seen with the twelve men. Or was he dreaming it? Could the faces be the same? Yes, they were, and they looked at him, right at him, but their eyes were not the same. . . .

Or maybe he, Linus, had made it up, made it up that they didn't look the same. It was hard to tell what was real.

They were at the chair. The back was tall. Linus felt himself being spun around, dizzy, then lifted off the floor and pushed back so he was sitting down. The guards pushed hard, so that the backs of his legs hit the edge of the chair. That hurt, and he tried to tell them, but the words that came out were not real, not words. Linus could tell from the guards' faces that they could not hear him. The guards were sweating, but Linus did not think the room was hot.

Linus felt his arms being grabbed and placed along the chair's arms. He heard the sound of straps and buckles, felt the leather on his arms. Linus could not understand why the sounds of straps and buckles seemed to go on and on, and why the guards muttered and puffed.

"Goddamn," one guard said. "Straps too big for a kid."

That made Linus want to laugh. He tried to laugh, but his laugh came out like a crazy sound, a dream sound. Then his arms stung as the guards gave up on the buckles and tied the leather in place. Linus felt his right pant leg sliding up, felt something wet being wrapped around his leg, then something wrapped tight over the towel.

Again, Linus heard the sound of straps and buckles, this time from down near the floor. He felt the guards tying the straps around his legs, about halfway between his knees and ankles. Linus wished there was a window.

The mask scared him, hurt his nose as it was pulled down over his face from behind. Blackness. He would never see anything again. But no one could see him either. He could cry, if he wanted to, and no one would see. He was being put to death.

Linus heard the guards walking away. He was alone. Someone far away coughed. Linus wondered how long. He was going to jump over a big ditch and go to heaven, way up north. . . .

Good-bye Ma, good-bye Pa, good-bye Will, good-bye Jewel. I pray for Ma, I pray Pa, I pray Will, I pray Jewel. . . . His stomach felt like he was getting ready to jump. There! A light. Sunlight over the catfish pond. There was a big fish he had let go, jumping high, high in the sun. Shining.

Junior was startled by the "whump" of the generator kicking on. He had expected to hear a sizzling noise, like bacon frying, but all he heard was the mounting whine of the generator.

Junior could not take his eyes off the colored boy's body twisting against the straps. Almost instantly, the head poked through the mask. Drool fell from the open mouth, tears streamed from the bulging but sightless eyes. Junior wondered if the tears had started before the current, or whether it was part of the dying.

Junior smelled burning hair, burning flesh, and (he was not sure) maybe urine and feces. A fan in the ceiling directly over the chair had turned on as the current started, and much of the smoke from the body—but only part of the smell—went straight up. For which Junior was grateful, as he watched the writhing, even though he wondered how he would sleep after seeing what he was seeing. How he would sleep that night, and the next night, and all the rest of the nights of his life if he lived to be a hundred.

Finally, the generator died down. The writhing stopped, and the colored boy's body slumped in the chair. The room was silent. Then—Junior could not believe it—the generator started up again, not as loud as before. The body twisted again, though not as much, and there was not as much smoke. Dead, Junior thought.

At last, the generator whined down and all was quiet. The guards who had led the colored boy to the chair came in, carrying a simple stretcher. They placed the stretcher next to the chair and untied the straps. Almost effortlessly, they pulled the small corpse from the chair and dropped it onto the stretcher. Junior watched, horrified but fascinated, as the head rolled to one side, as though the neck bone had been turned to sawdust. Expressionless, the guards marched out with the body.

Suddenly, the people who had watched began to cough and clear their throats and mumble as though they'd been waiting for the body to be removed. Feet shuffled as the men rose, slowly, from the witnesses' benches.

Junior stood up and wondered for a second whether his legs would hold him. He was glad for his father's arm across his shoulders.

"It ain't the prettiest thing in the world," the sheriff said quietly to his son. Then, to the others, the sheriff nodded solemnly. "Over now. All of it," he said.

He waited until everyone was out of the room. Junior wanted to get outside, out in the fresh air, more than he had ever wanted anything.

"Let's go, son," the sheriff said at last. "I'm thinking I'll need a jug of peach wine tonight. Maybe two. Don't care if I'm sick tomorrow, truth to tell. You can join me if you like."

BOOK TWO

BOOK TWO

CHAPTER 18

Columbia, South Carolina

Late March, 1988

The soil of South Carolina lay below, in the mist. It was a rich soil, James Willop knew—incredibly rich with the blood and bones of slaves and slave owners, interred under different circumstances, surely, but equal now in death.

As the jet circled, James Willop studied the mist, growing fainter by the minute in the morning sun, and wondered if the mist were any different chemically from that which rose, say, from New Jersey or Ohio or California. The South Carolina mist must be, in a way, the essence of sugar and rice and indigo, Willop thought, remembering what he had read about the colonial agriculture of the state below.

And if the blood and bones of slaves and slave owners (much of it assimilated by the earth, long since part of it) gave rise to the mist, how would that affect the content? Willop wondered if anyone had ever thought seriously about such things. Surely, the mist must be more from the blood and bones of black people, Willop reflected, since not many decades ago—and for centuries before that—the blacks who tilled the soil far outnumbered the whites who owned it.

With such thoughts, Willop tried to keep his nerves in check as the plane circled in a wide arc over Columbia. A rainbow shone in the window. One moment the rainbow would be right there in front of his eyes; the next moment it would be gone; then it would come back again.

The day was clear now. Blue sky and bright sun on a quilt of brown and green. He did not rest his eyes, not for a second, as the plane wheeled. He looked to the horizon and back and out again. In that way, he thought, his eyes might sweep over the grave of Linus Bragg.

A stewardess with a voice like syrup said the temperature was sixty degrees—ten degrees warmer than New York had been on this early-spring morning. The ground came up fast, concrete now, runway markers, black skid marks from the tires.

The plane bumped, the engines whined, and the butterfly feeling in Willop's stomach began to go away.

"Welcome to Columbia, South Carolina," the stewardess said.

"Did you have a pleasant flight, sir?"

"Fine, thank you," Willop said to the woman behind the counter. "I believe you have a car reserved for Willop, James B."

"Sure do. A compact all set to go. Are you here for business or pleasure?"

"A little of each." He liked her light brown hair, blue eyes, the smile. Braces, for God's sake! She didn't let her braces keep her from smiling. Well, good for her. He wanted to say more.

"You from these parts?" he asked.

"Born and raised," she said. Her eyes, bright and inquisitive, locked onto his. She was expecting him to ask directions, or something.

Willop wanted to say something more, to repay her friendliness. Then he imagined how the woman's father, and grandfather, and great-grandfather might have felt.

He said nothing.

He put his suitcase in a locker and found the cocktail lounge overlooking the runways. It was early, but what the hell. He would not break his promise to Moira to be careful on the drinking, but just now he could use something. He ordered a double Scotch and a water chaser, and looked absently at the television set in the corner. Every time a plane went by, the colors on the screen jumbled and bled. No one seemed to notice. He wondered again whether he should have told Moira to use a fake name for the flight reservations and car, then told himself it didn't matter.

The Scotch began to sink in.

"Care for another?"

"No, thanks," Willop said crisply. He was sure he had seen something in the white bartender's eyes, had seen the question: Is he white or black? I sure am, Willop felt like telling him.

The Scotch was not always good for him, but this day it was. Smoke in the nostrils, fire in the stomach. Friendship, courage. Peace. At least until it wore off. He had a bottle in his suitcase.

It was the perfect combination of things to make him nervous: driving an unfamiliar car into an unfamiliar city with no particular destination. Actually, Willop did have a destination. He wanted to find a hotel that was respectable (or at least not too unsanitary) but a cut or two or three below the well-known chain motels. His plane ticket and car rental had already stretched his budget, pushing his credit-card load uncomfortably close to the limit.

He had one other reason for wanting an obscure hotel. Perhaps it was paranoia, perhaps prudence, or maybe both. But he did not want to be too easy to find.

Finally, he found himself on a busy street that was neither slum nor thriving business section, but something in between. It was a bit seedy and ... old. Yes, that was it. A part of town that was like a thousand, or ten thousand, tracts in cities across the country. Prosperity and gaiety (fickle bastards) gone to the suburbs, leaving a suffocating drabness.

Willop spotted a hotel sign and pulled into an empty parking space at the curb. He watched for a few minutes, noting who went in and out of the hotel. A few black men, a few white men, black women, white women. They had one thing in common: They were old. No, two things. They looked poor, too. Maybe lonely; that's three things, Willop thought. Ah, shit. If there ain't any queers or drunks or loonies, I can stand it.

A few minutes of grace remained on the parking meter, so Willop locked the car and went into the hotel.

Way off in a corner, several old people sat, motionless, perhaps even uncomprehending, before a badly focused television screen on which contestants were hinting and guessing and pressing buzzers to win prizes. The television noise, some cigar odors, and (encouragingly) a smell of distant disinfectant—these were of the present. Everything else in the lobby, from the deep ruts in the floor, made by once-happy travelers long in their graves, to an old painting of a train platform where men and women dressed for the 1930s were climbing aboard a train, told of a past so dead as to be almost beyond memory.

The clerk was an old black, dark as a horse chestnut, short and knobby. He eyed Willop suspiciously.

"I need a room," Willop said. "For tonight only."

"Rate's better if you stay five days or more," the clerk said.

"No thanks. Just for tonight."

"Twelve dollars. Cash in advance. Sink and a towel in the room. Soap, too. Bathroom the end of each hall."

"Phone?" Willop asked.

"Pay booth in the lobby. Give you change when you need it."

"Here's your twelve. And here's an extra single for telephone change."

"Room 2C, upstairs and to your left. Checkout's at noon."

"One more thing. Where can I park my car?"

"Car?" The old clerk was astonished, then wary. "Ain't nobody stays here if they can afford a car. . . ."

"It's okay," Willop said. "It's not stolen and I'm not wanted for anything. It's just a low-budget trip, okay? Now, where can I park my car?"

"Alley behind the hotel. Drive to the first corner, turn right, then turn right again first alley you see. Nobody'll bother you back there."

"Terrific," Willop said. "Got a bellhop to help me with my luggage?"

The clerk did not smile.

"Just kidding," Willop said.

"Two dollars extra to park your car. Cash in advance."

Willop had seen worse hotel rooms. This one had a bed whose saggy mattress was covered by sheets that at least seemed to be free of semen and blood. The sink was moderately clean, and a fresh bar of soap lay on a fluffy towel on an ancient dresser. A quick inspection of the floor beneath the bed and behind the dresser revealed no huge balls of dust, no mouse turds, no roaches. The window overlooked the alley, affording a view of the car, and the fire escape seemed to be sturdy.

Man, I am living, Willop thought. Maybe I can get room service to send me up some sandwiches and beer.

He washed his face and went down to the phone booth in the lobby, note pad and pencil ready.

Willop had never been that great at working a phone, whether doing an investigation or trying to get a plumber to come to his apartment for an emergency. The detectives and reporters on television, or in the cheap paperbacks, operated at an effectiveness level he could not comprehend.

"J. Alfred Prufrock musta had more balls than me," he said in the quiet gloom of the booth.

The tattered phone book was especially worn in the "South Carolina, State of" pages (people calling to complain about welfare checks or something?), but Willop found a general-information number.

He hesitated before dialing. Should of called from up north. No, not so. He had to make the trip anyhow. Cut the shit and let us begin.

"Good afternoon, State of South Carolina."

"Yes, can you connect me with your corrections department? I'm calling from a pay phone."

"Certainly. Hold, please."

Silence for several seconds, and several more seconds.

"Department of Corrections."

"Yes, I'm calling for information about a criminal case. . . ."

"Certainly. Are you a relative of an inmate under Department of Corrections control?"

"No, no. I just need some information."

"In that case, perhaps I'd better switch you to our public relations office."

Without waiting for argument, the operator switched him.

"Public relations, Jim Baker speaking."

"Hi. I'm trying to get some information about a case. . . ."

"You a reporter or what?"

"Reporter, uh, and writer. Freelance right now."

"And your name?"

Willop had an instant to decide whether to use an alias. It was no decision, really. He had little faith in his cleverness, so he opted for the truth.

"Willop, James B."

"How can I help you, Mr. Willop? If this is a current case, it would help me a lot if you knew what county it came out of."

"It's not current. In fact, it's from over forty years ago. It was a pretty big murder case at the time. This was in 1944."

"Damn, that is a long time ago, all right. Might have to refer you over to archives, though no telling what they'll have. Or you might try the county clerk's office in the county where it was tried."

"Right. I'm going to do that. But you can understand how, with something so long ago, it pays to touch base with anybody who might help. This case ended in an execution."

"Ain't surprised a bit to hear that. South Carolina has always been pretty good about frying people. Even more so back then."

"You don't approve?" Willop felt he was getting somewhere.

"Can't say I do. Saw all the death I wanted to see in 'Nam. But never mind that. If you give me the name of the guy who got zapped, I'll give you everything we got on him. Which probably won't be much."

An operator cut in. "I'm sorry, your time is up. Deposit another twenty-five cents, please."

Willop fumbled for another coin. "Give me a minute," he said.

"That's okay, Mr. Willop. Just give the number where you're at and I'll call you right back."

Willop read the number gratefully, hung up, and sat in the silent, hot phone booth. Within a half minute, the phone rang.

"Hi," Willop said, immensely relieved.

"Now then," Baker said. "Suppose you give me the name of the executee."

"Bragg, B–R–A–G–G. First name Linus."

"All right. Now, I might be away from the phone for a minute or so. We gotta long drawer here with files on everybody who sat in Old Sparky. You just hold on."

Heartened, Willop did not mind the wait this time.

"You from up north?" Baker said when he came back on the line.

"From Newark, New Jersey, most recently."

"Thought so, 'cause of your accent."

"And you're a native Carolinian, I take it."

"Born, raised, and live in Columbia. Now then, all I got here is a little bitty three-by-five card. Says that Linus Bragg was delivered to the state prison May second, 1944. Then, hmmm, there's another notation that he was delivered here again, on June fourth, 1944. Oh, I see. Second time he was delivered directly to death row. First time was just for general custody, probably. . . ."

"That was for his protection," Willop said. "So the people back home wouldn't lynch him."

"That right? Protection, huh. Imagine that. Anyhow, here it says he was electrocuted on June sixteenth, 1944, with the required number of witnesses present. Body delivered to the Mason Funeral Home in Columbia—"

"Mason Funeral Home in Columbia," Willop repeated, scribbling in his excitement. "Any street address?"

"None here. 'Course, that outfit might not even exist anymore, it being that long ago. Black only funeral home, no doubt."

"Any other information?"

"Linus Bragg. Height five feet one inch, weight ninety-five pounds. Eyes maroon. Can that be right? Five-one and ninety-five pounds? Born December twenty-ninth, 1929 . . . Why, shit, that didn't make him but . . ."

"Fourteen," Willop said.

"Damn. What'd he do to get the chair that young?"

"Some people say he killed two little white girls. In a little dinky place an hour or so east of here."

"Damn. Sure way for a colored to get the chair back then. That's all the information we have here."

"You've helped me a lot. Anything else you can tell me? Anything at all?"

"Got a picture of the little bugger if you want to drop in and take a look."

Jim Baker was a big man with an unfashionable crew cut, beefy ears, and a face the color of ham. His smile was toothy and broad and his handshake just short of crushing.

Willop thought Jim Baker was friendly in part because he was completely confident about his physical appearance. He envied him.

"Nice to meet you, Mr. Willop," Jim Baker said.

"Same here." Willop thought Jim Baker's eyes measured him for a moment, but they were friendly eyes all the same.

"What's your interest in the little fella here, if you don't mind my asking?" Baker said, putting a tan envelope on the counter in front of Wallop.

"Oh, a little history, a little research into the past. Nothing much more."

Jim Baker said nothing, for which Willop was relieved. He opened the envelope and took out the picture.

An ordinary face, an ordinary colored boy (looking at the picture from so many years ago, Willop would not have thought to call him black, or even a Negro), an ordinary expression. No, not quite ordinary. There was a hint of sullenness, a hint of despair.

"Young-looking, ain't he?" Baker said. "And small. Look how them prison clothes hang off his shoulders."

"This was taken just before he was executed," Willop said.

"Yep. I wasn't even around then. Long damn time ago."

"Long time," Willop said. He stared at the picture, but no matter how intently he stared, the picture remained just what it was: a slightly overexposed prison mug shot in tones of gray that softened an already soft, boyish face that had neither edges nor guile.

"Killed two little girls?" Baker said.

"So they say. I got the Columbia paper to send me a couple of clips. Stories from back then say he killed them near some tracks where they were picking flowers."

"He was after a little somethin', was he?"

"So they say." One could certainly not tell by looking at the picture that here was a boy (and a killer?) with a burgeoning sexuality so fierce

128

that it had driven him to slaughter two innocents. But then, Willop thought, one never knew.

"I could get that copied for you," Baker said.

"I guess not." Willop thought he could look at the picture for an hour and not learn anything more. A moment from long ago, crystalized forever. Willop wondered what the boy behind the face in the picture had been thinking; wondered if the boy imagined, even for a moment, that someone would be looking at his face all these years later and wondering.

"Tell you what," Baker said. "I got a few other things to do now, but if you want, you can sit down here and use the phone. Just go easy on any long-distance calls. Okay?"

"That's very nice. I just might make one or two local calls."

Willop did, and found that there was no Mason Funeral Home, and that the Funeral Directors Association had no record of one in recent years. Then he called the state archives department and found that there was nothing on file about a criminal case involving one Linus Bragg from more than forty years ago.

"Now, that isn't really too surprising," said an archives employee, a man who sounded middle-aged and knowledgeable. "If there was no appeal filed, and if there was an execution fairly soon afterwards, most likely the material was just thrown out."

"Well, I am ninety percent sure there was no appeal," Willop said.

"Then I'm sure there's nothing still around here. Maybe in the county where it happened, though. See, if the lawyer, whoever he was, had appealed, why then a transcript would have been preserved. I mean, the lawyer himself would have ordered up the transcript, and then there would have been all sorts of additional paperwork generated. But without an appeal ..."

"I see."

"Of course, without an appeal, it all became pretty academic to the fellow who was executed," the archives man said, chuckling at his little joke.

"Thanks anyhow," Willop said, hanging up without laughing in return.

There were no more phone calls to make. It was late afternoon (Jim Baker would be closing up shop soon), and the Scotch Willop had drunk was beginning to wear off. It was definitely time to go.

"Thank you for everything," Willop said, shaking hands with Baker.

"Just doing my job. Good luck in your research."

Willop wanted to say something more to Jim Baker, to tell him that if more people were like him, the world would be a much better place. Then Willop canceled his own notion. He really didn't know Jim Baker at all, certainly didn't know how he talked about nonwhite folks outside the office.

Besides, for all he knew, Jim Baker's parents would have been glad to kill Linus.

Late afternoon. Too soon to go to bed, too late to start a drive into foreign territory, to the hamlet where Linus Bragg had lived. Willop stopped at a mom-and-pop store, bought a prepackaged ham sandwich and two cans of soda to go. On his way back to the hotel he stopped at a drugstore and bought a newspaper. Only after he'd tucked the paper under his arm did he realize he had just obeyed an old habit that was no longer relevant: As a newspaperman, he had always bought a paper whenever he was in a strange city, just to compare it to the New York papers and to the *Newark Tribune*.

Now he was an unemployed newspaperman, the *Tribune* having gone belly-up the week before. Willop mocked himself: Hey, maybe I should stop at the Columbia paper and see about a job. No, if they turned me down, it would just activate the butterflies in my stomach.

Back at the hotel, he chewed the ham sandwich slowly, sipped on the soda, and decided he needed to talk to Moira. So he went down to the lobby and called her collect.

"Hi."

"James. I was hoping you'd call. I guess you got there safe and everything."

"Yep. I'm in Columbia. At a hotel you might call ... unpretentious. Just for tonight."

"Get a good night's sleep if you can."

"Do my best. Anything new?"

"Well, the Mayor called me at work. He was very nice. Said again that if he could do anything to help ..."

"He already told me that. Damn, he sure knows how to keep up the pressure."

"That's why he's a politician. It's your choice."

"May not have one."

"Put it out of your mind for now, as much as you can."

"You're right, again."

He told her about Baker and the picture of Linus Bragg and made the hotel sound a little better than it was. She told him it had turned colder up north. She said she could hear rain lashing the window of her apartment. He didn't know if that made him feel closer to her, or farther away.

They said good-bye and he went back to his room. After a few minutes, he thought he had read all of the paper that he cared to read, so he poured himself a little Scotch. He lay down, sipped the drink, and remembered that he had not studied the editorial page, something he always did with an out-of-town paper. He picked up the paper again, but before his fingers had even found the right section, he reminded himself that he had no professional reason to read it.

He threw the paper toward the wall; it fluttered apart in mid-air and fell to the floor. Damn ...

He knew he was lucky: It was a lot easier to find a new job in your early thirties than in your early forties, or fifties. He knew of *Tribune* people who would have to tell their sons and daughters they weren't going back to college next fall. ...

Willop took another sip and tried to relax as his head sank into the pillow. God, what a day that had been. Talk about your world changing ...

He had played golf that morning with Newark Mayor Delmar Springs, fascinated as always by the Mayor's smooth, powerful swing and his seemingly effortless way with people. About halfway through the front nine, a white golfer had shouted a greeting to the Mayor from an adjoining fairway.

"Say what?" Springs shouted back, smiling and waving. Then he turned back to Willop and the smile disappeared. "He sells stationery. Wants to do business with the city. He asked me if I wanted to join his club, too."

"Might be a better course than this," Willop said.

"Fuck it. My father used to caddy for him, long time ago. He never would have invited me to join twenty years ago, now would he?"

"I guess not."

"In golf and life both, you gotta avoid the unplayable lies."

That blend of idealism and bitterness had attracted Willop to Springs and made his offer so seductive. The Mayor was in his early forties, honest as well as calculating, charismatic and had built a solid constituency among whites as well as blacks. Whether he ran again for Mayor or, as Willop thought more likely, ran for Congress, he would need a full-time, shrewd press spokesman. Of course, if he ran for Congress and won . . .

Willop knew that Moira had wanted him to take the offer, or at least consider it. The offer had been tempting even before that day on the golf course.

Willop had been on the ninth green, near the clubhouse, standing over a two-foot putt that would have given him a forty-nine. As he studied the green, he was vaguely aware that one of the Mayor's errand boys had driven up and called Springs aside. The messenger whispered something into the Mayor's ear, and the Mayor walked over toward Willop, stopping a few feet away. Willop looked at him, and saw something in his eyes.

"Something wrong?"

"Sink your putt, man," the Mayor said.

"What is it?"

"Go on, make it."

But Willop saw something in the Mayor's eyes, and the Mayor knew he saw it, and so he picked up Willop's ball. "That's a gimme, man."

"Okay, what the hell's going on?"

"Your paper just died."

The Scotch wasn't treating Willop too badly, so he poured himself a little more, lay down on the bed again, and took a short sip.

Actually, the *Tribune*'s folding shouldn't have been a big shock. The paper had been slipping for a decade or more, unable to keep a solid city-based readership and unable to cultivate a loyal suburban following as the Newark area changed. Willop knew he should have planned better, should have left the *Tribune* for a more solid paper, should have been bolder. ...

Of course, Moira was kind of stuck in Newark, at least for the time being. She was an assistant at Legal Aid, and until she saved enough to go to law school ...

His first thought, after hearing Springs's words, were that his housing series would never be published. He had worked on it for weeks, had honed and polished and rechecked every fact, every paragraph. And he had plumbed his conscience, making sure that he was not being too easy on the administration of Delmar Springs.

It was the best reporting job he had ever done. It might have won him a prize if it had been published. Now, it existed only in the form of a computer printout he had sneakily made in the *Tribune*'s funereal city room the afternoon of the closing.

Willop gulped the last of the Scotch in the glass and vowed that the drink would be his last of the day.

He had said guilty good-byes to the *Tribune* people he liked best—guilty because he had told them he might stop in at the neighborhood bar that served as the *Tribune* watering spot, when actually he had no intention of doing so. He detested the cliché of the newspaper wake.

All Willop had wanted to do that afternoon was empty his desk and leave the *Tribune*. Why stay close to a corpse? So, still in his golf clothes, he had sat at his desk, dumping the contents of the drawers into a wastebasket. But first, from the back of the top drawer, the one he always kept locked, he took out an envelope. It was a white, business-size envelope (at least it had been white; it was gray now with age and finger smudges), and it was addressed to "My Son James." It had been written more than twenty years before, when he was a schoolboy, by his mother, and only given to him after her death. The fold lines of the writing paper were sharp-edged from the years.

James,

I write this for you to keep and save till someday you be able to act. Even tho your smart (the teachers sayd your english is good, which I am very proud of becase it is so important) you probly wont understand this whole thing now becase your to young. That is why I will not show this to you now but keep it till you are older but I belief i must put words down now. I am remembring how my own mother passed away and how surprised I was when she did. We dont always know when things take place. So I write now when I have time. When I was little girl I lived near a place in South Carolina where they cut wood. It was very peaseful and quiet, way out by a swamp and away from most people. We did not have to much but we were happy most times, our folks and me and my brothers, Linus and Will. You will never see your uncle Linus on this earth becase he be in Heaven.

They kill him for a thing he did not do. They say he killed two little girls over near where they cut wood but we know in our hearts he did not. He never had chance to show it and our folks, they not unerstand how it can be. Linus so young. He not to much older than you when this be taken place.

No one care then, it was the war and all and no one know what happen way out there by the mill away from every one. No one care, but our mother and father never same after, they put us on big train and send us up north away from every one with hate in there hearts for us.

We never go back to that little peaseful place where there so much hate for us. Hate for something he not do. May be some day you can find out The Truth and tell every one. This so much to ask you to take up, such a load, but I feel you can. I feel I must say, or no one will know. Your uncle Will is not the one, he not have a head like God bless you with. He who God give most to, he carry bigger load. My mother say that, long before she die.

My feeling bigger than words I can use. Some day you unerstand more on why I ask this of you and just know for now I love and am proud of you. I hope it be a time before you see this, yet I wish also you can see it now. There is no telling how God He works His Wonders! If you find this out, your uncle Linus will rest easy in Heaven at last waiting for all of us.

With love,
your Mother

His mother had not had so long to live after writing that. But Willop would not think about that, not tonight.

He had kept the letter in his desk at the *Tribune* for a long time, telling himself that he would investigate, one day. But the time never seemed right. Early on, of course, he was too young, too inexperienced a reporter to have dared suggest such a story to an editor even if the story had not been about his own family. And when, not so suddenly, he was no longer a cub but a journeyman, there were too many other stories to write, closer to home. . . .

Closer to home. Where was that?

So he had never written, never even gone after, the story he should have pursued. Now he was going after it when he didn't have a newspaper to publish it, and when he had to pay his own way. Or let Moira pay it . . .

God, he owed her a lot. She had done so much, said so much, to boost his self-esteem. It bothered him to reflect on his own neediness.

He got out of bed and went to the sink. The mirror over it was dirty, but he could see his tan face clearly enough. With shame, he recalled how he had wanted things both ways: The minority scholarship program had made it possible for him to go to college, but once there—and for long after—he had thought himself blessed to have straight hair and skin no darker than a white lifeguard's.

He did not want too many people to know. Was that why he had pulled some punches in his reporting, why he had never written, never even tried to write, the story hinted at in his mother's letter? He dared not probe his soul too deeply with that question.

Willop guessed that it was better to repay a terrible debt late than not at all. And if he got anywhere on his mission, there would be no place to hide, no chance to pass for anything but what he was.

CHAPTER 19

Willop didn't sleep too badly, all things considered. After getting up, he dressed quickly, closed his suitcase without worrying about the wrinkles in his clothes, washed his face, and brushed his teeth and was out of his room in ten minutes.

He plunked the room key on the lobby counter without looking at the clerk, got into the car, and drove out of the alley with a feeling of relief.

No more excuses for delay ...

Willop stopped at a diner to buy rolls and coffee, which he took with him. Soon he was headed out of Columbia. He drove with the window open. Clean, Carolina air. Not much dirtier than when the slaves and their owners used to smell it, he thought.

Driving on Interstate 26, he saw buds on the trees. He guessed that spring had arrived here several weeks before it would up north.

When Willop heard the siren, he looked in the mirror and saw the car. Unmarked, no red gumball, the trooper hatless. Willop was alarmed, and puzzled. Wasn't doing more than sixty, he thought. Don't think about asserting your rights, he told himself.

"License and registration." The trooper had short hair and ice-blue eyes and smelled like chewing gum. His hat was on now, the strap pressing into the back of his neck.

"Didn't think I was speeding," Willop said, his attempt at casualness ruined by a croak.

"You weren't. Pulled you over 'cause your right brake light didn't light up when you slowed down for that work crew back there. Ask a gas station to check the fuse. Have a good day."

Immensely relieved, Willop drew in a huge gulp of air and let it out slowly.

He came to the I-95 interchange. I could stay on I-26, he thought, and go all the way to Charleston and the ocean. Supposed to be a pretty city, Charleston.

He turned onto I-95 and started north. Before long he came to Lake Marion. He drove slowly over the bridge, savoring one of the loveliest sights he had ever seen. A wide swath of water lay blue in the sunlight. The shore was a gold-orange where the evergreens didn't quite meet the water. In scattered boats, fishermen slumped in lazy pleasure. For a moment, he wished he was one of them.

He turned onto a two-lane that ran almost parallel to I-95. The signs advertised pecans, peach wine, and fireworks. Before he knew it, he was in Manning. Must be where all the action is, he thought, amused. But he found the smallness, the lack of traffic, the nonaggressiveness of the drivers compared to those around New York and New Jersey oddly disturbing—the inside-out of what someone from here feels when he goes to New York, Willop thought.

Willop spotted a motel that looked, at least from the outside, inexpensive but clean. A shy, pretty woman who looked to be Asian checked him in and gave him his key. Did she study my face the way I studied hers? he wondered.

Willop was pleased to find that the room had a cable hookup to the television set, a sink with glasses wrapped in paper, and a toilet with a strip of paper over the bowl. Almost as much class as you'll find in Yankeeland, he thought, rebuking himself for his snobbishness.

It was too early for him to call Moira, though he wanted to hear her voice. He unpacked, standing the bottle of Scotch next to the sink. Smoke in the nostrils, fire in the stomach—next best thing to human warmth . . . But he had to make it last.

He lay down on the bed, shook off his shoes, felt his legs loosen. He would not let himself fall asleep.

Willop thought back to the feelings he had had driving over the bridge across Lake Marion and seeing the fishermen. It was a yearning (there was no use lying to himself about it) to belong. Belong here? In South Carolina?

Well, wait a goddamn minute. They had newspapers in Columbia and Charleston, and you didn't have to be a white Protestant to get a job. Not anymore. Then Willop recalled (he would never forget) the stories he had overheard in his early childhood, tales of lynchings and burnings and castrations—many of them true, he had come to realize. Other kids get scared by Hansel and Gretel and witches being stuck into ovens, Willop thought. Me, I get the real thing. . . .

He shuddered at the memories. And they caused him to remember something else—a sign he had seen back there, between the signs for fireworks and pecans.

Willop put on his shoes, locked the room, got in the car, and drove back down the uncrowded road.

The gun shop had a tacky sign and a wood exterior that badly needed paint. The man in charge was balding and white, middle-aged, with a paunch covered by a dirty T-shirt. He scarcely glanced at the identification Willop offered him, nodded blankly and without apparent interest as Willop selected a cheap, short-barreled .32-caliber revolver. Along with it he bought a box of cartridges and a small cleaning kit. If his days in the Army had taught him anything, it was that if he ever aimed at somebody and pulled the trigger, he wanted the weapon to fire.

He paid cash and drove back toward the motel, realizing on the way that he was getting hungry. He stopped at a fast-food place and bought a cheeseburger, french fries, and milk to go.

Back in his room, he spread his meal on the table and ate—ravenously. His hunger satisfied, Willop found himself with time on his hands: It was late afternoon. The workday in Clarendon County, South Carolina, was without a doubt drawing to a close.

No, Willop thought. I should do something; at least break the ice.

He looked up the number and dialed.

"Sheriff's office. Dispatcher Bestwick speaking."

Young black woman, Willop realized at once. "Good afternoon. Is Sheriff Bryant Fischer in, please?" Willop had found out the name before flying south.

"Sheriff Fischer is gone for the day, sir. Can anyone else help you?"

"I should really talk to him. . . ."

"I do expect him in tomorrow morning."

"Okay, I'll call then. Thanks a lot."

That done, Willop took out the revolver and cleaning kit. He flicked the cylinder open, into the loading position, then back to the firing position and pulled the trigger. Action a little sluggish. Using the tiny oil can, he lubricated the weapon carefully, wiping the excess oil along the barrel and on the outside of the cylinder, being careful not to get any on the handle. He worked the cylinder and tried the trigger again. Much better.

The weapon had been the Mayor's idea. He had called as Willop was packing.

"Come by my office in a half-hour," Springs had said, hanging up before Willop could say anything.

Willop had found the Mayor in his shirt-sleeves, head down and frowning as he sat at his huge oak desk.

"Hear you're taking a trip," Springs said without looking up.

"How . . .?"

"I'm the Mayor, man. Business or pleasure?"

"Well, not pleasure. Sort of, uh, freelance . . ."

"Freelance what?"

"It's an old case. Looking into an old case . . ."

"A criminal case."

God, Springs had a sixth sense. Maybe that's why he's lasted this long. . . .

"Uh, yeah," Willop said. "Doing research, sort of . . ."

"Sure. Strictly academic." Springs's unerring bullshit detector had effortlessly sniffed out the evasion. Willop was grateful to him for not digging deeper.

The Mayor leaned back in his chair. "The police commissioner and I have both reviewed your application—"

"What?"

"—and find it perfectly in order, as do the prosecutor's office and court officials. So here are your credentials."

"Credentials?"

"Showing that you are a special deputy. They probably won't hurt, and they may help. For one thing, you'll have no trouble carrying a weapon. . . ."

"Oh, Jesus."

"Jesus won't help down here," Springs said. Leaning forward, his eyes flint-bright, he almost whispered, "South's changed some since my daddy's day and . . . whatever. Still the South, and you're still . . ."

"Yeah," Willop said quietly.

"You might not need the papers, much less a gun. Just don't forget where you're going. If this was twenty, twenty-five years ago, man, you could be in deep, deep shit."

"I guess I owe you."

"No, man, you don't," Springs said, sounding almost angry. "If you think there's strings on these papers, I'll rip them up right now."

"No strings." Willop was moved. "Anything else?"

"Some advice, my man. If it ever comes down to it and it's you or somebody else gonna die, better to be tried by twelve than carried by six."

Willop took off his shoes, turned on the television, and lay on the bed, his head propped on the pillow. A white man, a white woman, and a black man smiled out from the screen. Their clothes seemed to have gone out of fashion, at least by northern standards, Willop thought.

"Fuckin' double-knit hicks," he said to the screen.

Shit, Willop. You ain't no dresser yourself.

The black announcer was doing the weather. He fumbled his words about the possible approach of a high-pressure mass and grinned with all his teeth as he corrected himself.

"Say what?" Willop said. "Man, you is an affirmative-action disgrace, that's what you is. . . ."

He picked up the revolver and drew a bead on the white announcer's forehead, then on each breast of the woman. Finally, he aimed between the black man's eyes.

Suddenly, he felt not just silly but ashamed. He was glad for the announcers' indomitable cheerfulness.

"Just kidding," he said to the screen.

He got off the bed, opened the dresser drawer to stow the revolver, and stood there. He was undecided, but only for a moment. As long as I bought the goddamn thing, might as well play for keeps, he thought. Willop opened the box of cartridges and slipped six rounds into the cylinder. Then he flicked the cylinder closed, hid the revolver behind his T-shirts, and opened the bottle of Scotch.

Willop woke himself up snoring and for an instant did not know where he was. There was still a little Scotch in his glass, but the ice cubes were long gone. A little after midnight. He went to the sink and splashed cold water on his face and thought he should go back to sleep. He checked the lock, flipped the door chain into place, and pushed the curtain aside to look out.

Moonlight shining off the few cars. And stars everywhere. Got to see, he thought.

He stepped into his shoes, not bothering to tie them, and went outside. The sky was blue-black with moon and stars. Never did see any sermons in stones, Willop thought, but anyone can see sermons in stars. . . .

His mother had loved the stars. Ever since she had told him, when he was too young to begin to comprehend, that it took light from the stars years and years and years to come to Earth—more years than a man could live, many, many more—Willop had been fascinated.

He wondered if Linus, his child uncle, had ever lain on the ground some nights, looking up at the stars, seeing them as he, Willop, was seeing them now. Four decades was only a moment, measured against star time. Somewhere, the stars and moon were shining on his grave, wherever that was. Perhaps on his last night on Earth (only a moment ago!), before he was killed and sent to the colored section of Heaven, Linus had looked out at the stars.

No. More than likely the cell walls were too high for him to look out.

Yes, Willop thought. I owe Linus something.

And would finding the truth, whatever it was, make Willop happy, not to mention his mother and Linus, wherever they were?

The night, so full of stars, was empty of answers.

CHAPTER 20

Willop showered quickly and, in the tiny dining room next to the motel office, downed a hurried breakfast of coffee, toast, and grits. Back in his room, he spread a dozen or so sheets of paper out on the bed. Some were copies of long-ago clippings from the Columbia and Charleston newspapers, others were his own pencil-scrawled notes of names and numbers gleaned from the telephone work he'd done back home.

Where to begin? Almost anywhere, he thought. Any detective work at all was probably more than had ever been done in Linus Bragg's case. Since he didn't have a time machine, Willop could never know exactly what had gone on back then, but he was willing to bet the "investigation" had consisted of telling a helpless black boy what he should say.

So do better if you can, he goaded himself.

The first call is always the hardest, he knew. But as soon as he made it, he was startled at how trusting the people were compared to those around New York. He felt almost guilty, it was so easy. Well, at least getting the names of the people still alive was easy. Or getting some of the names. Some had moved away and were God only knew where, and others had long since died.

But Willop was surprised at how many names of people living right around Manning and Alcolu he was able to uncover after only an hour or so. His technique was simple, almost ingenuous. He would mumble a phony name, then something about an Army buddy or old classmate or a combination, and that was that. He had names.

Of course, there was no way of telling yet how many still had most of their marbles left, Willop thought. Come to think of it, how could he be sure they hadn't all heard he was coming and were stringing him along. . . .

No. Start thinking that way, Willop thought, and you'll be sure of nothing. Which, come to think of it . . .

Maybe he should just cut the bullshit and start using his real name and tell the goddamn truth about exactly who he was and why he was there.

Oh, no. That was fine for Columbia, for someone like Jim Baker (come to think of it, why had he been so sure about Baker?), but this was smack in the middle of South Carolina, hard by a dirty little swamp.

Finally, Willop had no more excuses: He was ready to make the call that made him nervous.

"Clarendon County sheriff's office. Dispatcher Bestwick speaking."

"Is Sheriff Fischer in, please?"

"I'm sorry, he's out of the office right now. Can someone else help you?"

Shit. "Well, maybe. I wanted to look at some old files, if that's possible. . . ."

"What agency are you with, sir?"

"I'm not. I mean, I'm doing some private research, sort of. . . ."

"Hold on, please."

Willop could hear a radio crackling in the background and the dispatcher talking into the radio. Then he heard the dispatcher talking, in slightly anxious and hushed tones, to someone nearby—asking some authority figure what she should do, Willop was certain.

"Yes, can I help you?" Willop was startled by the loud booming male voice, full of command presence.

"Hello. I was wondering if you might be able to help me on some research. . . ."

"Well, who are you?"

This guy talks so loud, he doesn't need a phone, Willop thought. "My name is Willop. I—"

"Who are you with, Mr. Willop?"

"I'm here on my own. Some private research."

"Private research . . . Well, you'll have to talk to Sheriff Fischer about access to his case files. I wouldn't presume to tell him how to handle a request like yours. He should be in this afternoon."

"Guess I'll have to call back. I gather you have some authority in the sheriff's office."

"I'm with the state police. but a request like yours, that has to go to the sheriff himself. No exceptions."

Willop found the voice, and the man behind it, authoritarian, totally in control, condescending, impatient, and all those things at once.

"May I ask who you are?" Willop said.

"Yes, you may. My name is Captain Stoker."

Oh, Jesus. Gotta be the sheriff's son. Born to the law and totally sure of himself. Willop did not want to deal with him yet. "Thanks for your help, Captain. I'll try the sheriff later."

"You do that."

Click.

Willop worked for a while on steadying his nerves, then opened the dresser drawer and took out the revolver. You never know, he thought.

It was time to take a ride.

Willop drove slowly, soon coming to a combination service station and general store. The car light; got to fix it.

"Give it as much unleaded as it'll hold," Willop told the attendant. "And fix the fuse on the right rear light, okay?"

"I only pump gas."

The belligerence in the old man's voice was startling. The man was thin and old, a turkey wattle for a neck, sunken cheeks, thin white hair.

"That's okay, Dad. I got it." A younger man, blond and smiling, had appeared. With a gentle hand on the shoulder, he dismissed the old man and steered him back toward the door.

"That's my dad," the younger man said, explaining but not apologizing. "He ran this place for years. Just starting to slow down a bit now. Fill it up and check the fuse?"

"Please," Willop said. He gave the man the keys, and the man flipped open the trunk. Within a minute, he slammed it shut again.

"It was burned out. Fine now. Five dollars for the gas and a buck for the fuse."

"Keep the change," Willop said, handing him seven. "And can you point me to the old Tyler sawmill?"

"Damn, I didn't think you were from around here. Only people call it that is people from around here."

"Well, years ago I was in the area for a while." Watch it, Willop told himself. Jesus, was he paranoid, or was that old man, now standing over by the corner, giving him a knowing look. . . .

The younger man gave Willop directions that sounded plain enough and thanked him for his business in a way that sounded friendly enough. Still, Willop was on edge. He figured he would be as long as he was in South Carolina.

Willop had driven only a few minutes when he began to think he was lost. The swamp on his left bothered him. Could be, but . . .

He spotted a long table under a green and yellow awning by the side of the road. A tired-faced woman, brown hair yielding to gray and the gray turning to wisp, sat in a chair next to the table. Her squinty eyes were small behind thick glasses. Next to the table was a large white sign lettered sloppily in red.

STRIPED BASS FESTIVAL, the sign said. BUY PECANS, CHOCOLATES, PEACH WINE AND GET CHANCES ON BIGGEST AND MOST FISH.

Guess I don't have to be too afraid of her, Willop thought, stopping the car.

"I gotta know," he said, sounding as friendly as he could. "What's the Striped Bass Festival?"

"You ain't from around here, obviously."

"Not exactly."

The old woman straightened slightly, adopting a posture for a stranger. "Every spring, people come from all over for the festival. Next month, it is. Best fishing for a hundred miles."

"I see."

The woman stared directly at Willop, as intently and unselfconsciously as an ostrich. Can't decide who I am, what I am, he thought. He guessed she was in her sixties and had lived nearby all her life. Strange . . .

"You can buy chances for a dollar apiece," the woman said. "Bet on the biggest fish that'll be caught. Case there's a tie, pick the hour and minute and day it'll be caught. Win a twenty-four-inch color TV."

"Got a TV already," Willop said.

"All the proceeds go to the Alcolu Volunteer Fire Department. That's who this stand benefits. I keep some from the pecans, chocolates, and peach wine and give a percent to the firemen. Striped bass chances, they're all sold for the fire department."

"Tell you what. Just give me a box of pecans. Help out the firemen ..."

"I'm on the auxiliary."

"Great. Say, maybe you can help me with some directions."

"Anyone can, I can. Lived around here all my life."

No pushover, this one, Willop thought. Eyes like a hawk. "Tell me if I'm going the right way to the old Tyler mill."

The woman's eyes brightened and she cocked her head. "Straight down the way you're going," she said, her voice taut. "You'll go under the interstate highway, then bear right. See a sign that says 'Alcolu.' Should see the mill then. First turn to your right."

"Appreciate it."

"The railroad owns it now. The mill ..." The old woman sounded hypnotized.

"Right. Well, thanks." Willop was so uneasy, he could almost feel the hairs on his arms standing up. Still, she seemed to know her way around, so he asked her the other directions he wanted. The old woman gave them in a voice clear as a bell. It was the eyes that Willop couldn't stand to look into.

"Appreciate it," he said, driving off in a hurry. Goddamn, I ain't seen so many strange people since I saw *Deliverance*.

All around him lay acres of grass shining yellow-green in the sun; the colors seemed to have been squeezed from a paint tube. Hundreds of yards apart. On either side of the road, farm houses anchored patches of soil so rich it looked black, almost wet. Willop breathed deeply.

The quiet loveliness of the place simply could not be denied. The air was cool and pure. Now, this is the way the world should be, he thought. It was almost impossible to imagine something evil and bloody happening in this place.

Several hundred feet away, the mill hummed and whined. Out of sight, diesel trucks could be heard revving up and moving away. Used to be horses here, Willop thought. Where'd the horses go?

Horses, hell. Man, where did all the people go? He knew that, all around him, where there was shining yellow-green grass, there had been a colony of shacks for the blacks—the colored, the niggers—who toiled at the mill. Gone now, the shacks. Gone, the people. Gone north, gone south, gone old, gone dead …

A railroad spur looped around the perimeter of the mill grounds. Willop began walking along the edges of the ties, faster as he got farther away from the road. He felt sweat on his forehead.

A church, there in a clearing, and smooth old gravestones nearby. A simple, clean, white wooden box of a church. Paint fresh. People still come here.

Oh my God, Willop thought when he saw the sign. Green Hill Church. His mother, his uncle, they had come here, sung inside there. No songs now, only the wind.

For a moment, Willop wanted to go inside. But he did not want to waste the time, and his knees were already weak.

On he walked. The spur started to swing back toward the mill, but Willop kept walking, straight away from the road. A path, there was a path. A path for children on bicycles. Down there …

Willop stopped, breathed deep. A breeze came by. Smells of dirt and grass, cut wood and … flowers? This time of year …

Hum of the mill, smell of cut wood. Birds. Willop felt outside himself. There were flowers down that way. He could see them in the distance. Pretty, down that path.

The breeze came by again. Smells of grass and water. There would have been the smell of blood in the air that day.

"Any ghosts down there?" Willop whispered.

He would go no farther. Let the spot where they died stay covered with flowers, he thought. I don't have to trample there.

Willop savored the breeze and the day one last moment, then wiped his forehead. It was time to go.

CHAPTER 21

The woman was white-haired, thin, and frail-looking through the screen door of the farmhouse, but she did not seem afraid of Willop. She said her husband was out tromping through the fields. With a shotgun. "Practicing on the crows for when quail season comes around. Mostly, he just walks for the exercise."

That sounded harmless enough, but it was still enough to make Willop nervous. Suppose Dexter Cody had something to hide, even after all these years. Willop remembered from his days on the police beat what a shotgun could do to a human body at close range.

Willop had parked on a hard shoulder in a gentle dip in the road a few yards from the house. After talking to Cody's wife and hearing that the old deputy had a shotgun, Willop went back to his car. He took the revolver from under the seat, loaded it and dropped it in his jacket pocket. He was not comfortable, carrying something to kill with, but he would do almost anything to keep from getting a shotgun blast in the stomach.

Willop locked his car. He looked up and down the road; nothing as far as he could see. Then he started into the fields, hoping Cody would not be hard to find, and hoping even more that he would see Cody before Cody saw him. He walked at an even pace, not hesitating, not hurrying.

Ideally, he would have gone to the sheriff's office first, found a cooperative clerk who would get out the old case file, and sat down to study the whole thing, paper by paper, hour after hour, if need be. Until he was steeped in it. But it hadn't worked out that way with the phone call. Real hard ass, that state police captain.

Light green, middle green, dark green waving in the breeze. A clean blue sky painted with long strokes of cloud. Suppose this guy is one tough nut and has something to hide besides, Willop thought. Well, then, I picked a great day to die in case he turns his gun on me before I can react.

Willop was not consoled by the thought.

He could feel the sweat on his forehead and under his arms. He wished he had paid more attention to his physical condition. He stopped, breathed deeply. His heart was pounding.

Scared.

On he walked. The breeze stroked the grass, fluffed the clouds high in the sky. A beautiful day to live, a beautiful day to die, if need be.

Up a gentle hill. Long, slow strides. No hurry. God, no hurry. The countryside, how beautiful! Could he stay here? Belong? Bring Moira here to live. Take her to Green Hill Church to pray? Jesus, what a crazy thought.

The breeze was a little stronger near the top of the hill; it dried the sweat on his face.

A shotgun boomed; Willop's knees shook. There, down the hill, just at the edge of a line of trees along a creek. The man was tall, thin, and his back was to Willop. He wore tan clothes and an orange cap that accented his thick white hair.

Willop started down the hill.

"Linus, boy, maybe we can start to find the truth," Willop whispered, hoping to muster courage from the sound of his own voice. The breeze whispered back, uncaring.

Weeds and grass swished away from Willop's feet. Closer.

It was never like this in the movies, Willop thought. A hard-ass detective walked into strange bars in strange towns, said strange words to strange men and women, beat the shit out of the men who got in his way, bedded down with the women . . . all before the first beer commercial. But he, Willop, was scared just about shitless.

The old man's back was still to him. Tall and lean, he moved awkwardly, almost as though on stilts. He was looking into the trees. The man crouched, pointed his shotgun into the trees for a moment, then changed his mind. He straightened up and cradled the gun across his arms.

"Afternoon," Willop said.

The old man's shoulders moved with the start, then he turned around slowly, his hunter's caution keeping his shotgun pointed away from the approaching stranger. The old man had clear, ice-blue eyes and shiny skin stretched taut across cheekbones. Old or not, he was formidable, and Willop could understand the stories he had heard about how tough and mean he could be.

"Who're you?" the old man asked.

"My name is Willop. I'm from up north. I want to ask you a few questions about a case—"

"I'm retired. Have been for some time."

"A case you were on a long time ago . . ."

"How'd you find me?"

He's a tough old bastard, Willop thought. And suspicious.

"Easy," Willop said, trying to smooth the nervousness in his voice. "You're still pretty well known around here, retired or not. And this ain't that big a community, so I just asked around."

Willop thought, from the look in his eyes, that the old man bought the explanation, one which, as a matter of fact, was true.

"What case?" the man asked.

"An old murder."

Willop could not stop his knees from shaking. Suppose the old man had something to hide. He, Willop, was the stranger, asking questions on the old man's property.

And if Willop were to get blown apart with a 12-gauge at point-blank range, the old man would probably have a lot of willing listeners. After all, his turf extended far beyond his own fields and hills.

"Uh, Mr. Cody, could I ask you a favor right off? I know it's silly, but guns make me nervous. Could you, uh, unload that shotgun? I'd really appreciate it."

Blue eyes staring at Willop, measuring him, retired Deputy Dexter Cody effortlessly worked the slide action, chucking glistening red shells out of the shotgun and catching them in his palm.

"That better?" Cody asked when he was done.

"Oh, yes. Thanks. I'm sorry. It's just the way I am." Willop kept his hand in his pocket, palm on the revolver grip, just in case.

"Funny way to be around here. Nervous about guns," Cody said.

"I guess so. The case I hope you can help me with was the one with those two little girls. Grade-school girls. Killed not too far from the sawmill in 1944."

"Colored kid did it. From the shacks they used to have over there. What's your interest?"

"I might be doing a book." Not exactly a lie, Willop thought.

"Ain't much of a book. At least, far's any story's concerned. Little colored boy, he wanted somethin'. Tried to take it, and they put up a fight. So he killed them. Confessed to it readily enough."

"Well, maybe it wasn't all that simple. . . ."

"Sure it was. Shit, the nigger confessed plain as day."

Bad enough, Willop thought, that he doesn't seem that eager to talk; he's gotta be a bigot, too. Well, what had he expected in the middle of South Carolina.

"What about the confession?"

"Simple as that. He confessed, like I told you. I softened him up a bit, made sure he was afraid of me. Then the sheriff went in and took the confession. Simple."

"And you and the sheriff had done some looking around before?"

"'Course. How'd you think we picked up the nigger in the first place? Went snooping around over by the shantytown where they all lived, all them mill workers. Asked around, we did. The sheriff, he was a damn good law man in his day."

"So somebody in the shanties . . ."

"Old man. Old crippled-up nigger." The old deputy's ice-blue eyes were alert and suspicious and Willop wondered if he detected a knowing look. "Anyhow, this old nigger—Crooks, his name was, I think, dead a long time now—he saw the nigger boy pulling a cow, real mean-like. By the nose, hard. Right around the time the girls were known to have gone down by the mill. Mean reputation, the kid had . . ."

Willop had learned from hearing witnesses at trials, and reading reports typed up by policemen, and in his own interviewing over the years, that you usually didn't get neat answers. It could be bewildering, even exhausting, to listen to people's answers, trying to sort out the irrelevant and the incongruous and hoping to recognize the seemingly trivial detail that might be all-important.

"His name was Linus Bragg, right?"

"Damned if you ain't right."

"So the old man, Crooks, said this Linus was mean. . . ."

"Mean as hell. Did some dirty, rotten trick on old Crooks once. Let the water out of his fish barrel, or something. So Crooks, he was an old fart, he had good reason to remember."

"So Linus was the only suspect? Right from the start?"

The breeze played teasingly off the grass. The trees soughed heedlessly, as they had done more than forty years ago, as they would tomorrow.

"Well, now . . ." Cody's forehead wrinkled.

"I mean, were there any loose ends?"

"Loose ends . . . depends on who you talk to, I guess. Always that way. Talk to a hundred people, get a hundred answers . . ."

Willop's breath caught in his dry throat and his heart beat fast. The breeze teased, and the trees soughed, uncaring, and this thin old man—a bigot to his bone marrow—couldn't make up his mind what kind of answer to give to the most important question Willop would ask him. "I meant, were there any other—"

"Back then, the niggers in the shacks all had stories. About this foreman, or that one. Pushing 'em around, screwing the women whenever they wanted. That stuff. Old Mr. Tyler, he owned the mill, he was good to 'em, but you know . . ."

"Know what?"

"Well, probably was some of that goin' on. The sheriff, he checked up on some loose ends. Damn good law man, the sheriff . . ."

"What loose ends?"

"Hell, I can't remember that. Ain't even sure if the sheriff told me, exactly. Besides, after the sheriff checked up, they weren't loose ends anymore."

"So the sheriff was satisfied the boy did it?"

"Hell, yes. Nigger confessed. Signed a piece of paper, then ate a big, hearty meal. That much I remember. . . ."

"Remember anything he said?"

"Didn't mean to, he said. Didn't mean to ..."

"Didn't mean to what?"

"Way I recall it, little bastard said he didn't mean to look at 'em, even. Something like that."

Across the creek a bird sang. Willop was conscious of the water slipping lazily over rocks, as it had done yesterday and the day and the year before, as it would tomorrow.

"He didn't mean to look at them?" He didn't mean to look. *To look.* A memory flickered in Willop's brain, a memory of terrifying stories told to little black boys about bad things that would happen if they dared look at white girls a certain way. . . .

"Didn't even mean to look. That's what the sheriff said he said. Kid sure did a lot more than look. We didn't mess around with 'em, not back then. Right to the chair. Sheriff, he kept the nigger from getting strung up, in fact. Plenty of folks was ready to hang the bugger. Or worse."

"Worse?"

"I've seen worse. You got any more questions?"

"I guess not."

"Damn long time ago. Deserved what he got, that kid. Black or white."

"I'll let you go back to your hunting," Willop said. He was tired and exhilarated and not a little relieved.

"Naw. About time for me to quit. Legs get tired." With that, Cody worked the slide of the shotgun another time, and one more gleaming red shell plopped into his hand. "I kept one round in the chamber," Cody said matter-of-factly.

Willop felt for the handle of the revolver, but his arm felt like cement, and he was not at all sure he could move it.

"Cautious old habits," Cody explained. "Now if you're done ..."

"Well, guess I am, for now. Maybe we could talk some more. . . ."

"Done all I want to," Cody said. His voice had gone hard.

"Understood," Willop said. "Thanks again. So long."

Willop tried to smile, tried to affect a casual farewell wave as he turned and started back toward the car. Not for a moment did he think of turning to see if Cody was still standing there; he was afraid he would see the shotgun pointed at him.

As he walked, Willop tried to remember how many strides he had taken. It wouldn't be that many, he knew, before he was out of killing range. The shotgun, so deadly within a few yards, would only give him a back full of skin-deep pellet wounds if Cody waited long enough. Ah, maybe he won't fire at all.

And then he was back on the road. He looked in both directions, then around him at the fields. He was alone. Willop got into the car, slumped in the seat, and discovered that his shirt was stuck to his back with sweat.

CHAPTER 22

Bill D. Stoker shut off the alarm, plugged in the coffee pot, and got into the shower. He let the water run as hot as he could stand it and thought of what he would put on his list for the day. Call about cable service; call Jen; call about ...

Shutting off the water, he forced himself to put the list out of his head. He had always kept himself organized that way, with lists (some on paper, some in his head), sometimes to Jen's considerable annoyance.

He could never put it into words as well as Jen herself had (yeah, she was good with words), but she had told him, in effect, that to put everything down on a list, or to be so endlessly organized and methodical, could get in the way of feelings. She had told him that a lot of times. Then her line had changed: She had started telling him that he *deliberately* put a lot of things down on lists so that he wouldn't have to face up to emotions. "And that gets in the way of a lot of things, including love," she had said finally.

Later on, when he had almost had it figured out, Stoker realized Jen said the last thing just about the time she was going to that therapist to learn more about her feelings. Sure ...

He was proud that the skin he was toweling covered (for the most part) good, lean muscle. Too many men, once they got to be sixty or so, figured it was okay to go soft in the body.

Not Bill Stoker. You didn't have to be a health nut or run ten miles a day or lift weights. Just stick to a few basic things, he always said: Use the stairs instead of the elevator once in a while; keep your dinners small; drink moderately. And it didn't hurt to jog once in a while and take long walks.

That reminded him: He would have to leave a note for Bryant Fischer, a tactful note, telling him that some of his deputies were getting a bit thick around the middle. Nothing serious, but better to catch it before it got serious. Little things had a way of turning into big things. Some of the hair and sideburns were getting a bit long also. . . .

He picked out a pair of comfortable slacks that weren't dirty and a shirt and a tie that didn't clash with either and sat down to his coffee, juice, and unbuttered toast. He had taken only a few sips when the stuff about the cable began to annoy him again.

Before the divorce, Jen had been the one who insisted on getting the cable TV service (he had had trouble justifying the expense to himself), but now he relied on it a lot. Not so much for movies and plays and things Jen hated Manning for not having, things which she had grown to like in Charleston and Atlanta on the business trips she took without him, but so he could watch the Atlanta Braves. Here it was, the baseball season starting, and he still did not have a good picture. Gotta get the cable people off their ass. He picked up the phone.

"Clarendon Video. Morning."

"Morning to you. Listen, I called a couple times already. Cable reception's lousy and I gotta have it fixed 'else I can't watch the Braves. Now, you folks gotta tell me when you're gonna get over here, because I'm on the road a lot."

The woman asked for Stoker's address, and he gave it to her.

"Is that a private home or apartment?" she asked.

"Apartment. Listen, just tell your boss Junior Stoker called again. Okay?"

"Yes, sir. Does he know how to reach you?"

"He better. And tell him to call me as soon as he gets that Clint Eastwood movie I asked him to reserve. Got that?"

"Yes, sir. What was that name again?"

"Stoker, Bill D. Just tell your boss Junior Stoker. Okay?"

"Yes, sir."

Stoker hung up, annoyed. If Manning was getting too big, so you couldn't deal with people person-to-person anymore, then there was no hope whatsoever. He always used "Stoker, Bill D." for his charge accounts and the like. "Junior," his lifelong nickname, pinned on him not because he was a junior but just because his parents thought it fit the younger of two brothers, he used whenever he wanted someone around

Manning to recognize his name. Now, it was getting so he couldn't even count on people to recognize his name.

Damn. It wasn't that long ago the old man hung up the shield. Was it?

He pulled into the lot next to the low, yellow brick building that housed the Clarendon County sheriff's office and jail. There was a parking space reserved for "Capt. Bill D. Stoker, South Carolina State Police," which, this morning at least, no one had usurped. Things were looking up.

"Good morning, Captain," Cheryl Bestwick said as he passed the dispatcher's station.

"Morning to you, Miss Cheryl."

Stoker had summoned more cheer than he really felt. For one thing, Cheryl Bestwick was an excellent dispatcher, and he wanted to keep her happy; for another thing, she was black. The word from headquarters, official and otherwise, was that you bent over backwards to be courteous to black subordinates.

Sometimes, Stoker remembered the advice his father had given him on treating the colored—the *colored*!—with the right mix of honesty and gentleness. Whenever he remembered that, he was touched by his father's old-fashioned rectitude, yet bothered in ways he couldn't put into words that his father had found it necessary to say such things regarding blacks. His father had never told him to treat white people with the proper blend of honesty and gentleness; that had been understood.

Well, what the hell. Now it was official policy that you had to be nice to them, the blacks. Bend over backwards, in fact. Which he thought he tried to do.

Cheryl Bestwick was in her mid-twenties, tall, round-buttocked, athletic. Black or not, she was something to look at, and Stoker was charmed by her, by the way she squared her shoulders when she walked, by her deep black eyes, her light tan skin and high cheekbones, even (and this was something he was a long time admitting to himself) her smell.

"That brother of yours, he still keeping that fastball down like he should?"

"Lord, Captain," Bestwick said. "Mama, she rave about Lyman all the time. Triple-A next year, she say. Then the big time soon after that."

"Well, he best not let anybody monkey with his arm motion. You tell your mama that for me, to tell Lyman not to let anybody monkey with his arm."

Abruptly, it seemed to him, there was no more time, no more room, for small talk with her. He went down the hall and turned left, into his corner office.

"Captain," Bestwick shouted after him from the other end of the corridor, "Mrs. Stoker on line two."

He was apprehensive. Jen called him occasionally from Columbia, where she was a buyer in a department store, but it was not like her to call him so early in the day.

"Hello," he said.

"Junior, I'm sorry to start your day this way. Thomas fell and hit his head. They think he suffered a mild concussion. Probably nothing serious, but I wanted you to know."

"Damn it. Wasn't anybody watching?"

"Well, sure they were. But it only took a moment for him to get up out of the wheelchair, you know how he is. It's not like taking care of a child. The people at the home were very apologetic."

"Good for them."

"I think it was just one of those unfortunate things."

One of those unfortunate things. Try as he might, Stoker usually thought of the life of his twenty-four-year-old retarded and institutionalized son as a long series of unfortunate things. Unfortunate he had been born that way, all the more so since it was their first and only child, and a late one at that; unfortunate that he had needed constant care, unfortunate that he and Jen had blamed themselves and each other. Unfortunate that his wife had complained bitterly that he, Junior, wasn't "learning to deal with it and accept," whatever that meant.

Well, maybe she had been right all along. He had been goddamn sorry and disappointed for a long time that he could not get the same enjoyment from his son that his father had gotten from . . . from Bob, goddamn it. More from Bob than from him.

"Everything else okay?" he said.

"Busy as hell. Last thing I needed today was the call from the hospital. Got a lot of stuff coming in for the summer season. Well, I just wanted you to know. Stay in touch."

After a few more pleasantries, they said good-bye. Jen sounded interested and happy in what she was doing. Much happier in Columbia than around Manning. Who could blame her? Mind like hers, college education, knowing stuff about paintings and books, she could probably land a good job in Charleston or Atlanta if she wanted. That possibility alarmed him, for some reason.

But he knew how to put unpleasant thoughts out of his head. He opened his briefcase and took out a small dictating machine and a black notebook, the latter containing jottings on thoughts he wanted to pass on to Sheriff Bryant Fischer. Fischer was only the second (no, third) sheriff since Hiram Stoker, but how things had changed. Miranda and probable cause and defendants' rights and science and computers and technicalities.

Stoker sifted through the reports left in his "in" box and was pleased. Fischer had trained his people to be meticulous and thorough, which made Stoker's job much easier. Stoker was the state police liaison with local law-enforcement agencies, and as such he could help determine how much state aid, in money and training, the local people got, or didn't get.

The fact was (and Stoker could appreciate the irony) he was just the kind of law man his father had found most troublesome.

But Stoker liked Bryant Fischer. He was a beefy law man from the old school, crew cut and all. He was only a few years younger than Stoker and shared his hard-ass feelings on drugs and respect for authority, and (Miranda or not) he could often frighten suspects into telling the truth.

"Hi, Bryant," Stoker said into the dictating machine. "Columbia suggests you send one deputy, two if you can manage it, to finger-printing classes scheduled . . ."

On another matter, he paused. Got to use tact, he thought. Or what passes for tact from me.

"Re the February twenty-eighth seizure of marijuana plants. Uh, good job by the deputies, but I suggest even stronger, I should say more detailed report-writing on this. Otherwise, you could be very vulnerable on the chain of evidence ..."

He paused again. Chain of evidence. Reports. More paperwork, less detective work ...

"Re theft of farm equipment ..."

So it went, through the morning. And then, not so suddenly, it was lunchtime.

CHAPTER 23

His back clammy and his legs weak (not so much from the little bit of walking he had done, but from tension), Willop was tempted to head back to the motel, take a hot shower, and down enough Scotch to fell a steer.

Instead, he drove into Manning and found the sheriff's office. He pulled into a visitor's spot next to an empty space reserved, so the sign said, for Captain Stoker. My big-mouthed friend on the telephone, Willop thought. For some reason, seeing the name on the sign made it seem doubly familiar. Willop was pleased to see that the space next to Stoker's, for Sheriff Fischer himself, was also empty.

He sat in the car for a minute or more, trying to relax, trying to rehearse, trying to tell his conscience what he was about to attempt was for a good cause.

What the hell, he thought finally. The law ain't always played fair.

"Yes. Can I help you?"

"Hi. I wonder if I could see Sheriff Fischer. . . ." She was pretty, Willop thought, spotting the name tag that said BESTWICK. Gorgeous face, skin the color of a new penny, athletic figure.

"I'm sorry, he's not in. Someone else help you?"

"Hmmm ..." Willop frowned, feigning surprise and disappointment. "I was hoping to look at some old material, actually. . . ."

"Well, who might you be?"

"I might be Mr. James Willop, distinguished visitor from Yankeeland."

"Well, I might be too busy for your smart-ass games." But she wasn't, and she laughed. Then her eyes brightened and her smile faded. "You're the one who called yesterday."

"The same."

"Well, Captain Stoker said that Sheriff Fischer himself has to okay that sort of thing. . . ."

"Don't make it sound so dirty."

That set off such a hearty, unself-conscious laugh that Willop liked her immensely. He would protect her all he could. . . .

"Sheriff Fischer, he's over to Sumter County, I think. I know he isn't expected back till late this afternoon. If he makes it at all . . ."

"How about the captain?"

"He's out on personal stuff. Won't be back for a while, and before he does he always radios in. Like clockwork."

Good, Willop thought. He wasn't ready yet for an encounter with Stoker—especially an unexpected one.

"His father was the sheriff," Willop said.

"That's right. You know him?"

"No. But I did some homework before I came down here. Old newspaper clippings and such."

"Hmmm."

Yes, Willop thought. She was studying his face. Yes, she was sure now. . . .

"They good to work with?" Willop asked. "Them honkies?"

Bestwick smiled slyly. "Yeah, mostly they is. The sheriff, he a big fella. Tough as nails, when he want to be. Mostly nice though . . ."

"Sort of a 'Cool Hand Luke' type maybe?"

She started to laugh, then stifled it when the radio crackled. Picking up the microphone, she mumbled something indecipherable to Willop but apparently understandable to whoever was on the other end. She put the microphone down and turned back to him, laughing anew.

"Funny thing," she said, "is that Sheriff Fischer, he really do wear them funny sunglasses. Like mirrors. Awful funny-looking, them mirror glasses under that crew cut . . ."

"Crew cut? No, come on. I mean, a crew cut?"

Bestwick's laugh showed malicious delight with just the tiniest touch of guilt.

"Well, how about the captain?" Willop went on. "He pretty straight? I mean, comfortabe to work with . . ."

Now, Bestwick's laughter was at hip-slapping level, and she made no attempt at all to conceal her mirth. "He so straight, it almost like he got a ramrod up—"

"That bad, huh?"

"The captain, he about the most uncomfortable man I know."

"Gee, over the phone he sounded pretty easygoing. I mean . . ."

"Shee-it." Bestwick laughed some more.

"Ah, I get it. I bet he tried to talk jive-talk to you. Am I right?"

"He pretty good at that, all right. . . ."

"I can tell. Seriously."

Willop let her laugh for a while. Then it was time for his move, win or lose. He pulled out the credentials Delmar Springs had given him and showed them to Bestwick, just long enough for her to see that they were official, or semi-official, but not long enough for her to examine them closely.

"No bullshit," Willop almost whispered. "I really need your help."

Bestwick put Willop in a small, windowless room at the end of a corridor. One wall was taken up by a blackboard, another by a cork bulletin board with various flyers and pictures and advisories. Willop sat in a stiff metal chair at a long table.

Bestwick pushed open the door and set a small cardboard box in front of him. Willop smelled mold and dust.

"Ain't much there, I bet," she said. "Don't look like anybody bothered it for a long time."

"I'll be careful of what's here."

"You gotta promise me not to take nothin' now, you hear?"

"Promise."

"You lock the door. When I gotta chase you out, I'll come and knock. If you ain't gone by then."

"I might be. Thanks again."

Willop locked the door, hung his coat over the back of the chair, and took an ancient manila envelope out of the box and carefully opened it. The tips of his fingers felt dirty, whether from the age of the envelope or just his imagination he could not tell.

"Clark-Ellerby homicide" had been scrawled in the upper left corner by—who? The sheriff at the time? His deputy?

Willop slid the contents onto the tabletop, then shook the envelope gently, certain that more papers would come out. To his surprise, none did. Jesus, he thought. A case like that, and this is all there is? Willop had covered courts and had been through God knew how many case files. A criminal case of any gravity or complexity would generate hundreds, sometimes thousands, of pages of police memoranda, photographs, indictments and superseding indictments, subpoenas, motions to quash subpoenas, motions to dismiss, trial transcripts, appeal motions—

Oh, of course . . . no trial transcript. Simple enough . . . no appeal had ever been filed, and they fried the kid just a couple weeks after the trial, which only lasted a day anyhow, so no trial transcript. And this was in 1944.

Damn, Willop thought. Things were a lot simpler then. . . .

With his fingers he shifted the papers. There, for God's sake, there was the same prison mug shot of Linus Bragg that Baker had shown him. God, look at him, Willop thought. A moment caught in time, long ago and yesterday.

Kid, did you ever dream you'd be causing me so much grief?

Willop found a note in ink on yellow lined paper: "Asked State Police to check suspicious traffic in and out of area since night before girls reported missing . . . nothing suspicious found . . . Old man name of Crooks (colored) says he believes one Linus Bragg is sufficiently mean. . . ." The note went on to say that Crooks's account would be followed up.

Seems like common sense, professional procedure, Willop thought grudgingly, acknowledging that the designation "Crooks (colored)" made the memo-writer no worse a bigot than anyone else at the time.

Again, Willop slid papers around on the tabletop, uncovering several more photographs. Before he looked (he already knew what they were, they could be nothing else), he raised his eyes to the ceiling and took a deep breath.

Willop had seen more than a few bodies at crime scenes and in wrecked cars, and he had seen many more photographs of bodies in various stages of decay—had seen enough of all that to face up to the fact that there was a certain attraction in horror, in evil. That he knew, and he was not ashamed of it, because he knew that it was part of the human condition. Also because he had not lost the capacity to feel weak in the knees, and in the stomach.

Jesus Christ. Every death scene had its own, unique horror. The picture of the little girls' bodies next to the ditch, their hair and clothes still soaked, their glassy eyes—Jesus, those eyes!—made Willop sad. Could he even dare to have children with Moira if there was even the slightest chance of something like that happening to them?

In other photographs, the girls lay nude on metal autopsy tables, their eyes the same: full of terror. The mouth of the older girl was half-open, almost as though the photograph had been taken while she was alive, the camera catching her lips in the act of forming a word. One of her bottom teeth was slightly out of line. Ah, poor kid. She should have had braces. Wonder if her folks were thinking about that, back then . . . Willop stared long at the autopsy pictures, his mind filling with sadness and futile pity.

He looked again at the photograph of the death scene. Way off in a corner, out of focus, was a fender from a World War II–era truck. And on the left edge of the picture part of a man's pant leg was visible, enough to show the full, floppy tailoring of the 1940s. Noticing those things made Willop feel better, reminding him that the horror he was looking at belonged, after all, in the long ago. Or most of it did. And if he was going to be any kind of investigator, he had better stuff his emotions in the closet.

He checked the back of the murder-scene photograph. "Bodies shortly after discovery by Pvt. Luke Reddy of Natl. Guard on 3/29/44." Willop took out a notebook and wrote down the name. Luke Reddy was likely long dead or long gone, but you never could tell. . . . Willop picked up a sheet of paper with the words "Autopsy Report" typed on top. Heights and weights of each victim . . . Cause of death "repeated blows to head by heavy instrument, causing numerous fractures and lacerations of brain . . ."

A present-day autopsy report would almost certainly state exactly how many wounds on each body, and the depth and width of each, Willop thought.

"No evidence of sexual violation ..." And that's it? Willop thought. No mention of what chemical tests were done, if any. A good defense lawyer today could tear this report to shreds. Hell, Willop could do the cross-examination himself: Doctor, would you say that the rest of your autopsy report is as thorough and detailed as your findings on possible sexual violation ...?

Nothing here about any water being found in the lungs, Willop thought. Or even any indication that the pathologist at the time even thought to look. So, Doctor, you're telling us that you don't know whether the girls were alive or dead when they were thrown into the water, isn't that correct? You don't know because you didn't bother to do any tests to find out. And would you say that the rest of your report ...

Willop could see that the head wounds were deep. Too deep to have been inflicted by a fourteen-year-old boy who weighed only a hundred pounds? Hard to say ... How strong does somebody, even a kid, have to be to cave in a head with a piece of metal? Willop had seen many men, and boys, smaller than he drive a golf ball a lot farther than he could.

He continued his imaginary cross-examination: So, Doctor, your testimony is that you didn't bother to do any fingernail scrapings of the victims, isn't that correct? And because you didn't bother, we don't know whether the girls struggled with their attacker, whether some of that attacker's skin and hair might have stuck under their nails, so that the real attacker would have a scratched-up face and a patch of hair missing, unlike Linus Bragg, who has no scratches. . . . Isn't that correct, Doctor?

Okay, Willop thought. Enough of the Walter Mitty routine. But *could* a kid the size of Linus inflict wounds that deep? Maybe yes, maybe no. Wouldn't the girls have struggled? Who could say? Richard Speck had killed eight young women in Chicago, one by one, with no help. . . .

Willop rubbed his eyes, got up from the metal chair, stretched his legs, and walked around the little room. None of what he had seen proved that Linus had killed the girls, or that he hadn't.

It seemed pretty obvious that Linus had not had any kind of defense in court—by today's standards. Though back then, maybe his defense wasn't so bad.

The confession, that was the big thing. There, a piece of yellow lined paper. "Confession of Linus Bragg in the deaths of Cindy Lou Ellerby and Sue Ellen Clark," it read, through the strikeovers.

Willop scanned the paper, soiled and brittle with age.

My name is Linus Bragg, and I can read and write and understand my rights.

On the afternoon of Friday, March 28, I saw the two young girls, whose names I later learned were Sue Clark and Cindy, picking flowers near the tracks down past the sawmill.

I approached them and made sexual advances and when they resisted me, I picked up a spike and struck them with it repeatedly. When I knew they were dead, I was in a state of panic. So I dragged the bodies, one by one, to a ditch and threw them in the water. I threw the bicycle in after them. Then I went and got the cow owned by my family, which I had been walking before this incident occurred.

I walked to my home near the mill, and on the way I met Mr. Crooks and talked to him briefly. I swear that I make this statement of my own free will, and that no one has attempted to threaten me or pressure me in any way.

Sure, Willop thought. Of your own free will, and in your own words, too.

With his fingertips, Willop shuffled the papers some more. He studied a sheet of notes, on yellow paper, in the same handwriting he had seen elsewhere in the file. Now, maybe to the guy who made these notes, forty and more years ago, this all made sense, Willop thought. Damned if I can make out much ...

In the upper left corner of the paper was the indentation left by a paper clip. Did the paper clip fall off, or was it removed, ten or twenty years ago? Forty?

And did the fact that the clip was no longer in place mean that somebody had taken something out of the file? Or did it just mean that whoever was looking was too lazy to put the clip back in place, and that all the papers were right there, on the table?

Willop drummed his fingers on the table. He was fighting to balance his common sense and his curiosity: It wouldn't do to stay here much longer, yet this was probably the only shot he would ever have of seeing the file. . . . Should he take some of the stuff with him, and to hell with his promise to Bestwick?

No. Besides, he wouldn't know what to take. . . .

Just a few more minutes. What to look for? What can I get here and *only* here? Got the lawyer's name, got the name of the guy who found the bodies, got some other names. Maybe something I missed in the confession. Read it again, word by word. . . .

"Left the stuff on the table back there," he said quietly to Bestwick. "Appreciate it."

"Remember . . ." she said.

"Relax. Our secret."

Willop got into his car and headed back to the motel. It wasn't a question of laziness; he needed to calm himself down before he unraveled.

CHAPTER 24

Back when he could talk, and when he had the audience (and the energy), he would talk about his boyhood. To his listeners, the things seemed so far away. But when the old man reminisced, either to others or silently, within himself, it was like pictures being held in front of his eyes.

He saw the wrinkled men, men who were old when he was a boy. They had fought in The War, and some had lost arms and legs. They told of biting hard into a piece of rawhide, going crazy with pain despite great gulps of whiskey beforehand, as the knives and saws went through flesh and bone.

Of course, for the longest time The War meant only one thing; nobody had to ask which war. Everybody remembered which one. To have fought in The War, even to have had a relative who fought, was something to be proud of forever, and the defeat was a tragedy to be embraced.

The images ran through the old man's head: sunshine on bugles and trumpets, on the brass fittings on the drums, on the brass spear points atop the poles around which curled the Confederate flags. Parades, then barbecues, then the old men—old when he was a boy—walking through the crowds, stopping to talk and tell stories. As long as he lived, the old man would remember the sun on the brass, on the red and blue and the white stars of the flags, the hot sun on those summer parades.

And those old men (now *he* was old!) wore their uniforms from The War, and the old man would never forget his boyhood wonder that they could have worn such heavy gray and butternut clothes while marching and fighting in the summer heat.

Now they were gone, all of them—long, long gone—and he was old. Think of that!

When he traced the course of his life, he remembered how it was that, gradually, those old men who had fought in The War became, not just old, but ancient, and how there were fewer and fewer of them. Eventually, there were only a few in all of Clarendon and Sumter counties. Then one or two in the entire state of South Carolina. And then, almost before he knew it, his own years having added up so fast, only a few in the whole South.

And then there were none. And he was old. . . .

Wait, now. That's only part of it. See, the old man told himself, that's how come you used to lose your listeners; the stuff about The War is only part of it. . . .

Television and the interstate highways, that's what changed things around here. That and the United States Supreme Court. For better or worse. Maybe both.

Japs and Germans, that's what people mean now when they talk about The War. At least people my age, the old man reminded himself.

What happened since *that* war, that's the stuff that's unbelievable. Wasn't that long ago (was it?) that a lot of folks had no electric or plumbing. Whites as well as the colored.

People didn't go to Columbia or Charleston 'less it was something special. Trip took way too long, cost way too much for most folks. Even if you could get gas, which you couldn't always . . .

The interstates, Godalmighty! Go to Columbia in the morning, come back to Manning at night. Even have dinner in Columbia, at a fancy place. A lot more people can afford that now. A lot more.

And television. Damn. See folks in Columbia or Charleston— Atlanta, even—and see how they live. The whole world. Used to be you were born in Manning, worked around here, got buried here.

And the colored. Working alongside the whites, sometimes bossing 'em. Well, say what you like, good or bad. Hard to believe, for someone my age. There I go again!

The old man had forgotten whether he was trying to talk out loud or just inside his head. Whether he was alone or had company.

Alone.

That big motel, over by Lake Marion. The old man could remember when they built it. Big place, took up some woods. Hard to believe, the motel sitting there. Television in every room.

People from all over, they stay there. They talk different. On their way to Florida or New York, God knows where. Passing through. Spending money.

The old man's son had taken him there for dinner a number of times. Hard to believe, his son affording that. Big steaks, free seconds on the salad. Air-conditioned.

Sometimes the old man thought he had missed a lot, like being able to afford dinner at a place like that. Twice his wife had been to that big motel place to eat, both times when their son treated them. She had not enjoyed eating there much; made her guilty to see that much money spent. She had ordered the cheapest thing on the menu. It made the old man sad to think about that. She was dead.

Amazing, all the things that had happened in the old man's life. His son had sensed that even though the old man was put off by the money and fancy table manners and funny accents at the motel eating place, he still liked going there. Just to see all the people with all that money to spend ...

After his wife died, the old man still looked forward to going to that place with his son, maybe two or three times a year. It was there, sitting with his son at a corner table and with no warning at all, that the terrible pain had come to his head, and his face had drooped and he had been unable to make words to tell what was happening to him.

The old man had to work hard to get the blanket all the way across his lap. His arms were stiff and his hands were warped by arthritis.

It tried his patience, getting that damn blanket the way he wanted it. Still, he preferred to struggle with it himself rather than allow that snotty bitch in the white uniform to do it for him.

It was the know-it-all way she said things that pissed him off so. Like this morning, in fact: "Sheriff, you best let me do your blanket for you, else you'll just get all worn out and cranky trying to get it right."

"No," he had said, clutching the blanket to his chest so tight his knuckles hurt, and that had ended that. Now, as he sat in the chair a few feet from his bed, facing the door, he almost had the blanket the way he wanted it.

Smells from the folds of his flannel shirt reminded him of being outdoors, of fishing. Today? Was he going today? With Bob? No. It had been weeks, months maybe, since he had seen Bob, let alone gone fishing with him. Longer ago than that, even. A year?

The thinking flustered him, mixed him up. It was something he could not always control, the thinking. Bouncing from one time to another and getting all confused; it embarrassed him, even when he was alone, which was most of the time.

Junior came to see him every now and then, more often than Bob. Junior always poured him a stiff one, just a tiny bit of water, and they would talk. Actually, Junior did most of the talking. Most of the time, whenever the sheriff tried to talk, it didn't come out right. Even when he knew what he wanted to say, knew exactly what he wanted to say, he couldn't get it to come out right. The side of his face, where there wasn't much feeling, got in the way, blocked his words, took the edges off them, slowed him down, so that sometimes—even when he started out knowing what he wanted to say—he would lose track before he could finish.

The best times were when Junior took him over by Lake Marion. Junior did that quite a bit when the weather was good. The old man loved to sit by the lake in the sun, smelling the water, watching the boats. It had not been so long ago—had it?—when he had gone out in the boat with Junior and Bob. Goddamn, there were times, over by the lake, sitting in the sun, when the sheriff recognized men in the boats and remembered when they were just little boys. Back when he wore the badge, back then.

It made the sheriff a little sad to recognize the fishermen that way (it reminded him of how old he was), yet it was reassuring, too. It meant he had not lost everything. Truth to tell, he had lost enough lately.

Never expected the wife to go as quick as she did ... Never expected that thing to happen in the restaurant that time, that thing that felt like a slap across his face and took away some of the feeling along his whole side.

Suddenly he heard steps outside the room. Bob, maybe! Oh, no, it was Junior.

"Hi, Dad. Can't stay too long, but I just wanted to say hello . . ." Why was it, Junior wanted to know, that he almost always felt awkward in the presence of his own father after all these years?

"Uhnnnn," Sheriff Hiram Stoker said, "Uhnnnn . . ."

"Good to see you too," Junior said.

"Uhnnnn," the sheriff said again, trying to ask his son where his brother, Bob, was. The sheriff thought he felt a little spit escape from the side of his mouth.

"Uhnnnn . . ."

"No, no. Don't try to talk, old fella. . . ." Junior Stoker turned away for a moment, trying not to feel annoyance toward his own father, trying to let his compassion dominate his irritation.

Junior Stoker sat on the edge of the bed and looked into his father's face. For a moment, the sight of the sagging throat skin, the liver spots on the cheeks and forehead, made him want to cry. My God almighty, where does a man's life go? he thought.

"Feel up to a little libation?" Junior said, trying to make it sound light. He reached under the bed and fetched the whiskey bottle that was always there. Then he took a paper cup from the rack on the table next to the bed. "Here, Sheriff," Junior said, handing his father a paper cup half full of whiskey.

The sheriff had to take the cup in both hands. His hands quivered, but he held tight. He loved the smell of the whiskey, and he loved having a son there to drink it with him.

"To long life," Junior said softly, raising the cup to his father.

"Uhnnn." It took the old sheriff a long time for him to raise the cup to his mouth. The whiskey was hot and good. He wished Bob had stopped by to have a belt. Maybe he still would!

The afternoon sun came through the window. Shafts of light fell across the blanket in the old man's lap. The sun was warm and good. It was a good day to be on the lake. To fish, to fish! If Bob got here pretty soon, there would be time to go to the lake and bait a hook while the bass were still biting.

"Uhnnn ... Bo ... Bo ..." It made the sheriff goddamn mad; no matter how hard he tried, he could not make his mouth form the rest of Bob.

"No, Sheriff," Junior said, "I don't think Bob is gonna get here today. Uh, maybe tomorrow." Junior paused; it was always difficult choosing the words. "I'll, uh, give Bob a call and see if we can set something up. . . ."

"Uhnnn ..." The sheriff was happy to hear that. He would give Bob hell the next time he saw him, give him hell (but Bob would know he was kidding!) for staying away so goddamn long.

"I, uh, talked to Jen today. Seems Thomas had a little fall. . . ." Junior Stoker paused, annoyed with himself. Now, why in God's name would he start to tell his father about that?

"Uhnnn ..." The sheriff was not sure what his son (his son?) was talking about.

"I'm getting a new Clint Eastwood movie pretty soon."

"Uhnnn ..."

Junior Stoker almost laughed. God, what would someone think, listening to this conversation? Guess I'd never make it as a guest host for Johnny Carson. Can't even talk to my own father. Not that it matters much. What the hell does he care about Clint Eastwood? Hell, what do I care about Clint Eastwood?

So it went, a conversation between father and son.

CHAPTER 25

Back at the motel, Willop dialed the number and almost prayed she would answer.

"Legal Aid. Moira Rosario speaking."

"I called because I just plain need to talk to you."

"James! You caught me right in the middle— How are you?"

"Been better."

"I'll make a few minutes to listen. Go ahead."

So he told her about the meeting in the field with Dexter Cody, how afraid he had been, how inconclusive it had turned out to be.

He told her about seeing the old case file. He told her how seeing the long-ago death pictures had broken his heart, yet given him—if he was really honest about it—a thrill of sorts. He told her about walking down past the mill, about seeing the church where his mother had sung, long ago.

Simple things, stupid things tumbled off his tongue—how he had kept his hand on the revolver handle while talking to Cody in the field, but that Cody—an old man!—had had him measured all the way, had kept a round in the chamber of his shotgun, just in case, and had seemed quite capable of pulling the trigger. An old man!

And more. To top it all off, Willop said, part of him longed to be part of South Carolina—to dig in its dirt and plant a backyard garden; to fish in the lake (he hadn't fished since he was a boy, for Chrissake!); to play golf and talk over the fence with neighbors and—yes—live there with her and have children.

"What's so bad about those things?" she asked softly.

"Nothing, I guess. I just feel like I'm coming apart."

"Listen, James," she said, all business. "Your circuits are way overloaded. You—"

"That's your answer for everything." He was sorry as soon as he said it.

"Just listen," she said. "You fly to a strange place on a strange errand, talk to all kinds of strangers, do and say things like you're not used to at all. . . . I mean, Jesus, of course your circuits are overloaded. Am I right?"

"Probably."

" 'Probably.' "

"I shouldn't have taken up your afternoon, just to argue. . . ."

"We're not arguing. I'm telling"—she interrupted the conversation for a moment to say something quick and businesslike in Spanish to someone else—"I'm telling you what you already know."

"Any suggestions? Seriously?"

"Pace yourself. Look at old clippings. Take a ride in the country. Give yourself a break from facing strangers. You'll be more effective."

"Right." And he knew she was.

"And treat yourself to a decent meal." She talked again in Spanish to someone else. "Listen, I gotta go. Take care."

"I love you."

"Me too . . ."

"Doesn't sound all that bad, does it? Living in some quiet place, having a garden . . ."

"We'll talk about it."

Click. She was gone.

Willop drove to the local paper, an offset weekly, and explained that he was researching an article on life in the rural South of several decades ago. Would it be too much trouble to look through newspapers from 1944?

"I picked 1944 because it was the height of the war, and I'm interested in seeing how the war dominated local life, if it did," Willop said.

"No trouble at all," said a cheerful young man. Willop guessed that he doubled as a reporter and official greeter. Probably still has his ideals, Willop thought.

The young man set aside his brown-bag lunch, went down a hall, and returned with several bound files, each about three feet by two feet.

"Not too much dust on them," the young man said. "We keep the storage room temperature-controlled and clean as we can. Take as long as you like. Sit at that table over there, why don't you."

"Appreciate it," Willop said.

Back in time. The papers were well preserved, not crumbling and yellow, so that they felt more like last week's papers than ones from more than forty years ago. In front of him now was a picture of a minister from Orangeburg, an earnest, slick-haired man in his late thirties, perhaps, who was taking a new assignment. Old man now, if he isn't dead. Retired with grandchildren, probably, Willop thought. Women's aid unit plans social ... Emerson Wells, a long-time railroad worker, dies at the age of eighty-two ... News for and about colored people: Negro soldier writes home to mother ...

And there it was: "Mill-Shanty Negro Held in Slaying of Girls." Mill-shanty Negro. Willop almost laughed. He had known some crusty old newspaper editors in his time (some were just plain bigots), but he had never seen a headline quite like that. Wonder what a mill-shanty Negro looks like, he said to himself. Easy: He looks like that picture of Linus that I saw in the Corrections Department.

"Colored Community Also Angered by Slayings ..." Oh, yes, I bet they were, Willop thought. Especially those who didn't want to be mill-shanty Negroes ...

"Early Trial Urged for Negro Accused in Slayings." Not bad, that. Almost sensitive by Old South, old-law standards, Willop reflected.

"Murdered Girls Laid to Rest ... Stunned, Angry Community Shares Parents' Grief."

Willop looked at the pictures of the girls—taken in school, probably—smiling in happy innocence. So different from the terrible pictures of the girls in death. Enough to break your heart, even after all these years, Willop thought.

And through it all, life went on. Of course, Willop thought. What else?

He remembered his own mother's death, how the day of the funeral, and for many days after that, he had been astonished that, while he was aching with deep, deep grief, the rest of the world went on. Not only went on but—and this was surely true—acted like it didn't care.

"Wife of Judge Heads War Bond Affair ... Hero Soldier to Speak." There was a picture of the hero soldier, in fact, looking much more like a tough, back-country lout than a hero, or even a soldier. Wounded at Anzio, decorated ... Well, good for you, hero soldier, Willop thought. Hope you had a nice life.

"Court Names Counsel for Accused Negro." So that's what he looked like back then, Willop thought. There was a picture of Judah Brickstone. Hair brilliantined in place, prissy, smug smirk ... Probably more at home doing—what? What the hell would a lawyer from around here do in those days? And why would he stay?

"Negro Convicted in Slaying of Girls ... Sentenced to Die."

And there was the sheriff, a bit on the plump side but a tough-looking *hombre* nonetheless, leading the desperate prisoner—how small he was! Willop thought when he saw the picture—to a car following the sentencing.

If Brickstone did anything at the trial, they sure didn't report it, Willop thought. But, to be fair, he had met reporters he wouldn't trust to accurately report a grocery list. God knows who covered this thing back then. . . .

"Many From Community Expected to Watch Justice Carried Out." Oh, yes, Willop thought. And I wonder how many slept that night after a good hearty meal. . . .

"Negro Goes to Chair for Slayings."

Well, there it was. Calm and without remorse, the account said. Holding a Bible the sheriff had given him. "Last Conversation Between Condemned and Sheriff Reported," the headline said.

"Linus, you know that you have only a few minutes to live, don't you?"
"Yes, sir."
"Well, are you guilty of the crime for which you were convicted?"
"Yes, sir."
"Did any officer from the time you were arrested up until now take advantage of you, threaten you, or punish you in any way?"

"No, sir."

"Was anyone else with you when this crime was committed? Linus, I asked you if anyone else was with you."

"No, Sheriff."

"Well, good-bye, Linus."

"Good-bye, Sheriff."

Driving away from the paper, Willop remembered Moira's advice about not overloading himself. But, having read the account of the last moments of Linus Bragg, he thought the least he could do was push himself a bit more. He owed that much, and more, to his mother.

Am I doing this right? he asked himself. Jesus, such a mix of science and hunch and—and aimless poking around. Or maybe not so aimless. God, who knew?

He found Luke Reddy's farm-equipment place easily enough, but Luke Reddy wasn't there. An aging, tired-looking man in a gray work uniform explained: "People ain't buyin' much farm equipment these days. I'm just kind of keepin' an eye on things. You can catch Luke over at the station, pretty certain."

"Where's that?"

When the man told him, Willop wasn't surprised that it was the same station where he'd stopped to have a new fuse put in for the car light. Seemed like everybody was connected to everybody else. . . .

"Fill it up," Willop told the same easygoing man who had tended his car a few days earlier.

"Hey, how's it going? Light working okay?"

"Fine. Luke Reddy here someplace?"

The station owner smiled and nodded in the direction of four gray-haired, stubble-bearded men sitting on benches and hunched over a sawed-off oil drum. They were playing dominoes.

Hands on his hips, hoping to look casual but feeling stiff, Willop approached them.

"Luke Reddy?"

"Right here." The man who looked up at Willop had thick glasses that made his eyes look grotesquely large.

"Maybe I could have a few minutes of your time."

"That's the sad thing. I got more time than I know what to do with." Luke Reddy chuckled at that, and one of the other men by the sawed-off barrel nodded and chuckled with him. The last man, the oldest of all, looked up, and Willop saw that he was the father of the station owner, the same old man who had given him the hard-stare treatment the other day.

"How's it going?" Willop asked him.

The man nodded, ever so slightly, but gave Willop the hard-stare treatment once again.

Fuck him, Willop thought.

"Buy you coffee?" Willop said to Luke Reddy.

"Naw, my treat. We got our own pot inside," Reddy said.

Willop followed him into an office smelling of grease and littered with batteries, fan belts, and hubcaps, some old and some new, and sat on the edge of a wooden desk.

"Black is fine," Willop said, taking the cup Reddy offered him. The coffee was strong and bitter.

"How can I help ya?" Reddy asked.

"Doing some research. Maybe for a writing project . . . On the way the South was back forty and more years ago—rural sections, I mean. . . ."

Luke Reddy's magnified eyes showed no guile.

"Fact is," Willop said, "I'm interested in that murder way back in 1944. The two little girls . . ."

"Oh, sure! Killed by that little nigger."

"You found the bodies."

"Damned if you ain't right! Now, how'd you know?"

"I've been studying. Look, do you remember any question, anybody ever asking, whether the black boy might have been innocent?"

"Shee-it!" Reddy waved his hand, more in patient amusement at Willop's ignorance than in disgust. "Nigger admitted he did it. Sheriff caught him soon afterwards. Went over to them shacks, over by the mill, niggers used to live there, the ones that worked at the mill—"

"I know that."

"—caught him in no time, got a confession real quick, sent him straight to the electric chair. Served him right, dirty little bastard."

"The sheriff ..."

"Hell of a man, the sheriff. Real good man. Straight and true."

"Not the kind to beat a confession out of anybody?"

"Oh, hell no." Reddy's face showed astonishment at the suggestion. "Fact is, a lot of folks woulda soon strung the kid up right away. From a tree. With or without all his parts, if you know what I mean."

"I can guess. But not the sheriff?"

"Told you. He wouldn't allow it to happen. Hell of a man, the sheriff. He was the law here. And fair to everybody. White and colored both."

"The, uh, colored ... A lot of them were pissed off at the kid too, I guess?"

"Oh, hell yes. Whites and colored got along fine, each minding his own business. Ones that worked at the mill—colored, I mean—had it good. Sure. Oh, hell. Everybody was shook up over that. Everybody ..." Luke Reddy suddenly began to cough, a deep, racking cough.

"You okay?" Willop asked.

"Good as a man with one lung can be." Reddy smiled, took out a soiled handkerchief, and wiped tears from around his eyes. "Gave 'em up too late," he said. "The cigarettes."

"Must be rough ..."

"Damn right. Own damn fault, though. What the hell, I don't worry none. Expect I got some time left."

"A good attitude." Willop could not help but like him for his indomitable cheerfulness.

"Used to think I had my share of troubles early, so's I wouldn't get any more," Reddy said. "Took a Jap bullet when I was just a pup. My wife, she passed on, kinda unexpected. Years ago. Then this." He pointed with his thumb toward his chest and coughed some more. "Get so's I'm used to living with one lung, more or less, and my business dries up. ..."

"Rough ..."

"Ain't the word for it. But what the hell. I'm just one of many. When it rains, it rains on everybody. But when it don't rain . . ." Reddy smiled sadly and shrugged.

"Some people around here wanted to hang the kid right away, you said."

"Oh, hell yes. See, there was talk, right after the bodies were found, that he'd . . . you know . . ."

"But that wasn't really true, was it? I mean, you found the bodies. The clothes were all in place."

"Yeah, that's true, I guess. Well . . ." Reddy frowned.

Press on this, Willop told himself. "That still bothers you? I mean, that talk?"

"Yeah, well, thing is we didn't know whether to believe the sheriff or—"

"You said 'we.'"

"Yeah, well . . ." Reddy coughed again. "Sure, I was as worked up as everybody else. Hell, I saw 'em when they was pulled out of the water. Jesus . . ." Reddy shook his head.

"But as terrible as it was, they weren't molested. Right?"

"Well, I guess not. Still, I don't mind telling you, ain't ashamed to admit it, some of us—"

"You and who else?"

"Well, several folks. You have to realize, the feelings back then. . . ."

"If you can remember anyone in particular . . ."

"Well, now, T. J. Campbell, for one. I remember him being quite outspoken, about how we ought to just take the nigger—"

"Who the hell was he?"

"Nephew of old Mr. Tyler, the man who owned the mill. All worked up, he was. T.J., that is."

"He good friends of the girls' families, or what?"

"No, no, no. Not really. Not good friends with anybody, particularly. Then or now."

"You mean he's still around?"

"T.J.? Oh, hell yes. Lives over that way." Reddy pointed.

"Excuse me, I don't get it." Willop's coffee was cold, his backside was sore from sitting on the edge of the desk, and he was getting tired.

"Get what?" Reddy's magnified eyes were puzzled.

"How this T.J. fits in. Keeps to himself, isn't all that friendly with the families of the girls, then he's one of the people making noises about a lynching. That's what you said."

"Never really came into his own, T.J., if you know what I mean. Never really fit in anywhere. There was kind of the expectation he'd be pretty well set, what with his uncle owning the mill and all and him being a foreman, but it never happened."

"How come?"

"Hard to say. Just never quite fit in, T.J. didn't. Used to be talk about him and the colored women over by the mill . . . You know." Reddy smiled slyly, and Willop shook off his disgust.

"So he didn't wind up rich or anything, when the mill was sold?"

"Oh, hell." Reddy chuckled and coughed. "If he is rich, he's even dumber than I thought. Lives like a goddamn bum . . ."

"So how come he was making lynch talk?"

Reddy shrugged. "Maybe it made him feel important. Like he knew more than we did. Telling folks he'd heard the nigger boy had violated them girls. After they was dead, even . . ."

"He ever say where he heard it?"

"'Damn long time ago. Seems like he said he'd heard from the sheriff's deputy. Guy named Cody. He lived over that way, retired a long time ago—"

"From Cody? T.J. said he got information from Cody? You're sure?"

"Hell, damn long time ago. You can ask old Cody himself, if you want. . . . I mean, T.J. might have been makin' stuff up. He had a big mouth sometimes. Sheriff never liked him at all."

"How come?"

"Sheriff, like I said, was a hell of a man. Good eye for people, mostly. Just plain didn't like T.J. Sheriff, he liked animals. Dogs and horses. T.J., he was mean to dogs and horses, if you can imagine a man like that. I can't, personally. . . ."

"Sounds like a sweetheart."

"Not hardly."

"He married, this T.J.?"

"No, not hardly." Reddy paused to cough again, and Willop could not tell whether he had laughed, too.

"Anything else you can tell me?" Willop was suddenly getting worn out, physically and mentally.

"No, not hardly."

"So I won't take up any more of your time."

Willop shook Luke Reddy's old, tired hand.

"Hope I helped you some," Reddy said. "Come see me any time."

"Thanks."

"Just a terrible thing, what happened back then. Never saw anything worse in my life."

As he drove back to the motel, Willop stopped at a drugstore to buy some aspirin. God, his head was aching. Just too damn much stuff crammed into it, he thought.

He swallowed two tablets right in the car, without water, and leaned back in the car seat, closing his eyes. Something was bothering him; something wasn't quite right.

Something he had seen in the old file, back in the sheriff's office?

Something in the old newspapers?

Something that Reddy had said?

Damn, what the hell was it . . .?

CHAPTER 26

Willop had the water as hot as he could stand it. Only his head was above the surface, and perspiration matted his hair and trickled down his face into the tub. The strange thing was that, even though he was almost immersed in wet heat, he could stand to have his arm out of the water only as long as it took to reach the tumbler of Scotch on the edge of the tub. A quick, hot gulp, put the glass down, then pull the arm back into the water. He shivered every time the arm was exposed.

The hot bath had seemed like a good idea: Relax the body, sort out things in his mind, decide who to talk to next. What he hadn't planned on was the mental videotape that started rolling through his head. Maybe it was triggered by seeing the pictures of the girls in death, or maybe he just liked to torture himself. Whatever.

The funny thing was that he had not seen the event in real life, yet the videotape was always absolutely clear and in color when it played in his head.

He saw his mother being stabbed to death.

Too late to rewind the tape, too late to speed it up. Here it comes, Willop thought. Just don't let it be in slow motion. There she is, smiling and waving, as she used to wave at him.

And there came the man, the man his mother didn't like anymore and had tried to stop seeing. He came up behind her, and there was the knife, horribly long, the kind butchers used, poised in the air. She was still smiling, her lips curved up in a smile. Then, in an instant, her mouth curved down, her eyes rolling back in her head as the blade found her heart. He saw his mother falling to the sidewalk, the knife stuck in her, the man pulling it out (the blade red and wet!), the man bringing the knife down again and hacking, hacking through his mother's coat until, at last, people pulled the man away. . . .

There, the tape was done. Willop prayed as hard as he could that the tape of the other thing, the earlier thing that had happened to his mother, would not roll tonight. That, he would not be able to bear.

Maybe Moira was right; he should get some more therapy.

He partially drained the tub, then refilled it to the previous level with hot water.

It would make no sense to try to see the old sheriff, Willop thought. Most likely, he wouldn't be able to just walk in on him. And even if the old bastard agreed to talk, what would he ask him: Sheriff, did you frame this kid? Then there was the problem of the sheriff's son. This is his territory, Willop thought. He scared Willop, more than a little.

Should he try to talk to the sheriff's son? Oh, sure. Let's see, what to ask him ... Captain Stoker, did you ever consider the possibility that your daddy, the sheriff, fucked up?

Drowsy and discouraged, Willop wondered whether it would be smarter for him to fly home tomorrow and hire a private investigator. Oh, right, makes a lot of sense ... How much can you afford to pay me, Mr. Willop? Well, I can't pay you right now, because I don't have a job, but my girlfriend ... well, she can't afford to pay you either. But it's a hell of an interesting case. . . .

He slid down into the water again, until the water was just under his lower lip. His face perspired freely. A purifying process, perhaps. Willop let his arms float and closed his eyes. His arms floating reminded him of the boats on Lake Marion. Floating. His whole body floating now. Willop felt drowsy, drunk and drowsy. He slipped off into slumber for a moment, but he woke himself with a snore. Water warm and good. The floating safe and good, in the arms of the water ...

The sound of the doorknob turning startled him. The knob was turning, slowly, slowly. The door was opening. Someone was there, in the dark. The someone could see him, naked in the tub.

Get the gun, get the gun and fire into the dark! Willop couldn't move. His arms were floating and he couldn't move, couldn't raise himself up from the tub enough to get the gun.

His mother appeared, smiling, glad to see him. He tried to move his arms, to cover himself, but he couldn't. His mother looked down at him, saw him, and the corners of her mouth turned upside-down, and her eyes rolled back, and she fell back into the darkness.

Willop screamed, and the scream made him able to move again. He flung his upper body out of the tub, banging his ribs and sending the Scotch glass crashing. The water sloshed back and forth crazily, some splashing on the floor, rocking his body from one side of the tub to the other.

The water was cold now. He waited for it to stop sloshing, then got out of the tub, stepping around the shards of glass. He took two bath towels, flicked on the room light just outside the door, and sat down on the bed. He dried himself quickly and turned the heat up.

Moira. He would call Moira. No, too late. She might be sleeping, dreaming her own dreams.

CHAPTER 27

The hardware store near the sawmill had displays of licorice, flashlight batteries, work gloves, and blue jeans up front. The area around the counter was the only part of the cavernous building that was well lighted, even in the middle of the afternoon.

Willop looked at the floor, worn smooth long ago from the feet of the mill hands and their families. Where he was standing now his mother and his uncle had once stood; their feet had helped wear the floor smooth.

"This used to be the company store, didn't it?" Willop said to the young woman behind the counter. "I mean, going way back when?"

"That's what I understand," she said, smiling. "I can't remember that far back, though. Can't come close. My daddy, he owns the store now."

"He here right now?"

"Nope. In town. Won't be back for a couple hours."

Though friendly, the young woman, who had sandy hair and wore a blue checkered blouse, was clearly bored.

"I guess a Mr. Tyler used to run the mill. And the store."

"Yep. Lock, stock, and barrel. Sold out to the railroad a long time ago, though. Got old and tired, I guess. You gonna buy anything, sir?"

"Sure. Give me a bag of those pecans. Small one will do. I hope you don't mind me asking questions."

"No trouble at all, long as I don't have anyone to wait on. You're from up north, I guess."

"I thought you were the one with the accent."

She laughed. "You originally from around here?" she asked.

"Uh, no. But I have some old connections, sort of."

The young woman let Willop's vague answer go unchallenged. The truth was, he had stopped at the store because he just had to see it, not knowing when he'd be this way again.

The young woman put the bag of pecans on the counter and took a dollar bill from him.

"I'm just here part-time," she said. "Helping out my dad. I go to the University of South Carolina. I'm just home on break."

"Ah. You coming back here to live after you get out of school?"

She laughed again. "Nooo, not me. Too small, too quiet, too boring. I mean, I've been to Charleston and Atlanta, even up to Yankeeland a couple times. Too slow for me here."

"Hey, how you gonna keep 'em down in Alcolu once they've seen Columbia?" Willop said.

A bell jingled and the door swung open. An old black man, bent and shuffling, but clearly once powerful, entered.

"Afternoon," the old man said.

"Hey, good to see you," the woman said.

"Got any licorice there?" he said.

"Saved the best for you." She took a few coins from the man and gave him several red strands. "And here's an extra for being one of our regulars."

"Obliged," the old man said, turning and shuffling out.

"Nice old man," the young woman said. "You seem awfully interested in local history."

"You get that way, living around the New York area. Everything's so crowded, you kind of like to find little, out-of-the-way places."

"Well, I guess," the young woman said. "Can't get much more out of the way than here, I suppose."

"Right," Willop said. Then, on an inspiration, he added, "I'm interested in regional dialects and accents, too. I do some writing, and I'm interested in how the various accents vary."

Terrific, Willop thought. Various accents vary; every time I try to get clever ...

"Oh, I agree," she said. "People around here talk different from the ones in Charleston, at least if you know what to listen for."

"Right."

"I'm quite interested in linguistics, actually. Have you read much in that area?"

"Not recently," Willop said.

"Well, anyhow ..."

"Thanks for the pecans. I'm going to depart before I bore you completely."

"Happy to talk. Not that busy in the afternoon."

On the wall behind the counter hung an old ax and sickle, an ancient chewing-tobacco poster, and, framed in wood and covered with dusty glass, a World War II poster showing a Flying Tiger fighter shooting down a Japanese Zero.

"I guess you wouldn't remember any of the shacks they used to have around here. For the mill workers."

"Not directly. The little community—it was all black—that's been gone for a long time. 'Course, a couple of the shacks are still standing. Mostly abandoned, though."

"Mostly?"

"I know at least one of them is still lived in. Right across the way. That old fella who was just in here. Used to work at the mill, in fact. Tyrone."

When Willop reached the old man's shack, he found him leisurely tending a small rubbish fire in his bramble-strewn yard. His cabin— light gray, one room, door half open to reveal a cluttered, dark interior— was barely thirty feet away.

"Hi," Willop said, louder than normal. He didn't know if the old black was hard of hearing.

"Afternoon." The old man paused for a moment.

"Can I have a few minutes of your time?"

"Time I got plenty of." The old black chuckled, but Willop sensed a suspicion that might be impenetrable.

"I understand you used to work over at the mill. Lived around here a long time."

"True enough."

"Can I offer you some pecans?"

"Teeth have enough trouble with licorice."

The old man was having none of Willop's smooth talk. He resumed his task of poking twigs and branches into the fire.

"I was hoping you could help me with something that happened around here a long time ago. Your name is Tyrone, right? My name is Willop." Willop would have offered the old man his hand, but it was no use. The man kept poking in the fire, scarcely looking up.

"What you want?" Tyrone said finally, more a demand than a question.

What the hell, Willop thought. Nothing to lose by getting it out. "I'm interested in a murder that happened here a long time ago. Down past the mill there. Two little girls."

"I ain't know nothin' about that thing," Tyrone said. But, unmistakably, his once-powerful shoulders shook for a moment.

"Well, maybe you know more than you think. . . ."

"Don't know nothin'. Told you that." Tyrone poked at the fire harder.

Open up to him, Willop thought. "Look, I'm trying to settle an old personal debt by asking some questions about the case. To see—"

"Man, I ain't got no reason to give a shit 'bout your debt. Anyone else's either."

Tough nut, Willop thought. Back off a little.

"You live here alone?"

"Look that way, don't it?"

"I mean, I thought maybe your wife—"

"Ain't never had no wife. Never had time."

"The mill took a lot of energy, I bet."

"Work hard, you get tired. Ain't a mystery 'bout that, no matter what they say."

Some smoke from the fire blew in Willop's face as the breeze shifted. He moved closer to the old man.

"You must be one of the last of the men who worked in the mill way back then. Any reason you never moved away?"

"Man live where he want to. Ain't never lived anywhere else. Ain't never seen a reason to. Hurt my back in the mill, long time ago, movin' a log, but Mr. Tyler, he let me stay on here."

"Nice of him. He's been dead a long time, I guess."

"Long time. But he let me stay. He tell the railroad, when they buy the mill, you leave that place alone over there, that little place where Tyrone is."

"So that's why you're here."

"Reason good enough ..."

Willop backed off, from the fire and the questioning. He chewed a few pecans, playing for time, thinking. He held out the bag to the old man again, but the offer was ignored. Screw it, Willop thought.

"You remember when those two girls were killed, Tyrone?"

"Everybody do. Everybody who was around here. Not many left anymore ..."

"What kind of day was it? You remember? Nice day? Chilly? It was March, I think."

"Beautiful day. Beautiful day. Pretty spring day."

"I can see you have a pretty fine memory. You have a window then, in the mill? A window you could look out and see the beautiful spring day?"

"Shit. Ain't no windows. 'Sides, I used to be mostly outside. By the pond, with the horses ..."

"I'll be damned. So you must have been outside that very day. Especially if you usually worked down at the pond and if you remember how pretty a day it was."

"'Course I be outside."

"Right around the time those poor girls were killed ..."

"I ain't the only one. Whole gang of us. Rudy and Lem ..."

The old man's voice had risen in pitch and volume. Afraid, Willop thought.

"But none of you heard anything."

"Ain't none of us heard a thing. Sheriff, he asked us. Happened down the way a bit, off the tracks. We didn't hear nothin'."

"You remember talking to the sheriff, then?"

"'Course I remember. Helped him get his car out of the mud, in fact."

The old man turned his back, walked a few feet away, and swept up another armful of branches and twigs. He began feeding them into the fire, not looking up at Willop.

"You know that boy? The one they say did it?"

"Probably seen him around. Can't say I knew him . . ."

"You must have known him a little bit, seeing he lived in the shacktown. Must have been a mean little bastard, to do a thing like that."

Silence, save for the low hissing of the orange fire as it fed on the twigs.

"The sheriff ever look for anyone else?" Willop asked.

"I never ask the sheriff his business. A good man, the sheriff. Ain't for me to ask him his business. Ain't for me . . ."

"He must have been glad you helped him out of the mud."

"Anybody be glad to get out of the mud. Any sane man . . ."

"That time when you helped him out of the mud. He ask you where you'd been, you or anybody else who worked on the pond? To see if you had an alibi?"

"Never ask me where I been! Never did! He knew I done nothin' like that!"

Sad, Willop thought. Old black man from the Carolina nowhere, thinks he has to defend himself after forty-plus years against something nobody ever said he did. Talk about broken spirits. . . .

"You all must have been pretty broken up, a horrible thing like that. Being acquainted with the fathers of the girls and all . . ."

"Any sane man be broken up. Any sane man."

"Mr. Tyler, he must have been sad."

"Any sane man . . ." Tyrone poked harder at the fire, the embers flying several feet. "Mister, maybe you got all day to talk crazy, but I ain't."

"I'm sorry, but this is really important to me."

"Well, it ain't to me. What's important is getting my place clean and proper-like. . . ."

Willop felt a deep sorrow for the old man. What he had, the cabin and the yard, were so little. There, Willop thought. That's how to get to him.

"Mr. Tyler leave you money, or did he just give some directly to the railroad? So you could stay here."

"Ain't your business."

"How about T. J. Campbell? You get along all right with him?"

The old man stood up, slowly, and pulled a glowing stick from the fire. He held it between himself and Willop as a threat, but it was no good. The face showed terror; old Tyrone was not used to thinking he had any rights, let alone asserting them.

"I'm sorry," Willop said. He meant it, but he was not through. "Guess I should go find T.J. himself . . ."

"I ain't never said a thing to you 'bout him. Or that thing back then . . ."

"Anybody ever ask you if you knew where T.J. was then? I mean, right about the time of the killing."

The stick had cooled, and the old man put it down. "Sheriff, he asked me. Told him T.J. was right close by. The truth."

"You saw him?"

"He told me. Told me he was right close. Right close. On his horse. Remember it plain, 'cause T.J. say he have trouble with a horse."

"He told you where he'd been, but—"

"Leave me be, mister."

"The truth is, he told you what to say."

"Leave me be, I said."

"Tyrone, would you be willing to sign a statement to all this? I mean, what you remember about that day? If it ever came to that?"

Triumph lit Tyrone's face. He smiled at last. "Told you to leave me be," he said. "Ain't gonna sign no statement, ain't gonna sign nothing. Not till Judgment. Never did learn how to read and write . . ."

Willop nodded, sadly. Then he handed the bag of pecans to Tyrone and walked away.

CHAPTER 28

Though he was a quintessentially sociable man, Judah Brickstone loved that moment when the door closed as his secretary went to lunch. It meant he was alone.

Time to put the brown bag on the desk, peel the hard-boiled egg and dust it with salt, arrange the carrot sticks on the waxed paper and salt them, too. Brew some tea. Save the apple for last.

Alone, until his secretary returned. Except that today the interlude would be interrupted by this strange Allison, who just had to see him on his lunch hour. All right, he would not fret. No sense spoiling the time. Time was meant to be savored.

He had been to Columbia, many times; been to Charleston, been to Atlanta. Indeed, the walls of his office were full of reminders of those visits. Pictures and plaques, charters and certificates, ribbons and citations. There, with Sam Ervin, just after Watergate. Over there with Strom Thurmond. Next to that with George Wallace (God, how they both looked younger! Especially the Governor, before the shooting ...)

Judah Brickstone had learned very early on that few things were as important as learning how to get along with all kinds of people, people as diverse as the ones in the pictures. And not just politicians and powerful folks. You had to be kind to the everyday folks, too.

He smiled at his own surfeit of feeling. His wife, Lou, poked fun at him for that, as did his son and daughter, as did his grandchildren, whose pictures had the most honored spots of all: on top of his desk.

The clock near the door ticked its perfect course toward twelve-thirty. Not long now before the stranger would arrive. Well, the stranger could just watch him eat his lunch; Judah would not hurry to be done before he arrived.

He had a hunch the visitor might be colored. Judah had not been sure, on the phone, but there was something in the voice.

Actually, Judah had the best possible reason to chew his modest lunch at his usual, relaxed pace. More than most folks, he had to watch what he ate, and how fast, and when. He had survived a heart attack and, a few years later, cancer.

Talk about getting things in perspective. Couple kicks like that were enough to make a man realize that how he spent his time was the most important thing in the world.

The heart attack had been the easy part, once he had survived it. Exercise just a bit more, relax more, lose weight. Ration the intake of bacon and eggs and ribs and yams and pecan pie—all that good stuff! Look thin for the doctor.

Which Judah had done. Which had only made the cancer that much harder a kick in the old behind.

Judah Brickstone felt the stranger's presence before he heard him.

"Ah, Mr. Allison, I presume," Judah Brickstone said, rising slowly from the chair and extending his hand.

"Hope I'm not disturbing your lunch," Willop said.

"Not at all. Things don't move too fast around these parts. Have a seat."

Judah sized up the stranger: a bit awkward, fairly strong build, though a bit flabby. Accent from up north, someplace. Clothes that did not suggest wealth (though Judah had learned long ago that they often did not). Most interestingly—Judah was almost certain of this—a trace of colored in his blood.

"I understand you're interested in land," Judah Brickstone said. "What kind of land?"

"You sure have a lot of pictures," Willop said.

"That's what comes from staying in one place for a long time." Judah smiled pleasantly.

"I guess so. Seems like you must have been here forever, getting to know all these folks. Politicians and regular people both, I guess."

"Plain folks is good folks around here. I draw up their wills, give advice on taxes sometimes, draw up paper for the county when it wants to sell bonds. All that. I been here so long that, more and more in recent years, I've tended to specialize in real estate. I know all the agents. Got a license myself, in fact. Been here so long, I practically know the county tax maps by heart." Again Judah smiled, though it took a shade more effort. He wished this Allison would get down to business.

"I'm impressed. All those pictures. Lots of well-known politicians. Regular folks. Even some black folks, over there behind that plant."

Odd remark, that last, Judah Brickstone thought. Now he was certain that this odd Allison fellow lived far away, and that he was most likely part Negro: Any white person his age who'd lived in Clarendon County all his life would more likely have used the term "colored."

"Well, I've been active in the state bar. Served on some state commissions, that sort of thing. What sort of land are you interested in?" Judah's patience had run out.

Good, Willop thought. Let him get uptight, then surprise him.

"Actually, I'm most interested in a plot about, oh, three feet wide and six feet long."

Judah looked right at Willop with an expression that showed he was baffled to the point of fear.

"A grave. That's really the little plot of land that brought me back here. Do you know I couldn't even find his grave? Maybe you could help." Let that sink in, Willop thought.

"I wish to God almighty I knew what you were talking about...."

"Oh, you know," Willop said, standing up and taking off his coat. Play this right, Willop told himself as he took the revolver out of his pocket and wrapped his coat around it so only the muzzle protruded.

"I don't, I swear...." Fear in his voice. Good, Willop thought. He just didn't want him to die of a heart attack.

"Look here," Willop said, sitting down again.

Judah saw the muzzle, and his eyes bulged with terror. "Gun ...?"

"Right, gun. Now listen. I'm going to ask you some questions about Linus Bragg, and you're going to answer them. To the best of your recollection, as you lawyers like to say."

"Linus ... Oh, my God. That colored boy ..."

"You got it."

"So long ago ..."

"Ain't it the truth. Now, how come you never filed a notice of appeal? Just doing that would have postponed the execution."

"There were no grounds. I mean, the boy confessed...."

"You saw the confession? And he told you he did it? Did he?" Got him good and scared, Willop thought. Just try to keep cool....

"Sure, I saw the confession. The paper, I mean. I mean, he didn't tell me exactly, like in so many words...." Judah Brickstone was practically stammering. This stranger's eyes were cold, like he could kill him without a second thought. Maybe if I tell him I'm sick, Judah Brickstone thought. Maybe if I tell him I've had a heart attack and cancer. Suddenly, Judah Brickstone imagined how a bullet would feel, tearing into his midsection, through it, and then—God! Just the thought was terrible—ripping through his bag, making his death messy and disgraceful as well as painful and splashing The Governor and Senator Sam ...

"All right. Just listen to my questions. You don't have a transcript of the trial?"

"No. None anywhere. No appeal filed."

"You didn't even bother.... Ever study the confession real hard to see if it sounded like a little colored kid?"

"No. No. Oh, God ..."

"Just listen. What did Linus tell you? About the killing?"

"He said, I think he said, he didn't mean it."

"Mean what?"

"To kill the girls. He didn't mean to—"

"No, I want his exact words. To the best of your recollection."

"He said, 'I didn't mean to ... to ...'"

"To look," Willop said.

"Uh, to look. Yes." There was surprise on Brickstone's face, surprise at the memory.

"So he didn't tell you he killed them?"

"Well, I figured he meant ... I mean ..."

"Little colored boys used to be told not to even look at white girls. You know that, Brickstone?"

Brickstone's face was white.

"All right," Willop said. "You never appealed. How come you never asked for a change of venue?"

"Why, I thought . . . I mean, there was no need. . . ."

"No need. You just figured a little nigger boy accused of killing two white girls could get a fair trial right in the town where the killings took place. Right?"

"Standards were different then. I mean . . . Oh, my God . . ."

"Never mind God. Just listen to me. Anybody ever offer you money not to seek a change of venue?"

"No! And if they had, I would have flat turned them down. And that's the truth."

Judah surprised himself with his courage. Well, if he was going to die, it would be with the truth on his lips. He remembered, too well, the long-ago conversation in the Calhoun House. But he had never been offered money, and he damn well wouldn't have taken it, and the whole thing had damn well caused him more grief than he deserved.

"All right. No money. How about political pressure? Any of that?"

"Yes. Sure. Look, emotions were very hot. It was an election year. Now, please, don't ask for a South Carolina political history, but—"

"Never mind that shit. Just listen. And answer." But first Willop had to throw him a good question. "Did you ever try to raise any reasonable doubt by asking how come two girls, one eleven years old, couldn't fight off a boy who weighed ninety-five pounds and stood five foot one inch tall?"

"Well . . ."

"I figured not. Ever ask how come this colored boy didn't have scratches on his face from the girls' struggling?"

"No."

"Think maybe a defense lawyer, a decent defense lawyer, would ask those questions today?"

"It's different today." Judah was gaining composure.

"You're not going to tell me," Willop said, "you're not going to tell me you were never pressured by anybody not to seek a change of venue. By anybody?"

"Well, yes, there were some. But I might not have anyhow. I mean ..."

A light in Willop's head. "Anybody who sought you out on this, anybody at all, were they a friend of Tyler, the guy who owned the mill?"

Almost as fascinated as he was afraid, Judah searched his memory. Yes, Cyril Hornsmith and old Mr. Tyler had been fairly thick back then. "I suppose," he answered finally. "There was one well-known lawyer. He had some connection with the Governor or something. Made his wishes known to me, this lawyer did, that he would prefer the trial not be moved. And he did know Tyler, yes. But Mr. Tyler knew a lot of people...."

"I understand that." Nevertheless, Brickstone's answer left Willop almost breathless. "And nobody ever promised you anything for not getting the trial moved?"

"No, and that's the God's truth."

"This T. J. Campbell," Willop said, "Tyler's nephew. You know him?"

"Sure, I know him. Knew Mr. Tyler, handled his will, in fact. So I knew T.J., sure."

"His will? You handled it? Tell me, did Tyler arrange for T.J. to be set for life, or just enough to keep him starving and a little better? Seeing as how T.J. seems to the world's biggest asshole."

Brickstone was silent.

"Tyler ever arrange for an old black, Tyrone, to live for the rest of his life near the mill? Maybe even have a little extra, enough to keep him in licorice?"

Brickstone was silent. His face was resolute.

"You hard of hearing?" Willop said, wiggling the revolver. "Oh, yeah. You are, aren't you? I asked you about the will."

"That's confidential. Between my client and me, even if my client's dead," Brickstone said at last. He was resigned to his fate and he would keep his oaths.

"Fair enough." Willop had underestimated Brickstone. Now, he had new respect for him. And he was satisfied, at least from what he could see in his face, that he knew no dark secret about T. J. Campbell.

"What do you want from me?" Judah said. "I don't claim to be the bravest man in the world, but I've been close to death before. I wish you'd end the suspense and tell me why you're here."

"I promised someone a long time ago that I'd look into the case. Investigate it. Which is a lot more than anyone else seems to have done."

"You're not going to shoot me?"

"Shit, no," Willop said, standing up. "Gun's not even loaded. Reason I wrapped my coat around it is so you couldn't see the empty cylinders."

"You tricked me."

"Sure did. Had to do it. Look at it this way, they tricked Linus. Only difference is, you get to live."

Satisfied, Willop turned to go. No, he had to leave Brickstone with something more. "Brickstone, I know you weren't much of a defense lawyer, but you don't lack for balls."

Alone, Judah Brickstone sat still for a long time, listening to the clock tick.

Willop drove a short distance from Brickstone's office before he pulled over and turned off the engine. He closed his eyes and breathed as deeply and slowly as he could. He had seen the fear in Brickstone's face, but he doubted that the lawyer had been any more frightened than he himself was.

It was not like the movies, when you pulled a gun on somebody and had total control. Not like that at all . . . Christ, what would he have done if Brickstone had pulled a gun out of his desk drawer?

Nothing. I would have done nothing. So maybe I just should have played it straight in the first place. . . . Oh, a fine time to wonder about that . . .

Slowly, his composure returned. He would have to get a look at that will. What the hell, must be a public document . . .

Willop had the same feeling he had often had years before while fumbling with an algebra problem. He had pieces of information, but he didn't know how to string them together in an equation.

No, the feeling was stronger than that. What the hell was it? Something from the old case file? Or the old newspaper? Maybe something that Reddy had said, or Tyrone ... Jesus, poor old Tyrone ...

Or something Brickstone had said?

Something ...

the feeling was stronger than that. What the hell was happening here? He did care. His age the old men were silly comforting to flagellate himself. You, your parents, your grandparents, he told himself.

Something.

CHAPTER 29

As Willop stood at the counter in the Clarendon County clerk's office, he was apprehensive. Two middle-aged women, wearing loose dresses, their skin like parchment, worked at typewriters a few feet apart. They ignored Willop for a minute or more, as did the thin, gray-faced man of sixty or so seated at a nearby table. He wore gray striped suit trousers that would have been stylish in the 1940s. Faded suspenders ran over humped shoulders, bunching up his faded blue shirt in the back.

God, Willop thought. These people *look* like they live here. Am I being uncharitable? Probably. Easier in a big city, he thought. Court clerks there were used to people coming in every day by the carload, asking for this and that, and they didn't give a damn. . . .

"Yes?" one of the women said at long last, rising slowly and not smiling.

"Good afternoon," Willop said. "I'd like to see a will that I believe is filed here."

"Well, who is the deceased?" the woman asked.

"Name's Tyler," Willop said, trying to sound casual and blowing it. "Used to own a big mill hereabouts, I believe."

It seemed to Willop that the woman's eyes instantly turned frightened and suspicious. Without a word, she turned and walked over to the other woman, bent over, and whispered to her. The listener's parchment skin wrinkled and, Willop thought, her shoulders shrugged. Willop was apprehensive. This was still the South, after all.

"Just have a seat," the first woman said to him.

Willop sat in a metal chair by the door, a few feet from the counter. Keep your head, he told himself. The worst they can say is no, but do not, do not, do not show anger. Unless you want a disorderly conduct charge and a jailhouse beating.

Willop tried to be comfortable in the metal chair, which he found impossible, and tried to look nonchalant, which he imagined was also impossible. There were several other clerks, bent over typewriters and index cards and tray-size metal baskets. They were all older than he, Willop thought; old enough to be set in their ways, their Southern ways. He did not belong....

"Here you are," a voice said at length. It was the woman; she had returned from somewhere, silently, and dropped a document, folded in thirds to the size of a business envelope and protected by a light blue cover.

Willop began reading: "I, Harrison Baines Tyler, being of sound body and mind, do on this twenty-fourth of May, in the Year of Our Lord One Thousand Nine-Hundred and Fifty-Two, hereby ..."

Tyler directed, in the virtually universal language of last wills and testaments, that his funeral expenses be paid (he wanted a plain casket as part of a plain service), that all his debts be paid, that all liens against his estate be satisfied. Willop noticed, as he read, that the paper was cleaned, unwrinkled, the folds of the paper apparently having been disturbed seldom, if ever.

Since Tyler's wife, Willop knew, had died before him, it might be interesting to see who got the money.... There was a bequest to the University of South Carolina, "my beloved Alma Mater," of five thousand dollars—not hay back then, or even now for that matter, Willop reflected. The South Carolina Chamber of Commerce was left one thousand dollars, as was the South Carolina Manufacturers Association. Easy to see where his heart was. And his politics ...

A sister in Raleigh was left ten thousand dollars, and a brother in Columbia an identical amount. Willop was not that good with numbers, but he thought those sums indicated no small wealth in 1952 in the middle of South Carolina. Now, how much did old T. J. Campbell get ...

"... and to my nephew, T. J. Campbell, who often sought to take the place of the son I never had, I leave the sum of fifteen thousand dollars ..."

Willop's skin almost tingled with fascination as he read the passage over and over. No matter how many times he read the words "who often sought to take the place of the son I never had," they did not come across as warm and loving. Oh, they could be interpreted that way, if the reader was expecting to find those sentiments on paper, but to Willop the words suggested something wonderfully, ingeniously ambiguous. And the amount wasn't much, not when compared to the brother and sister, not when you considered that Tyler had no son. . . .

And the amount certainly wasn't much when you looked at the bequests to charity, Willop thought. There they were, the Cancer Foundation, the Red Cross, and—

Oh, my God. Willop stopped reading, in astonishment. He blinked and read again, and the words were the same. Man, the guy had a sense of humor, if nothing else. . . .

Slumped in the car across the street from the courthouse, Willop tried to sort things out. He wondered if he was losing it all: He had used a fake name when he saw Brickstone, but he had blown whatever cover he had by asking to see Tyler's will. No, wait a minute . . . No one in the courthouse had asked for his name. . . . Yeah, but there aren't that many strangers come into town and ask to see—

Shit. Tired and frustrated, he slapped the dashboard with his hand, so hard that his palm stung. He needed to get back to the motel for a rest. Maybe take some time off, treat himself to a nice dinner, like Moira had said . . .

On his way to the motel, he drove past the newspaper offices. He thought of the stories he had read. Then he thought of the pictures of the little girls, smiling.

And that made him turn around.

* * *

Willop was out of breath and trying not to show it when he asked the friendly young man if he would mind terribly getting out the 1944 bound file once again, just for a minute, so he could double-check something. No trouble, the young man said, showing Willop to a corner table.

Willop smiled, trying to appear casual, as the file was placed in front of him. Turn the pages . . . farther back . . . no, not this far . . . there!

Willop stared again at the pictures of the girls. Smiling. God love you, Cindy Lou. . . . You'd be older than me today, wouldn't you? Tell you what, kiddo: There's not a damn thing wrong with your smile.

Willop drove past the sheriff's office. Good. The parking spaces for Stoker and for the sheriff himself were empty. He turned around and pulled into the lot.

Bestwick was there, alone. She smiled, though Willop thought she was a bit more wary than the time before. He told her he needed one last favor: Could he see the file on that old murder case just once more? Just one little thing he had to check, and it was pretty important. . . .

Again, Willop locked himself into the room at the end of the corridor. This time, he ignored almost everything, except for the pictures of Cindy Lou Ellerby.

There, there, child . . . I see, I do see, at long last. . . . You didn't have a bad tooth before the attack, did you? And since there aren't any cuts around your mouth, I'm figuring you broke your tooth biting your killer, even though whoever did the autopsy didn't pick that up.

Is that what you're trying to tell me, child?

Across the years, Cindy Lou's heartbreaking death face stared back.

"Bless you, Cindy Lou," Willop whispered to the empty room. "Hope you were able to give him a real good chomp."

Willop slipped out of the room. When he passed Bestwick, he pointed toward the room to tell her the file was still there and nodded his thanks.

CHAPTER 30

There were few things better in the world than a good, hot shower. Plenty of soap—good, pure lavender aroma—and plenty of warm water to relax the muscles, take away the tension inside, too.

A good, hot shower could even make him forget nasty things that happened a long time ago, some going back to when he was a boy and some to . . . later on.

In his bedroom, he put on a clean pair of work jeans and a clean flannel shirt. He liked the feel of jeans and flannel, loose, comfortable. A man could feel relaxed.

His bedroom was a private place, very private. The walls were cedar-paneled; they were not only handsome to look at but smelled good. His bed was narrow and compact; no need for a big one, and he didn't toss and turn much. He used queen-size sheets, though, because they could be tucked in real, real tight at the bottom and along the sides. He liked the feeling of the bed tucked in real tight. It made him feel . . . safe.

In one corner of the room stood a low, dark cabinet, and on top of the cabinet was a small refrigerator. The cabinet held bottles of whiskey, brandy, and wine, and the refrigerator held beer and soft drinks; in the freezer section there were several containers of ice cream. He got a kick out of it, whenever he thought how luxurious and personal he had made his bedroom. Those folks who imagined he didn't know how to have fun . . . ha!

Next to the cabinet and refrigerator stood his easy chair. It was positioned just right, so that he could reach into the refrigerator or cabinet and hardly have to move. Best of all, the chair faced the wall over the bed, faced it exactly right for the times he tacked up a sheet to watch a slide show.

The windows had black shades, so that he could give himself a slide show with very little trouble. He had a big-screen television set, too, and a video-cassette recorder, which he used sometimes to tape football games. The hitting was good to watch, and he sometimes ran the same play over and over. Just as much fun were the shots of the cheerleaders. He loved to run them over and over, back and forth, slowing up the tape, sometimes stopping it, so that he could look for as long as he wanted. In that way, he did possess them, almost. . . .

Sometimes he watched men's tapes. He didn't mind driving all the way over to Columbia to get them; he didn't want people around Manning knowing what he watched.

The television and VCR were a godsend. Years before, he had had to create the scenes he wanted in his own mind, using the town girls as props. Years before, whenever he would play one of those scenes in his mind, he would try as hard as he could to slow it down, to savor it. But he always hurried too much near the end, to get to the hitting. . . .

He no longer bothered playing such scenes in his mind. He had outgrown them. And the girls he had used in the scenes, those who had stayed around Manning, had all gotten fat anyhow. So he ended up with the last laugh. Why, some of their children were prettier to look at. Yes, some of their children . . .

He frowned at the memory of a mistake he had made. He had invited a little girl to his room—for ice cream and a slide show. She had made a fuss, had started to cry for no reason, no reason at all, only because he had gotten tongue-tied and maybe said a couple of things he hadn't meant to. . . .

That had been a mistake, all right. She had calmed down, once he gave her a ride back to the playground. Nothing had happened, so there was nothing for her to cry about. But it had been a mistake. . . .

Another mistake had been bringing that woman to his room. Well, she was the one who had made the real big mistake. When he met her in Columbia, she was willing enough—no, eager—to come with him, all friendly like, after taking the money. She had taken a drink and seemed interested in watching a slide show. He hadn't minded, too much, when she chuckled at him staying in the bathroom, getting ready.

What had done it was her asking why there were no mirrors in his bedroom. Because I have one over the sink in the bathroom, and I don't need one in the bedroom to look at myself, he had said, puzzled at the question.

She had laughed at that. Laughed louder and louder and not stopped. Making fun. Well, he had had the last laugh, that was for sure. He did not feel the least bit sorry for her. She had brought it on herself. . . .

He decided to relax a little before treating himself to a show. First he tacked the sheet up over the bed, then he pulled down the black shades. There, the little tasks were done (setting up the slides in the tray, that was fun, not work), and so he sat down in the easy chair. There . . .

What to have? He was not thirsty enough for a beer. . . . Whiskey? No . . . Maybe a glass of brandy. Yes, that was just the thing. Having only to shift his sitting position a little, he reached into the cabinet, took out the bottle of brandy and a big glass, and poured himself some.

He loved how the brandy felt, in his throat and nose, in his stomach, right down to his toes. In his very blood, even. He thought of it as a fire burning on a river; it was like the brandy set his blood on fire.

It was certainly a good thing to have before a slide show. . . .

He sipped the brandy slowly, slowly, deliberately putting off the pleasure of the slides. Pleasure delayed was all the more enjoyable. The brandy made him feel warm. . . .

Time for a slide show! Now, where was Florence? Out, probably. Yes, she was, he remembered. Just as well; he was not really in the mood tonight to cuddle the old cat on his lap.

He had to reach down into the cabinet, behind the bottles, to get out the two boxes. One box was black; it held the ordinary pictures—of fields and roads and woods and streams and fences and cows and blue skies. Regular pictures, some taken by him and others just slides he had picked up here and there.

The other box was red. It held slides taken (almost all of them) by him, mainly with a zoom lens.

The trick was to decide how many slides from the black box and how many from the red box to arrange on the slide tray. Usually, he liked to use about one red-box slide to every four black-box slides. That way, there was just the right amount of suspense.

He counted out the black-box slides, then carefully pulled out one-fourth as many red-box slides. He had to be careful, because he pulled out the red-box slides without looking at them. He had come to know them by heart, and if he knew in advance which ones were going into the tray, and where, it would take away some of the fun.

He shuffled the slides carefully, not looking, so the ones from the black box and those from the red box were mixed. Then carefully, carefully, still not looking, he arranged the slides in the circular tray. There, all ready for the show.

He got himself all set with a full glass of brandy—the fire in his blood was warm and good—and turned out the lights.

Click. A cow grazing, over near Sumter.

Click. Old mansion, way over near Charleston.

Click. Just a sky over a field.

Click. Buildings in Columbia, nothing special at all.

Breathing hard, he paused. Now, figuring the law of averages, the next slide up ought to be one from the red box, since the first four had been from the black box. But you never knew, you never knew. . . .

Click. Just a farmer on a tractor, way off the road.

He paused again, sipping. He had to laugh at himself, he was feeling so excited, not knowing. But that was the whole point. He was almost sure the next one up . . .

Click. A fireworks stand by the road. He laughed again. All right . . .

Click. Oh, yes. There, there, there. That one. Playground picture, taken from far away with the zoom lens, her going down the slide, smiling, not caring that her legs, all of her legs, were showing, and why should she, she did not know. Hmmm . . .

Click. The bridge over Lake Marion.

Click. Oh! His favorite of all, the one on the teeter-totter. Dark eyes, raven-black hair, dress blowing up just a little. Oh . . .

Click. Old dappled horse, looking at him and nibbling grass.

He let his body slump deep in the chair. Once in a great while, he would back up, go back to a slide that was especially good. The teeter-totter one was his favorite, but he didn't want to hold up the rest of the show.

The thumping on the front door startled him.

His house was shaped so that he could look out one bedroom window and see the front door. He pulled the shade back just a little. . . .

Well, I'll be damned. What brings him here?

CHAPTER 31

Two sheriff's department cars and an ambulance were parked by the road when Stoker got to the Cody farm. Sheriff Bryant Fischer was waiting for him, mirrored sunglasses in place and sleeves rolled up to show hairy, fencepost-thick forearms. The kind of sheriff the old man would approve of, Stoker thought.

"Old Dex, who would have thought it?" Stoker said, getting out of his car.

"Don't know too much," Fischer said. "Wife found him. Out all night, apparently. She thought he'd walked over the hill to drink and play cards yesterday, after going crow hunting. Which he did almost every day."

"How long ago did she find him?"

"Less than an hour. We're taking plenty of pictures. Lab team and coroner on the way. Looks like he was chasing a bird and tripped. Shotgun went off under him as he fell. Blew away a good part of his head."

Stoker said nothing, but he was already puzzled.

Fischer led him through tall grass, and Stoker felt a hint of the hay fever he had had occasionally as a child.

The body lay in a clearing near a creek. The corpse was face down, legs stretched out. Around the head a puddle of blood had soaked into the ground. Stoker could see the butt of the shotgun protruding from beneath the corpse; the muzzle was concealed.

"You done some hunting, Bryant. Anything look funny to you?"

"Well, I ain't thought to look for anything funny yet, to be honest. . . ." Fischer's voice betrayed embarrassment, which Stoker would try to soothe.

"Tell you what I mean," Stoker said. "Just came from a visit to my daddy. Kind of reminds me, when he was sheriff he always said, knowing

I wanted to be a law man, to use common sense, start off looking for the obvious and know when to look a little deeper."

"What you see?"

"You done some hunting, Bryant. As have I. As did old Dexter here. One of the first things you learn is how to carry a gun so you won't shoot yourself if you fall. Now, it would have been pretty damn tough for him to fall that way, the gun right under him—"

"If he'd been carrying that shotgun the way an experienced hunter probably would."

Stoker was glad Fischer had caught his drift fast enough to finish his thought. "And if he'd been running after something, all the more likely the gun would have landed way out in front of him, assuming he tripped," Stoker said.

"Come to think of it, Cody was too practiced a hunter to be running and carrying a loaded shotgun."

"There you go. Too old to do much running, for that matter. And why would he? This here's crow season. Old Dex, he just shot 'em for practice. Hell, he wouldn't run after a quail, even."

"Damn suspicious thing. I don't recall the last homicide around here."

"Well, I guess we don't want to jump to any conclusions. Could be an accident. Wouldn't be the first time an accident didn't seem to make sense. Hell, that's why they call 'em accidents."

Fischer frowned and got down on one knee. "Look here," he said, using a pencil to point. "For this kind of damage, he would have had to carry the damn gun real, real low. Hard to imagine ..."

Stoker turned away. "Do me a favor and don't turn him over till I'm gone," he said.

"We'll run a check on his card-playing buddies," Fischer said. "Make sure they can prove where they been and all ..."

"Right." As he suppressed a sneeze, Stoker had another idea, though he wanted to avoid the appearance of meddling. He remembered how his father had chafed at state police interference. And now I'm on the other side, Stoker thought, not without humor.

"And we'll take some plaster casts on the road out front there," Fischer said. "Off chance some tire prints will show up."

Stoker finally sneezed. Then he looked down at his shoes and pant cuffs. Dust stuck to his shoes and, amid the laces and on his cuffs, clung scores of tiny burrs and seeds. "Know what, Bryant. We should have the boys take some samples of the grass and burrs and seeds and whatnot around here. Put 'em in those plastic envelopes."

"In case we make an arrest and find a pair of pants with burrs and such."

"You got it."

Stoker heard laughter coming from below, down near the road. He looked to see two men coming up the hill, carrying a stretcher. They were chuckling, chatting amiably, probably enjoying being outdoors. And, Stoker had to admit, it was a lovely day to be outdoors. But it bothered him, the laughter in the presence of death.

"Do me a favor and ride back to headquarters with me, Bryant. I'll wait for you by the road."

Stoker was quiet on the ride back. His mind had more than it could handle.

"How's your daddy?" Fischer asked.

"Oh, pretty good. You know how it is. Most of the time I think he's all there. Ain't getting any younger."

"Don't know anybody who is. Hell of a man, your daddy . . ."

Fischer was quiet for a while, perhaps sensing that Stoker needed the quiet. Stoker was grateful.

Stoker took a shortcut on the way back to headquarters, going down a seldom-used dirt road, and saw a pickup truck parked next to an abandoned house. "Don't that beat all," Stoker said. "I remember that house from when I was a kid. Don't recall anybody living in it then, truth to tell, and that ain't yesterday. . . ."

Coming closer, they saw that a bulldozer was poised at one corner of the structure. As Stoker slowed to watch, the machine coughed and roared and leaned into the house. Wood snapped, metal shrieked. The bulldozer backed off, readying for another assault, as the house sagged.

"My daddy and me, we used to drive by that," Stoker said. "Now they get around to tearing it down. Tell you, Bryant, things move slow around here." Stoker drove on, glancing once more in the mirror at the bulldozer and house. Something ticked in his head. His daddy had always told him to play his hunches.

"Know what, Bryant? We should run a check on any prisoners getting out recently after long terms. I mean, ones who might've been sent up 'cause of Dex. And damned if I'm not gonna get out the old files to look through the cases he worked on."

As soon as Stoker opened the door to his office, he smelled the dust from the files. There they were, lying on his desktop, just as he had asked the clerk: two long cardboard boxes and one shorter one. Slips of paper chronicling mischief and misery and death from bygone years.

Stoker saw the clerk's note on top of one of the boxes:

Captain, here are the files on cases Dexter Cody investigated. The first box covers 1950 through 1954, the second '55 through '59, and the last 1960 and part of '61, when he retired. Earlier than 1950, you have to go to the basement files.

He started with the latest files, pulling the manila envelopes out of the long boxes and spreading the contents out on his desk, piece by piece. The papers consisted of everything from indictments, complete with seals and official language, to pink slips of paper saying that an assistant prosecutor had returned the call of an assistant public defender at a certain hour, and so on.

There was a certain sameness to most of the files (few had to do with truly serious crimes), and yet as Stoker worked back in time, the differences became apparent. Drug cases, for instance, were relatively common near the front of the files. But as Stoker's thumbs and fingers traced through the months and years, getting dirty gray in the process, there were fewer and fewer of them.

Stoker dialed Bryant Fischer's extension.

"Sheriff Fischer."

"Bryant, did old Dex ever have anything to do with drugs? You ever hear anything like that?"

"Oh, hell no. Shit, he retired before drugs were much known around here. No, hell no."

"Well, anything new from the coroner?"

"Talked to him not ten minutes ago. May be a while, he says, before he has anything definite. If ever."

"If ever?"

"Well, could end up cause undetermined, probably accident. I mean, we may not be looking at something that'll ever be satisfied one way or the other. . . ."

"Hmmm. All the same, it does seem strange. Guy hunts all his life . . . Listen, good-bye for now. I'm going through old case files. Just for the hell of it."

Stoker's thumbs and fingers went back to work. The older cases carried routine references to "Negro," none to "black." Back a few more years and the paperwork was thinner: fewer references to pre-trial motions and hearings, no mention whatever of public defenders. Race was mentioned so openly as to be almost startling. Here was a prosecutor questioning three young blacks about a stolen car ("Now one of you boys may get a free ride in this case and the other two are going to prison. You boys decide who's gonna do what. . . .").

And no interference from a defense lawyer, Stoker thought. Defense lawyer? Oh, hell no. Way before Miranda, before Gideon even. No wonder.

So many names. Some popped up time and again, either as witnesses or defendants. Troublemakers. Some had died, some had moved away, taking their trouble-making to some other cops. Some had just gotten older. Some had even stopped making trouble.

Stoker's back felt stiff. A waste of time? No. His father never thought hunches were a waste of time. Ah, good old man. You were all right in your day, good old man. It was Stoker's version of a prayer.

He got up and stretched his back, then went to the door and shouted down the corridor: "Bestwick."

"Yo, Captain?"

"Put me down for a tuna on rye and a soda."

Back to the files. Cody's name appeared again and again, as did his father's, once he got far enough back in time. Stoker smiled at an old glossy picture of his father and Dexter Cody, flanking a handcuffed black man who had axed his wife to death and fled into the woods. It was not the recollection of the crime that made Stoker smile (actually, he winced at the crime-scene photograph showing the victim lying on a kitchen floor, her head at a crazy angle), but the close-cropped hair and full trousers his father and Cody wore.

Long, long time ago. Stoker wondered where he himself had been at the precise moment the picture was taken. Shit, in his twenties? A teenager? Goddamn, the time had just slipped right away. His time and his life had just slipped right away. . . .

He stared at the face of the black. Fatigue, resignation, a touch of sadness. Perhaps some contrition, though it was hard to tell. Ah, poor bastard. Back then, he probably knew what the price was going to be. Sure enough, Stoker's fingers found the documents attesting to the fact that the defendant was delivered to the state prison in good health. In good health, that is, until he was put to death by electric current . . .

His father had never talked much about the executions he'd seen, and he'd seen a few. Junior Stoker had seen just one, that one time, with that kid. He shuddered at the memory. The worst thing had been the face, coming out of the mask, the tears . . .

A long time ago. An eternity. Whoever could have told how things would turn out. Blacks, whites, together all over now. Even in the sheriff's department.

Stoker wondered if his father had ever regretted taking him along that day, to watch the execution. His mother had been against it, Junior knew that. Junior himself wasn't sure if he regretted having seen what he had seen. Some of the younger law men, those who had never seen an execution, occasionally tried to get him to talk about it, but he chose not to. It made him feel sad, about his father, about life in those days, about himself, about the certainty of death. . . .

The old man, he would have been a damn decent law man today, Stoker thought. Despite the civil righters and the liberals, a damn good one.

Once he got to thinking about his father, it was tough for him to climb out of melancholy, so Stoker was relieved when he came to the end of the files. God, what a dull little place this is, he thought. All the crime I went through, right here on this desktop . . . Why, shit. A day's worth in New York or Houston. An hour's worth . . .

A knock. "Here's your lunch, Captain," Bestwick said, laying a paper bag on the desk. "I'll get someone to put them files back. You be needin' the really old ones?"

"Not right now. Oh, I don't know. . . ."

There was something uneasy in Bestwick's manner, Stoker noted. Perhaps she sensed his sadness. She closed the door quietly. Stoker unwrapped the waxed paper, and the smell of tuna fish blended with the smell of old paper telling of old heartaches. He ate slowly, and his gloom deepened. It wasn't just thinking about his father that did it. Face it, he said to himself. In the sanctity of your small office with your so-so sandwich in your so-so day in your so-so life. This place, this damn, dull little place to live, is in your bones. Boring bones, at that. No wonder Jen got sick of it. And you. There. Honesty.

He picked up the phone. "Bestwick, let's do have all the old files, right back to the year one, when you get a chance."

"Right, Captain." Over the phone, Stoker heard the sound of a siren on the radio.

"What's that?"

"Some kinda fire over by the mill, Captain. Doesn't sound like much."

"Right."

"And Captain. Sheriff Fischer says there's only a couple of prisoners that've been released recently that sound even remotely promising. I mean, in connection with Mr. Cody's death. They're being checked out."

"Fine."

In a down mood, and with a little down time on his hands, Stoker called the video place and found that someone would indeed come to fix his cable, and at a specific day and hour, and that the Clint Eastwood movie he had requested was indeed in. (A Clint Eastwood movie! No wonder Jen had left! She was right! Hell, Stoker thought, a man has to laugh at himself a little. . . .)

Then he called about his son and was told that he was resting just fine, and that everyone felt bad about the fall, but that it was just one of those things. Just one of those things . . .

And then Junior Stoker wondered how, and when, and if he would tell his father about Dexter Cody's death. Well, that would depend partly on how he had died: If old Dex had died accidentally, and there was no more to it than that, well, the old man could handle that. But if it turned out that he had been murdered (why did Junior think that?), then it would be a lot tougher to explain to him.

Damn. Gotta explain things two or three times to my father; gotta explain things two or three times to my son. Can't win.

The phone rang. It was Bestwick.

"Captain, the deputy over by the mill says that fire's a fatal. Old black fellow name of Tyrone."

CHAPTER 32

Junior Stoker had read once, a long, long time ago, that Ulysses S. Grant—in the Confederate version of Civil War history an unfeeling butcher who triumphed only because he sacrificed thousands of Union soldiers in the Battle of the Wilderness—was in reality a deeply sensitive man who could only eat meat if it was fried to a blackened crisp.

God, a blackened crisp . . . The image was almost enough to make Junior Stoker throw up, after what he had seen today.

He parked his car in his apartment-building lot, thankful that he encountered none of the other tenants on his way in. The last thing he needed was questions about the burned body from decent citizens transformed into voyeurs. He checked his mail slot. A thick brown envelope with something hard inside. Stoker was momentarily puzzled. Opening it, he saw the film cassette and a note from the manager of Clarendon Video. "Junior," the note said. "Sorry for the delay. Here's the Clint E. film you've been waiting for. Happy viewing. Best, Don M."

Stoker laughed. Any other time, he would have been delighted; the movie would have guaranteed him a full (or at least not an empty) evening. Maybe a little violence is what I need, he said to himself, mockingly. In a movie, blood doesn't smell. Neither does flesh, either rotten or burned . . .

Suddenly, he thought he was going to vomit. He leaned against the wall of the building, closed his eyes, swallowed hard twice. The feeling passed; he was Captain Bill Stoker again, Captain Bill Stoker of the South Carolina State Police, Captain Bill Stoker for whom highway deaths and shooting deaths and cutting deaths were supposed to be routine.

He squeezed the film cassette hard. Maybe he would watch it tonight and maybe he wouldn't. There, that was better. He was himself again. "Go ahead," he said, "make my day."

221

Stoker took the bottle of rye whiskey from its spot in the cupboard under the sink, and poured himself an inch and a half of whiskey.

One thing that bothered Stoker so much was that Tyrone had never had a great deal in life. Therefore, one could argue, he was entitled to a slightly easier, or at least more dignified, death. But smarter men than Bill Stoker had made the point that life was not fair. So why should death, be fair?

Being black and that age around here was hard enough, Stoker thought. Never having a wife and kids ... well, Stoker could understand what that was like. At least understand part way ...

All right, never mind. It was time for Junior Stoker to think like a cop. Now, how the hell would Tyrone burn himself up in his own little cabin like that? Sure, he liked a corncob pipe now and then, and sure, he liked to tidy up his yard by building a little fire for the twigs. Just for something to do, like as not. And sure, the wood in his cabin was probably pretty dry. Tar on the roof, dry wood, tired old man who liked to build fires in his yard, liked to smoke a corncob pipe, maybe smoked in bed sometimes ... Sure, there were all the ingredients for an accidental death by fire.

Bullshit.

He went to the sink cupboard again, poured himself another inch of rye, and picked up the phone.

"Me, Bryant. Sorry to bother you again. Like you ain't got enough stuff to do today."

"What's up, Junior?"

"Damn thing's fishy, that's what's up. Tyrone burning himself up like that. Don't make any sense to me."

"Well, hold on, Junior. After you left, we found an empty whiskey bottle, glass all cracked, under the body. Now, you know how easy it is. Get a little hooched up, smoke in bed, or maybe a spark from his yard fire ..."

"Whiskey bottle, huh ..." Junior Stoker was just starting to feel, and welcoming it, the hot glow of alcohol. And he was a lot younger, in a lot better shape than Tyrone. Probably ate better, too ...

"Way we look at it, Junior, the old fellow passed out, set his mattress on fire, probably died of the fumes before the flames got to him."

"I guess that isn't too much to hope for, in retrospect," Junior said.

"No. Well, look, Junior. We'll give things a good going over. I mean, we think we know what happened, but we'll give it a good look-see. I mean, we gotta get along okay with the state police...."

"You turkey," Junior said. "We'll be in touch."

Junior hung up, finished the whiskey, then went to the refrigerator and took out a can of beer. Ah, there was some cold chicken. He could probably stand that tonight. White meat, no blood, cold, bland.

Tyrone had never had much, had never seemed to want much (who could tell?), had never caused any trouble. Never caused any trouble. What a thing to say about a man. Here lies a man who never caused any trouble....

Junior felt very much alone, and so he picked up the phone again and dialed Jen in Columbia.

"Hi," he said when she answered. "Just thought I'd, uh, check on Thomas."

"Oh, Bill, hi. Umm, I haven't heard anything new. Just what I told you ..."

"Ah. Well, I was over to see my dad today, so I didn't get a chance—"

"How is he? Your dad."

"Oh, pretty much the same." Junior thought his ex-wife sounded distracted, nervous. He could hear the sounds of dishes and silverware in the background.

"Well, give him my love...."

"Will do. We, uh, have some excitement over here. At least you could call it that, by our—"

"Oh, what's that? What's happened, I mean?"

Junior sensed an abruptness, a nervousness over the phone (not that he considered himself that perceptive; it was just that they had been married a long time). He was puzzled and upset.

"Well, a couple of deaths. Accidents, maybe. Or maybe not. Dexter Cody. Remember him? Used to be my dad's deputy. Shot himself accidentally, it looks like. Then there was an old black fella, got burned up just today in a fire over by the mill. His cabin—"

"No, that's okay. The oven timer's on. . . . I'm sorry, Bill. I have someone here for dinner."

"Oh, excuse me," he managed to say without his voice breaking. A deep breath. "I'll let you go. Keep in touch."

"I will. Thomas would probably enjoy a visit. . . ."

"I know. Bye."

Ah, Bill D. Stoker, boring captain of the state police and thorough investigator, so you don't know yourself quite as well as you thought. You were supposed to be over her, supposed to be happy for her new life and new success without bitterness, without pangs.

So how come you feel like a stake was just pushed through your heart?

This calls for a third trip to the sink cupboard, he thought. But when he saw the bottle, he left it alone. I'll just mellow out, slowly, on another beer or three or five, he thought.

Bill D. Stoker thought of his brother Bob. Without warning, the thought crept in, and he was afraid he might cry. It had been so long. . . .

Gotta stop this, he thought, draining the beer.

Lord, how the alcohol can bring on the sadness, Junior thought. He wondered if that was what had happened to Tyrone. Maybe he had just been overcome with the sadness of everything, and so—

Jesus. Am I stupid or what? Junior asked himself, yanking the phone off the hook again.

"Bryant, it's me. Where did you say that whiskey bottle was at Tyrone's cabin?"

"Under the body, Junior . . ."

"Under?"

"Under . . ."

"And the glass from the bottle, you said it was all busted?"

"Yeah . . ."

"Well, was it all burned, like covered with carbon?"

"Well, no. Pretty clear glass. We knew right away what kind of bottle it was. . . ."

"So then Tyrone didn't fall asleep, pass out, smoking in bed, did he? 'Cause he couldn't have done that and fallen down on the bottle. And we know he fell on the bottle before the fire, or else the bottle would have been all covered with carbon."

"Jesus, Junior . . ."

"Ain't that right, Byrant?"

"Jesus, Junior . . ."

"Right. And you know what else? All them years, back since I was a kid, Tyrone's been living over by the mill, used to work there—"

"And all that time nobody ever seen him drunk."

Junior was happy for Bryant, happy that the sheriff had been able to finish his thought.

"You got it."

"Jesus, Junior . . ."

"Right. And you know what else? How come we got two suspicious deaths hereabouts all of a sudden? Ain't but, what, thirty thousand people this whole damned little county, can't remember the last time somebody killed somebody else—"

"And now we got Cody *and* poor old Tyrone dead."

"Right." Again, Junior was happy the sheriff had finished his thought.

"Jesus, Junior . . ."

"Right. Listen, come to think of it, I don't like the way the cabin all seemed to go up at once. Like somebody used an accelerant . . ."

"A who?"

"Fancy term I learned at an arson seminar in Atlanta once. It just ain't right, none of it. . . ."

"Junior, I'll have my men snoop around some more. Damn straight, you're right about nobody ever seeing Tyrone drunk. I mean, shit, a big deal for him was buying up a handful of licorice at the hardware store there."

"There you go. Ask the hardware people when they saw him last. Whether he smelled of booze. Whether any strange people been hanging around."

"Jesus, Junior . . ."

"I know, what's it all mean?"

"Somethin' ..."

"Yeah. Listen, first thing tomorrow have somebody get out the rest of the files for the cases Dex worked on. I already looked at 'em back to 1950. Might as well go through the rest."

"Jesus. You think ...?"

"Ain't got the slightest, truth to tell. All I know is, we got two old, dead men around here. Come to think of it, I'm gonna call state headquarters tomorrow and see if I can get us an arson expert. Don't know why the hell not. And don't worry. You'll still be running the show, with help from me."

"Okay. I'll get my people on the other stuff first thing. Them old files, too. You'll have 'em when you come in tomorrow."

"Terrific." Junior was going to say more, but he heard voices and laughter on the phone. "Oh, I'm sorry, Bryant. You must have company...."

"No, no, that's okay. Business first. My daughter is home from college."

"Oh, ain't that grand. Well, her dad is a first-rate cop. You tell her that."

"I been telling her...."

Both happy for Bryant Fischer and envious, Junior mumbled a couple more pleasantries and hung up. Just when he got to thinking things were simple—crime and feelings both—something happened to change his mind. He was sad that he would never have a daughter, or a son, home from college, sad and angry and jealous about Jen, sad and sick about the death he had seen not many hours ago....

Ah, but there was his salvation. He was not a half-bad cop, in a world (even a quiet, Clarendon County world) that could use some not-half-bad cops. He would have plenty to work on, plenty to think about tomorrow, and the day after that....

Meanwhile, he was getting hungry. He took out the chicken, some whole wheat bread, some cheese, some lettuce, some mustard. Maybe he would have some prune juice later, just to keep things moving smoothly ...

Maybe he could make another trip to the sink cupboard. Yes, he had earned it. He took out the bottle, poured himself an inch and drank it neat. Next he piled chicken, bread, cheese, lettuce on a plate and put the plate on a tray; put the mustard jar and silverware next to the plate; took out another can of beer and put that on the tray; grabbed a handful of paper napkins.

Into the living room. Set the food tray on the table in front of the easy chair facing the television set. Take out the cassette of the Clint Eastwood movie, put it into the video-cassette player.

Open the can of beer. Turn on the movie.

"Go ahead," Junior Stoker said to the television screen. "Make my life."

CHAPTER 33

Stoker barged through the front door, much more briskly than usual, much more briskly than he felt, considering his hangover. He startled Bestwick.

"Oh! Morning, Captain . . ."

"Hi, Bestwick." Stoker was momentarily puzzled, for she was not in her seat. She was, rather, out in front of the counter, stapling something to the bulletin board. God, that time of year again, he thought as he recognized the large cardboard cutout in the shape of a bass. He would have to set a good example and buy several chances on the festival. He had resisted attempts in recent years to enter the fishing competition.

"Captain, all the old case files between 1945 and 1950 are on your desk. So musty and mildewy, they made me sneeze. That's enough for you to start on, I guess. . . ."

"Should keep me busy," he said. With one more glance at Bestwick's generous curves, he went down the corridor, stopping at the soda machine to get something to cool his pipes.

God, he was getting old. It seemed the bass festival came up every month instead of once a year. Jesus, how long had it been since he had fished on the lake with his father—his father, who kept asking to go out on the boat with him and Bob. . . . A light was flickering in his brain, and while he could not tell where it was coming from or what it meant, he knew it was significant.

Now, what the hell had bothered him . . .?

That cutout of the fish that Bestwick was putting up. A long time since he had fished with his dad on the lake and, of course, Junior Stoker would never forget that one day, when they were met on the shore by that bunch who would gladly have lynched, or castrated, that black kid. . . . Now when the hell was that? I wasn't but seventeen, so that had to be—

Oh, Christ. I'm not only getting old, I'm getting stupid. Stoker fumbled with the keys to his office. Once inside, he ignored the case files already on his desk. Sure, it all seems too farfetched to believe, he thought. Sure, and my dad always said that the truth was odder than fairy tales, if you lived long enough.

Stoker picked up the phone. "Bestwick," he shouted. "I need the files from 1944. And I mean right now."

There, Stoker thought. There it was, a manila envelope, dirty now with age and from being handled.

He studied the notes and looked at the awkward, self-conscious signature of a black adolescent from many years ago next to the more rigid, controlled signature of his father, and he smiled. He smiled, too, at the language of the confession. The words were his father's, of course; young teenagers, white or black, today or over forty years ago, just didn't talk quite that way. Besides, Junior could easily detect his father's stylistic gaucheries.

He picked up an envelope which, he could tell at once, contained several photographs. He shook the contents onto his desk. Instantly, he was horrified and, almost, ashamed. Junior Stoker had never seen the photographs of the victims' bodies next to the tracks, hair and clothes still soaked.

The autopsy pictures were even worse. Looking at the hideous wounds, the innocent, prepubescent bodies lying nude on the metal tables, eyes glassy from the moment of their terrifying deaths, Junior Stoker was embarrassed. He ought not to be looking; no one should. It was as though he had never before seen a human body, or a picture of a body, instead of hundreds of bodies and hundreds of pictures.

He would go to the girls' graves and pray, someday soon.

He put the pictures back in the envelope and looked again at the mug shot of Linus Bragg. He stared at the face, a child's face, frozen forever in time. A killer's face, the law said. Junior Stoker hated the boy he saw in the picture, and understood the need for revenge that could make people kill.

With a clarity that made him heartsick these four decades later, Junior Stoker remembered the morning of the trip to Columbia with his father. Going to watch that boy sacrificed on the altar of vengeance.

What a lovely Carolina morning, not too hot. He would have enjoyed the ride more were it not for one of his earliest experiments with peach wine two nights before. And the dog in the road. That dying dog with that poor colored family. My God, whatever happened to them? Did they still live around here, those kids? Grown-ups now. Who knew, and who cared? Junior Stoker did.

He had never loved his father, the sheriff, more than he did that morning. Truth to tell, as his father used to say. Junior remembered how his father had comforted the colored children, what he had said to them.... The dog had been merely a hint of the death Junior Stoker was to experience that day. Death, and then more tragedy ...

But that was over forty years ago, he thought. And he ought to be more concerned about investigating the deaths of Dexter Cody and Tyrone than about taking a trip through time. Well, suppose there wasn't anything to investigate, that Dexter just fell on his shotgun. Wouldn't be the first guy to do it.

No. Too much of a coincidence. Dexter Cody, a hunter much of his life, killed with his own gun. Just about the same time a pathetic old black man died down by the mill near the scene of a long-ago murder.

Too many coincidences. Oh, they happened, all right. Coincidences. Junior Stoker believed in them. But he didn't see them as an explanation for two violent deaths in a quiet little county.

Actually, Junior Stoker had long ago lost the capacity to be surprised by crime. Horrified, sickened, depressed—all of that. But not surprised.

He remembered a case he had read about several years before. A woman had been experiencing severe nervousness and terrible nightmares in which she saw the face of her long-dead father staring up at her, as though from the bottom of a muddy pit. Under hypnosis, she began to recall a night from her childhood. She remembered being awakened in the middle of the night and seeing her mother and a man dragging a long box down the hall past her room. The next morning, her father was gone, and her mother said he had just run away and would never come back. The years went by, and the girl grew up, but she never got over the sense of loss about her father.

But what, the hypnotherapist pressed her, was the muddy pit that had claimed her father? The outhouse behind her mother's old farm, the patient said finally. And so the police went to dig (the outhouse was long gone and the pit filled in and planted over), and they found the skeleton of the missing father.

The mother had been all sweetness, serving lemonade to the diggers, but when the searchers started pulling bones out of the earth, the old woman walked into the nearby woods and shot herself in the head.

No, Junior Stoker was not surprised anymore.

The phone rang. "Captain," Bestwick said, "Sheriff Fischer says he'll be in touch as soon as he can. He's gonna stop and see Judah Brickstone. Seems Judah met up with somebody connected with an old case of his. The guy was pretty mad, like Judah cheated him or something. Judah's afraid the guy's gonna come back and hurt him. . . ."

"Thanks, Bestwick." Stoker chuckled; he had long had a grudging admiration for Brickstone's smooth, ingratiating manner, and an envy for the way Brickstone prospered because of it, especially by Clarendon County standards. So now Brickstone has someone mad at him. Probably a new experience for him.

Stoker was about to close the envelope on the Ellerby-Clark case when something caught his eye. It was so apparently inconsequential that it had not registered before, even though, he now realized, he had indeed seen it. The yellow piece of paper with his father's notes showed the imprint of a paper clip in one corner, though the paper clip was no longer there. Stoker looked at the back of the sheet and saw some old pencil smudges.

No, not smudges, he suddenly realized. The marks were the obverse, the mirror image, of whatever had been written, or printed, on the paper that had once been clipped to the paper he held in his hand. So it wasn't just a paper clip that was missing but, naturally and much more important, a piece of paper. How I do get smart in my advancing age, Stoker thought.

Holding the old yellow sheet by one corner with just a thumb and forefinger, Stoker went into the men's room. Standing under the bright fluorescent light, he held the old pencil smudges close to the mirror. "Ck Camp for poss," it read.

The "ck" seemed clear enough to Junior Stoker. It meant "check" and was an abbreviation he himself used all the time. The longer he looked at "Camp," the more he wondered if the "C" was lower-case, perhaps a reference to a logging camp or an Army camp. "For poss" could mean "for possession." No, Stoker thought. "Possession" was a word modern cops heard all the time, what with drugs and all. In my dad's time, it probably would have meant "possibilities."

Stoker was intrigued. He recalled stories, from his childhood and teenage years, about the logging camps and, once the war started, Army camps—how they brought together big groups of men, and how when you had a big group of men you were bound to have some who were untrustworthy, or dangerous. So his father, all those years ago, had written a note to himself about them.

Only, Junior could not remember any big Army or logging camps around Manning or Alcolu. . . .

The phone rang as he reentered his office. It was Bestwick again. "Captain, lady over at the courthouse says a stranger was in there, looking at some old will. . . ."

"Well, that getting to be against the law all of a sudden?" Stoker was annoyed at the interruption.

"Beg pardon, Captain. No, it ain't against the law. Just that the woman in the courthouse was suspicious, the man being a stranger and all . . ."

"Sorry, and I don't mean to bite your head off." Stoker tried to make it an inviolable rule (though his temper occasionally got the better of him) not to snap at a subordinate; it was the worst way to kill initiative.

"No problem, Captain. Uh, what do you want me to tell her?"

"Well, does she feel in some kind of danger? I mean, I guess there ain't nothing for us to do if this guy ain't breaking any law. . . ."

"Well, I don't know, Captain. The lady, she was just puzzled 'cause she can't remember anybody ever coming to look at Mr. Tyler's will before. Before my time, Captain, but I guess he used to own that sawmill. . . ."

"Shit," Junior Stoker said.

It seemed to Junior Stoker that the court clerk was embarrassed but grateful for the attention.

"Captain, I'm sorry. I know you're busy, and I hope I did the right thing. . . ."

"You did just fine. Tell you what. Let's just have a look at that old will and see just what it was our friend might have been interested in. I don't see any harm in that, do you?"

"No, sir."

Hardly ever looked at, Stoker thought as he handled the crisp, stiffly folded but almost unwrinkled legal paper. Now, then: Here's a piece of paper the people outside the Tyler family don't give a good goddamn about, and now we got some stranger in here asking to see it. Now, what the hell does that tell you? Stoker was damned if he knew the answer, but he knew the will might hold a clue.

Stoker found it depressing, reading the will. It made him feel guilty. If he got hit by a truck tomorrow, his own affairs would be left in a bit of a tangle. Shit, what to do about Jen (he owed her something, goddamn it), and what to do about—oh, God, what to do about Thomas? Not to mention . . .

At first glance, old Tyler's will seemed routine enough. But Stoker was surprised that his nephew, T. J. Campbell, didn't get all that much, despite a lot of kind words from Tyler about his nephew trying to be his son and all that. . . .

So the old bastard could be generous after all. Charities didn't do all that bad by him, and neither did the university. Wonder if the school spent any of that on a couple of good linebackers. Oh, hell. Long time ago . . .

Jesus. Then Stoker saw it. His knees felt weak.

His red radio light was flashing when he got back to his car.

"Go ahead, Bestwick."

"Captain, Sheriff Fischer wants to talk to you right away about that man who bothered Judah Brickstone today. Says it's urgent."

"Put me through."

Bryant Fischer told him in a matter-of-fact way that Judah Brickstone had told him about a visit from a man who spoke mysteriously, and with more than a hint of menace, about a murder case over forty years ago and an innocent child and—

"Yeah, that figures, Bryant," Stoker said. "I catch on to everything just a step too late. Jen always said ..."

"Huh?"

"Never mind. Listen, this same guy was just over here at the courthouse, checking up on old Harry Tyler's will. I ain't checked Judah's description of his visitor with what the courthouse people remember, but I don't have to. I know it's the same guy. And guess who handled Tyler's will way back a long time ago."

"Judah, probably."

"You got it. Oh, guess what else. Tyler left a tidy sum to the NAACP. Imagine that."

"Who would've figured. What's it mean?"

"Don't know. Listen, I'm heading in."

When Stoker got back to headquarters, a note was waiting on his desk, telling him to call the medical examiner's office. He did, and found that the autopsy on Tyrone had detected an injury on the back of his head near his neck, an injury serious enough to have rendered him unconscious, or even to have killed him. The medical examiner was reasonably certain the injury had been inflicted before the fire since the wound was too serious to have been caused by a fall.

Stoker got hold of Fischer again and suggested he send a deputy over to the mill area to see if anyone had met a stranger, especially one who resembled the man who had visited Brick-stone and the courthouse.

Stoker was pleased that Fischer had already begun checking the motels in the area. Then (suspending his own rule that investigators should share their information rather than hide it from each other) he went to see his father, the sheriff, to see if the old man could remember what he had meant all those years ago when he jotted "ck camp for poss."

"Hello, Mr. Stoker, and how are you today?"

"Just fine, thanks."

"Your father is being just a bit difficult," the starched, plump, middle-aged attendant said in a maddeningly cheerful voice.

"That so?" Junior couldn't blame his father a bit.

"Yes, indeed. Said he didn't want any of that nice vegetable beef soup—"

"Uhhnnn...."

Junior could tell from the tone of the grunt that his father was, indeed, angry.

"—and I told him he just had to eat something or I surely wouldn't pour him anything from that bottle." The attendant said "that bottle" as though she was referring to opium or heroin instead of whiskey.

"Well, he sure does know what he wants sometimes. Ain't that right, old sheriff ..."

"Uhnnn ..."

There: The old man's tone was softening, Junior thought.

Sheriff Hiram Stoker damn well knew he had all his marbles, at least for today. He hadn't liked the vegetable soup because it was cold, and the pain in the ass in the white uniform had not made the slightest effort to understand him.

It was goddamn unfair, and it frustrated the sheriff no end to not be able to tell her how goddamn unfair it was.

"Hell, this soup's cold," Junior said as he picked up the dish. "No wonder you don't have much of an appetite...."

"Uhnnn ..." Junior understood! The sheriff instantly felt better.

"Well, let's just get it warmed up. Tell you what, I'll pour you a little something to go with it, too. How's that?"

"Uhnnn ..."

Junior opened a bureau drawer and took out the heating coil he had stashed there. A heating unit was against regulations, but Junior didn't care. It was just the thing to make his father a cup of hot chocolate on a chilly winter day—or heat up his soup. As the coil did its work atop the bureau, Junior got out the whiskey, dusted off a tumbler, and poured his father a half-inch.

"This'll clear your throat a bit there," Junior said.

The old sheriff lifted the glass, slowly and carefully, and sniffed the contents. Then he took a gulp.

"Bet this'll taste a lot better now," Junior said, offering his father a spoonful of the rewarmed soup. "I'll serve you a couple of ladles and then let you get back to that amber stuff. . . ."

The sheriff wished he could tell Junior how grateful he was that Junior understood so much about what he wanted, and when. He was a good son, and it was too bad the three of them— Junior, the sheriff, and Bob—couldn't get together more often. . . .

No, no. The sheriff knew he was mixed up, had jumbled all the things up from one time to another. . . . Never mind.

This is going to be tricky, Junior thought. Got to keep the old man from getting too excited, because if he gets too excited he wouldn't be able to distinguish his "yes" grunt from his "no" grunt. And he didn't want to upset him.

"I meant to ask you," Junior began tentatively. "I know I was a teenager at the time, but like most teenagers I didn't pay a lot of attention. I mean, I might have forgotten some things. . . ."

The sheriff knew Junior was being slightly deceitful; Junior was never a clever enough speaker to fool him. But then, Junior was his son.

"You, uh, remember any big Army camps hereabouts, back during the war?"

"Uh . . ."

"I didn't think so either. Well, how about any logging camps?"

"Uh . . ."

"No, huh. Hmmm. Uh, tell you why I asked. I was, uh, looking through some old case files just recently. Just for old times' sake, if you know what I mean. And I, uh, saw a note in one. 'Check camp for poss,' it said, assuming you meant 'check' when you put down a 'C' and a 'K' like that. Anyhow . . ."

"Uhnnn . . ." The sheriff was agitated. No, no! That's not what he had meant at all, not at all! How could he make Junior understand. . . . He could print it out! It might take him half an hour, but if he could get

Junior to give him pencil and paper, he could print it out. Of course, it would take a while. . . .

"So, anyhow . . ." Junior began. He stopped short when his father's arm suddenly swept across the table, spilling soup and whiskey onto the floor.

Oh, goddamn it! Sheriff Hiram Stoker thought. "Uhn . . ." Son of a bitch, I'm sorry, Junior. No, no, goddamn it. Leave the mess alone. "Uhnnn . . ." No, just get a pencil and paper. Clean up later . . .

"That's okay, old fella," Junior said, mopping the mess up with paper towels. Well, enough. He just wasn't in the mood to put up with his father's tantrums. Not today. "Listen, I'm gonna get going. I'll stop in again real soon. . . ."

"Uhn . . ." Goddamn it. Sometimes Junior was really thick.

Junior Stoker was sad and annoyed, doubly annoyed. He hated to see his father not quite in control of himself, which made Junior annoyed both at his father and at himself, for not having more patience.

It was a relief for Junior to find his message light flashing when he got back to his car. Anything to take his mind off the visit with his father . . .

"Stoker here."

"Captain, hold on for Sheriff Fischer."

"Junior, we're getting somewhere. Young woman over at the hardware store, the one right near the mill, remembers Tyrone coming in the other day. To buy licorice, like he always does. Anyhow, there was this stranger in the store at the time. Said he was interested in local speech patterns, or some such. Young woman didn't buy that story at all. Says the guy left just after Tyrone did."

"Well, run a check and see if he looks like the guy who was interested in Tyler's will and the guy who visited Judah Brickstone."

"We did and he does. Positive. Traced him to that motel run by them Asian people. Know the one I mean?"

"Sure. Listen, be careful. We got two bodies around here already. Make sure we got plenty of backup."

"Too late, Junior. He checked out already."

"Goddamn. Meet me there."

Two sheriff's department cars were conspicuous in the motel parking lot. Well, probably doesn't matter, Junior Stoker thought. Guy probably checked out in the first place because he thought we were on to him. Wonder if he has any notion how slow I been about this thing ...

Bryant Fischer was waiting for him outside the motel room.

"We vacuumed up the rug," Fischer said. "Pulled up some stuff that looks like seeds and burrs and such ..."

"Like in Cody's field," Stoker said.

"And we got the maid to pull all of this morning's bags out of the dumpster. Found these."

Stoker held up a transparent plastic bag containing several crumpled white circular pieces of cloth: gun-cleaning patches.

"Yeah, he's been cleaning a gun, all right," Stoker said. But something bothered him. "Don't see any dirt, carbon, on the patches. Nothing to indicate it's been fired."

"We'll keep looking. Used his real name, apparently. Willop, James B. Credit card's the same one he used to rent a car with over at Columbia airport. Used it to buy his airplane ticket down here, too."

"How about a return ticket?"

"Ain't bought one yet. Police over at Columbia been alerted. Airport security, too."

"Good. Be interesting to see what a computer check turns up."

"In the works," Fischer said.

"Wonder what the hell he wants, exactly. Other than to kill some harmless old people ..."

"Could be he's crazy as a shithouse rat, Junior. Motel lady said he looks like warmed-over death in the mornings. Tired, hung over, whatever. Like he's got a lot on his mind."

"Well, I know what that feels like. Uh, Bryant. I was thinking on my way over here. If this guy's looking up old-timers, and one fella who's dead already is Dexter Cody, then ..."

"Right. Already arranged to have your dad's nursing home watched. He'll have a guard there for company most of the time. I gave orders already not to say anything about any details around here so as not to upset him."

"Thanks for thinking." Stoker felt grateful and humble. Also tired. "Let me know what the computers find," he said, turning to go.

"I'll be in touch."

Something still nagged at Stoker. "Keep looking for gun patches that are dirty," he said.

CHAPTER 34

Willop was glad he had called Moira. He had planned to buy a cheeseburger or a bucket of chicken or some fish and fries and bring them back to the room.

No, she had said. He should take a hot shower, put on some good clothes (if he still had any), take a leisurely, sightseeing ride, and go out to dinner.

What for? he had asked. Because you're tense and exhausted, she'd said.

How could she tell?

At that she had laughed. Then she'd suggested that he leave the little motel he was staying in and check in to a better place. She would send more money, if necessary.

It had taken him fifteen minutes to shower, get dressed, and pack. He bought a newspaper at the machine in front of the motel office. Just for the hell of it, Willop looked in the real-estate section. Amazing, what you could buy down here compared to the prices around New York.

Of course, you still need a job.

Willop drove in the general direction of Lake Marion (he had already decided to try the restaurant over at the big motel, maybe even check in there), but in a circuitous route. He wanted to see some neighborhoods.

He turned down a road he hadn't driven before, then turned onto a cul-de-sac. Several houses at the end stood shrouded in pines, facing a circular court. Yards big enough for privacy, especially with the trees, but houses grouped just close enough to give a feeling of togetherness ...

Jesus, Willop thought. Is that what I want?

One of the houses had a for-sale sign in front. Willop stopped, checked the realtor's name on the sign, then easily found the advertisement in the paper. Damn, could that price be right? Four times as much for that house in Jersey. We could probably scrape up enough right now. . . .

Willop got out of the car, stood next to it, breathed deep. Pines and clean air. Birds.

What kind of work could he do here? Hell, he was a broken-down ex-newspaperman. And what about Moira? No, she wasn't the problem on that score, she was a lot more willing to take chances. He was the problem. . . .

Hey, what about the people in these houses? They work around here, don't they? Were they all smarter than he was?

Willop heard a door open a few houses away. A young woman leaned out of the entryway. Ah, there, calling to her little girl in the front yard, telling the child to come inside. The woman saw Willop, stared at him, face uncertain. Willop raised his arm, forced a smile. The woman waved back and smiled a big smile.

Yes, he and Moira could live in a place like this. They could have a yard, fence it in for the kids to play in, get a dog. . . .

Willop thought of Moira, wanted her standing next to him, wanted to put his arms around her. He could almost smell her perfume and her hair and her skin. Oh, man. No time to get horny . . .

He drove around some more, loving the quiet. From somewhere he heard a siren, maybe two sirens. Damn, ain't heard that sound much, he thought. There, that was just another example of how much more tranquil it was down here. . . .

Willop thought of his mother, wondered if she had loved the smells and the sounds around here. He didn't like to think of her too much when he thought of South Carolina. . . .

Without planning to at all, Willop thought of Bestwick. No doubt about it: She smelled great, and she was really built.

No you don't, he told himself. Don't even think for a moment . . . Yes, he was missing Moira. . . .

She had helped him a lot, Bestwick had. Maybe it meant she liked him a little. Willop liked that thought. Or maybe it just meant she wanted to help one of her own. Whatever . . . Willop hoped she had not risked too much. He would remember, and maybe pay her back, somehow. Or maybe use her again ...

The traffic was light on the way over to the big motel by Lake Marion, and Willop reflected again that life could be a lot less congested, a lot slower, here, or someplace else away from the New York area. As he played the soft music on the car's FM radio, Willop thought that if Moira was just sitting next to him now, his evening would be complete.

There was valet parking at the restaurant, and the young man who took the car and gave him a claim ticket was smiling and friendly. So was the restaurant hostess, who told him it would be just a few minutes, and she could seat him over near the window if he liked, and would he like to have a drink at the bar while he waited?

The bar area was in a dark-oak motif, and the walls were decorated with Civil War scenes by Currier and Ives and color photographs of famous stock-car drivers. Cluttered but cheerful.

Feeling in the mood to really relax, Willop asked the cheerful bartender for a martini on the rocks with the top-shelf gin, whatever it was, and not enough vermouth to hurt anything.

"I've been using the same bottle of vermouth for five years," the bartender said.

It was beginning to sound like Willop's kind of place.

He was about half done with his drink (the bartender hadn't been bullshitting, he really did know how to make a martini) when the hostess came by to show Willop to his table. She seated him over near the window, and he sat down in a fine mood. He resolved not to let Moira's absence bother him, but rather to savor the thought of her. The gin seemed to make the task easier.

A young waiter brought him a menu, and Willop said he could use another martini just like the first one, and he slumped into his chair to decide what to eat. The death of the *Trib* and the decision he had to make about Delmar Springs and when he could afford to buy a new car were little problems that he could handle. And he would have a life with Moira. He would ...

Willop ordered prime ribs and a baked potato and asked if he could have a Caesar salad, even though he was alone and the menu said it was normally made for two. The waiter said sure, they did it all the time, no problem.

Willop took a gulp from his second martini (the bartender hadn't lost his touch) and felt altogether good about himself for the first time in—how long?

He studied the people at the other tables. There was a man alone, just like him. Probably on the road on business. And there was a family: father and mother in their, oh, early thirties probably; freshed-scrubbed kids, a boy and girl, learning which fork to use and behaving just right. And there, there was a couple out on a date, for God's sake. The way they smiled at each other ... Maybe they were already married and it was their anniversary or something....

For a moment, Willop considered asking the waiter to see whether the couple would have a drink on him. No, no, don't overdo it.

Willop was on the bottom half of his second martini. Ah, good friend, you're fading fast. He felt the gin in a good way, so far, but he would be careful. Probably not order another drink till after he'd eaten something.

The Caesar salad was not the best he'd ever had, but it wasn't bad. The beef was almost as rare as he preferred, and the flavor was good. He'd eaten worse meals in New York, and for twice as much.

He chuckled at himself when he realized how sentimental he had become. Well, part of it was the gin. Nothing wrong with that. But most of it was from his talk with Moira.

He realized, as he'd savored the last of his beef and scooped the remnants of the potato out of the skin, how deeply he loved her. It seemed to Willop that if he could have Moira with him permanently (or as permanently as you could have anything in life), and have a house with a little bit of lawn and enough room in back for a garden, and some neighbors to have over for some beer and hamburgers on summer nights ...

Man. Then if there was enough time left over for some golf, and a couple of decent guys to get out with ...

Dammit, Willop thought. I want that, and sooner rather than later. I mean, what else is there?

Well, there's a couple of kids and going to PTA meetings and saving up for college.... Yeah, there is that. The trick is figuring out whether all that other good stuff is harder or easier to come by if I go with Delmar Springs. Yeah, that was the trick card in the whole deck....

But Willop was in too good a mood, he had his priorities too much in order, to let the decision about Delmar Springs vex him. Hell, plenty of people would love to be wrestling with a decision like that.

He was going to make things permanent with Moira, and they were going to settle down, no matter what kind of work he—they—did, and where. Just look at the people around me, he thought. Plain people, family people. Good people. And I'm gonna be like them. I might even discover God, or He might discover me.

Willop let himself think about the puzzle. Yes, he would chew on it a little, maybe see a fresh angle or two, but he wouldn't let it consume him. Not tonight, anyhow ...

Maybe he should just call the sheriff, ask for an appointment, tell him everything he had found out. Or maybe that hard-ass Stoker, he might have more pull. Wonder if he's enough of a pro to try to look objectively at what his daddy did. Can't count on that ...

But what could I tell them? Willop thought. That Brickstone did a half-ass job? Shit, I ain't asking for a new trial. . . . Or tell them to just do some detective work, forty-plus years later? Sure, that's it. And while I'm at it, I can just tell them I'm nuts, because they'll think that anyhow....

The tooth in the autopsy picture. Like maybe the older girl bit the guy. Well, maybe she did. They missed it at the time. So what? And now they're going to go all over Clarendon County—maybe Sumter, too—and ask all the older men to hold their hands out so they can check for bite marks? Sure, that's it....

I can tell the sheriff and this guy Stoker that the old deputy, Cody, seemed kind of shy about answering any questions. And so what ... Hey, tell 'em about that old Tyrone, how he didn't want to be bothered with me. No, more than that. Like he was hiding something, or afraid ...

Something did bother Willop, but he couldn't quite pin it down. Or maybe it wasn't one thing, but two or three things he couldn't connect. . . .

Goddamn, Willop thought. It ain't like it's on Perry Mason. . . .

What cop anywhere is going to check into a case that was already stamped "solved" more than forty years ago? There, that was the point. Cops everywhere, they all claim they got plenty to do keeping up with today's crime.

Maybe I should just write what I find, try to sell an article to *The New York Times* Sunday magazine. If it was good enough, and I got some civil-liberties lawyers to notice it, especially some angry young black ones . . . Hey, maybe. At least tell the world what happened, even if it wouldn't do any good. Whoever said Truth and Justice went hand in hand?

Willop was wondering whether to have the pecan pie plain or with vanilla ice cream when he overheard some conversation from the next table. There were a man and his wife and their two young sons, ages twelve and ten or thereabouts. The father was explaining in a serious way, in quiet tones the boys could pay attention to, about death. That much Willop had discerned without even trying. There had been a death in the family (sounded like an uncle, maybe, or a grandfather), and the father was talking to his boys man-to-man.

Willop saw the waiter coming. He would order the pie with vanilla ice cream on it, and never mind the calories.

". . . so just remember the lesson. It only takes a moment, just a tiny bit of carelessness with a gun . . ."

"I know."

Willop tried to tune out all other sounds.

"Well, I know you know, son. All the same, if you're wanting a gun for next Christmas . . ."

Dishes clattered nearby. Shut up, shut up, Willop wanted to shout.

". . . thought he knew all about guns, too. Probably handled them all his life, being a deputy and all . . ."

"Would you care for some dessert, sir?"

Willop ignored the waiter, trying desperately to hear.

"...and now he's dead as can be. All because of a little carelessness. Dead by his own gun ..."

"Sir? Some dessert?"

"Uh, no. Thanks. Just give me the check."

Mechanically, Willop gave the waiter a credit card, realized after the waiter had gone how stupid that had been, that they would be able to trace him easily from the credit card if they (who?) were looking for him. But Willop didn't care. The fear had deflated him like a punch in the stomach.

He left the tip in cash, stumbled out of the dining room, bumping a couple of tables but not looking down to beg anybody's pardon, ignored the hostess's good-bye smile. He waited for an eternity while the kid brought him his car, then gave him a dollar tip and drove away. Not too fast, not too slow, Willop thought. Just away, away, away ...

He drove back toward the motel he had left, then thought no, no, no, they would look for him there. He was a fool, in way over his head....

Down a side road ... Must not, must not go into a ditch ... Careful in the dark ... Familiar. Why? Oh, the road to the mill, to the mill. Ahead was the hardware store, used to be the company store, a big shape there in the dark. Right across is Tyrone's shack....

No! Nothing there, no shack, nothing standing against the night blue ... Slow the car, slow the breathing, open the window, can't hear any night sounds over the breathing ... Smell, smell, smell the smoke, the wet ashes of the wood, and Tyrone.

Roll up the window and drive, drive, drive.

CHAPTER 35

Willop drove away from Manning, toward Columbia, avoiding the main roads. He would be safer in Columbia; more people, he could disappear more easily, until he figured out what to do. . . .

But no, they would find him there easily. He couldn't go near the airport, they would have it staked out. . . . Who would? Stoker and his cronies? Was that it? Was he the one who had something to lose in all this? Or . . .

Jesus, the car . . . Trace it so easily if he even went near Columbia . . .

Would they (he?) try to kill him, or just frame him? Maybe both . . . Frame him, then arrange a jail suicide . . .

Ahead, he saw a little store with a gasoline pump out front. Light still on . . .

He pulled over, parked in front of the gasoline pump, went inside, tried to act casual. Only customer in the place . . .

Need the tank filled, Willop told the man. Help yourself, the man said, then come on back and pay me. Need some black coffee to go, Willop said. Coming up, the man said. Best damn coffee anywhere . . .

Willop paid the man, made his good-bye as friendly-sounding as he could, got into the car, and drove off. The coffee was sitting in the well between the seats. He'd need it later, because he was going to find a road heading north, and he was going to drive out of Clarendon County, out of South Carolina, was going to drive all night, heading north, north, north. . . .

There was no comfort in the empty roads, only terror. It would be easy to pick him out; he would be stopped on an ink-black stretch of lonely road, and he would be handcuffed. Or maybe just killed on the spot, and nobody would have to know. This was South Carolina, still South Carolina. . . .

He was falling into the trap, doing what he (they?) wanted, running, running. . . .

He had gone less than a quarter-mile from the store when he saw it: a little white house by the side of the road with a sign out in front. Room for rent. Vacancy.

He braked hard, had to back up a few yards, turned into the driveway, shut off the engine and the lights. Dark, quiet, only the trees.

Willop felt naked under the porch light as he pressed the bell. He rang it again, again, again. Please . . . The door swung open. An old black woman, must be over seventy.

Willop was glad she was black, glad that she seemed to be able to tell he was black. Willop smiled, and meant it, he was so relieved.

Just need a room for tonight, Willop told her. "I found myself kind of stranded," he said, an explanation that explained nothing, yet with his smile might explain anything: kicked out by his wife, can't afford a motel, hiding from his girlfriend's brother . . .

The old woman didn't care. Pay in advance, she said. Pull your car around back. He parked the car so it couldn't be seen from the road, got out his suitcases, followed the woman upstairs, nodded as she pointed out the bathroom, told the woman that, no, he didn't smoke.

The room was just big enough for the bed, a dresser, a chair, and a small closet. It looked clean and smelled of furniture polish, though that didn't quite mask the smells of people grown old with the house.

Willop locked the door; took out the bottle of Scotch; took out the gun, loaded it, put in on the chair next to the bed; stood his suitcase in front of the door; slid the dresser over (quietly, so she couldn't hear) so that part of the dresser was in front of the door. He took off his shoes, turned off the light, lay down on the bed, his head propped up on the pillow. He felt for the gun, felt secure that it was right there.

Willop realized then that he had left the coffee in the car. He would not go back for it. He would need the Scotch tonight, even after the martinis at dinner (so long ago!), to sleep, to sleep.

He slept on his back, which he almost never did, awaking every so often with a start, holding his breath, listening for sounds in the dark. There were none. Back to sleep . . .

Finally, with one of the wake-ups, he sensed that the room was no longer ink-black, the night outside the single window had merged with the first hint of dawn. Back to sleep ...

Another wake-up, the room gray with early morning now, and sounds from below in the house. Just the old woman. Back to sleep ...

But only for a little while. The next time Willop opened his eyes, it was still gray in the room, though a lighter gray, but he knew he was done sleeping, even though he did not feel rested. He got out of bed (the room was chilly), hurriedly put on the same clothes he had worn to dinner (so long ago, last night), and went to the bathroom. The woman had left a clean towel and washcloth on the edge of the tub. Willop washed his face, rinsing again and again with the warm water, ran his fingers through his hair, dried himself. God, he felt like hell.

He closed his suitcase, put on his jacket, stuck the gun in the pocket, went downstairs. A clock ticked in the old-smelling house.

"Morning," he said to the woman, who was standing in the kitchen.

"Coffee's free," she said, more loudly than necessary. "Give you a full breakfast for three dollars. Bacon, toast, juice, and grits. Ain't very busy ..."

"Maybe some toast," he said.

Willop saw that she wore a hearing aid and thick glasses. Good ...

The old woman moved her head and shoulder to tell him he could sit at the kitchen table. She put a big mug of coffee and a plate of toast she'd already made in front of him. The coffee was strong.

"You here alone?" he asked.

"Just me," she shouted.

Good, Willop thought. He took out his wallet. "Here's five bucks. Three for the breakfast and two if I can use your phone to make a couple of calls."

"No long distance?"

"Collect only."

"Phone's in there."

Willop ate a couple of bites of toast and, without asking permission, took his coffee into the living room. The phone was on a stand near a window that looked out on the road. He sat down and dialed.

249

"Collect from James," he said when the operator cut in.

One ring, two, three, four ... she couldn't have left for work yet. ...

"Nobody's answering, sir."

"Keep ringing."

Another ring, another, another. Maybe ...

"Hello?" Moira sounded harried.

"Collect call from James. Will you pay?"

"Yes. James?"

"Hi."

"I was in the shower. Where are you?"

"Still you know where."

"Are you in trouble?" There was something wrong in her voice. ... Couldn't be explained just by her having to step out of the shower ...

"I might be. That's one reason I called, so in case I get arrested or ... anything ... you can tell someone—"

"James, I don't think we should talk very long."

"What's wrong?"

"Delmar Springs called last night. To tell me that the police got a request from someone in South Carolina to run a computer check on you."

"Great."

"Why would they do that?"

"Couple people turned up dead around here."

"Oh, James ..." She was crying.

"I haven't wasted anybody."

"Oh, James. Be careful."

"Yeah, I will."

"Someone may be setting you up."

"What an understatement ..."

"Just come home. Please."

"You know, my mother was right. It's still South Carolina, and I'm still—"

"Can you come home?" She was still crying.

"How? No way I can get on a plane. They'll be looking for me. Can't drive the car I rented ..."

"Then just give up. Call the police, or the sheriff, or whatever. Tell them where you are and let them come and get you."

"You know, that probably would be the most sensible thing."

"Please ..."

Because he couldn't bear to hear her cry, and because he was afraid someone might be trying to run a trace on the call, he told her in one breath not to worry, that he loved her and good-bye, and hung up.

He finished his coffee, looked out the window at the road, and picked up the phone again.

The sensible thing to do—the only sensible thing—would be to call the sheriff's office and tell them where he was. Hey, he could tell her to tell them he was waiting, that he wouldn't resist. . . .

"Clarendon County sheriff." A woman, but not Bestwick.

"Bestwick in today?" Willop mumbled.

"Not till three o'clock."

"Thanks." Willop hung up. Should have just said who I was and where I was, he thought. . . .

It was stupid—no, goddamn reckless—to even think of calling Bestwick.

The information operator said there was only one Bestwick in the Manning area.

Willop dialed.

"Hello." Her.

"Can we talk?"

"You ..."

"Please. Just for a minute."

"I shouldn't. I never should have ..."

"Please. Please."

"They're looking for you."

"I didn't kill anyone. I never would."

"They think you might have."

"Supposed to look that way. Don't you see that?"

Silence.

"Don't you see?"

"You should come in."

"Hey, I'm the stranger around here. They're looking to blame someone. I'm the right guy. That's how cops are. Cops any place . . ."

"You should just come in. That way, they can't hurt you. But you wouldn't tell them I showed you— Oh, dear Jesus . . ."

"Take it easy."

"Jesus . . ." Now she seemed close to crying. No, she was tougher than that.

"I promise I won't tell," Willop said. "All I want is to talk to you for a minute, and for you not to tell."

"Dear Jesus . . ."

"Right. Dear Jesus. Listen, I talked to that Cody guy once, just once, and he's dead. Same thing with that poor old Tyrone in the shack. Somebody killed them, right? No accidents."

"They think maybe you did."

"No. I told you. Listen, I keep hearing about this T. J. Campbell guy in every other conversation I have around here. What's with him and Cody and Tyrone?"

"Deputy Cody, he never have any truck with T.J. that I know of. . . ."

"How about Tyrone?"

"Tyrone, he just live over there in the shack. Not want nothing else that I know of . . ."

"Figures. Listen, did anybody ever think T.J. might have, you know, had something to do with that thing that happened a way long time ago around here?"

Long pause. "You mean that thing I showed you in the files?"

"Yeah. That thing."

"Not that I know of." But there was something in Bestwick's voice.

"You're trying to say something else," Willop said.

"My mama, she a young girl in the shacks way back then, and her mama tell her she have to watch out for the white foremen. Especially Mr. T.J., because he the one who most like to . . . you know. . . ."

"Yeah, I know. Well, how come nobody ever asked the people in the shacks about him?"

"You know. Back then, they think that just nigger talk. Anyhow, nobody ever asked, I know of. You better come in. I can't talk to you no more."

"Thanks."

"Promise you won't tell. . . ."

Willop knew he should leave her dangling, leave her afraid. That way, she would be less likely to tell the sheriff and Stoker he had called. . . .

"I promise," he said. "I promise."

So what now? Willop thought. What he should do, what Moira wanted him to do, was call the sheriff's office and have them come and get him. Sure. It could all be straightened out, couldn't it? No way he'd be convicted, if they would only listen . . . He could explain the visits to Cody and Tyrone and Brickstone and looking at Tyler's will. . . .

Maybe he could even persuade Stoker and the sheriff to do a good investigation of T. J. Campbell. Sure, after more than forty years . . .

Isn't this the craziest damn thing, Willop thought, because just then he remembered a golf tournament he had seen on television years before. Young, strong golfer, never a winner before, has his biggest decision on a par 5: whether to lay up short of a wide creek to set up an easy wedge to the green, or to take his biggest fairway-wood shot and try to go over the creek and reach the green in two. The golfer had disdained the easy shot, had gone for the green, reached it in two shots, got an eagle that won the tournament.

Ah, but he had won as soon as he chose to go for it, Willop thought. *That* was what had made him a winner. . . .

Willop picked up the phone. He would call the sheriff's department—but not to turn himself in.

"Clarendon County sheriff." Same voice as before.

"Hi. I'm an old friend of Dexter Cody. Are there any calling hours at the funeral home?"

"Yes, sir. Going on right now, in fact."

"Good," Willop said.

Maybe the old woman had believed him and maybe she hadn't when he told her he couldn't start his car. Whatever. She had been happy enough to take the twenty dollars Willop offered if he could use her car for a little while. He had even promised to fill up the gas tank; well, maybe he would and maybe he wouldn't. Her car didn't run that great, and it had been a long time since he had handled a stick shift.

He only hoped the car would last until he got to Cody's house.

Willop parked behind several other cars by the side of the road. If he had guessed right, Cody's widow and whatever other relatives he had would all be at the funeral home. Probably somebody minding the house, maybe a neighbor ...

Good, Willop thought as the door swung open. The person opening it was a small woman in late middle age. Black.

"Hello, I'm sorry to bother you at such a time," Willop said as unctuously as he could. Then, showing his credentials, he went on: "The sheriff sent me over just to pick up some papers that belonged to Deputy Cody. Won't take but a few minutes ..."

"They's all at the funeral home," the woman said uncertainly. "I'm just a neighbor."

"Yes. I see. Well, you're welcome to review my credentials," Willop said, holding his thumb over part of the credentials so she couldn't study them too closely. "Or you can check with the sheriff's office...." The last was a pure, all-or-nothing gamble, but Willop had no choice.

"Guess it's all right. Folks'll be back in a half hour or so." She held the door open for him.

"Thank you again ever so much," he said. "Sheriff Fischer and Captain Stoker asked me to come by."

"His desk is in there." She pointed to a small room just off the kitchen.

Willop wandered over to the room she'd pointed out. At the desk, he stooped over, pulled open the drawers, fingered through sheafs of letters and utility bills and unused envelopes and long-ago snapshots and addresses. ...

Crazy, Willop thought. Crazy to come here, crazy to think I could find anything. He felt sweat on his back.

"Find what you need?"

The woman was by the door, not ready to challenge, no longer convinced.

"Think I need to look in his room," he said. "Upstairs?"

"Well, I don't know...."

"Told you, the sheriff asked me to come."

Then Willop was by her, going through the kitchen, past condolence pies and cakes and casseroles stacked on the table and window ledge and on top of the refrigerator, bounding up the stairs, two at a time.

There, his bedroom. A smell of an old man: his work clothes, his field clothes, hunting clothes, all of it too-seldom washed, or maybe just worn too many years. Those smells blended, Willop gradually realized, with the smells coming from downstairs—the mountains of food and, from somewhere, flowers. Together, the smells almost made him vomit. Willop felt like a ghoul.

This drawer for underwear, this for socks, this for flannels, the bottom drawer for a box of old coins, woolen longjohns ... He had no right....

The closet. Smells of old boots and slippers and shoes. There, an old steamer trunk. God, don't let it be locked.

The trunk was secured only by the clasps. Willop dragged it out into the room so he could explore better. He could smell his own sweat now, over the other smells....

Willop flung open the trunk; the top banged against the closet door. The woman downstairs might be calling the sheriff now....

Top shelf of the trunk filled with letters, paper, old photographs in browns and grays. There, a much younger Dexter Cody, thin and bony and awkward in an ill-fitting suit, standing next to a young woman, plainly dressed, holding flowers, trying to smile. Oh, his wife, their wedding day, long ago. He had no right....

Willop lifted the shelf out of the trunk and flung it to the side. It clattered on the floor. People might be back from the funeral home any minute....

The bottom part of the trunk was stuffed with envelopes, mostly old and smudged with fingerprints, and shoeboxes. One shoebox filled with small, long-ago gray and brown photographs of picnics and people standing on porches and with one foot on a running board and waving and at a county fair or something. . . .

Willop could smell his own sweat. He had no right. . . .

A big envelope full of letters; woman's handwriting, addressed to Cody's wife.

A sheaf of letters, held together by a rubber band, more women's handwriting.

Never mind being delicate . . . Scoop up an armful of stuff and toss it on the floor to see what else is in there. . . .

More envelopes on the bottom—manila, thick, and business-size—like from an office . . . Where had he seen that kind of envelope before?

The sheriff's office! Same kind of envelope he had seen with the case file . . .

Willop's fingers trembled. He was running out of time, he almost cut a thumb on the metal clasp of the envelope, he could smell his own sweat. . . .

Pictures. Terrible pictures, and not small like the others. Pictures of a black woman, head almost cut off, lying in her own blood. Axed to death.

Lots of cops kept their own private scrapbooks, Willop thought.

Picture of a farm accident, mangled body lying next to a conveyor belt and some machinery . . .

Pictures, pictures. Pictures of two little girls lying dead next to a ditch. Jesus, the same pictures he had seen in the sheriff's office. Same pictures. Was that how Cody got his kicks?

Another big envelope. Not pictures, just a bunch of papers, all sizes, some with clumsy typing, some with handwriting.

The long-ago handwriting of Sheriff Hiram Stoker.

Willop had seen the papers before, in the file of the Ellerby-Clark homicide. Cody had copied the file.

And here was a piece of paper Willop hadn't seen before. A piece of yellow lined tablet paper. In the sheriff's handwriting.

Shld be kept confid. Inter. of one Tyrone (col'd.), a millwrker, seems to acct. for whereabouts of other col'd. wrkers at time of killings, as well as other possibles. Tyrone also accts. for presence of T. J. Campbell. Tyrone recalls T.J.C. being near pond, says he is sure because he can recall T.J.C. having to hit horse ...

Willop's heart pounded in his ears. He had not seen this piece of paper before. He was sure, sure, sure ...

The sheriff had at least thought it might be somebody else, thought it could be. . . .

What had Tyrone said that had gotten him killed? What had he told Willop?

Jesus.

Enough. He had no more time. Willop left the trunk contents strewn on the floor, ran down the stairs, through the kitchen filled with pies and casseroles.

The woman was holding the phone. Was she starting to call, or already done? Should he stop her? No.

"Thank you," Willop said. Then out the door, into the fresh air, still no one else in sight, start the car, the clutch bucking and the car lurching, but taking him away.

CHAPTER 36

The old woman's car was jerky and stalled out every so often, and it occurred to Willop that one way or the other, it might be the last car he would ever drive again in his life. He would have to ask Moira about irrelevant thoughts in tense moments, if he ever saw her again. She knew a lot more than he did about psychology. . . .

Willop stopped the car not quite in front of the house. He wished he had had a bigger breakfast, because he knew he was running mainly on adrenaline. That and the thought of what had happened to his mother and Linus and Tyrone.

He checked the revolver. Loaded this time, for sure. He told himself he would kill without guilt—more important, without hesitation—to save his own life. He told himself that, but he wasn't sure. Was there still time to call the sheriff?

No.

A quiet street of cracked asphalt. Several small houses, none too close. Most of the lawns a little ragged. Old people, perhaps.

With his hand in his coat pocket, around the handle of the revolver, Willop walked toward the front door. He saw no movement at the front window. Surprise him, he thought. His steps felt unsteady. He was afraid. No. I'm not dying, not today. Not if I can help it. Not yet . . .

Willop stood at the door, his legs trembling. He felt lightheaded. Got to do it now, before the fear makes me change my mind.

Willop knocked. Nothing. Another knock. The door swung open.

And there he is, Willop thought. He had tried to picture him, but had never come up with a consistent image. The man in the door looked sickly and old, repulsively so. A flesh-colored hearing aid, bigger than a cigarette lighter, hung around one ear. Thick rimless glasses framed watery eyes. Thin, graying hair, slicked down and damp, like he had just come out of the shower. A couple of ugly purple growths on the face, one over the left eyebrow and one pushing like a grape out the left side of his nose.

"Yeah?" the man said.

"T. J. Campbell?"

"Yeah. Who're you?"

"My name is Willop," he heard himself say. "I need to talk to you."

"What about?"

"Something that happened a long time ago."

Willop saw T. J. Campbell read something in his face. Willop thought Campbell was about to turn, like he was reaching for something, so he put his foot in the door and yanked the revolver out of his coat pocket, ripping some of the fabric.

"What?" Face white with fear, jaw going slack, Campbell backed into his own house, steered by Willop, who held the revolver next to the grape on his nose. Surprised the shit out of him with the gun, Willop thought.

"You are without a doubt the ugliest thing I ever saw," Willop said. "What do you say I shoot this fucking wart off for starters?"

"What ..."

There, Willop thought. Terror and bewilderment all over T. J. Campbell's face. He's so goddamned scared, he won't see how I'm shaking.

"How's a smelly old buzzard like you get any?" Willop said. "But I guess we know, don't we?"

Backwards, step by step, Willop facing him down, until T. J. Campbell came to a chair.

"Sit," Willop said, as though he were speaking to a dog.

T. J. Campbell slumped into the chair. Willop sat down on a sofa a few feet away.

"Now, then, just relax," Willop said. Can't let him have a heart attack, he thought. "We have a few things to talk over."

T. J. Campbell's chest had been heaving. Now his breathing eased a little, and some color returned to his face.

Willop could feel the sweat on his back. The sofa he was sitting on smelled, as did the rest of the room, of stale breath, dirty skin, dirty clothes. Dirty thoughts?

"You're alone here," Willop said. It was a statement, not a question.

"I ain't rich. Take whatever—"

"Shut up. You know I'm not here for money. Besides, you sure as hell didn't get rich when your uncle sold out. Shitty little house, lousy furniture. Even your wallpaper sucks. . . ." Willop stopped to catch his breath.

"I'm not rich. . . ."

"I know," Willop said. "I checked your will. Damnedest thing, your uncle leaving all that money to the NAACP. I guess we know why he did that, huh?"

Silence.

"Your uncle felt disgusted with you. Probably guilty, too, for covering up. Him and that lawyer, Hornsmith. Am I getting warm?"

Silence.

"Only reason a white man from these parts would leave money to the NAACP back then was because he felt guilty. Ain't that right? It was also your uncle's way of showing how much he hated your guts, how much you made him sick, he was so disgusted with you. That's right, too, isn't it?"

T. J. Campbell looked like he would cry, but he bit his lip. Willop thought he saw his eyes harden, like he was calculating. . . .

"You were a foreman back then," Willop said.

"For a while."

"I know. You used to boss the niggers at the mill. Go to the shanties and collect the rent. Didn't you?"

"Yes."

"Ever get any pussy in them shanties?"

T. J. Campbell twisted his face to keep from crying in anger.

"You ever think of screwing my mother?" Willop asked. "Or was she too young then, even for you?"

T. J. Campbell bit his lip hard.

"I know, I know," Willop said. "You weren't the only one who did that around here, back then."

Got to be careful, Willop thought, as Campbell's eyes showed hate as well as fear. Got to keep him afraid ...

"Aren't you curious who my mother was?" Willop said.

"No," Campbell whispered.

"What?" Willop raised the revolver slightly, glad that Campbell avoided looking at it so that he could not see how Willop's hand trembled.

"Yes, I mean," Campbell stammered.

"Her name was Jewel. Last name Bragg, same as my middle name ... Never mind that. My mother's brother was Linus Bragg. You know who he was, even though you only saw him once. Ain't that right?"

"Oh, my God ..." T. J. Campbell shook his head and started to cry for real. Willop thought he cried like a child.

"God doesn't figure in this. I used to wonder how a god could let something like this happen. Then I gave up trying to figure. ..."

"I never meant ..." Campbell sobbed loudly.

Willop felt tired, old, almost sick to his stomach. "I know, I know. You never meant to hurt those two girls. It just happened, didn't it?"

Campbell sobbed and nodded his head yes.

"It just happened, and you figured you could blame it on a little nigger kid."

Campbell trembled and sobbed.

"You knew just what to say to my Uncle Linus, didn't you? Back then, little black kids were told by their parents not to even look at white girls, else they'd get their parts cut off if a white man caught them. You knew that."

Tears and snot dripped from T. J. Campbell's face into his lap.

"So you told him it was his fault, that you'd kill not just him, but his mama and daddy. Maybe rape his sister, my mother, if he told. Something like that. Right? Right? You'd better answer. ..."

T. J. Campbell nodded yes.

"Sure, Linus was there. Maybe he wanted a little look, nothing more than that. Then he saw you, or you saw him, and you figured you could keep him quiet, let him take the blame. Right?"

Silence.

"And the way you did it," Willop hissed, "you told him he shouldn't have looked. Then you threatened to cut him, down there, cut him right on the spot. Right? Maybe you even grabbed him, down there, and said if he told he'd get his parts cut off, if he told what he saw. Right?"

T. J. Campbell slumped in his chair.

"Sure," Willop said. "I can almost fill in the words. . . . Linus, him being just a poor nigger kid, was scared shitless. Out of his mind, almost. Probably did go out of his mind before it was over. Which was just what you were counting on."

T. J. Campbell rubbed his cheeks and eyes with the back of a blue-veined hand.

"So," Willop said, "poor Linus was taken away, fried in a chair without hardly a trial. Like everybody figured he was guilty from the start."

"It wasn't supposed to happen," Campbell whispered.

"Hell no. Wasn't supposed to happen. But as long as it did, you figured a nigger kid might as well take the blame. . . ."

Willop could feel sweat from his hand on the revolver handle.

" 'Go back there,' my mom said in her letter. 'Go back to that mean little Carolina town, reopen the whole thing, find out what really happened. . . .'"

T. J. Campbell's face was in his hands. His shoulders shook as he cried.

"Always told myself I'd go back one day, but I never really meant it. Until . . ." Willop paused. He himself was close to breaking down, and it would never do to let T. J. Campbell know.

T. J. Campbell had stopped crying. He wiped his face with his sleeves.

"And when I started to find the trail, old Tyrone went to you, like a good loyal darkie, to tell you about it, just like he gave you an alibi way back then. Right? Only, you couldn't afford to have him around. Just like you couldn't afford to have that old deputy, Cody, around. Tell me something. Was he blackmailing you? Or was he a cop to the end and gonna turn you in?"

"You can't make me tell. Anything."

"We'll see," Willop said. "Guy I feel sorry for is Tyrone. Nothing clever about him. Didn't want much. I couldn't figure what he said to me that was so important. Then I got it, finally."

Willop paused, breathed deep. He wondered if T.J. would guess.

"Tyrone said something about how you had trouble with a horse. Just went right by me, he said it so fast. Wasn't a horse. It was that little girl's teeth. Bit you so hard, one of them broke. Must have hurt like hell. Bled. That's why you had to make something up about trouble with a horse. Hey, want to show me your hands?"

The last thing Junior Stoker had wanted this day was a call from his wife, but he had been worried about his son, Thomas, and so he told her he could talk for a few minutes, even though he was buried under work.

Thomas was much better, Jen said, and one of the doctors wanted to try some new drugs. Stoker had never met the doctor (he had let that end of his life slide, let Jen pick up the slack, he thought guiltily), but Jen said she trusted him.

"I don't know," Stoker said. "About them drugs ..."

"You're not much for trying new things," she said matter-of-factly.

"This is our son we're talking about, and these are drugs we're talking about." God, he didn't like this conversation, it was the worst possible time. Then, because he was rattled and recalled the hurt from their last conversation, he said, "Besides, you can always get someone who's more willing than I am to try new things." There, the words were out, no calling them back.

"You're a goddamn fool. Bill, you know that? Mixing one thing with another. The person I was with when I talked to you was my boss. I'd invited her over for dinner. That's right, I said 'her.'"

Stoker was both embarrassed and elated.

"Are you still there?" she said.

"'Course I am. Guess I should apologize. But you can't blame me for being worried. About you and Thomas both ..."

"All right ..."

"And I got a lot on my mind, which of course I don't blame you for. I went to see my dad and he was a real pisspot. Knocked over his soup and whiskey, and of course I got all pissed off 'cause I had to clean it up. Tried not to let on, but of course he could tell I was pissed...."

"I know," she said, her voice more gentle. "It's tough sometimes."

"Anyhow, you think those drugs might help and you trust the doctor, let's go ahead." Then, in a sad afterthought, "What's to lose?"

"Nothing, I think. We'll talk some more, Bill. Take care."

As soon as Stoker hung up, there was a knock on his door and Bryant Fischer came in.

"Results, Junior. We got some results from the computers."

"Hey, I told you. Computers are here to stay."

"Look here," Fischer said, spreading a printout out on Stoker's desk. "Our boy himself hasn't been arrested yet, but look here at these people with the same last names. We already verified it's the same last name...."

Stoker's phone rang. "Yeah," he said, annoyed at the interruption.

"Sorry, Captain," the dispatcher said, "but I got Deputy Morris on the line. He's been with your father, and he says it's urgent."

"Put him on." Stoker took a deep breath. Had the old man suffered another stroke? Died? Junior felt guilty for having been so impatient. No, if the old man had died, it would be some nursing-home official calling, not a deputy.

"Captain, Morris here. Your dad was agitating like crazy. Took me the longest time to figure out he wanted paper and pencil to write something down. Anyhow, took him forever, but he finally scrawled the word 'camp,' then an equal sign, and then 'T.J.'—"

Junior felt like a whip had cracked his face. "Well," he said, "I'm a goddamn fool, Tell my dad I understand and I'm sorry."

Junior cradled the phone. Of course; so simple.

"Look here, Junior," Bryant Fischer was saying. "This entry here, this is our boy's mother, as it turns out. Ain't that something ..."

"Bryant, let's you and me get on over to T. J. Campbell's place as fast as we can," Junior said. "I'll explain on the way."

On the way, they got the radio call about the intruder at Cody's house. Stoker hoped they would be in time.

They saw the old car in front of Campbell's place, and Fischer parked the patrol car half a block away. They got out and closed the doors quietly.

"Let me go around back, Bryant. You take the front." They checked their service revolvers.

"I don't know what to expect," Stoker said. "I'm not really satisfied our boy Willop is a killer. Not satisfied he isn't, either. He's got a gun, and if he waves it my way, even casual-like, I'll pull the trigger. Expect you to do the same."

"Understood."

"Well, I can't remember the last time we did any shooting around here. I'm nervous."

They nodded at each other, to show they knew what they had to do and that they wished each other good luck, and then Stoker was tiptoeing along the hedge next to Campbell's house.

From inside the house came a loud shout, followed by someone else's scream.

Stoker trotted around back, tiptoed two steps at a time onto the porch (there's a gasoline can, he said to himself; got to check it out ...) cocked his revolver, and took a deep breath so his arms would be steady if he shot.

"Tell me, goddamn it." Stranger's voice from inside. Where had he heard it before? On the phone?

"No!" T. J. Campbell's voice. Scared out of his wits.

"Tell me ..." Lots of hate there, Stoker thought. May have no choice but to shoot.

"Don't ..."

Stoker elbowed the screen door open as quietly as he could. Ah, the inner door wasn't locked. He opened it slowly, catching the stale smell of the house as he stepped inside.

"You killed those girls and you killed my uncle. Now you're gonna tell about it...."

"Please ..."

Very close, the voices just around the corner from the tiny kitchen (dirty dishes, Stoker noticed). Stoker went into a crouch, locked his elbows. A long, crisp step to the entrance of the living room.

The stranger was exhausted, on the edge, Stoker thought. Could do anything. Careful ...

"Say yes," Willop hissed, holding the revolver under Campbell's nose. Campbell's face was full of fatigue as well as terror.

"Police," Stoker said. "Let the gun drop or you're a dead man."

Willop shuddered, turned his head slowly toward the voice.

"Now, or you're dead. Last chance."

Willop let go, and the gun thudded to the floor.

"Now stand up, slowly, and lean on the sofa. Bryant! I got him. Come on inside."

"He would have killed me or framed me," Willop said. "Just ask him."

"We'll ask him," Stoker said quietly.

Willop had never felt such a mixture of elation, relief, and fear. He wondered what would happen to him.

Bryant Fischer banged through the front door, his revolver already holstered. "Nice," he said softly to Junior.

CHAPTER 37

Willop sat on the smelly, dilapidated sofa. The words of the Miranda warning, read to him by Stoker, had been a distant echo. Willop could not begin yet to fathom all of his feelings. All he knew, for the moment, was that he was dead tired. He wondered what would happen to him.

T. J. Campbell had been taken into another room, where he was being watched by a deputy.

"You know who I am?" Stoker asked.

"I figure you're Stoker," Willop said.

"You got it. Stoker, Bill D., captain of investigations with the South Carolina State Police."

"Son of the former sheriff."

"That too. You know, since you came to visit I got two dead people and lots more trouble than we usually have."

Willop shook his head and laughed. Appreciating the joke might make things easier.

"Nothing funny about what's been happening," Stoker said.

"I didn't kill either damn one," Willop said. He shook his head and laughed again, to himself. He recalled scenes from old, old Western movies in which the man with the white hat was jailed for a crime he didn't commit. The man with the white hat would call his horse over to the cell window, tie a lariat around the bars, and have his horse back up, yanking the bars loose.

Then the man with the white hat would ride off and find the real killer (who wore a black hat), all in time for the final cereal commercial. . . .

"Ain't nothing funny about this," Stoker said again.

"Know where I can find a horse?" Willop said.

Stoker shook his head sadly. Willop was clearly out of his mind, on drugs, dead tired, or all of the above.

"Bryant," Stoker said, motioning for Fischer to join him in a corner. "I think we should seize the gasoline can on the porch. And I think we should look in the garage and check T.J. 's car. See if the tires got any mud, then see if any tread marks from the road in front of Cody's house match them tires."

"Jesus ..." Fischer said.

"And look through T.J.'s clothes. For seeds and burrs, like in the field where Cody was. And vacuum the house here, too."

"Uh, we got any probable cause, Junior?"

"No. But we may have some pretty soon. Or I'll get a warrant. One way or the other, we'll toss this place. I just don't want anything disturbed."

"Well, what will the gas can show?"

"Nothing, maybe. But you can see T.J. hasn't cut his grass lately. So if he bought a couple gallons of gas lately, and there's a lot less than that in the can, that tells us something. Now, there ain't that many gas stations around here, and people know who T. J. Campbell is. Gotta be someone who remembers selling him that gasoline ..."

"Which you think he used to set fire to Tyrone's cabin."

Stoker shrugged. He walked the few steps to the easy chair and sat down, facing Willop.

"What happens to me?" Willop said. "Not that I give a damn." But he did.

"Not sure yet. Menacing poor Judah Brickstone like that wasn't too smart. Could be a high misdemeanor ..."

"The gun wasn't loaded."

"Yeah, well he thought it was. Like to scared him shitless ..." Junior paused, embarrassed by his unintended bad joke. "Them fancy credentials of yours notwithstanding, you got no right to run all over my county, getting information under false pretenses, trying to do the work of professional law men."

Willop chuckled, bitterly. "You 'professional law men' hadn't done much with this case in over forty years," he said.

"True enough," Stoker said. "And since you arrived we got two dead people here."

Willop was getting some of his energy back, enough to know he didn't want to go to prison for the rest of his life. Or go to the chair, like Linus ...

"Listen," Willop said, "I didn't kill anybody...."

"We know you went to see Cody, and Tyrone, along with Brickstone."

"I didn't kill anybody."

"You had plenty of reason to kill Cody, seeing as how you think he railroaded your uncle...."

"So? How about Tyrone. Why would I kill a pathetic old Uncle Tom?"

"Because you were mad at him for not coming forward sooner," Stoker said, testing. But his own words didn't ring true. "You could have come to us. Should have, with your information...."

"Yeah, well, I thought about it. Then I thought the better of it."

"Were you prepared to kill T.J.?" Stoker asked. On a hunch, he went over to the closet.

"I don't know. Why?"

"'cause if you weren't, and we hadn't showed up, you could be dead." Junior took the shotgun out of the closet, broke open the barrels, and caught the shells in his palm. His dad had told him to always play his hunches.

"Jesus," Willop shuddered. "How'd you know?"

"I'm a professional law man," Stoker said. "We ain't fools, you know."

There was a shuffling noise from the other room.

"Steady," a deputy said, then led T. J. Campbell out and looked uncertainly at Stoker.

"We'll need to have T.J. come along and give us a full account," Stoker said.

"He wants to go to the bathroom," the deputy said.

"It's his house," Stoker said. A moment after Campbell went into the bathroom, Stoker said to the deputy, "Listen close. Don't let him open a medicine chest."

Overhearing, Willop looked into Stoker's face and smiled. "You're thinking about what I said," Willop said, feeling a weight fall off his chest.

Stoker did his best to keep his face expressionless. A moment later, there was the sound of a toilet flushing, and T. J. Campbell emerged from the bathroom, stooped and pale.

"Guess we're finished up here, Bryant," Stoker said. "Let's seal this place up and get going."

Willop was handcuffed ("Don't try anything, and you'll be treated just fine," Stoker told him) and put in the backseat of a patrol car next to a deputy. Campbell, supported by Fischer and another deputy, was put in another car. God, he looks old and tired, Stoker thought.

Junior drove clumsily for the first few minutes; part of it was the adrenaline he was still feeling from the guns-drawn facedown with Willop, and part of it was simple awkwardness. He didn't know what to say to Willop.

"Not very goddamn smart," Junior said to Willop at last, "coming down here and waving a gun under people's noses ..."

Willop said nothing.

"'Course, I guess you figure you had plenty of reasons," Junior ventured.

"You read me my warnings," Willop said. "Is this off the record?"

" 'Off the record.' So, you used to be in the newspaper business?" Junior looked in the mirror, saw that Willop was startled that he knew.

"Oh, yeah," Junior went on. "I know you used to be a reporter. Once we got our act together, we did some pretty good checking on you."

They rode in silence for several minutes, the deputy sitting stiffly next to Willop. Finally, Willop said, "What's the outlook for me? I mean, as far as charges. Seems like it should count for something if I uncovered some facts you didn't know about...."

"I don't know exactly," Junior Stoker said. Which was the truth.

By the time Stoker pulled into his regular parking space, Fischer and the other deputy were leading T. J. Campbell into the building. Campbell seemed to need their support.

"Bryant," Stoker hollered as he got out of his car. "Let T.J. rest on that cot in the room at the end of the hall." Fischer nodded and waved.

Stoker led Willop through the door, past Bestwick, who had just come on duty and looked, Stoker thought, oddly startled, and down the corridor to his office.

"Captain, you want me in there with you?" a deputy asked hesitantly.

"No," Stoker said. "Uncuff him. I'll be all right."

Willop sat in the chair that Stoker indicated, rubbed his wrists, and studied the white walls and fluorescent lighting.

"I never killed anybody," Willop said. "I'm not even sure I could."

"Oh, you could," Stoker said. "Trust me on that. A lot of decent people kill, as well as those not so decent."

"Never even fired that gun," Willop said. "Hey! You can run tests and prove that for yourself."

"Sure we can," Stoker said. "That'll only show you didn't kill anybody with that gun."

"Even so . . ."

"How come you didn't come right to me from the start?" Stoker said. "How come you had to play detective yourself? Maybe you really were interested in killing. . . ."

Willop laughed, bitterly. "You have any idea how black people feel about the law in the South? Even today? I mean, Jesus Christ, Stoker . . ." Willop reminded himself who Stoker's father was.

"Well, times change," Stoker said. "We got col—black people working here. Try to treat them the same . . ."

"Do you remember?" Willop said. "Remember the killings? And the execution?"

"Remember?" Stoker chuckled mirthlessly. "I'm the sheriff's son. I remember when it happened, remember driving over to Columbia with the boy . . . My daddy stopped and bought him a chocolate bar and a Bible. You know that? Not that he had to or anything. He just did. Good man, my daddy . . ."

"You remember the execution?" Willop pressed.

"Watched it, for God's sake. Only one I ever saw, only one I ever wanted to see. Had nightmares about it for a long time afterward. That and—" Stoker stopped; his feelings were too full, and he didn't want to share them with Willop.

"How was he, right at the end?"

"Good as can be expected, and that's the truth. Walked in and sat down, carrying that Bible. Think he was doped up a bit, maybe. When they shot the juice to him, his face came out. . . ."

Stoker didn't want to say any more, and Willop didn't want to hear any more about that.

"They say my uncle confessed. You really think those are his words? You really think a black kid, a nigger kid, used those words back then?" Willop said.

"The sheriff paraphrased, kind of," Stoker said.

Willop tried to keep his contempt from showing.

"But my daddy never beat any confession out of anyone," Stoker said. "And that is the goddamn truth."

Got to be careful, Willop thought. Jesus, yes, be careful. I am in the middle of nowhere in the middle of South Carolina. . . .

"Can I ask you something?" Willop said. "Just hypothetically. Assume, just for a second, that I didn't kill Cody. Then do you think Cody was killed, by whoever did it, because he was going after the truth, like a good law man? Or was he trying to blackmail somebody? He had a copy of the whole case file, photographs and all, in his trunk. And—"

Willop stopped himself. He had been about to mention that Cody's trunk held something the original case file didn't, but he didn't want Stoker to know Bestwick had shown the file to him.

"I don't deal much in hypothetical stuff. Leave that to the lawyers. Tell you this much, Cody was a funny duck in some ways. Not the easiest guy. But I can see him being on the right side in this. Might be he was always suspicious of T.J., and T.J. knew it, and figured he had to kill him once he'd done away with Tyrone. Long as we're talking about hypothetical stuff. Anyhow, Dex was a law man, straight and true, in his time."

"In his time ..."

"All you can ask of anybody. That he be good in the time he lives. Back when my daddy was the sheriff, people thought a lot different about things. Here, sure, but other places too." Stoker thought of his father in his prime, and was proud. "Don't forget. My daddy didn't have fancy computers and stuff like we do today."

Suddenly, Willop felt like he had been stripped naked. "So you know everything about me?" he asked.

"Never know everything about anybody. But we know a lot. How the family moved to Newark, New Jersey. How your other uncle, Will, was killed in the riots up there in 'sixty-seven ..."

"Family never had a chance," Willop said softly. "Their folks, they died young. Never the same after ..."

Stoker wanted to be gentle. "I've seen it," he said. "Seen how bad things follow some folks. It's the truth. Sometimes hard luck follows families around. Seems like if a bad thing happens, other things ..." Stoker bit his lip; some of his own memories were intruding.

His soul naked, Willop asked, "You know about all the rest? I mean, my mother ...?"

"We know about her being killed."

"Jesus ..."

"And your father running off."

"My step-father, you mean."

Stoker was embarrassed, almost ashamed.

"You know the rest," Willop said.

"We know about her, your mom, being raped near Fort Dix, New Jersey, yes. The name came up when we punched in ..."

Now Willop wanted to get it over with. If he said it quickly, he might be able to do it without breaking down. "Always bothered me, not knowing exactly who my father was," he said, then took a deep breath. "One of them five or six white guys. Can't really be sure."

Stoker stood and turned away, an intruder on someone else's grief.

"Hey," Willop hissed, "suppose she'd been a white woman raped by a bunch of nigger soldiers. Think maybe there woulda been a trial then?"

"Could be," Stoker said. He owed him that much, at least.

The phone rang. "Captain," Bestwick said, "Sheriff Fischer wanted me to find out if you need any sandwiches and coffee?"

"How do you like your coffee?" Stoker said to Willop.

"Black," Willop said. "Naturally."

"Couple black coffees," Stoker said into the phone. "And ham, tuna, anything."

Stoker hung up, sat down again, looked at Willop. "Never had a case quite like this," he said.

"Hey, Captain. There's just two of us in this little room right now. What do *you* think happened? I mean, that day the girls were killed."

"I'll be goddamned if I know, goddamned if anybody ever will."

"We both know he didn't get any kind of trial. . . ."

"Well, at least he *got* a trial," Stoker said, defending his father.

"Right, right. Okay . . ."

"Today, well, a lot of things would be different. I'd never want the chair for someone that young, you want to know the truth. Not sure I'd want it for anybody . . ."

Outside, the corridor suddenly clattered with sounds of footsteps, pushing, shoving . . . something. The door to Stoker's office flew open and Bryant Fischer's face appeared, not tough and hard, but a way Junior had never seen it. Heartsick.

"God, Junior, I'm sorry. T.J. must've taken some pills in his house. Snuck 'em in the bathroom, I guess. Jesus, and we were watching . . ."

"Get a doctor," Stoker said matter-of-factly.

"On the way. Jesus, I'm sorry . . ."

As if in a dream, Junior saw a stretcher bearing T. J. Campbell, blanket-wrapped, only his face showing, being wheeled by. Eyes closed, head to one side, skin blue-gray . . .

No need to hurry, Stoker thought.

CHAPTER 38

Stoker arranged for Willop's rented car to be returned because he, Stoker, wanted to see Willop get on the plane. Part of it was simply courtesy; then, too, having used some discretionary powers to see that Willop wouldn't be charged with anything, Stoker wanted to watch him leave his jurisdiction. And there were things he wanted to say to him, or at least try to say.

Sitting in the car next to Stoker, Willop felt empty. "Maybe I shouldn't have come here at all," he said. "Three people dead who wouldn't be if I'd stayed home."

"Not your doing," Stoker said.

"Yeah, well whose then?"

"T. J. Campbell's. T.J. died by his own hand. Tyrone ... well, poor old Tyrone, he'd be alive if he'd trusted in the law a bit more. Come to us instead ..." Stoker stopped talking when he heard Willop's quiet, bitter laugh.

"Yeah, I know," Stoker said. "Too much to expect a poor old black guy to trust in the law much ..."

"Yeah, it is. After Selma and Birmingham, it is. ..."

Stoker was about to say that Selma and Birmingham were a long time ago, but he stopped himself. With all that had just happened, they didn't seem that long ago.

"You know any Catholics?" Stoker asked.

"Sure. Why?"

"I've known some. The serious ones, especially the priests, they sometimes talk about the Sorrowful Mysteries. Hell, I don't even remember what that means. But I never forgot the term. Sometimes it seems to sum life up pretty good. Like today."

"You could say that."

"Just did."

They rode past gently sloping farmland. Occasionally, they passed a general store or a small gas station.

"Pretty in a way, ain't it?" Stoker said. "Same way we came back then, with your uncle. Whenever I'm not too rushed, I like to take this way, instead of the interstate. Makes me feel more part of the countryside. For better or worse. Am I making any sense?"

"Part of the countryside?"

"I mean, not that I have any definite feelings on religion or anything, but the older a guy gets, the more he wants to feel a part of things, sort of. . . ."

Junior Stoker remembered some of his father's awkwardness with words and was ashamed; he was no better.

More and more, Willop sensed Stoker's vulnerability. "You married?"

"Separated. My job kind of got in the way, not that it was the only thing. We have a son, Thomas. He's never been well. . . ."

"Well, I guess I owe you," Willop said. "For not jumping to too many conclusions. And you might have saved my life."

"My job."

"Yeah, well, you did it right."

"Seems like you must be a hell of a reporter."

"That's what Moira says when she's trying to encourage me—"

Moira! God, she must be worried sick. He would call her from the airport. So much to tell her . . .

Stoker made an unexpected turn, so abruptly that Willop thought it was on a whim.

"Someone I'd like you to meet," Stoker said.

* * *

Junior Stoker knocked.

"Come right in," a woman's voice said. "The sheriff's just finishing his lunch."

"Hi, old sheriff," Junior said. "I brought along a visitor."

Willop stepped into the room and looked at the man—old, frail, skin shiny and tight across the face—who, probably more than anyone, had sent his uncle to the electric chair.

"Uhhnn ..." the sheriff said, raising his hand from the chair slightly.

Willop took the hand, gently, and shook it.

"Hello," Willop said softly. He could not hate this man.

"My dad, he used to be the best damn sheriff in the state," Junior said. "Fair shake for everybody, and nobody gave him any shit. Ain't that right, old fella?"

"Uhhnnn ..."

"That woman who just left, old Dad doesn't care for her," Stoker whispered to Willop. "Lets his soup get cold, talks down to him without meaning to."

"Uhnnn ..." Sheriff Hiram Stoker was annoyed. He didn't want his son telling his private business to a stranger (who was he, anyhow?), and besides, his son had not yet apologized properly for not having understood him during his last visit.

"Right, Dad," Stoker said. "I should have paid more attention. That what you're trying to tell me? I admit it."

"Uhnn ..." The apology out of the way, the sheriff wanted an explanation. What had it all meant, his son Junior asking about T. J. Campbell? Why, he, Sheriff Hiram Stoker, had checked into that just last— Oh, no. Longer ago ...

"Soon as I get a chance, I'll explain everything, Sheriff," Junior said. "Right now, I was just driving my, uh, visitor over to the airport and I wanted to stop in. ..."

Willop sat on the edge of the bed, near the end, and studied the old man. He would have been big, powerful in his prime. Perhaps Linus had been afraid of him. Or, if the sheriff had shown kindness, maybe Linus looked up to him. ...

"Mr. Willop here, he was just in Manning doing some research on, uh, some local history," Stoker mumbled.

Goddamn liar, the sheriff thought. My son Junior is a goddamn liar. I don't know what that stranger is doing here, but he ain't just doing research. . . . Have to get Junior to tell me the truth, goddamn it. Bob wouldn't lie. . . .

"Uhnnn . . . Bo . . ." Was Bob coming today?

"Not this time, Dad," Junior said, recognizing his father's attempt to say his other son's name. That was strange; his father seemed more confused today than usual.

No, goddamn it, the sheriff thought. I haven't lost it all. Swing back and forth in time now and then, but I haven't lost it all. Junior still has some explaining to do.

"I guess you know as much as anyone about these parts," Willop said to the old man. His own voice sounded stiff and wooden, like his words, but it was the best he could do.

"Uhnn . . ." Something about this stranger . . . Junior would have to explain.

"Let's have a little something," Junior said. He stood three paper cups on the table next to his father's bed and poured an inch of whiskey into each. He handed one to Willop and held out another to his father, who was slow in taking it.

"Well, here's to being happy and doing the best we all can," Junior Stoker said, hoping he could live up to both ideas.

The sheriff had trouble raising his cup. The whiskey smell was faint, and he was surprised when Junior reached over with a tissue to wipe off his chin. The sheriff hadn't realized he had spilled on himself.

"Here's to truth and justice," Willop said, draining his cup. Imagine, he thought. Me drinking a toast with the sheriff . . .

Junior looked at his watch; if they left now, they could still make another stop and be on time for Willop's plane. Besides, his father was looking tired.

"Sheriff, we're gonna push off," Junior said. "I'll be back soon for a long talk. Promise."

"Good-bye," Willop said.

In the hall, the plump attendant was waiting for Junior. She motioned to him, and Willop walked away to give them privacy.

"Captain, I have to tell you something," the attendant said, softly. "I see a change in the sheriff."

"A change?"

"Yes. A lot of little things that add up to a change. His signs are still all right, but in my experience ..."

"Right. Well, I guess it's no surprise, is it?"

"No. Just wanted you to know."

The sheriff could not hear what they were saying, outside his room, but he was sure they were talking about him. That annoyed him; he would make Junior tell what is was. . . . Damn, he hated to be a problem.

The whiskey, just that little bit, was making him tired. He would take a long nap this afternoon. Yes, it was getting harder to do even the simple things. And yes, he thought sadly, it was getting harder to keep everything straight. But he had not had a bad life, truth to tell.

The sun bathed the fields in a light that turned the grass yellow-green. The same sun that had shone, not so long ago, on slaves and slave owners alike, no doubt comforting both, Willop thought.

"Day like this, makes you glad to be alive, don't it?" Stoker said.

"Yeah, it does. . . ."

"My dad, he's slowing down a little. . . ."

"Thanks for taking me to meet him."

"Well, I figured you came all this way, might as well meet ... the sheriff."

"I can see he was a big man when he was younger," Willop said.

"Tough, too. But a good man, for all that. He knew everybody around Clarendon County. One of the reasons I kind of stuck close to home is that you get to know everybody. Makes being a cop easier, in some ways ..."

"Because you know everybody?"

"Partly. Plus, any stranger comes to town, he stands out. Now you, you stopped and got directions from an old lady selling pecans along the road. Right?"

"How'd you find out?"

"I'm a cop, remember? Now, you would have stood out for her in any event, because you're a stranger here. But when you asked how to get to the mill and how to find Cody's place, you really stunned her."

"How come?"

"Name's Marcia Overpeck. In her sixties, not as old as she looks. Had some tough times. Used to be Marcia Ellerby. Sister of . . ."

"Jesus."

"Told you. Small community, lot of lives touch each other. Married a guy who worked for a tobacco company. Seemed for a while like he had it made, good money and all. Then he got sick and died. Cancer. Wasn't much of a smoker, himself, either . . . Anyhow, the scar stayed with her, with her family. What happened to her baby sister, I mean. Parents were a little bit sad all the rest of their lives. . . ."

"So were Linus's."

"Back there with my dad, that toast you made to truth and justice. Sad thing is, and I don't have it all figured out yet, probably never will, but they don't always go together."

Stoker turned onto the interstate, and Willop recognized that they weren't far from Columbia. The traffic was denser, moved faster, and the buildings were higher than Willop had been used to for a while.

Then Stoker surprised Willop by turning off the interstate into the parking lot next to a tall, white modern building.

"This here's the veterans hospital," Stoker said.

* * *

Stoker led Willop down a long corridor with sparkling green and black linoleum and white walls. As they went by rooms, Willop saw men in pajamas, mostly old men, some very old, but a few who were in their thirties. Vietnam, Willop thought.

Nurses and orderlies passed them, smiling and nodding as they recognized Stoker. Near the end of the corridor they turned into a room illuminated by sunlight streaming through a window. A white-haired, pajama-clad man who looked to be in his mid-sixties sat in a wheelchair. The sun shone on his face, and he seemed to be in a deep sleep.

"My brother, Bob," Stoker said softly.

Willop saw that part of the man's forehead had been surgically repaired, almost as if the doctors had had to fill in a huge dent.

"Piece of a German shell got him," Stoker said. "A shade more to the left and he would have had just a small scalp wound. A bit more to the right and he would have been killed on the spot."

"Sad," Willop said.

"Happened in France, just after D-Day. We got the telegram the day of the execution. Waiting for my dad and me when we got back. My mother, she was afraid to open it until we got home. . . ." Stoker paused, took a deep breath. "'Course, he was actually wounded days before that, but it was the day of the execution that we found out. Awful day that was . . ."

"Your parents, they must have been . . ."

"My dad always liked Bob a little better, actually. Used to bother me, but it doesn't anymore. They were never the same, my folks. Oh, they adjusted, whatever that means. But my father, especially . . . a part of him died, it really did. See, my dad always dreamed, prayed, that Bob would come home from the war and then they'd go fishing again and all that. . . ."

"Instead, he came home like this."

"Pretty much. When he's awake, he seems aware, sometimes. At least I think he is. I don't know. . . . Folks used to hope—" Stoker had to stop.

"Thing that hurts to think about," Stoker went on, "is that guys with his kind of wound in Vietnam, well, he would have recovered, most likely. What they know today, what they can do . . ."

"Ever think it would have been better if he'd been killed?" Willop asked softly.

"Used to think that. Thought how much nicer it would have been, my big brother dead, maybe under one of those white crosses in Normandy. Then, gradually, I thought different about it. I mean, he's my brother, and he's alive. Oh, I can't visit with him or anything, but he's here, living. He breathes and he feels the sun on his face. . . . Does that make any sense?"

Stoker carried one of Willop's suitcases into the terminal. Just before they got to check in, Stoker heard the public-address system: "Will Captain Bill Stoker of the South Carolina State Police call his Clarendon County office at once. . . ."

Bestwick answered. "Captain, your wife called. She wants you to meet her at the Holiday Inn in Columbia at six o'clock for dinner." A pause and giggle. "I already told her you would."

Stoker smiled. Then Bestwick put Bryant Fischer on the line, and the sheriff told Stoker a few things, none of which surprised him.

"Trouble?" Willop asked.

"No. Just found out that T.J. bought three gallons of gasoline at Winkler's service station not many days ago. The can we found had a lot less than that, so . . ."

"Makes it look like he might have set the fire. How'd you find out about the gas?"

"Old Leon Winkler. Son of the present owner, been around forever. Used to wait on my dad, in fact."

"Sure. I had a fuse changed there."

"Same place. Sure enough. Anyhow, the sheriff— Bryant Fischer, I mean—tells me the soles of T.J.'s boots have burrs and seeds, like in the field where old Dexter was killed. And we may get something on the tire tread."

"Great," Willop said. "Listen, I have to make a call."

"You go ahead. I'll see when the next flight is."

Moira answered her office phone on the second ring.

"It's me," he said softly. "I'm almost on my way."

"James! Are you safe? Did you find—?"

"Found out some stuff. Other stuff I didn't. Lots to tell you. And we have a lot to talk about. . . ."

"James, I'm so relieved." She excused herself for a moment to say something in Spanish or Portuguese; things were back to normal. "Oh, James. I am so glad. . . ."

"Me too."

"Listen. Delmar Springs called."

"Tell him I still haven't decided."

"No, not that. He says you should meet him on the first tee Friday morning at nine-fourteen."

The passengers were lining up to board.

"So . . . I'm clear?" Willop asked.

"Far as I'm concerned. That's what I'm gonna tell the grand jury."

"You know, I never found Linus's grave. . . ."

"Tell you what, Willop. I'll do some checking myself. Next time you're in town we'll stop and see it."

"Next time?"

"Friendly place, Clarendon County. Expect you'll want to be coming back to visit."

All the passengers except Willop had boarded.

"Listen, Captain," Willop said, embarrassed. "I want to thank you for playing it straight. I mean, I think I got more than a fair shake. . . ."

"Just doing my job, that's all. Got pretty good training from my daddy . . ."

"Guess I should go," Willop said.

"Just one more thing," Stoker said. "Want you to read something." He reached into his pocket and pulled out a yellow clipping. "This was a telegram sent to the Governor just before Linus was executed. See, there had been a case up at Parris Island. White boy raped and killed a girl. Got a prison term instead of the chair."

Stoker handed the paper to Willop, who read:

> I am a White man. I believe in the right thing among white or colored. Now I am pleading with you for the life of the little Negro boy age fourteen that kill the two little white girls. They gave the white boy that kill the little girl in Parris Island twenty years in prison. A sentence in prison would be fair for the Negro boy. Please Governor try to save this boy's life.

"What do you think?" Stoker asked.

"A good man, whoever wrote this," Willop said.

"Had to be. And it was a South Carolina man wrote it. Over forty years ago. Plenty of good in people back then, too. Just different times."

"Different times," Willop agreed.

They shook hands, said good-bye, and Willop went down the tunnel to the plane.

He was glad his seat was by a window. Soon the jet took off, and as it ascended, the buildings and houses were harder to see. The plane turned before heading north, and Willop saw farmland and grass—the rich earth that had received the blood and bones of slave and slave owner, black and white. Together now.

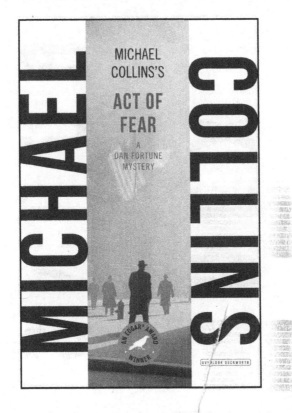